WRATH OF THE WREYA

SABRINA ROZNOWSKI

For my husband Chris and my best friend Adrianne, for pushing and supporting me until this mess was finished. Thank you.

And to my baby, Alex, you made my first dream come true, and I'm so glad you're with me while I chase the next one. I hope you enjoy the story.

Arcadia
Pyrrha
Brax
De
Syri
The Fo
of Ga
The Continent
of Kell

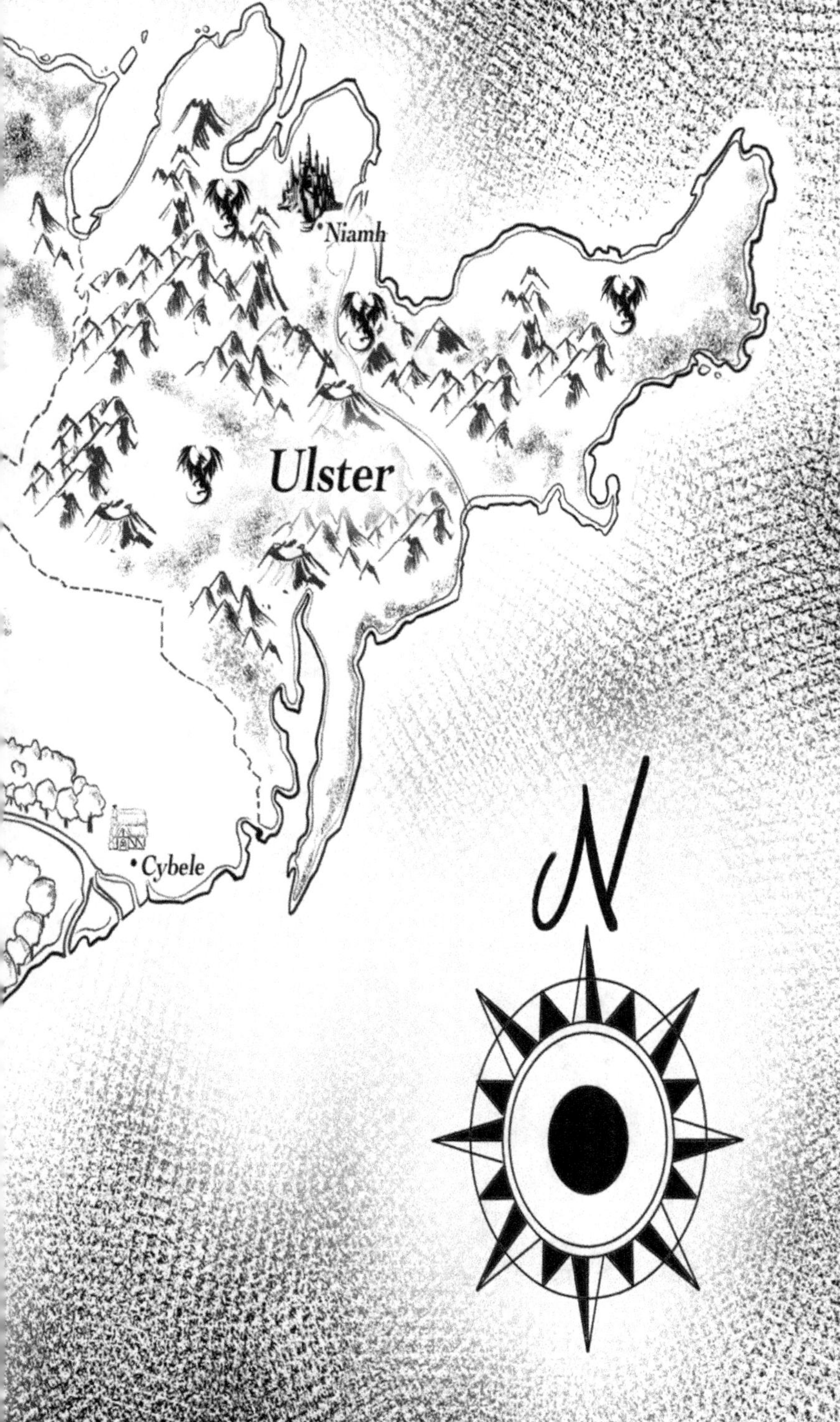

Niamh
Ulster
Cybele
N

THE FOREST MADE
HER A WARRIOR:
THE WORLD MADE
HER A
HERO.
REYNA

In a kingdom
ruled by cruelty,
Kindness
is his
Rebellion.

Derrick

CHAPTER 1

Reyna left the forest of Gaia as the evening sun began to set, leaving a burning glare across the sky. She took the simple dirt path worn into the earth over hundreds of years by her ancestors. As she crept along the well trodden path, her horses Andromeda and Orestes followed behind her. Orestes carried a heap of furs she needed to sell in Cybele on his back.

Reyna knew, after years of traveling through these woods, that brigands and the king's spies could be hiding behind any tree or bush. While no one but the Wreya, her people, dared to go into the forest, its outskirts were prime real estate for anyone who enjoyed harassing the Wreyan women emerging from the forest.

Leaving the protection of the forest always set Reyna on edge. She felt the forest shift and settle behind her. Its magic erased any trace of her existence from its soil.

Cybele stood as a dark smudge in the distance. The Wreya had been trading with Cybele for hundreds of years. It was the only village left that would do business with the tribe of warrior women.

Reyna's body relaxed as she reached the open, grassy plains. She patted Andromeda's flank. "We'll be nestled down safe behind Cybele's walls soon," she murmured.

The horse snorted in response.

"I know." Reyna sighed, "I want to get back home to Syrinx as soon as possible, too."

Reyna dismounted Andromeda just outside the rustic gates. Her long braid swung about before finally resting at her thin waist. As the shadows of the impending night stretched before her, the town came into sharper view. Smoke curled into the air. Tendrils of the scented breeze reached out to tempt her nose. Reyna's stomach growled. Mutton and pork, her favorite.

She headed for The Mangy Wolf Inn and Tavern, where she always rested for the night before trading her furs with Morken, the local tanner and blacksmith. The Mangy Wolf was much cleaner than its name implied. The owners, Zachius and Sarah, took wonderful care of their patrons. Sarah's cooking was the only decent food for miles.

As Reyna approached the stables beside the tavern, she dug a coin out of her purse and flipped it to the stable boy. "Be gentle when you unpack them. I'll need them boarded and fed for the night." Reyna noted the boy had lost weight since she'd seen him last.

The small boy nodded and hurried to take Andromeda and Orestes' reins. Her horses were in good hands.

She made her way into the tavern. Reyna's eyes narrowed upon spying the red and yellow cloaks of King Julius' guards. They had been coming through the villages more and more often. Overeating and leaving less and less for the locals each time they came through. Three of them leaned on the heavy oaken bartop, slurping down ale, leering at the other patrons. Their thin, weasel-faced counterpart danced about like a king's fool between the tables, bumping carelessly into other patrons. Sarah held her breath as the soldier tripped over his own feet and crashed head-first into a chair. The other guards roared with laughter.

Reyna's jaw clenched and she furtively darted to the back of the room.

"Another round!" One guard called out, ordering drinks none of them would pay for.

"Don't cause a scene," Reyna ground out in a whisper to herself.

Sarah and Zachius were great people; kind, loyal, and protective. Reyna wished she could do more to protect them and their beloved establishment from the king's men.

With a heavy sigh she sat in a dark corner of the common room, scowling at the soldiers from beneath the leather hood of her cloak. Sarah gave her a bowl of rabbit stew with a hunk of fresh bread on the side.

"On the house," she insisted, then flitted away. Reyna dug in. The ride had taken nearly a full day, and she was famished.

"Still eating like a half-starved wolf, I see," a rich, deep voice greeted her as she gulped down a large piece of carrot from the bowl. Her gaze flicked up, and she grinned.

"When it's Sarah's stew, I can't help it," she replied.

Anteros, Reyna's best friend, stood in front of her. His thick, disheveled black hair looked as if a wind storm had torn through it. It fell across his gentle blue eyes, and a loose strand tickled the broken, but still handsome nose. His muscles flexed as he uncrossed his arms from in front of his broad chest.

"Aren't you going to invite me to join you," the blacksmith's apprentice teased. "No wonder no one visits Syrinx. The Wreya are all so rude!" He gave her a wink as he sat down.

Reyna swatted at him. "I was just coming to that, you brute. And who says we Wreyans want some meat slab of a *man* to come visit us anyway?" she teased back, and the two laughed together.

"Oh yes, I almost forgot! All men are disgusting boors who thirst for blood and a warm body to lay with," he chuckled.

Reyna shrugged, holding a straight face. "You're not wrong."

"Hey, now. We're not all terrible," he frowned.

She laughed. "That remains to be seen."

Anteros let out a quiet chortle. "Your wit is a shade too sharp and a hair too dry," he grinned. "I'm never quite sure when you're joking."

Sarah flitted in with a tankard of mulled mead for Anteros. Reyna's eyebrows shot up. "Since when do you drink mead?" she frowned as he took a sip. The Anteros she knew had always prided himself on not drinking spirits.

"Since the men in town make sport of me for not joining them," he replied, his shoulders slumped. "I drink here once or twice a week, just to keep up appearances."

"Gods, Anteros. This is why the Wreya stay in Syrinx, hidden from men who want to control everything and everyone around them." Reyna sighed. She recognized how lucky she was to have grown up with the freedom to live a simple life. In fact, it was Wreyan law.

"Rey, I want more than what Morken has planned for me. I know he needs me to take over the forge and I don't want to let him down. When my parents died, he took me in and treated me like the son he never had. I love him for that... but I want to travel, see the world," Anteros said. Reyna raised an incredulous brow and put a comforting hand on his bicep. His cheeks flamed beneath her skeptical gaze and gentle touch. "Alright, maybe I want to be like the old heroes; protect those who can't protect themselves. I know it sounds stupid," he confessed. "But, why can't I get a say in how I live my life?" Anteros grew wistful, looking far younger than his nineteen winters.

Reyna bit the corner of her lip. "It's not stupid. If it makes any difference, you're a hero to me."

He gave her a grateful smile. "You know it does."

"You should stay here. For now, at least," Reyna said. The guards' behavior crept back into her thoughts, unbidden. "Julius is a tyrant, and he and his men are getting worse. Braxis was only the beginning. Cybele will likely be next. The way his cloaked cads behave, it's only a matter of time. My people have seen this again and again, throughout our history. Freedom has to be fought for, and defended. It needs champions."

Anteros huffed out a breath. He was quiet for a long time. Reyna wanted to say more, but held back. Anteros, she knew, did not come to decisions lightly. He would need to think on her words.

Finally, he sighed. "I know you're right," he said, "but now is not the time to discuss such thoughts. Not here. Not where there are other ears to listen."

He took another long breath. "It's late. I'll see you after you finish at the tanner tomorrow, okay? Let's take a walk like we used to, before you go back home to Syrinx."

"I'd like that," she nodded with a wry grin. "Then you can tell me all about Anteros the hero," Reyna smiled and swept her upturned hand through the air, like a merchant revealing her finest goods. Anteros shifted from one foot to the other, glancing around to see if anyone had heard her. He seemed embarrassed that she would sing the praises of a fictional hero, so she touched his arm and added with sincerity, "He sounds wonderful."

Anteros got to his feet, cheeks flushing once more, and hurried to the door. Reyna smiled to herself and sighed. *Stop it, Reyna. What would he want with a gangly wraith of a girl like you? Your hair is so curly you have to bind the tresses up into a braid just to tame them. You're a mess. A wild Wreya. And he's...*

Reyna closed her eyes, remembering the night she'd first realized that Anteros was more than just another *man.*

"Your eyes match the midnight sky," he'd grinned, tucking a loose strand of her dark hair behind her ear. She could still feel his breath against her cheek, even though years had passed between then and now.

Reyna shook herself from her thoughts. "Stop being so

weird. You're Wreya," she muttered.

A deep yawn rocked her where she sat. She finished her stew, got up and made her way towards the stairs. Zachius met her with a long, glowing taper, and led her to her room. He bid her good night, and she locked the door behind her as he turned to leave.

Reyna, exhausted and stiff from her long day of travel, un-buckled her sword belt and laid it beneath the bed for easy access. One could never be too careful. That done, she fell into the soft bed, blew out the candle, and fell into a deep sleep.

Cybele came alive with the rising sun the next morning. Reyna woke to chickens clucking, merchant voices hawking their wares, and donkeys braying as they hauled their carts. She dressed quickly, gathered her things, and went to the stable.

"You've done a wonderful job," she said. The stable boy from the night before grinned at the praise, and his eyes grew wide as eagle eggs when she flipped him another coin. "For a job well done."

He still hadn't found his voice by the time Reyna grabbed

both horses' reins and made the short walk to the tannery.

"Be with you in a moment!" a gruff voice called out as she shut the door behind her. Morken looked and sounded like a great big bear, even in the most jovial of moods. But he was always fair with his prices, and kinder than almost any man Reyna had known.

"Take your time, Morken. My pelts won't die of boredom," she laughed.

A loud thump and a muffled curse came from the back room. "That you, Reyna? Where have you been this season?"

Reyna winced. "I had to find pelts that were worthy of your skill."

Morken laughed as he came in, wiping his hands on a sheepskin cloth. "I've never met a hunter so picky as you. But, better late than never, eh?" he teased. "How many do you have?"

"Sixty-seven." Reyna held her breath. She usually brought around eighty.

"One hundred and fifty drakes."

Reyna's mouth fell agape. She stood up, stunned. "Morken, that's too much!" she protested.

The older man just shrugged and stood waiting for her answer. Reyna shifted. Her people could desperately use the coin.

"Are you sure, then?" she asked.

He nodded, a twinkle in his eye.

"Alright," she capitulated with a grateful smile. "But I still say it's too much, you stubborn old man."

"Pshaw. I pay for quality, and your pelts are the best every season." Morken gave her the bag of coins.

Reyna clasped his hand. "Pleasure doing business with you, Morken. You're a decent man," she said, her voice solemn.

Morken raised a brow, understanding the significance of the compliment coming from a Wreya. Reyna smiled before heading back to the horses.

"Make a good bargain?" Anteros asked, materializing as if out of thin air.

"Of course. Morken is far too generous to me," she said, the weight of the money bag ever present at her hip.

"I'm sure your pelts were worth every drake," he grinned, reaching out to take Orestes' reins.

The two fell into a companionable silence as they walked through the market. Reyna sensed unease and tension thickening the air the closer they got to the town's center. The shopkeepers were on edge; the crowds were unusually quiet. Reyna halted the horse and narrowed her keen, dark blue eyes.

Anteros pulled Orestes to a stop as well and lowered his voice. "What is it?"

"Not sure." She took a deep inhale and clenched her jaw. Reyna ground out, "Let's go find out."

A crowd gathered in the road a few dozen feet away. As they

came upon the edge, screams rang out. The two friends dashed into the mob and pushed their way through. At its center, they saw cloaked soldiers towering over a bruised and bloodied elderly woman on the ground.

She sputtered and coughed, crying out, "Please! Stop! I beg you!"

The men laughed and jeered as one strode up and kicked her hard in the stomach. She shrieked and doubled into herself as her body rolled on the cobbled street. Anteros balled his fists. A scowl shadowed his face.

Captain Ryell Mythos turned to the horrified crowd. "You see? This is what happens when you don't pay for the king's protection." His red and gold cloak billowed in the wind as he squatted down next to the crying woman.

She whimpered, "He's not... our king."

"And where is your ruler? Hmm?" Mythos chuckled. He made a show of pulling off his fine leather gloves, taking his time and relishing every second. "This is why you *need* a king." He slapped her with the glove, laughing as her head snapped sharply to the side.

Reyna's jaw clenched. Mythos had gone too far. She opened her mouth to say something when a voice boomed.

"That's enough!"

It took Reyna a moment to realize it was Anteros who stepped forward, drawing his sword from its sheath with a soft hiss.

The captain smirked as he got to his feet. "Be careful, boy-"

Anteros cut him off, seething. "Around here, we protect each other. There is no payment for decency and kindness. We don't sell our honor to the highest bidder." Anteros spoke with dangerous softness. The crowd went still.

"Is that so?" Mythos scoffed. "Tell me, farm boy, can your pathetic *protection* rival that of the king's trained soldiers?" He beckoned Anteros forward, drawing his own sword.

The old woman scrambled to the crowd's edge as the two men began to circle each other like wolves vying for alpha dominance. The captain lunged forward, swinging his blade in a downward arc. Anteros quickly raised his arm to block, turning his blade at the last moment to draw a thin red line from the captain's forearm. Reyna's heart leaped as she watched and brimmed with joy when she saw Anteros' grin.

He jumped to a stranger's defense with no thought for himself or the danger before him. He doesn't even realize how heroic he can be.

Mythos' face clouded with rage as he slashed out at Anteros' middle, but the younger man jumped back and scored another shallow cut on the captain's thigh. Reyna hissed a quick "Yes!" under her breath.

Anteros was the best swordsman she knew. This buffoon in silks had no chance. Reyna watched, mesmerized by the dance of swords, the melody of metal ringing on metal. The ferocity of the blows grew by the second. The captain feinted to the left, then tried a backhanded cut. Anteros parried, hooked his leg behind the captain's knee, and tugged, sending the man sprawling onto his pompous ass.

Anteros' sword hovered just over an inch from the captain's throat.

"You tell me," he growled. "Am I on par with the king's soldiers, *sir*?"

Mythos grimaced as Anteros backed out of the circle. He sheathed his sword and walked back to Reyna with his head bowed.

"That was amazing!" she beamed. "You saved that woman." She went to hug him.

Anteros lifted his hand and shook his head. "No, Rey. When they come back, it'll only get worse for her. I should have kept my nose out of it." Behind them, armor clanged, and another dozen sheaths hissed.

Anteros spun around. Other than the two helping Mythos to his feet, the rest of the guards had drawn their swords. And from the murderous gleam in their eyes, Reyna knew Anteros would not be taken prisoner.

Reyna cried, "We've got to get you out of here!" She swung up on Andromeda's back, and Anteros vaulted onto Orestes. Both horses bolted. Reyna cut through the streets on the most direct path towards the Forest of Gaia.

"After them!" Mythos shouted to his men, cursing.

Reyna and Anteros spurred their horses on. Reyna called out, "I can talk to the Wreya, I'm sure they would grant you sanctuary. At least for a short time. My people have no love for King Julius."

Anteros said nothing. A dark grimace clouded his handsome face. She knew he hated to flee, but for the moment, it was their only option for survival.

Faster, Reyna urged her horse forward. *Please, we need to be faster.*

They reached the outskirts of Cybele just as the sound of galloping horses thundered up from behind.

"We're almost there!" Reyna shouted. "Once we reach the forest, its magic will protect us!"

Anteros nodded and kicked Orestes hard. "We can make it!"

Reyna's vision narrowed on the forest's edge. The shouts from behind seemed muffled as she focused on what was ahead.

Fwip! Anteros' mouth fell open, his eyes going wide. Blood poured over his chin as he let out a muffled groan.

"Anteros!" Reyna cried, looking about wildly for the source of the blood, for the wound that threatened her friend's life.

Anteros fell forward, over Orestes' neck. Reyna's eyes widened at the arrow in his back. She watched in horror as his body went slack. He slid off the horse, dangling by the stirrups from his feet.

"Get up!" she screamed. "Damn it, Anteros, get up!"

Reyna pulled back on Andromeda's reins with all her might, but nothing she did would slow her horse. She watched, praying that any second, he would rise up and follow her. Anteros didn't move.

She watched as the soldiers caught up to him. The sun glinted off the captain's blade. A clean slice through the air sent the sword deep into Anteros' back. A scream tore through her throat as Orestes reared up in defiance, then fell atop her childhood friend.

The soldiers glared, their swords swung up as they charged after her. All sound dissipated. Reyna's ears were pounding as the adrenaline rushed through her. Hot tears smeared her face and were whipped away in the cool wind as Andromeda raced her back home.

CHAPTER 2

"Derrick." His mother passed by the back of his chair. She gave him a sad look and squeezed his shoulder before gliding out of the hall, her ladies in waiting trailing her like ducklings.

Derrick tried not to scowl as he looked up at the high table. His father, King Julius, was busy laughing at his own bawdy jokes. His thick, wavy, black hair and chocolate-colored eyes would make him handsome if his soul hadn't rotted him from the inside out. He had the brutish, thick-shouldered body of a warrior, though still lithe and quick on his feet.

Derrick took a deep breath, looking over at his brother, Stravos. A serving girl, maybe sixteen winters young, sat on Stravos' lap. The girl looked miserable, which only seemed to please his brother more.

The older boy, it seemed to Derrick, had grown into a mirror of his father– though his strength was quieter, more thoughtful. Stravos moved with languid ease. He seemed to hypnotize his victim, then struck hard and fast. The man was a snake.

Derrick balled his hands into fists beneath the table as he watched the girl squirm, tears building in her wide eyes. His face contorted with each unwanted squeeze.

He's a bloody monster. No better than our father, Derrick thought, bitterness and bile rising in his throat.

Stravos, oblivious to his brother's mounting anger, spoke to the officer next to him. "And what news do you have of Syrinx?"

"We still cannot find the village, sir." Stravos glared at the officer. Flinching, he explained, "None of the Wreyan savages will pledge loyalty, let alone tell us how to get into Syrinx."

"And they survived this insolence?" Stravos growled.

"Well, yes— I mean, not *all* of them, sir. They are quite skilled..." Seeing the murderous rage behind Stravos' eyes, he added with haste, "The people of Cybele are finally ready to join our cause."

"Good. Without any allies those stubborn Wreyan wenches

will have to submit." Stravos adjusted in the chair with a smug grin.

As the men continued talking, Derrick slipped an apple up his sleeve and stood up without ceremony.

"If you'll excuse me," he said, his voice as quiet as his feet. He walked out without another word.

The people who had been sitting to either side of him said nothing as he moved to leave.

Ah, yes. It is I, the royal ghost, who haunts the halls of this hellish castle, he thought to himself. He tried to control his ragged breathing, to unclench his fists before his fingernails dug moon-shaped crescents into his palms. Usually, Derrick would go to his chamber to read after dinner. But the idea of reading in the comfort and safety of his room, seemed...*wrong* as that young girl was being put on display for Stravos' pleasure. He had to get out.

Derrick turned towards the entrance hall. His gut twisted. *What will that poor girl have to endure tonight?*

He sighed as he reached the freedom of the outdoors. He put the young woman out of his mind. He could be of no help to her. His interference would only make things worse for both of them. After his father and brother snored off the night's revelries, he would have her assigned to other duties.

Derrick crossed the manicured lawn and made his way to the stables.

"Your Highness." A small boy with bright red hair bowed to him.

Derrick raised a black brow. "Are you a new apprentice?"

"Y-yes, sir. I-I mean, my prince," the boy stammered.

"'Your Highness,' technically," Derrick chuckled. "But you can call me Derrick."

"Oh no, Your Highness," the boy bowed deeper, trembling before him.

Derrick frowned, then added as gently as he could, "I won't hurt you. Please, stand."

Slowly, the boy rose. "H-how can I help you, Your Highness?"

"I'll need my horse saddled, please." Derrick gave him a soft smile.

"Right away!" The boy took off as if all the demons of hell were on his heels. Derrick barely saw the back of his ragged tunic whip around the corner of the stall. He stepped into the cool darkness of the stables to wait.

The warm scent of sharp yet musty hay, paired with a sweeter scent akin to a rose reached him. He closed his warm brown eyes and listened to the horses. Their soft whinnies and the swishes of their tails soothed his heart.

His eyes opened at the staccato clop, clop of hooves. His beautiful palomino pranced at the end of her lead. Her coat shone like burnished gold. Derrick turned to the little groom.

"Thank you," he said with sincerity.

The boy gave a squeak of fright, dropped the lead rope, and disappeared. Derrick sighed. New servants always assumed he was like every other man in the Dragonspear family. And who could blame them?

Heavy shuffling headed his way.

"What did you do? Threaten to roast him over an open flame?" Matthias grinned as he came out of the shadows of the stables.

"You know me better than that," Derrick replied, his demeanor stern. "I prefer a vat of boiling oil," he winked.

Matthias was covered in scars along his arms and face; each won during battle. He had straw-like blond hair that hung down into his eyes. Granted, anyone foolish enough to laugh at that would be frozen by his glacier-blue gaze, then pummeled to death by his hammer-like fists.

Matthias was the closest thing to a friend Derrick had in the castle. Though it had taken three years to break him of the "Your Highness" formality.

"Well, either way, Arlen probably won't stop running till he gets to Arcadia. Seriously, though, what did you say to him?" Matthias raised an eyebrow at Derrick as he continued polishing an old bridle.

"Nothing! I swear. I just tried to thank the kid."

Matthias laughed.

"It's not funny!" Derrick burst out. "I hate when people are afraid of me. All because of *them*," he spat.

"Alright, alright, don't get your pantalettes in a twist," Matthias grinned. "I'll have a word with him."

"Thank you, Matthias." Derrick ran a hand through his short, dark hair.

"Sure. Once he's done running for the hills!" Matthias roared with laughter once again.

Derrick scowled at him. He unclipped his horse's lead rope and threw it at Matthias before swinging himself gracefully into the saddle. Matthias caught it before it hit his face, which made him laugh even harder.

"Come on, Apple, let's get out of here," Derrick clucked.

He gave Matthias a farewell wave as the horse took off at a gallop. As Derrick rode Apple, they became one. Riding the wind, running faster than sadness or guilt or bottled rage... they were both free.

Derrick was six years old when she'd crossed the leagues to enter the lands of Niamh, all the way from Arcadia's vast desert country in the west. Niamh was a harsh, brutal land, riddled with active volcanoes that housed the world's last dragons. Traversing the lands of Niamh as a foal made Apple a Dragonspear, as much as Derrick.

They rode across the stark, barren grounds just outside the castle. No fence, no physical boundary penned them in. But

Derrick knew how far they were allowed to venture before incurring his father's wrath. Still, he felt free on the scant few miles that distanced them from his cold, unwelcoming home.

Apple's powerful muscles shifted beneath his legs. Her lungs worked like bellows in her chest. Derrick's tense body relaxed as she galloped farther and farther away. He focused on her stride allowing his concerned mind to clear.

After a while, he pulled Apple back to a trot. "You ready to go home, girl?" he asked, patting her flank. She slowed enough to turn her head and nuzzled him. "Alright. Come on, then."

The sun had begun to set. It would be dark by the time he got back to the castle. Derrick swung up into the saddle and lightly touched his heels to Apple's sides to increase her pace. Apple obliged, and the pair began their journey home.

The moon shone large and waxing from behind the monstrous clouds as Apple sped along the barren ground. Derrick pulled her to a stop for a moment to take it in.

"They'll never understand it, will they, Apple?" Derrick shook his head. "Beauty is not something that should be taken for granted. Especially not beauty like this."

Apple huffed out her agreement.

The guards patrolled the tops of the walls outside the castle as they finally approached. They did not acknowledge the prince as he entered the gates. *The Royal Ghost does not need greeting,* he thought with a frown.

Derrick continued on to the pitch-black stables. The stable boy had gone home for the night. Derrick lit a lantern and led Apple back to her stall.

He took off her bridle and all her tack, then hung everything on the pegs against the boarded wooden wall. He took a soft brush and ran it over her body, starting at her flanks. Apple nuzzled him, and he chuckled under his breath, "I know. It's been too long since I've gotten to take care of you myself."

After he'd combed her mane and tail, he took a leather cloth and rubbed her down, knocking off any loose hair before bending down to polish her hooves. He patted her head and kissed her velvety nose before closing the door to her stall.

With Apple attended to, Derrick made his way up the gravel trail to the quiet castle. On nights like tonight, the *Royal Ghost* could go wherever he pleased. His lips curved ever so slightly at the thought.

Derrick padded on silent feet down the dark corridor towards the war room. His boots slid over the stones like liquid silver, and he clung to the shadows. Warm light and dark laughter spilled out from behind the wooden door.

Derrick shook his head. They were already drunk... *Am I too late?* he wondered, pursing his lips together.

While the rest of the castle slept, King Julius and Prince Stravos went to the war room for discussions they preferred to keep amongst themselves. Arrogant as they were, they left the door open...for no one would dare to spy on them. But a ghost? A ghost could hear everything.

"The nerve of him!" Stravos slurred his words.

Derrick crept closer.

"*'Your Majesty! It simply can't be done!'*" King Julius mocked in a high-pitched voice. "I don't care how they do it, but they *will* do it," he growled.

"Have they made no progress, then?" Stravos hiccoughed.

"No. Not a single egg," Julius sniffed. "I don't understand. Why is this so difficult? Observe the dragons. Learn their habits. Grab an egg once the mother has left. It shouldn't be that hard!" Julius slammed his fist onto the table.

"Incompetent fools. They should have had *one* egg by now! Why are they taking so long?" Stravos slammed a fist down on the table, punctuating each of his words, "I. Want. My. *Dragon!*"

His father slumped into his velvet armchair. "Patience, son. I've sent a unit of my best soldiers to the caves to take charge of the situation."

Derrick went cold, as if a chunk of ice had slipped down the back of his tunic. The acrid taste of bile crawled up his throat, threatening to choke him. His thoughts raced as he slipped away from the door. *A dragon egg? How? They've been missing for over a century.*

Derrick's late night reading had taught him that dragons

were highly intelligent creatures. Long ago – though no text could put a precise time on *how* long ago – they had even lived alongside men. Now, for reasons the books' authors had not speculated, the dragons no longer held love for humans. The creatures had disappeared, leaving no trace behind.

Even if they find a dragon's egg, its mother would not allow them to take it... Gods, what does Stravos want with a pet dragon?

Head spinning, he slid away from the door. Derrick didn't stop until he had made it to the safety of his own chamber. He threw the bolt on the door behind him. Not that the bolt would really be much protection; the castle was riddled with secret passages. Though he'd never found so much as a hidden broom closet.

Exhausted, Derrick pulled his shirt over his head, then took off his deerskin trousers. He put on the lighter, linen pants he slept in.

A quiet knock came at the door moments after he crawled into bed. Frowning, Derrick got up and padded barefoot across the room. He slid back the bolt on the door. The door opened and a slender figure brushed past him, dressed in black.

"Derrick, you have to leave!" The soft voice came from beneath a black veil.

"Mother?"

She held up her finger. "There isn't time. Your father is

planning your death as we speak. You have to leave *tonight*."

"What?" Derrick couldn't begin to wrap his head around her words. "What are you talking about? They're too busy trying to find–" He shook his head, stopping from incriminating himself. "No. You must be mistaken. I'm the Invisible Prince. The Royal Ghost. No one here pays attention to me. Father doesn't see *me* as a threat..."

"Son," she said, her voice thick with tears, "he fears that the heart of the people will be with you when you come of age. And he's right. They will *demand* that you rule. The little projects you've been allowed to do as prince have always been to better the people's lives. They love you, and that *beast* sees it."

Derrick thought back to his last project: he sent the leftover food from the castle to the local villages. It had felt incredible, but it didn't solve anything. Soon after his father rescinded Derrick's order and he was chastised for showing "weakness".

Still, inciting rebellion hadn't been his intention. Derrick didn't have the *courage* to stand against his father, let alone rule in his stead.

"Mother, why? Why me? Our people hardly know I exist," Derrick insisted.

"More people know about you and your kindness than you think. There are groups forming, even now, who want you on the throne." Fear flickered across her face. "I'm proud, but— I cannot lose you." She took his hands in hers. "You are the one good thing I've done with my life."

Derrick shook his head. His mother had to be mistaken, or at least misinformed. "No. I don't want it. I'm nothing, a nobody."

His mother's green eyes softened. "That, my son, has never been true," she sighed. When she spoke again, her voice resumed its edge. "Matthias has packed your provisions. Apple is saddled and ready to go. Now, get dressed and take some extra clothes." She lunged forward and threw her arms around him, almost crushing the breath from his body. "I love you, Derrick." Tears rolled down her cheeks as she tore herself away from him.

He could feel the same welling up in his own.

"I will pray every night, to any god who will listen, to keep you safe." She held her hand to his cheek for a moment. Then she was gone.

Derrick stood, staring at the back of his door. In his heart, he knew he needed to do as she said. But he couldn't help but wonder at the validity of her concerns. After all, his brother and father never gave him the time of day.

And yet, her words rang like alarm bells through his stunned thoughts. *Am I really in danger?*

His mind raced as he dressed with urgency in the clothes that he'd worn earlier. They were the simplest clothes he owned and would blend in while he was on the run. There was no doubt King Julius would put a bounty on his head once he left the castle grounds. From a chest by the bed, Derrick grabbed a second set of roughspun clothes, rolled them up as small as he could, and threw them into a leather satchel.

Derrick took one last look at the chamber where he'd grown up. With a shaky sigh, he slipped from the room and retraced the familiar steps to the stables.

As he crept along in the dark, his thoughts turned to his mother. What would happen to her? If his father ever found out that she had warned him... No one was safe from the king's wrath, not even his own wife.

"Derrick?" a voice hissed. "Is that you?"

Derrick jumped, a panicked scream rising up inside him before recognizing the voice. "Matthias. Yes, it's me." He swallowed the knot forming in his throat. "I can't ask you to do this for me. My father will-"

"Think nothing of it. I will do whatever it takes to protect my future king." Matthias checked over everything that he'd packed.

Derrick froze at those words. "It was you. You told the people about me..." His mind raced.

Matthias interrupted his thoughts. "Me and many others," he grunted. "Focus, Derrick. We aren't far from the border. Once you cross, head southwest until you reach the Forest of

Gaia. There are plenty of villages all around it. Cybele, for one. They have close ties with the Wreya."

"Not anymore—"

"Lies told by a man who wanted to keep his head. Listen, it will be easy to lose yourself there. No one will recognize you or suspect who you may be. Whatever you do, you *must* gain the trust of the Wreya— get them to fight with us before it's too late. Most importantly, do not attempt to enter the Forest of Gaia on your own. It will end in certain death. The forest is too wild, and they say its magic keeps men from ever returning. You need a Wreyan guide to get you through. It's why your father has yet to take the land."

"How do *you* know all of this, Matthias?"

"I picked up some things here and there." He shrugged. "Remember, *southwest*. Be careful and may the power of the dragons shield you, Your Highness."

Derrick climbed into his saddle. "Matthias, since when do you call—"

Matthias slapped Apple's flank, sending her off at a gallop into the dark night.

CHAPTER 3

Pain lanced through Reyna, tearing her heart to pieces. Nothing felt real. Her cheeks numbed; her mind rushed through the images of Anteros' death, again and again. One second he was there, the next... *gone*.

It happened so fast. I should have done something. How did I not stop it?

Knowing she could not have foreseen the horror didn't stop the guilt from settling onto her shoulders like a heavy cloak. Tears streamed down her face onto Andromeda's tawny mane. Her heart felt raw, a cold dead weight in her chest. But she pressed on, weaving into the tangled green Forest of Gaia.

The shouts of the soldiers grew more distant as she plunged deeper into the trees and undergrowth. Unbidden, Anteros' jaunty grin rose from her memories...

"What would Ephiny say about us hanging out so much?" Anteros gave her shoulder a gentle shove.

Reyna laughed. "She'd probably say, 'What are you doing? He's a man. What use is a friend who is so weak?'"

"Ouch!" Anteros gripped at his heart. "You wound me."

"Well... you're the exception to the rule," she shrugged, feigning innocence.

He gave her a cocky smirk. "And why is that?"

Reyna took a moment of honest consideration before answering. "You're not like the rest of them. For one, you never drink. Two, I've never once seen you get angry."

She paused as she noticed Anteros looking at her. She felt her heartbeat quicken.

"I'm glad I'm the exception," he grinned, breaking the silence. "And I'm especially glad you've taken over Ariadne's old job."

"Me too. I enjoy spending time at the blacksmith's forge. There's something very powerful and humbling about watching the metal being made malleable, and the intricate inlay of chain and plate that creates armor. Besides, Mother's getting older and I don't want her making the trip." Reyna's thoughts dragged her into a hidden place in her heart, leading her to

reflect on other reasons.

"*And I do love a good haggle,*" she added with a small smile.

"*That, I believe,*" he said, raising his brows.

"*Hey!*" she protested, giving him a soft smack on the arm.

"*What? I mean, you do love to argue, and even more you love to win.*"

"*You know me too well,*" she sighed.

And he had.

He always had.

The horse sprinted on, racing through the hidden trails she'd traveled so many times before. Reyna, folding into herself, blocked out the world. Her grief, her overwhelming sense of loss, dredged up another memory…

Reyna had joined her motherAriadne in Cybele, to learn the ropes for trading furs. They'd finished with their work for the day and small, energetic Reyna bounced off and around the tables at The Mangy Wolf.

"*Reyna, get down!*" *Ariadne insisted.* "*Go outside and play. Just be back here by sundown.*"

Reyna needed no further encouragement. She ran out the door and into the bustling city to indulge her favorite pastime: exploring the inner walls and outer lands of Cybele, a place so unlike her home.

Squinting up at the early afternoon sun, she found herself at a ramshackle fort made of chunks of wood and clumps of leaves.

Reyna went up on tiptoes, creeping closer to investigate.

"RAAARGH!" A little boy charged forth, holding a stick up high like a sword.

Reyna bent low and swung her leg out, sweeping the boy's own legs out from under him. She pressed her foot to his chest, kicking the stick from his hand.

"Whoa!" The boy coughed. "Can you teach me how you did that?"

"No." Reyna stated, crossing her arms over her chest.

"Can you at least let me up?"he pleaded.

She rolled her eyes, lifted her leg and helped him to his feet. "You men are all idiots."

"Sorry. I thought you were one of... them. The king's..." The boy's voice fell to a whisper.

She put out a hand. "No need to explain. I'm Reyna."

"Anteros." He grinned, shaking her hand with a firm grip.

Reyna smiled at the memory. From that day on, they had been secret best friends. Reyna had never been bored on a trip to the village again.

The trees started to thin around her. She still had a while to ride, but she could tell by her surroundings that she was almost halfway there. Reyna blinked back tears.

"Are we ever going to stop meeting in secret?" Anteros slashed out with a wooden sword as Reyna parried.

She grinned, "Maybe. Who knows? Now stop trying to dis-

tract me." She swung, knocking him back into a thick oak tree.

Anteros, eyes wide, fought for a gasp of air. "I have to admit, you've gotten really good at this," he wheezed.

"Thanks." Pride filled her, though she tried to keep it from showing on her face. The Wreya never used swords, and she enjoyed Anteros' lessons on using a blade.

The young man rubbed his side. "Let's take a break. I have something I want to show you."

"Tired already?" She raised a gently mocking brow.

He shook his head. "It's your name day, isn't it?"

She crossed her arms over her chest, suddenly leery. "Why?"

He rushed to the woods and pulled out something hidden in the brush.

"I made this for you," he said. He handed her a long, heavy object wrapped in a thin hide blanket. "Careful, she's sharp."

Reyna could feel the hilt beneath her hand even before she unwrapped it. "Anteros," she gasped. The long sword gleamed in the sunlight. The pommel had tiny leaves from the fairy trees found in the Forest of Gaia pressed into the tightly wrapped leather. Elegant, yet dangerous vines were painstakingly carved into the sharp blade. It was thin, balanced... perfect. "You made this?"

His gaze darted away and his cheeks pinked. "For you."

"I love it," she beamed.

His chest puffed and his eyes sparkled. "Oh! And this. It

seemed fitting." He handed her a wooden pendant, carved with twin swords crossing in the middle of a circle. Her eyes grew wide as he leaned forward and tied the leather cord around her neck. "There. What do you think?"

"Did you carve this?" she asked, staring at the pendant.

He nodded, then smiled. "What will you name her? The sword, I mean."

"I don't know yet. Maybe Little Anteros?" she teased.

"Maybe not that," he chuckled, his voice cracking.

Reyna put the blade down carefully and hugged him. "Thank you. From now on when I want to meet with you, I'll ride to our clearing and raise it high so you'll know I'm there, waiting for you." Her hand crept to her new necklace, fingers caressing the wood.

"I like that," he said as he pulled back from their embrace.

A hot branding iron pierced Reyna's chest. Anteros was dead. She would never hear his deep voice; never see his warm grinning face again.

She began to sob. "I can't even give him a proper burial..."

Even postmortem, Anteros would be charged with treason. His body would be hung outside the gates until nature and scavengers reduced it to bare bones. Only then could his family take him down and bury what remained.

"This is my fault, girl," she said to Andromeda. The mare huffed in response, slowing her pace to a trot. Her body shook with sobs. "I should have gotten him out of there sooner. I should have stopped at the village gates and killed every last soldier so he could get away!" Reyna gulped in hot air, again and again, trying to steady her breathing. Her heart thundered and her chest tightened. "What have I done? I-I let this happen..."

Reyna rode through the trees, slumping over Andromeda's neck. She bit her lip, and her mouth filled with the taste of salty metal.

Wreyan horses knew the way back to Syrinx. Andromeda led them through the dappled paths without Reyna's guidance.

As she drew closer to home, Andromeda slowed to a walk, her sides heaving. Reyna looked up, wiping at her face with her sleeve. Her eyes felt gritty and raw, as if full of sand. She pulled at her windblown hair in a vain attempt to gain control of it.

Hiccoughing, she slowed her breathing and closed her eyes. Now that she was home, she would have to tell her mother what happened.

CHAPTER 4

Fairies flitted about over her head, the tinkling sound of their flight mixing with the cheerful buzzing of Syrinx as her home came into view. Her mind couldn't grasp how there was still happiness in the world. It didn't make sense. Her best friend was gone. Nothing would ever be right again.

She locked fresh sobs behind her teeth, and pasted on a false smile. Every now and then she waved when someone called her name.

Syrinx bustled around her, with women working at their daily chores. Some skinned animals and butchered the meat, then passed it off to be salted and stored. Others carried baskets of fruits and vegetables from the community gardens down by the river. The sights and sounds of home comforted her, though the wound in her soul still ached.

"Reyna!" Ariadne called from the animal pen under their treehouse.

Reyna's head snapped up, and her heart sank. She knew she would have to tell her mother ... and Reyna knew this conversation would not go well.

"Hello, Mother."

Ariadne's eyes snapped up, like a deer scenting the hunter. "What happened?"

A sob escaped Reyna at her mother's question. Ariadne was there in an instant, wrapping her daughter in a strong, protective hug.

"I'm sure, whatever it is, it can't be as bad as you think," she said, her voice softening. "Let's go up and I'll make some tea."

Reyna let Andromeda's reins slip out of her nerveless fingers. She nodded.

Ariadne began the climb, picking out hand and foot holds in the rugged bark, as did all the Wreya. Reyna, on the other hand, went to the rope ladder that hung from the branches, an accommodation reserved for the old and injured. She heard a few gasps behind her, and she knew rumors would be flying before the sun set. She didn't care.

By the time she made it to the platform, her mother had already poured steaming hot water over elderberry leaves, and stood waiting for her. She offered her mother a feeble smile and sat down. Ariadne leaned against the wall, silent and expectant.

Reyna took a sip. Her mother's tea was always good, but she could not bring herself to enjoy it. Nor did she allow the pleasure of the wooden cup warming her hands more than a cursory acknowledgement. The cup had been carved by Ephiny, their queen. A scrolling *E* at the bottom marked the wood with pride. She studied it, trying to find the words to begin.

"Anteros... he's gone," she managed though the words were strangled. Then, tea forgotten, Reyna buried her head in her arms. Bitterness crept up from her soul as she once more began to cry.

Ariadne crossed the room and rubbed her hand in soothing circles on Reyna's back.

"So that was the boy's name," her mother said to herself. She sighed. "I know there's nothing I can say that will take the pain away... but I'm here for you, my daughter."

Reyna spun in her chair and threw her arms around her mother's waist, sobbing into her tunic as she had when she was a child. Ariadne held her until her tears ran out.

"He was my best friend," she wept, not hearing her mother's words at first.

"Wait..." she gasped, realization dawning. Reyna stared up at her mother's face. "You knew?"

Ariadne smiled. "Mothers always know."

Reyna's guilt gnawed at her. *If I hadn't said anything... hadn't cheered him on... he would be alive right now.* She wanted to put a voice to these words. But pain shot through her heart, swift and sharp as a dagger, and once again, she could not speak. Her thoughts must have shown on her face.

"We must see the queen," her mother told her gently.

She blinked at her mother through tear-stained eyes. "Why?" She didn't relish the idea of having to admit her guilt and ineffectualness to anyone.

Her mother nodded, her answer in the movement. Reyna sighed, and stood up.

"Fine," she grumbled. Even a broken heart could not assuage her fiery temper.

Reyna's hands grasped the sturdy bark and she made her descent. Once her feet hit the ground, she was thankful she hadn't used the ladder again. A large group of women gathered near the base of the tree, muttering amongst themselves, their eyes filled with concern... or worse, pity. Ariadne scowled at them and they scattered like a school of fish.

They headed beneath the intricate patchwork of woven bridges that connected the trees around them. The forest towered above, limbs and branches dotted with Wreyan houses of all makes and kinds. Some of the sturdier, older trees held two or even three homes, each one as unique as its owners, and built by their own hands. Bridges connected each level for ease of access between the structures.

The queen's treehouse sat in the largest tree in the clearing, an ancient elm so massive even twenty women standing around its base couldn't surround it. Empty treehouses, used for emergency shelter and storage, surrounded the queen's abode. Despite its occupant, the treehouse was the same size as all the others.

Reyna could feel prying eyes watching her and her mother. She found herself squaring her shoulders and lifting her chin as they approached the royal residence. They began the climb, leaving the ground and a cacophony of whispers behind them. The ascent showed the queen reverence and a symbolic fealty, something Reyna needed to exhibit before she explained herself.

They reached the queen's platform. A guard stepped forward, spear held loosely in her

hand. Her expression remained a careful blank, but her deep brown eyes sparkled with mischief.

"Varia, Reyna needs to speak with the queen," Ariadne stated without pause.

"Business or pleasure?" Varia asked, her voice honeyed and warm.

"Business, I'm afraid."

Varia's face turned grim. She gave a curt nod and stepped aside. After a moment, Ariadne gave Reyna a gentle push forward. With a reluctant sigh, she walked in.

Queen Ephiny didn't sit on a throne, and she did not shout orders like a general to the men in his army. These traits made her unique among royalty. Her requests, however, were still taken as commands by the Wreya.

Reyna had visited the Queen several times before, but never for a reason this grave. She stepped into the audience chamber, her mother at her heels. Ephiny sat at a desk, poring over scrolls. She kept her graying blonde hair swept back in a casual braid, and her tunic did little to veil her well-muscled arms. It was clear that she was a warrior as well as a leader. She looked up at the sound of their footsteps.

"Ah, hello, Ariadne. Reyna! How are you, child? To what do I owe the honor?" she asked kindly.

Reyna could not meet the queen's eyes. The silence stretched on, and Ephiny's smile slipped.

"What's wrong?" her voice dropped.

"There was an... incident in Cybele. Reyna was involved," Ariadne began.

"I was not involved, I just witnessed it!" she said, hands balling into fists at her side. Words failing her, she made the mistake of looking up.

Ephiny's gaze felt like a heated iron hook, pulling Reyna's confession off her tongue by force.

"There was an old woman," she burst out. She paused, searching for how to say what she needed. "The soldiers – King Julius's thugs – were in town." The words came out disjointed and foreign. The events played out in her mind all over again. A border of red surrounded the memory; tears welled in her eyes. "My friend... he stood up for her. The old woman." Reyna's voice thickened with pride, even as tears slipped from the corners of her eyes. "We left. The soldiers followed us... He was shot... in the back. "

"You know our laws, Reyna," the Queen frowned. "Even bearing witness to such a crime reflects poorly on the Wreya, and it puts our honor into question. But what you did was worse. You aided a criminal in his escape. I know you're not of Wreyan blood, but these laws govern you, too."

"Criminal?! Anteros was a *hero*. We had to stand up to those soldiers, to show King Julius that he can't treat people like that!" yelled Reyna.

Ephiny shook her head sadly. "We have enchantments of protection from our shamans and traps surrounding our village for a reason. No man can pass them."

"It's not enough." Reyna's thoughts spun. *How do I make her understand?* "We have to take the fight to Julius, to cull the hordes of soldiers so they can't assault innocent people anymore! We must avenge Anteros!"

"Reyna." The word was barely audible, but Reyna heard the note of warning in her mother's voice. Reyna had been screaming at the queen of her people, questioning her judgment and the rule of her law. Such an act could be considered treason.

Ephiny's tone, by contrast, was subdued and moderate, befitting her station. "I understand that you are angry. That you've lost someone you loved."

Reyna felt herself blush. The queen was right. She did love Anteros. Even if she'd never allowed herself to acknowledge it

"But we are a peaceful people. We no longer fight in the wars of men. We fight for our own, and only when we are threatened," the Queen continued. "There is no reason to put our people in needless danger. We are safe, here, in the forest. I won't risk the survival of my people to avenge one man."

"Would it matter if the soldiers had threatened me? Would you fight then?" Reyna dared to ask.

"*Did* the soldiers threaten you?" Ephiny's calm, gentle reply made Reyna want to lash out at something.

"No. Not directly. They chased after me because I was helping Anteros, but he was their target," she answered, though honesty lost her cause. "But I think they might recognize my face if I went back in the next moon or so," she muttered.

Ephiny let out a held breath. Reyna saw that she had been

hoping for that exact answer. It made her anger boil back to the surface.

Reyna erupted, "We shouldn't be standing by while others are hurt! It's selfish to protect ourselves while all of Ulster is in danger!"

Ariadne moved swifter than Reyna could react. She grabbed her daughter's arm and forced her onto her knees before the queen. Her fingers dug painfully into Reyna's shoulder.

"Please forgive her, Queen Ephiny," she said, her own eyes downcast. "She didn't mean to speak out against you and your edicts. She is young. Passion guides her thoughts more than reason."

A pregnant silence filled the air. Reyna realized she'd pushed too far.

At long last, Ephiny stood. She walked over to Reyna and put a hand under her chin, forcing Reyna to look into her eyes. The queen studied her, and defiance met Ephiny's gaze.

"I will forgive her," Ephiny began. Ariadne drew in a shuddering, relieved breath. Though Reyna couldn't see her mother's face, the sound filled her with guilt. Ephiny let go of her chin and Reyna's gaze dropped to the floor. "The girl has received punishment enough today. No one deserves to lose someone they love to such violent acts. Her words are nothing more than grief lashing its way out at everyone around her." The queen returned to her desk, her every movement graceful.

She seated herself and focused once more on her scrolls. The audience had ended.

Knowing that she could be punished for breaking the rules and not waiting for a dismissal, Reyna wrenched herself out of her mother's grip, turned, and ran from the room, from the house. Rules be damned. She didn't care. They couldn't help you when you needed it anyway. She followed the bridges between the trees until she neared the training grounds, then climbed down to the ground below. Her legs churned under her as she sprinted for the one place she could let her anger out without an audience.

She arrived at the empty training arena, winded but still furious. Practice dummies carved from dead wood, whose magic had been used up and could no longer service the forest, stood in a row at the end of the arena. She drew her sword, contemplating one of the wooden figures. The lines and knots of the head seemed to flow into Mythos' leering face before her.

Reyna's rage bellowed out of her, chest heaving from the exertion. She launched herself forward, hacking at the shape with wild, ungainly strikes. Over and over she swung, tears blurring her vision, her breathing becoming rough and ragged.

Half an hour passed before her swings began to slow. Another hour before the sword fell from her exhausted hands. Her fingers felt sore and stiff with the vibrations of the unending blows.

Her strength gone and her anger spent, she sank to her knees, hunched over in her grief.

"You're pathetic," a voice growled behind her.

Reyna's head jerked up and around. "What do you want?"

"The queen has decreed that you are not to leave Syrinx." Varia scowled down at Reyna, eyes heated. "You *loved* a *man?*" She asked without wanting an answer. Then she spun on her heel and began to march away. Pausing, she threw over her shoulder, "Your outsider blood makes you not only weak but stupid. You'll never be a *real* Wreya." Then she melted into the trees.

Pulling herself to her feet, Reyna stumbled into the forest. She clenched her teeth to keep in more sobs.

She ran, blind, deeper into the trees she had always thought of as her home. But she lost her footing and collapsed to the earth, as though even the forest itself scorned her. She screamed her anguish into the dirt and leaves, pounding her fists against the uncaring ground.

She lay for a while, her grief once more spent. Finally, she sat up. Her hand crept to the necklace she never took off.

The necklace her dearest friend had made her.

She yanked at it, ripping the leather strap away with a clean break. She began to dig, hands scrabbling into the dirt, fresh tears running down her cheeks. When she was satisfied the impromptu grave was deep enough, she dropped the pendant in. She covered the pendant over with slow, unsteady hands. After a moment, she pressed a kiss to the freshly smoothed earth.

"Goodbye, Anteros. You may be gone, but you have a piece of my heart with you... Even in the shackles of death itself."

CHAPTER 5

Derrick rode through the twilight in a daze, his thoughts speeding through his head as fast as Apple's legs beneath him. Matthias' earnest face haunted his thoughts. *Is my friend right?* he wondered. *Would the people of Niamh really put me on the throne?*

He shook his head. Had he ever even thought about sitting on the throne? Of course. But thinking and doing were two different things. Derrick could never stand up to his father. Or Stravos, for that matter.

Derrick gave the reins a gentle tug, and Apple angled her gallop west, changing direction once the castle passed behind the horizon line. He hoped he had properly laid a false trail by riding south until he was out of sight of the turret guards; he'd never left the castle grounds before, and had to rely on the adventuring books he read and studied instead. The maps hanging in his father's chambers had all shown the Forest of Gaia lay far west of Dragonspear, so he did his best to stay on course using the faint, waning moonlight from above.

With no hint of dawn in the sky behind him, he rode on. Derrick remembered reading that traveling by night would help avoid detection. He patted Apple and murmured, "Sleep is a luxury we'll have come morning, girl."

Apple's gallop remained steady, though Derrick feared he pushed her too hard. Occasionally he would slow her to a fast cantor, trying to relieve her stressed muscles. Still, he found the steady hoofbeats and lungs working like bellows beneath him soothing. So soothing, in fact, that he felt his eyelids drooping. He jerked his head up with a panicked gasp, fear jolting him awake. At least, for a little while...

When the first streak of pink shot through the clouds Derrick found an old barn off the side of the road and snuck inside. The warm scents of leather and sweat, musk and hay rushed to greet him. A cadaverous cow stood in her stall, lowing a pained "good morning" to him. Her udders hung shriveled and lifeless from her thin body.

A sad whinny came from the stall beside her. Derrick turned. An ancient horse, sores covering his bony back, looked to him for help. Derrick's heart swelled with pity.

"I don't know what happened to the two of you, but I'm so sorry," he said, his voice soft.

He patted the cow's head, then scratched behind the horse's ears. He led Apple past them, a touch of embarrassment shading his cheeks, and slipped her into the very last stall. He found himself a stack of hay and crawled halfway inside, hiding as best he could. The moment he found a position where the hay didn't poke every inch of him, he fell asleep.

As the sun rose outside, beating down its bright rays, a little girl came out of the run-down hovel near the barn. She was small for her age, and though she looked underweight, she was covered in lean muscle. Yawning, she brushed at her bruised cheek and made her way to the barn. She went to get the old nag out and harnessed, so her father could plow the almost-barren fields.

The girl wandered in, gave the cow an affectionate pat on the nose, and headed to the other stall. A flicker of movement caught her eye, and she froze. Something was moving in the back of the barn! Sweat beaded her brow and her hands shook. In the gloom, it looked like a ghost. A ghost... horse? Its eyes locked onto her own, and her knees began to tremble.

Swallowing her fear, she took a brave step forward. The horse twitched its tail as it watched, but gave off no sense of malice. She took another hesitant step, and it responded with a soft whicker. The fear left her all at once, and she grinned.

"You're such a pretty pony," she breathed. "Where did you come from? Did the fairies leave you here?" Her voice lilted with longing. Hope stole into her heart as she opened the stall door and let herself in.

She had to step over a large pile of hay to get to the horse's side. It was itchy, and it poked at her ankles. On her second step, the hay let out a loud yelp. The girl jumped back in alarm, an involuntary shriek escaping her. The pile of hay shifted and heaved. She shrank back against the closed door of the stall.

"Ouch!" A distinctly male voice growled out of the straw.

Tears started to roll down her cheeks. "Oh, gods! I'm gonna die because of a horse. The horse of a demon! A hay demon!"

Derrick did his best to claw his way out through the stalks of hay without reburying himself. After a moment of struggle, he managed to pull himself cautiously to his feet. The girl crouched against the door, her face in her hands, crying. He felt horrible.

"I beg your pardon, miss. I didn't mean to frighten you. Are you hurt?" He kept his voice as gentle as possible.

She gave a loud hiccough, then peeked through her fingers. She craned her neck up to see him.

Derrick dropped down to a knee in front of her. "Is that better?"

"Are you a demon?" she asked, her sunken eyes wide.

His mouth dropped open before he burst out laughing, "A demon? No, miss. Not even close. I am simply a weary traveler who sought shelter in your barn last night. I am willing to pay you for it, of course. You have only to tell me how much."

He held out a hand to her. After a moment, she took it, letting him help her to her feet.

"I don't... Y-you'd have to ask my father." She shivered a little.

Derrick's jaw tightened at her expression. He knew all too well what that shiver meant. He'd shivered the same way, only a day or two ago.

He took her hands and gently tugged her closer until they were eye to eye. His voice had dropped into something tender. "What is it that you need most? Not your father. You."

She sniffed loudly, but squared her shoulders and stared right back into his eyes. He praised her silently for having the strength to still stand up for herself after everything she'd been through. He knew that he didn't.

"Food," she whispered. "He keeps most of it for himself." She tugged one hand away from him; it flew up, covering her mouth. Her eyes grew as wide as dinner plates, and she flinched away from him.

"I'm not going to hurt you," he told her. "Is there some place that you have where you can hide things without him finding them?"

She looked around, making sure that they were alone before she nodded.

"Good. Then this is for you and only you, alright?" He reached back into the hay and retrieved his saddlebags. He pulled out a loaf of bread, some dried beef strips, and two apples. Her eyes widened even more, although he would not have thought it possible.

"For me?" she whispered.

He nodded, pressing the food into her hands. She stood there, staring up at him. Then she dropped the food, tore open the stall door, and ran out of the barn.

Derrick's head was reeling. *What just happened?* "We'd better get going, Apple. Poor thing might be getting her father."

He hid the food in the dark corner between the door and the wall of the stall. He gave Apple a quiet nudge and swung himself up into the saddle.

"So much for traveling only at night..." he sighed. His eyes burned, half-lidded with exhaustion.

Apple pushed gently through the barn door into the open field. With a cluck from Derrick, she leaped into a gallop.

Derrick's thoughts remained on the girl as Apple quickened her pace. A pang of sadness shot through his heart as he envisioned her malnourished face, her obvious inner strength. She was a kindred spirit. He wanted to take her to his mother. It broke his heart, leaving her there. It broke his very soul.

He hung his head in shame. He wanted to be courageous, wanted to protect her. Instead he worried for his own safety.

"Did we do the right thing?" Derrick asked Apple absently, tugging her reins lightly to slow her down so he could have someone to talk to. She whickered in reply. "My father's men are scattered throughout all of Ulster. If her father had recognized me..."

Apple huffed.

"I know, I know. I'm a coward."

The horse gave him a shriek of a neigh, as if his words were an insult to her as well.

"Well, it's true. I don't understand for the life of me why the people want me in power. Or why, for that matter, my father would think I would ever try to take his power away from him."

Apple whinnied, and Derrick continued, his tone darkening. "I hate him. I hate how he treats our land and our people. But, there's no standing up to him. It's just not possible," he stated, with such definitiveness that Apple shook her head back at him.

They rode on until they neared the outskirts of a thriving metropolis. Activity surged around them, and they passed many busy travelers with minimal notice. Derrick pulled his cloak over his head anyway, keeping as much of his face hidden as possible.

Derrick had spent years reading up on the surrounding towns and villages. He'd pored over maps for several hours, dreaming of life outside the castle. Now that he was living that dream, he had come to realize that it wasn't as glamorous as he once thought. Without a map, he was horrible with directions. He prayed he was still heading the right way.

Derrick shook himself from his reverie and frowned. Over the hustle and bustle of his fellow travelers, the streets of the upcoming city sounded...empty. No merchants shouted their wares. No women sang as they swept. No one hung laundry or did their shopping. No happy children played or chased each other over the cobblestoned fairway.

Apple sensed the tension too. She slowed down, taking each step with caution.

The city came into clear view, and Derrick understood the silence. Mud, soot, and... stains he didn't recognize spattered the dilapidated buildings. Cracks broke the smooth facades, and many of the structures stood eerily empty. *This* wasn't what he'd read about. *This* was a skeleton of a town. The whole place made him uneasy.

The women kept their eyes downcast to their ragged, threadbare dresses. Men stooped under the weight of hard labor and disappointment. The few children on the street panhandled instead of played. Soot covered their faces as well, hiding their sunken cheeks. They held out grime-caked hands. "Please sir, could you spare us a coin or two?"

He must be in the wrong place. Did he get turned around? Derrick's gaze darted around, looking at the few open shops along the fairway. Broken signs and cracked steps met his gaze. No repairs had been made in months. Possibly years.

How long has it been like this? His heart clenched. *This* was what his father had done. *This* was how the king held onto his kingdom. By taking everything a great city had to offer and grinding it into the ground until all that was left was... *this*.

Apple shied away as a woman tossed out the night's waste, the stench overwhelming. Everywhere he looked, the same fear and pain that the little girl had in the barn shown on the people's faces. He needed to get out of here. The longer he stayed, the more the devastation crippled him.

CHAPTER 6

Someone was following her. They took great pains to hide any noise or hints of their passing, but Reyna still heard them. She paused, bending down as if checking her boot laces. There. Just slightly to her left, and maybe thirty yards behind her. In the blackberry bush. A flicker of movement and just the *tiniest* rustle of branches...

Reyna exploded to her feet, drawing an arrow from her quiver and nocking it in her bow in one fluid motion. She drew the string back to her chin, the tips of her bent fingers kissing the corner of her mouth. She sighted down the arrow, settling on the dead center of the blackberry bush.

"Come on out. You get one chance and one chance only. I don't take kindly to being followed." Reyna had to fight the smirk that wanted to bloom on her face. "Come on out... Denali."

Silence followed, only for a second. Then:

"Oh, come on! How do you always *do* that? I was being so careful, too!"

Reyna unstrung her bow, returning her arrow to the quiver, and crouched down, opening her arms. With a burst of energy and speed, a small figure came hurtling over the leaves and dirt. Seeing the little girl raised Reyna's spirits a modicum. Denali was a ball of happiness that it was impossible to ignore.

"I know you were. Oof!" Reyna's voice cut off as the little girl barreled into her, knocking her back a step.

"I'm never going to be able to sneak up on you, am I?" Denali asked, defeated.

Reyna took a good look at the girl, nine winters old, the only child currently in the village. Her curly blonde hair was tightly braided with rebellious whisps escaping along her face and the top of her head. Her eyes were a bright, spring green; her smile a warm beam of sunlight. Denali was female, of course. Wreyan women only gave birth to girls. It helped to swell their numbers, albeit slowly.

Reyna put a hand on her shoulder. "Never say never, little

one. You're going to grow up and be the best warrior the Wreya have ever seen. Just you wait and see!"

"You really think so?" Hope lit her eyes, and she gave Reyna that brilliant smile.

"Absolutely." Reyna nodded. The little girl gave a satisfied nod, then held out her hand to Reyna. She took it, forcing a smile back.

Denali's grip tightened. "I'm so sorry, Reyna. I know how much you liked him." Reyna froze. "You know news travels fast," Denali continued, her tone defensive. "I wasn't spying! I promise! I just wanted to come see if you were okay. I thought I might be able to cheer you up."

"I'm sorry, Denali. Everything's too fresh to be cheerful right now," she tried to explain. "I know it's been a few days, but...grown-ups have a hard time letting go of sadness some-times." The little girl's face fell. "But that doesn't mean that I can't enjoy the day with you," she added, trying to be concil-iatory.

Denali's brow lifted and her face resumed its naturally joyful state.

Denali was like a little sister to Reyna. She'd sworn to protect Denali after first seeing her wrapped in her mother Marlee's arms.

They barely made it a dozen steps before Denali was jump-ing with excitement. "Reyna, Reyna, Reyna! Do you know what today is?" Denali blurted the answer before Reyna could guess, "It's my birthday! I'm ten! That means I start my warrior training in a few weeks! And guess what? Mother ordered me a big bun for breakfast today. She got it from the bakery in Cybele! It was so delicious, full of cinnamon and raisins..." She closed her eyes, savoring the memory of eating it.

Reyna laughed. "Where's my bite?"

"I was going to save some for you," she began. Her face fell, then reignited as she added, "But it was just so *good*! I had to eat it all."

"That's okay, fierce one. You can do whatever you want today. The whole village will want to see to it you're spoiled."

Wreyan children were considered a small miracle, as Wreyan women rarely tried to become pregnant. Part of that was because of the traditional mistrust of men ingrained into them from a young age; part of it was the Wreya kept so busy running their village that they just didn't have the time to woo a potential suitor. Very few of them had jobs that required travel to the towns beyond. Like Reyna.

And Reyna herself was *not* ready for motherhood. *At all*.

The two of them strolled along, making easy conversation, until suddenly, Denali froze. Her eyes fixed on something in the bushes, and her mouth hung open in a little "O." She tugged on Reyna's tunic and pointed.

"Look! A cait sith!" Reyna crouched down to Denali's level

and looked in the direction the little girl pointed. A black cat with a white mark in the shape of a sunburst sat in the shadows of a large bush, cleaning its paw. Sitting down, the animal was as large as Denali herself. Its big ears twitched, and its eyes were riveted on the girls.

"Maybe we should go back another way," Reyna suggested. The cats could become ferocious when startled. Denali nodded, and started to back up slowly. They circled wide, Reyna listening with cocked ears for any sign of pursuit. Once she deemed them to be safe, she breathed easier.

"What an interesting birthday, huh? I get a year older and now I'm going to die." Denali laughed.

"That's not true! Those stories are just stories. That's the first time I've seen a cait sith. I always thought that I'd like one for a pet, but now that I've seen one..." she trailed off.

"Not so much?" Denali chuckled.

Reyna laughed. Denali shivered and shook her head in agreement.

Another dozen minutes passed, and Reyna spotted another living being. It was *her* turn to nudge Denali and point.

"The fairies are coming out to celebrate with you, too. It's a special occasion when the only child in the village has a birthday," she teased.

Two wood sprites fluttered above them, their beautiful dragonfly wings sparkling in the sun. They were dressed in their usual forest greens, and waved down at the girls. They waved back.

These creatures Reyna liked. They loved to dance and sing, and often came to perform at special occasions in Syrinx. They had a small market area – it couldn't be any bigger, the clearing where they kept it was filled to the brim with tiny stalls and high-pitched voices hawking goods – where the Wreya could go to trade with them. There was no work finer than fairy-made cloth or shoes. Reyna's favorite pair of boots came from that market.

The village came into view. Denali coughed, and cleared her throat. Reyna frowned and stopped walking.

"Are you alright?"

"Yeah! It's nothing! I probably got some extra flour caught–" *Cough*. "In my throat from the bun." She tried to smile, but instead gave a hacking cough that bent her little body double. "I'm just going to run home and get some water."

"Oh, yeah? I bet I can beat you home!" Reyna challenged.

"Never!" She gave Reyna a hug and dashed off. Reyna watched until Denali was out of sight, coughing every few steps. Reyna followed her, but hung back enough so Denali would win. Besides, she wanted to sift through her thoughts.

That cough didn't sit right with Reyna. Something was wrong. It had been wet, and rough. It couldn't have come from dry flour. Maybe Denali was coming down with a cold?

By the time Reyna rounded the trunk of Denali's tree, the little girl was nowhere to be seen. Man, she was fast! Grinning, Reyna climbed up the trunk, bypassing the first treehouse and stopping at the second level.

"You got me! You won fair and square!" Reyna called out as she walked through the door.

"Oh? I didn't know I was out to get you," Marlee laughed, setting aside her knitting and getting to her feet.

"Marlee!" Reyna met her halfway across the floor and enveloped the older woman in her arms. Though relatively close in age, Reyna still looked up to her like an older sister.

"Hi, Reyna! Want to stay for dinner?"

"Oh, no, but thank you for the invitation. Didn't Denali come in here? I was chasing her."

Marlee gave her a puzzled look.

"No... just you," Marlee laughed. "She probably ran off to cause more mischief. She's a feisty one."

Grief caught Reyna unaware, then. Marlee's words brought Anteros' feisty, mischievous face to mind. She gasped in a breath, holding a sob that threatened to erupt from her. Marlee caught her as she buckled.

"Reyna! Are you alright? What happened?" Marlee led Reyna to the chair she'd just been sitting in. She sat at Reyna's feet, holding the younger woman's hands in her own.

"I... I..." Marlee waited for her to get the words out, but Reyna couldn't get them past the hard lump in her throat.

"Is it about that man that was killed?" Marlee asked gently. Reyna nodded, and the dam in her chest broke open and she sobbed out all of her pain and grief. Marlee sat there, holding her hands and listening, letting Reyna unburden herself.

"Thank you, Marlee. I know that I can always count on you." Reyna wiped the tears from her cheeks as she hugged her friend. "I'm sorry. I better go. I think I have something I need to do."

Marlee nodded, giving Reyna a sad but understanding smile.

Reyna had done her best to keep her grief at bay. Yet still it attacked, catching her off guard, crippling her without warning. She felt broken; worse, she felt like everything she'd ever learned about waging war was useless. How could you wage war on your emotions? They didn't follow any of the rules.

She couldn't let her heartbreak govern her any longer. She needed to build walls around her heart, otherwise she wouldn't survive. The only place she could do that, she knew, was in the forest. She chose a different path from the one she'd taken to bury Anteros' necklace. That way lay more pain, and memory, and all the emotions she needed to harden her heart against. Brick by brick, the wall went up, shutting out the rest of the world.

Reyna walked the Forest of Gaia for hours, letting her feet choose the speed and direction. She focused on her breathing, taking long slow breaths from her nose and letting them roll out from her mouth. She focused on her rage, tempering it, burning her grief in its righteous flames. And she focused on herself, her taut strength, her iron will, her unbending sense of justice.

Upon emerging from the primal forest, heart somewhat healed and hardened, she decided to once more visit the queen. She needed to go to Anteros' funeral, to get closure and send him away. It didn't matter what Varia had told her in the training grounds. She would make herself heard and understood. Ephiny *had* to let her go.

It took only minutes for Reyna to find her way back to the royal tree. Varia blocked her way as she tried to enter, a disgusted look contorting the guard's face into a sneer.

"What do *you* want?" she spat.

"Attitude now that my mother isn't here? I expected no better of you," Reyna bit out. "I came to speak to the queen."

"But *is* she your queen?" Varia asked, her tone vicious. "I mean, you're not even Wreyan. Are you."

Reyna gritted her teeth until her jaw popped. She glared at Varia.

"Ephiny doesn't seem to mind. And maybe *that's* why I'm a better warrior than you are," Reyna said sweetly. She ducked around Varia before the latter could work out the insult, and continued into the queen's chambers.

When Reyna reached the door to the queen's study, she closed her eyes and took a deep breath. She squared her shoulders, fixed a respectful look to her face, and knocked.

"Come in!" called Ephiny.

Reyna opened the door, relief at the queen's cheerful tone flooding her. She hadn't realized how much she needed to hear that.

"My queen," Reyna said, bowing her head.

"Reyna! What can I do for you, child?" A look of sympathy and a sad smile bloomed on her face. "Are you doing alright?" Reyna nodded, the pain bouncing off of the walls she had built so sturdily.

"First, please let me apologize for my earlier behavior," Reyna said with another supplicating bow.

Ephiny nodded, giving Reyna a small smile. Reyna took that as a good sign, and continued. "I have a request."

Ephiny raised an eyebrow warily but said nothing. Reyna swallowed, and took another deep breath. "I want to ask permission to go to Cybele and see Anteros laid to rest, when his body is ready for burial."

Ephiny shook her head sadly.

"I'm sorry, Reyna, but I can't grant that. Your face could be recognized, and you are, in their minds, a fugitive. I can't allow you to call attention to the Wreya for such a personal reason."

She paused. "I really *am* sorry, Reyna," she said softly.

"That's not fair!" Reyna burst out. "I–"

"That is the best way for me to protect *my* people!" Ephiny cut her off sharply, whipping her head up.

Reyna's cheeks grew hot and her mouth snapped closed. Once again, she didn't bother bowing or waiting to be dismissed, but spun on her heel and ran out of the room. She was beginning to make a habit of that, apparently.

Ephiny didn't call after her. And even if she had, Reyna wasn't sure whether or not she would have stopped.

"Running away with your tail tucked between your legs?"

Reyna ignored Varia, pushing past her and sprinting along the connecting bridges until she found herself far away from the queen's domicile. Storm clouds formed overhead, and Reyna laughed. Fitting. The weather matched her sour mood exactly.

I should check on Denali. The little girl was Reyna's ray of sunshine, and damn it if she didn't need some light. Reyna headed across the pattern of bridges that led to Marlee's home.

When she reached the door, she gave it two sharp raps with her knuckles. No answer. She repeated the knock. Still no answer.

"They aren't living in the tree right now."

"What?" Reyna turned to look at the passing redhead who'd

spoken.

"They moved to one of the ground huts. Denali has come down sick. Her mother didn't want her falling off a ladder."

"Th-thank you," Reyna stuttered, excusing herself. She swore under her breath. She *knew* something had been wrong. Flour...humpf. Reyna climbed down the nearest ladder, her hands and feet moving so fast she practically fell down the tree.

The hut looked dirty and unmanaged on the outside; it stood to reason that the inside wouldn't be much better. A cooking fire sat in front of it, like any other hut. But a pot still hung over it, something so charred and burned inside that it stuck to the bottom.

"*This* is the hut?" Reyna mumbled. She knocked softly, hoping she would not disturb Denali if she slept inside.

"Yes? Oh, Reyna!" Marlee collapsed into her friend's arms. Reyna wrapped her up in a comforting hug, determined to be the same source of comfort that Marlee had been to her just a little while ago. "Oh, Reyna, I don't know what happened, someone found her! They just found her on the ground, collapsed, and I wasn't there, I was home, I should have been there, I should have been there for her..." Marlee's words faded into sobs. Reyna stood there, holding her, numb.

I should have done more. I should have followed her home. Instead of mooning over some man, *I could have done more to help Denali.*

"Would it be alright if I saw her?" Reyna asked gently.

"Of course, I'm sorry, I'm such a mess right now…"

Reyna nodded, and Marlee led her into the hut. Reyna saw Denali wrapped up in blankets, laying on a low cot, a bucket of water next to her. Reyna sank to the ground and put a hand on Denali's forehead. She was burning up with fever.

"Oh, Denali," Reyna sighed. "What's happening to you?" Tears welled up in Reyna's eyes and she thought back to the happy, bouncing girl that had tried to ambush her that morning. Outside, a slow rain began to fall.

Denali gave a soft cry, jerking Reyna out of her reverie and pulling a startled gasp from her mother. Its delicate fragility tore at her heartstrings, and Reyna began to sing softly.

It wasn't something that she did very often, because it always garnered strange reactions from the listeners. As she sang an old lullaby her mother had once used to pacify her, Marlee joined in, her own voice thick with fresh tears. Reyna wished for the little girl to find the peace of sleep.

After a few verses, Denali's whimpering stopped, and her brow smoothed. Reyna sat still, listening to Denali's even breathing…and the soft rain falling outside.

CHAPTER 7

Derrick had ridden all night, his mind turning restlessly through the events of the last couple of days. He would need to find someplace to hide once the sun rose... maybe get some sleep. Although they had set a hurried pace for a few hours, he'd slowed to let Apple catch her breath. After all, slow progress was still progress.

There was no way that Derrick could stand up to his father. He knew his mother was right, that he had been marked for assassination. Her voice sounded in his head. *All the programs and initiatives that you've put into place are helping the people. That's why your father is afraid of you. That's why the people want you.*

Derrick chuckled under his breath. King Julius? Afraid? *That* was impossible. His father feared nothing and no one. The conviction of those thoughts silenced his mother's voice. Still, a small part of him wished it was true. He wanted to make his mother proud.

But he knew himself to be a coward. Had his mother and Matthias not gotten him out, he would have been so paralyzed by fear that he would most likely have stayed in his chambers, waiting for the assassin. Shame consumed him again. He had been conditioned to fear, to cowardice. Ever since he'd tried to stand up to Stravos.

Derrick continued to ride, lost in thought, until he came to a small village. Every town or village would be a risk; any attentive villager or passing King's man could catch him and send him back to his father. But he'd been on the road for weeks now, and he needed to be around people. Even if it *was* dangerous.

He sighed, hunching his shoulders. He withdrew into his dark hooded cloak, embarrassed to be nothing more than a sheltered prince.

His eyes darted back and forth through the village streets, looking for trouble. What he saw broke his heart all over again instead. And on the heels of that pain and sorrow came anger.

Stalls stood along the streets selling stunted vegetables, tough meat, and moldy cheese. Children ran rampant with no one to care for them, hunger and fear clear upon their faces. He noticed a distinct lack of pickpockets; with a jolt, Derrick realized that these people had nothing of value. His eyes fell upon many oft-patched pieces of clothing. About half of the people still had holes where the material had been worn through with continued use.

The signs over the small shops were weather beaten and badly in need of repair. The blacksmith's shop no longer had a sign at all, instead relying on a horseshoe nailed to the wooden door. Many of the shops were boarded up.

A few elderly people huddled in threadbare blankets. Some shook and shivered, others coughed from illness, and no money to buy medicine. *What a painful and cruel way to die,* Derrick thought, anger and hatred burning through his veins like liquid fire. How could his father not know the state his people were in?!?

The answer hit him with such force he almost fell from his saddle. His father *did* know. He just couldn't be bothered to care. He lived in luxury while his people starved.

A young woman sat at a stall near the end of the main road, her eyes locked on the ground, despair and hopelessness clinging to her like a heavy cloak. She sat on an empty apple crate with a small table in front of her, shriveled apples and mealy pears on display. Derrick dismounted and walked over. She only raised her eyes to meet his face once he was standing right in front of her.

"Are you interested in any fruit, sir?" she asked, a tiny spark of hope in her voice.

"No, ma'am," he answered quietly. Her face crumpled in disappointment. He cast his eyes down in embarrassment, and saw her swollen belly. It had been hidden from him by the table.

"I was wondering if you could point me in the direction of the Forest of Gaia." Derrick couldn't bear to look at her directly. Knowing her hardship and not being able to help her tore at his soul. As his eyes roamed, hidden by his hood, they fell on the village notice board that stood a dozen paces or so to his right. He froze. His own face stared back at him, a reward attached to the sketch done in a very familiar hand.

"If you follow the road out of town, you'll come to a fork a few miles out. Stay to the left," the poor woman responded, her voice toneless.

Derrick took two coins from his money pouch and handed them to her, leaning over the table. When he pressed the coins into her hand, gently folding her fingers over them, she gasped, eyes darting up under his hood. She looked from him to the sketch and back.

This is it. All of his mother's and Matthias' efforts for nothing. *And all it took was one act of kindness, one scrap of pity.*

Tears sprang to her eyes. She put the coins into the pocket of her ragged dress and whispered, "Thank you, Your Highness. Good speed on your journey." Then she bobbed him the slightest hint of a clumsy curtsy and sat down.

It touched him. That small show of fealty led him to believe she wouldn't reveal his secret. Even for the substantial reward his father had set for his capture.

"Thank you. Best wishes to you and your little one."

She looked down and stroked her belly with a shaky nod.

Climbing back into the saddle, he followed her directions. He told himself that the tears now pricking his eyes came from the red dust being flung into the air by Apple's every step.

The next three villages all looked like twins of that first. He managed to get directions from all of the villages, paying a few coins to the person who'd helped him each time. He didn't regret the money he was losing; only that he wouldn't have enough to give every single person some. He didn't know how long it would take to get him to the forest. If he could help one person per village, then he wanted to make sure that he had enough to do that.

Finally, Derrick came to the last village he planned to stop in before trying to gain entrance to the forest. The wooden sign at the gate ahead read, "Cybele". He found a stable for Apple, and rented a room at the inn for the night.

"Welcome to Cybele, sir." The man taking his money gave him a strange look, but Derrick couldn't read it. He'd noticed his wanted poster on the board, as usual; but he hoped that this time he wouldn't be recognized. He had the beginnings of a beard now, and his hair was longer. And *much* more shaggy.

"Thank you," he mumbled, trying to withdraw further into his hood anyway.

"I'm Zachius," the man said, "and that's my wife, Sarah. We own the place." He raised a hand to get an older woman's attention, and she bustled over with a warm smile.

"You poor thing. You need a hot meal. Will you be joining us?"

It warmed his heart that this couple was so kind and welcoming to him.

"I would really appreciate it. But I think I'd like to take a look around first, if that's alright?"

"Of course! You just come back and let me know when you're ready for your supper. If you have any questions or need anything, don't hesitate to let us know." She flounced away when another patron called her name. Pulling his cloak over his head, he went out to explore the village.

The women here wore bright colors on their dresses, and easy smiles on their faces. Men stood outside of the shops, bargaining for supplies. One was buying flour with sheep's wool; another was at the blacksmith's shop, picking up a set of horseshoes with a sack of wheat. Everything about Cybele proved a stark contrast to when he'd first began his journey. Derrick began to wonder if he'd finally outrun his father's reach.

He relaxed, if only a little, and continued his walk until he stumbled upon a bakery. After a brief perusal of the shop's delicious-looking goods, he bought two sweet rolls from the pink-cheeked owner. He pocketed them for later, when he was back on the road.

As he left the building, though, he froze. A trio of soldiers stood right outside, acting suspiciously. One inspected the supplies neatly tied into bundles on a small wagon, while the other two looked around, letting their gazes sweep back and forth. To Derrick, it seemed like whatever they were doing, they didn't want to get caught. He ducked his head quickly... but not before he saw the soldier by the wagon add a small package to the supplies from a hidden pocket in his cloak.

Derrick moved quickly, trying to put as much distance between himself and the soldiers as he could, and found himself back at the stables.

"Hey, girl. We're almost done." He rubbed Apple's nose as he spoke, stashing his treats on top of his other supplies. "You can have a nice, long rest soon."

She gave him an affectionate nudge of acknowledgement.

He made sure she had plenty of water and fresh hay, and went back to exploring the city.

He saw a woman selling cheese a little further along the road from the stable. She gave him a raised eyebrow as he approached. He dipped his head, hoping she wouldn't recognize him. He hurriedly made his selections and paid her, then walked away, his heart in his throat. He threw a few covert glances over his shoulder and saw that she was still watching him. He swore under his breath. She'd made him. Right? Or was she just suspicious? Either way, he needed to lose himself in the village.

Derrick kept walking at an even pace, waiting until the cheese stall was out of sight. Then he spun on his heel and ducked down the row of houses behind the market, heading back to the tavern. His mind raced as he examined his options. If she'd made him, the guards would be coming soon. If not, he should hurry anyway – he hadn't liked the way the woman had looked at him, and she probably wouldn't be the only one who deemed him suspicious.

He needed to get something to eat and get the hell out of there before he brought down all the soldiers in Cybele on himself and Apple. If nothing else, then he would at least leave with a full belly.

The smell of fresh bread hit him as soon as he walked into the tavern, and he took a long, deep breath in appreciation. He saw a small, unoccupied table towards the back wall, half hidden by shadows – prefect for a man keeping to himself. Derrick had made it halfway across the room towards it when a man the size of an outhouse, and with the accompanying smell, lurched to his feet in front of him. His hair was greasy and unkempt, and his gut protruded out from under a bat-tered tunic that had seen better days. His belt looked like it was valiantly fighting a losing battle in trying to keep his trousers up.

"You're nothing but a dirty cheat! I won't sit around and let you rob me a second longer!" he roared. As he stumbled, he knocked into Derrick, sending him skittering back a few steps and knocking his hood back across his shoulders. Frantically, he grabbed at it, tearing it up over his head with such force that he felt a little surprised he hadn't ripped the damn thing clean off.

The angry man stared at him, a bewildered expression on

his face. He looked lost and confused.

"I'm sorry for bumping into you, sir," Derrick said to him. He waited a second to see if the man would raise the alarm. When he didn't, Derrick continued on to his table. He breathed a shaky sigh of relief. He was safe...for now.

"What can I get for you?" He started as a serving girl appeared before him. She laughed, a sound like music in Derrick's ears. "A little jumpy, aren't we?"

He nodded, allowing a small smile to cross his face. "A little, I guess. I don't want any trouble. I'm just passing through."

"Oh, don't you pay any mind to Lem. He can get loud when he's in his cups, but he's harmless. Wouldn't hurt a fly. Let me fetch you some dinner." She whirled away before he could say another word.

Derrick closed his eyes and willed himself to calm down. Nothing had happened. Even if the man had seen his face, he hadn't called any attention to it. Besides, the man was drunk.

He had just about convinced himself of the girl's words when she returned with a half chicken roasted in garlic, a hunk of fresh bread, and a steaming baked potato with butter on top.

"Thank you! This looks wonderful!" he said, with the enthusiasm of a man who hadn't eaten a whole meal in weeks. She gave him a sideways look, then took the coins he offered her.

"You said you were just passing through. Where are you headed?"

"The Forest of Gaia," he answered around a mouthful of chicken. Courtly manners stood no chance against an empty stomach.

Her eyebrows shot up in surprise. "You're a very brave man, then."

"What makes you say that?" Derrick asked, confused.

She gave another musical tinkle of laughter. "The forest isn't safe. Only the Wreya know their way around, and can come and go as they please. Many men have tried to find their village, and never came back alive. The king himself even sent a few groups of soldiers in."

The mention of his father made his heart race and his hands begin to sweat. He checked to make sure his hood was still up.

She continued, "The forest protects them. The Wreya, I mean. The only safe passage through is to have one of them with you." And she flitted away, leaving him mouth agape to stew on her words.

That was information Matthias should have given him. Granted, if he *had* told Derrick, the young prince might never have left. What was he supposed to do now? Apprehension crept over him, inch by inch. A memory resurfaced in his mind's eye... Matthias *had* told him. He'd mentioned that he needed a Wreyan guide to find the village. But he'd only said that Derrick would get lost...not that he would disappear.

Not that he might *die.*

Suddenly, the tavern door burst open. Men in red and gold uniforms streamed in, looking around the room, hands gripping sword hilts, eyes narrowed. The leader dragged Lem in by the collar. The poor man blubbered and tried to find his feet.

And Derrick had thought the cheese woman would be the source of his trouble.

Zachius strode forward to confront the soldier. "You know that I won't tolerate any fighting in this tavern, Mythos!" the innkeeper shouted. The room went deathly quiet.

Derrick's heart raced. He had to get out of there, immediately. The captain seemed distracted. He had to make a break for it...

There! A window, two tables over. If he could just reach it, he could throw himself through and escape. He got to his feet, so slowly it barely looked like he moved at all. He prayed he wouldn't be noticed.

"I'm only here to pick something up. A filthy excuse for a boy. Then I'll be on my way." The captain shook Lem, whose hands fell from a red, blotchy, tear-stained face.

"There! That's where he was sitting!" Lem pointed.

Mythos' eyes followed Lem's finger... then he scowled when he saw that the table was empty. Derrick, almost to the window, almost to freedom, prayed that the captain wouldn't look around.

The fates didn't feel inclined to grant his wish. Mythos' eyes swept the tavern, a practiced hunter searching for prey, and came to rest on Derrick. His face lit up with a sudden, cruel grin.

"Ah. Just what we've been looking for." He released Lem, who fell to the floor, sobbing. "Men!" The soldiers around Mythos fanned out, coming towards Derrick. Their casual pace flooded him with shame. It seemed his coward's reputation had preceded him. A candle's flame of courage ignited in his chest at that thought. *Be brave. For the first, and maybe the last, time...be brave.*

With a wild cry, he ran the last few steps to the window and launched himself through it.

The paned glass shattered under his weight, slicing his skin in a dozen different places. Blood sheeted down his face, and he felt it bubble up on his arms and chest. Each cut stung so much he felt like he was coming apart at the seams. He landed on his hands and knees, hissing in pain as more shards embedded themselves into his sides, his palms, his knees.

He jumped to his feet, forcing the pain to the back of his mind, focusing on his escape. He ran as fast as he could to the stable, not daring to look behind him.

He'd barely reached Apple's stall door when white hot pain bored through the bottom of his foot. He screamed again, but didn't stop moving. A rusty rake, used for mucking out the stalls, poked its now-bloodied tines out of the straw near Apple's stable door. Barely giving the object a glance, Derrick threw the saddlebags over Apple's back, buckling only the straps necessary to keep the tack and saddlebags on. The rest he left hanging. He jumped into the saddle as the men reached the door.

"Halt! Off the horse, Your Highness!" A sneering voice; a voice used to quivering obedience. A voice like his father's.

Wild adrenaline pumped through Derrick's veins. Anger, hot and impetuous, bubbled in his guts. It was something new that he'd never felt before.

"Come on, Apple. We've got to get out of here," he growled, his mouth near her ear. Then, head raised with a roar of word-less fury, he kicked her sides, launching her out of the stable and into the street. Some men leapt to the side. Derrick didn't stop for the ones who didn't. He clung to Apple's back and pointed her to the dark sea of trees just outside the front gate of the city.

He was going to make it. After coming all this way, he re-fused to stop now. No matter what the serving girl had told him. He would see this plan through until the end.

He had to.

CHAPTER 8

There was nothing Reyna could do for Denali right now except to let her rest. Time would tell if she would get better... or worse. She tried to turn her mind away from the little girl, and the pain and suffering she must be going through. Unfortunately, with her mind being forced from that subject, it immediately circled back around to Anteros and the injustice that surrounded his death. Reyna still fumed over the queen's refusal to help the people of Cybele, or even allow one of her own to avenge an unrightful death. Her hands balled into fists as she seethed.

She needed to talk to her mother. Ariadne usually had a calming effect on her. Besides, her stomach was growling.

She went to the animal pens under their tree first, patting Andromeda and checking to make sure the gate was closed.

"Hey, girl," she murmured to the horse. "Are you recovered now from that... horrible day? It's been a few weeks, I know. I'm sorry I haven't really come to see you." The horse nuzzled her for a moment, letting Reyna know she'd been forgiven. Reyna smiled and patted her again before heading up the tree.

The smell of roasted turkey made her stomach rumble in earnest, and she couldn't help the little moan of excited anticipation that escaped her.

"Finally decided to come home, have you?" Ariadne asked, as Reyna entered. "I wasn't sure if you'd be here. You'll have to get your own plate."

"I'm sorry, mother. I was visiting Denali. She's really sick. She didn't even know that I was sitting there next to her." Reyna sighed, looking down at her hands. "And I know I've been spending a lot of time in the woods lately. I just...can't be around people right now."

"I can understand that, my love." Ariadne gave her a sad smile.

"I went to see the queen today," Reyna said, not letting her tone betray her feelings. Ariadne stiffened but said nothing. "I asked her if I could go to the burial."

"What did she say?" Ariadne asked.

"She said no!" Reyna burst out. "It's been weeks! No one will remember my face! It's not fair, I was his best friend! I should be there!" Her voice rose as she spoke, and she finished not far from a roar.

"Shhh. You don't need the neighbors to hear you," her mother chided.

Reyna blushed. Reprimanded by her mother as though she was still a child of Denali's age. Worse still, Ariande was right. "Yeah. That's all I need. More talk going around."

"Reyna..." There was a warning in Ariadne's tone.

"What?" she asked, trying to sound innocent.

"Don't do anything foolish. I know you're still grieving, and that it hurts just as bad as it did when it happened. But that doesn't mean that you need to go and lose your head. "

Reyna offered a noncommittal grunt in response. With the two of them being so close, it wasn't a surprise that Ariadne had an instinctive feeling for what her daughter was thinking most of the time. She also knew when to push, and when to leave her daughter alone. The two finished their meal in silence, then Reyna excused herself to bed.

She lay there for hours, staring at the ceiling, still restless. All her anger and grief needed an outlet, and she didn't have one to give it. That restlessness came directly from her anger, and she knew it. Every single day that she'd spent in Syrinx since Anteros had been killed, she saw Mythos' face. Alive with cruelty. And the sword... striking down her best friend.

She shook her head. He had to pay! As much as she loved her mother, she was about to disobey her. She was about to do something foolish. She was going to murder the fiend. To avenge Anteros.

The village was silent. Only the songs of nightingales lauded Reyna's passing. Heart pounding, she slunk in through the open doorway, eyes darting around for any sign that her mother was awake. Nothing.

A large knapsack hung from a peg by the door. Her fingers shook a little as they reached for it. Holding her breath, she managed to free the leather cord from the nail. The scent of herbs and crumbles of recently foraged mushrooms still remained. Reyna shook out the bag, praying the sound didn't summon Ariadne, then set about filling it with anything she might need.

Considering what she was planning to do, she knew she wouldn't be welcomed back.

Food and a water skin. Check. A small cooking pot, a knife, rope, some medicines, and other odds and ends. Silent and swift, she finished by grabbing her bow and quiver of arrows, strapping them to her back with practiced ease.

Reyna padded to the doorway of her mother's room one final time. The moon peeked in through the open window, making Ariadne's golden hair look like molten silver. Reyna frowned, her voice barely audible.

"I hope I can make you proud. I love you." She inhaled softly. "Thank you for everything. Goodbye, mother."

Ariadne's chest rose and fell with the ease of a peaceful sleep. Reyna turned and left the only home that she had ever known.

She hopped gracefully to the ground. She darted into the shadows, listening for anyone nearby. Only silence met her straining ears. She slipped into the trees and the darkness swallowed her.

She knew the Wreya would send out a search party for her the moment her mother noticed she was missing. Leaving Andromeda behind helped cover her flight, but she had to keep moving, had to use the cover of night to mask her trail for as long as it could. Reyna struck out towards the northeast, making sure to stay far away from any game trails that she came upon to hide her tracks.

Dawn had begun to lighten the world around her by the time she thought it safe enough for a rest. She unslung her knapsack from her shoulder, and dug around in it until she found her water skin. She took only a few mouthfuls, choosing not to eat any of the food yet. She had no idea how far she'd have to go while on the run.

A gentle breeze blew loose tendrils of her hair around, and she felt light. She was free! No rules to keep her from meting out justice... It was almost dizzying.

Then her stomach tightened at the thought of leaving her tribe, thoughts of the cruel punishment she would receive simply for wanting to save her friend. No, leaving the Wreya was her only option, if she wanted to follow her heart and do what she felt was right.

A sudden doubt assailed her. *Could* she leave the only home she'd ever known? The place that held so much love and warmth? So many memories of her childhood? A tear slid down her cheek, sparkling in the last rays of moonlight.

She gritted her teeth. *Yes*. She could. Her heart had been shredded by Anteros' murder, and now she had the chance to make sure no one else had to feel as she did. It was for the greater good; no matter what her sentimental heart wanted to tell her.

A strange noise startled Reyna out of her reverie. She paused, her brows furrowed and her ears pricked.

There it was again! It sounded like something between a moan and a growl. Reyna did her best to judge which direction it came from, then struck out towards the mysterious sound. After a few moments of fruitless searching, she began to wonder if this was the right direction after all. She couldn't hear the noise anymore.

Whump! She jumped. It sounded like someone had run into a tree trunk. She whirled around. The thick limbs of an oak tree were bending themselves almost to the ground, whipping through the air. They looked like they were straining to reach something. A strangled scream reached her ears. She headed towards the commotion.

As she drew nearer, she saw vines writhing like snakes over a form on the ground. Muffled groans and yelps of pain came from the lump. A few vines slid away, and Reyna saw that it was a man. *A man being pummelled by the forest.* She snorted out a laugh. Served him right. He didn't belong here. She turned her back on the idiot and began to walk away when a panicked whicker caught her attention.

A beautiful palomino stood not far away, clearly agitated. The man must have ridden her this far before the forest instituted its protections. Horses had a good sense of direction. This one would either find her way to Syrinx or back to the village she'd come from. Probably Cybele, since it was closest. Reyna turned to go, but the horse darted in front of her, blocking her path.

"What's wrong, girl? Do you want to come with me? Ok, then. Come on." She took the reins and walked two steps before being jerked to a halt. The mare refused to move. She tossed her head and stamped her hooves, standing her ground.

Reyna looked into her eyes and saw a deep sadness pooling there. Then the horse took a deliberate step back...towards the man. Had that been an accident? Or was the horse trying to tell her something?

"We're going this way," she said gently, taking another step and tugging softly on the reins. The horse again balked, then took two deliberate steps backwards.

The lump on the ground was struggling feebly. She wondered if the man in the vines was being crushed or strangled. Not that she cared, but she was curious.

"Alright, then stay here." She dropped the reins and started walking.

The horse neighed insistently, sauntering back into her path.

"You're really not going to let me leave, are you?" she asked, irritated. The horse gently put her muzzle against Reyna's chest and pushed her towards the man.

"Fine!" Reyna threw up her hands and headed towards the pile. "I'll look at him, ok?" If the horse loved him that much, then she didn't really have a choice now, did she? Not even animals deserved to have their hearts broken.

As she drew nearer, the branches pulled back, and the vines slithered away like snakes. They revealed not so much a man as a total mess.

He had black hair, all matted with blood. She couldn't see the color of his eyes, because they were closed, and one had even swollen shut and bruised. His shirt had been cut to ribbons, and she saw blood drenching almost every inch of it. She bent down, moved a corner, and gasped. His chest was riddled with glass shards, the majority of the shallow cuts infected. Her fingers brushed the outline of one of the wounds.

Two figures stood at the top of a mountain, the sun glinting off their swords. Clouds of smoke billowed out behind them and a blood red sun set behind them.

Reyna reeled back as if stung. What just happened? The bite of magic still stung her fingertips. She looked at them. They *looked* normal.

They should be seared red from the jolt I just got.

"Who are you?" she whispered. Now, she had no choice. She had to bring this man to Syrinx. He needed a healer. Badly. She picked him up gently, eliciting a strangled cry from him, and loaded him onto the insistent horse's back. Sighing heavily, she turned her steps towards home.

Her thoughts spun wildly during the hours it took to get back. Mostly about what she would do if anyone mentioned her being gone so long. After all, she wasn't supposed to come this way again. She'd already made peace with that in her heart. Now here she was, slinking back like a dog with its tail between its legs.

When she stood outside the healer's hut, she knocked loudly.

"Come in!" came a hard, strong voice. Reyna felt thankful that the healer's hut was on the ground. There was no way she'd be able to get him into a tree house...

"I just want to bring in someone who needs help! I'm not staying!"

"That's fine!" The voice came from the store room in the back. "Put her on the table and I'll be out in just a second." Reyna didn't bother to correct the gender of the patient. The healer would know soon enough. She lifted the man's body, groaning, onto the table, then turned her back on him and stalked out, washing her hands of the matter. She wanted nothing more to do with him.

There was something just...*wrong* with him. There had to be. Why would he have had magic if he wasn't a sorcerer of some kind? Reyna shook her head. It didn't matter. He wasn't her problem anymore.

"There she is." The sarcastic singsong voice assaulted her seconds after she left the hut.

"What do you want? Don't you have anything more important to do than annoy me?"

Varia glared at her.

"As a matter of fact, I do. I'm to bring you to the queen. Maybe I'll get lucky and you'll get kicked out of the tribe this time," the woman sneered.

Reyna gritted her teeth. It took everything in her to keep from punching Varia right in that smug face of hers. She followed Varia all the way to Ephiny's tree house.

"Reyna, what have you done?" Ephiny asked, voice low and dangerous.

"He needed to be taken to Naida. I did my best..." A wave of exhaustion hit Reyna. She realized she hadn't slept the night before, and had been on the move all day...first from Syrinx, then back to it.

Ephiny stood in front of her, eyebrows raised. "Where have you been? And more importantly, where did you find that boy?"

"I was taking some time to myself." Reyna rubbed her eyes.

"Why?! What would you need time to yourself for?"

"To grieve!" she snapped. Her voice hitched. She refocused, answering the Queen's second question. "I found him while I was walking in the woods."

The queen stared her down. Reyna met Ephiny's's eyes steadily, maintaining her silence, daring her to challenge her statement, daring her to call out her weakness. Reyna sighed. She'd come up with the lie easily enough, but it was a double-edged sword; it hurt her, too.

"Your thoughtless actions have put all of the Wreya in danger! How could you bring a man into our midst? A stranger! I've let your actions slide so far to coddle your grief, but enough is enough!" Ephiny put her head in her hand. Her voice gentled, just a shade. "Your punishment for not thinking is to be responsible for him. And if anything happens to my people because you brought him here...I will hold you fully responsible."

Reyna opened her mouth to defend herself, to argue, but Ephiny gave a sharp flick of her hand. She was dismissed.

Three days later, rumors continued to circulate about their male visitor and Reyna's scandalous decision to bring him to Syrinx. Reyna cursed the wounded boy: saving him had put everyone's eyes on her, and there was no way she could attempt to leave again.

Now Reyna stood in the healer's hut, staring down at the boy. Okay, not staring, so much as glowering.

"What? Afraid he might die?" Varia had once again managed to come up behind her in silence while Reyna stewed in her thoughts.

"No."

Varia turned disbelieving eyes on Reyna. " You're so soft where men are concerned," Varia spat. "If you care about and trust them so much, why don't you just move to the nearest town and become one of their brood mares?"

Reyna's hand lashed out, faster than a striking snake, and cracked Varia across the face. Varia's head rocked back hard enough that her teeth audibly clacked together.

"Don't ever call me a brood mare. The next time you disrespect me, I will challenge you to combat. And trust me, Varia, I won't lose." Reyna said all this in a voice dangerously soft, like poisoned silk sliding down the polished edge of a sword. Varia stared into Reyna's cutting eyes, then growled in answer. She stalked away, her hand clutched in a defiant fist, refusing to touch her bruising cheek.

CHAPTER 9

Derrick's eyes fluttered open. A woman stood before him, more beautiful than any he'd ever seen. He must have died. The forest must have killed him, and this angel had come to escort him to the Fields of Bliss. It was too bad he couldn't tell Matthias that he'd been right.

The dark haired angel turned to look down at him, scowling.

"Who are you?" she demanded.

"My name isn't important." The words scraped his throat, and his chest burned inside. He looked around. He could see trees and other women through the open door. He also noticed that the second woman had disappeared. His heart raced. Then he groaned at the fresh stab of pain. He wasn't dead... he was in Syrinx! He must be! His hand went to his throbbing face, feeling the stubble there. It came away red with blood. "Ugh. I must look horrible. Any chance I could get a blade and some water to shave?" She didn't answer. "Or just some water to wash? I'd like to look a little more presentable when I go to petition the queen."

That got a reaction out of her. Her face clouded over. He wanted to laugh, but he knew that would hurt, so he bit the inside of his cheek instead. "What makes you think you have any right to see the queen?"

He blushed, not able to meet her eyes any longer. "I...um...don't want everyone overhearing my business."

"Well, without knowing your business, you're not going. I'm your warden while you're here." His eyebrows shot up in surprise, and she sneered at him. "I'm not any happier about it than you are. If you want to talk, fine. We talk in the woods. Just know that if you try anything, the forest won't be the only thing trying to maim you." He wanted to tell her that the guards had already done a number on him, but somehow, he didn't think she would appreciate the joke.

Instead, Derrick gulped. That got a grim smile from his...warden?

Captor?

"Would you be willing to speak on my behalf then? Since you're my... warden." He winced, feeling a stab of pain in his leg.

"Why would I do that? I don't even know you," she growled, flicking a tight braid of hair over her shoulder. His heart sank. Maybe being able to stay wasn't going to be as easy as he'd thought. He felt boxed into a corner. He wouldn't be able to stay unless he talked to the queen. And it seemed like this woman wasn't going to let him do that until he told her who he was and what he wanted. Could he trust her to keep his confidence?

He didn't have a choice. He would just have to try his luck. He took a deep breath, and immediately regretted it. His chest felt like someone had stabbed him with a thousand needles.

"So, should I follow you? To the woods, I mean," he prompted. She stared down her nose at him and sighed.

"Fine. Get up."

He clambered to his feet, albeit a little unsteadily. She led him into the woods, just outside the village. She stopped, turned, and glared at him.

"You try to run..."

Derrick seemed to be having trouble finding his feet. As they reached the edge of the forest, he tripped on an arbitrary root sticking up from the ground. The warden's hand shot out towards him. He startled so badly that he jerked away hard, falling over, face first into the dirt. He heard her laugh softly, as if she was trying to hide it. She hadn't touched him. His face flamed. Looking up, he saw that her hand was still there, waiting. Which made him *beyond* embarrassed.

Back at court, any fast movement like hers had spelled pain. It was hard to believe that the same movement could be used to help, not hurt.

His stomach tightened with unease as she ducked under branches and leaves, leading him back to where the treacherous tree branches had seemed to go out of their way to knock him from Apple's saddle. "You're... not planning to leave me out here, are you?" Fear creeped into him, clenching his bowels in an icy grip. In an odd way, the feeling made him almost homesick.

Reyna chuckled darkly up ahead. He looked around, frantically trying to find landmarks to commit to memory.

"Don't bother. You won't find Syrinx by yourself. The forest will see to that." He stumbled over another root. How did she know what he was doing? She'd never even turned around.

"What, uh, *exactly* does that mean?" he asked nervously.

She still didn't turn to face him, but he could hear the smile in her voice as she answered. "It means that only a Wreya can lead you to the village."

"What if someone has an important message to get to your

people? If they have to wait for one of the Wreya to bring them to Syrinx, won't that message be delayed?"

This time, she *did* whirl around, so suddenly that he froze in his tracks.

"Is that why you're here? To give us an important message?" The scorn in her voice was almost a physical slap to the face.

"No. I'm not here to give anyone any messages. I..." he swallowed his embarrassment. "I'm here to beg for sanctuary." He waited for her to turn again and lead them deeper into the woods, but she just stood there, arms crossed over her chest, glaring at him. "Is this where we're talking, then?"

She gave him a curt nod, waiting for him to continue. He took a deep breath to steady himself, shoving his fears and doubts down as far as he could. " I... just barely got out of a dangerous situation." He paused, expecting her to ask questions. But she remained silent, an impatient look on her face. "My father wants to have me assassinated. My mother learned of his plans and warned me. She actually helped smuggle me out." Derrick's voice broke. Would his mother be punished for helping him? He couldn't know, would probably never *know*. He left his mother with a murderous tyrant. His cheeks flushed crimson.

"What kind of father sends an assassin after his own son?" she asked, disgust dripping from her words.

"The kind that doesn't love his son," Derrick said, his eyes on his shoes. He couldn't bring himself to meet her gaze. "The kind who worries that people will love his son more than him." He glanced up and saw Reyna's brow furrowed at him in confusion. "King Julius," he finished, spitting out the name.

Her jaw dropped. He waited for her to recover.

"No. That can't be true." Her stance relaxed and she let out a laugh. "You should be a bard; you tell such wonderful stories."

"It's the truth!" he snapped. She opened her mouth to argue, but he cut her off. "I can prove it." He reached into his left boot, fingers going all the way to the ankle. He pulled an item from it and closed it in his fist before she could see more than a glimmer of gold. "I didn't want anyone to know. My father's soldiers are hunting me. Wanted posters are posted in every town I've encountered on my way here." Derrick paused, his eyes going misty. "My father's men finally found me in a tavern in Cybele. I jumped out of the window to get away."

"The glass..." Reyna whispered.

"Yes. I guess those cuts got infected..." he trailed off, holding out his fist to her.

Wordlessly, she reached out and he dropped something into her hand. He watched her face as she looked at his signet ring. The ring that marked him as being in the Dragonspear bloodline.

Her eyes locked onto the golden spear set in a flaming ruby, cut to resemble flames. "You're the prince," she said flatly. Her eyes didn't move from the ring.

"Please, call me Derrick," he said, trying to be friendly. "You see now why I've come to Syrinx. I'm looking for sanctuary."

Her face clouded again, and lightning flashed in her eyes as she looked upon him once more.

"Why didn't you fight back?" she snarled. Derrick gaped at her. "You said that the people love you, right?" she continued through gritted teeth. "I've heard of some of the prince's... I mean, *your* initiatives. They've really helped people. Why didn't you rally an army, or even some mercenaries, and stand up to your father? You could have changed things! You could make it so nothing like..." she stopped, looking uncomfortable.

"Like what?" he asked softly, studying her features. Reyna's hardened face fell, those distrusting eyes glazed over with grief.

"You just could have changed things, alright?" she snapped, her features murderous once more.

"No one wins against my father," he said "He didn't hesitate to try and murder his own son! My mother might be dead, because she helped me escape! If I stand up to him, then what? More people die, because of *me!* No. I don't want any part of it! My father wouldn't give my followers a swift death. He'd drag it out over days, make an example of them. He'd make me watch as he tortured every last person that stood with me. I won't allow that to happen. I can't."

"So, you just ran away? You're a coward," Reyna spat.

"If I hadn't, I wouldn't be alive right now! As it is, I almost died anyway!" he shouted. Softening, he mumbled, "I have *you* to thank for keeping me alive."

"What's the use of having a life, if you allow someone else to control it?" she demanded.

"I don't know," he shrugged. That was a question he'd asked himself before; he hadn't had a good answer then, either. "I tried to change things, once. When I was younger..." His thoughts went back to that horrible night with Stravos. He shuddered. "It didn't go well. And that was something so small in comparison to what you're asking of me."

Reyna sighed. "I've always known King Julius to be cruel. But, why not use the people's love for you for his own gain? Why would he want you dead over something that could be an asset?"

"Because the people want me on the throne. He will never let that happen. Besides... Look at me. I can't even protect myself." He gave her another pitiful shrug.

But Reyna's face lit up. "That's it! If the people want you on the throne, we need to make that happen! That would completely reshape Niamh! Soldiers could be replaced by decent men, who actually know what justice *is*. Not twisted wretches who abuse their powers."

"*No*! I want no part of any uprising," he said, waving his

hands, his eyes wild with sudden fear. "And I won't say another word on the subject."

She looked him up and down, and he just *knew* that she was judging him in her silence. "Fine," she said after a moment. "Why, then, would you even think to try and come here? Do you know nothing of the Wreya?"

"You all have the safest region in all of Niamh. It's the only place my father's men would not find me." Derrick hung his head. He didn't know much else. His books had given him surprisingly little information where the Wreya were concerned.

Reyna rolled her eyes. "Have you ever heard of the Wreya taking in a man before?" she scoffed. "Though I guess Ephiny may see value in keeping the prince safe. "

"Alright, I can—"

"I'm not finished," she growled, talking over him. "*If* she allows you to stay here, then you can expect to learn how to fight. You'll have to contribute to the community, including the daily tasks that we rotate among ourselves." He opened his mouth to say something, but Reyna shot him a warning look. "Ephiny will give you duties to perform that are exclusive to you." She started to walk away, then threw over her shoulder, "And when you petition the queen, if you don't tell her the truth, I will. And trust me, you'll wish you stayed with your father if that has to happen." Reyna gave him a savage grin.

"Time to start thinking about what you want to say. We're going to see the queen. Now." She increased her stride and marched away, her head high.

The minute they came out from under the trees, the second woman from the hut stormed over to them.

"Queen Ephiny wants to see you." She shot Derrick a look that said he was lower than the dirt under her boots.

With his mind churning like a whirlpool, Derrick didn't even notice when they arrived at the foot of the ladder. He stared at it for a few seconds, before shaking himself out of his stupor and grabbing the rung in front of his face. He followed Reyna up, concentrating on the rungs in front of him, and not the powerful legs and... other parts above him.

The surly woman stood at the top of the ladder, waiting for them. She looked down her nose at Reyna, then led them towards the queen's audience chamber. Reyna offered Derrick a sarcastic bow, directing him to follow the other woman.

"Wait here," the guard snapped, letting herself into the chamber and shutting the door in their faces when they made to follow. A short moment later, she returned, and grudgingly held the door open for them.

The audience chamber of the queen was *much* different from his father's. He felt sheepish in his ignorance. The woman he took to be Queen Ephiny sat in a wooden chair behind a desk covered in scrolls, quills, and a bottle of ink, rather than a gilded throne. There were no seats for other nobility to sit in and watch the show. There were no shackles sunken in the floor for the sentencing of criminals... or torture for the king's entertainment. This room looked warm and inviting.

"Welcome! You needed to speak to me?" Ephiny asked, eyes darting from one face to the other. She looked wary; trying to read each expression for clues as to the situation and how to act on them.

"My queen, this man has a request to make of you." It was the first time he had heard Reyna speak with deference and respect. It took him a moment to remember that it was *his* turn to talk now.

He took a deep breath, standing as straight as he could. "Your Highness," he began.

"Let me stop you right there," she interrupted, not unkindly "I don't need any honorifics. Just speak freely." Though the queen looked young, she had a regal air about her. Her green eyes looked like the softest of spring meadows, her hair as blonde and barely graying. She stood up straight, proud. It was something that Derrick wished he could do.

"Thank you, Your... ma'am. I came here to seek sanctuary." He told her what he had told Reyna, hoping that she wouldn't react the same way.

Her face betrayed nothing. She was silent as she took in the information, then she sighed.

"It's not up to me, Prince Dragonspear."

The man's heart sank at those words, but he plowed on anyway. "Please, call me Derrick. I would rather as few people as possible know my bloodline."

"As you wish, Derrick. As I was saying, something of this magnitude is not something that I can decide by myself. It will require a nature reading."

Reyna made a strangled sound low in her throat. It made him more than a little uneasy. A nature reading? What did that even *mean*? And did it mean that there was no one that he could do his best to convince of his plight?

"Varia!" Ephiny's voice startled him, and he stepped to the side so he wouldn't be blocking the view of the door.

"My queen?"

"Please fetch Lyra. Tell her to bring her ingredients."

Varia's eyebrow rose in shock before she bowed and left the room. Derrick felt his stomach grow even more queasy. What did she mean by "ingredients"? What were they going to *do*?

Minutes later, Varia returned, leading a shorter woman with sandalwood hair into the room. This, Derrick presumed, was Lyra.

"My queen. You summoned me?" Lyra had a small leather pouch slung around her waist, hanging from a matching belt.

"Yes, we need a nature reading. It'll be two-fold," the queen explained. "I need to determine the truth of this man's words,"

Ephiny threw Derrick an apologetic look, "as well as advice on how to answer his request."

Lyra nodded, dropping down to the floor in the middle of the room and assuming a meditative pose. She began taking things out of her pouch. She brought out a small flask of water, a little bag of dirt, a feather, and a piece of wood. Next, she pulled out a small silver plate, and another small pouch of what looked like various herbs.

"Everyone, please sit down," Ephiny said, coming around the side of the desk. Derrick looked to Reyna, unsure, and followed her lead as she sat down. Ephiny came around and sat in front of Lyra, facing the twosome, with Lyra in between. She gestured for Lyra to begin, then shifted her gaze to Derrick and Reyna, holding a finger to her lips.

"Spirits of nature! Heed my call. Your humble servants request your presence!" Lyra lifted her arms, then began taking herbs out of her pouch, taking care to find the right ones before putting them on the silver plate. The four of them sat in silence. The women remained motionless, but Derrick shifted uncomfortably. He glanced over at Reyna, and opened his mouth to ask what they were waiting on. Before he could speak she gave him a sharp shake of the head. He closed his mouth and stared forward.

Suddenly, a spark of light exploded on the silver plate. Reyna and Derrick jumped. Lyra began to mutter under her breath.

The scent of herbs permeated the room. How had the herbs caught fire? Derrick looked at Reyna with wide eyes. She studiously ignored him.

Lyra began to sing in a language Derrick didn't recognize. She lifted the feather. Her voice grew light and airy. For each item she held, her tone changed. It became low and gravelly for the dirt, slow and smooth for the water, then sharp and harsh for the piece of wood. She gently used the flames from the silver plate to set the wood on fire. After giving it a moment to smolder, Lyra blew out the flame on the stick and set it down. Smoke began to billow up from the herbs, reaching its tendrils out to Lyra, flowing into her mouth. Lyra fell back, lying still as a corpse on the floor. Derrick jumped up to help her, but Reyna's hand snaked out and latched onto his bicep, gripping painfully. He had to bite down on his lip to stifle a gasp at the sudden spike of pain. She let go as he sat back down.

"We are here, and we are listening," rasped Lyra, in a voice clearly *not* her own.

"I come before you today to humbly beg for your help," began Ephiny. Derrick's heart began to race. Nature spirits were speaking to them through Lyra! It was unheard of! "Are Derrick's words true?" Ephiny asked, respectfully.

"Yesss...the boy speaks true," rasped Lyra. Ephiny nodded to herself, as if she'd anticipated that answer.

Derrick felt a burst of gratitude. Ephiny had known nothing

about him, and yet, she'd believed him. It was something that had never happened to him before, and he found that he liked it.

"We thank you for your answer. My second question: should we shelter this boy in our community?"

"Ah...*that* is a good question. One that we cannot answer for you." Ephiny's face fell. "We *can*, however, weigh your options for you. If he stays, he will become his true self. He will grow into a leader, much respected by the people. If he leaves, he will follow the darker path of fate."

Ephiny's face still bore disappointment. She'd been hoping for a clear and direct answer.

"We thank you for deigning to speak to us. We will burn incense in your honor tonight in appreciation." Ephiny reached for the silver plate to extinguish the fire when a small bolt of lightning leapt from the plate to her fingers. She squeaked, recoiling in shock.

"We are not finished," growled Lyra.

"I have no more questions for you," Ephiny said, confused.

"No, but you have brought before us the two humans whose fate will change the realms. Both of these young humans' lives are tied to an ancient talisman called the Draco Lingua." Reyna's and Derrick's eyebrows rose in tandem.

"Long ago, nature spirits created the first dragons. A male, Cadmus, and a female, Tanis. Dragons roamed far and wide when the first humans were created, and it caused war between the two races. In order to make a truce, Tanis met with the human's king. She offered to use her magic to make him a powerful talisman, one that would give the king the power to speak to dragons. One that would only work for the rightful heir to the line.

"Tanis created a silver arrow, which she bade the king shoot into her heart. When she died, her body disintegrated, leaving only her skull. It shrank to the size of a human heart, and appeared around his neck.

"But the talisman was lost, long ago. It now rests in the cave where Cadmus and Tanis lived. Whoever has the Draco Lingua, will prove to the world that they are the rightful heir to the throne. Only the one who is worthy to rule can find it. The quest for the talisman is one that these humans must go on together if the world of Man is to be righted." Lyra came back to herself then, sitting up and gasping for breath.

"Thank you, Lyra, for your service to us. You may go. Leave everything." Ephiny rubbed her temples. Lyra bowed her way out then slipped silently through the door. Reyna and Derrick both sat in shock. "The spirits have never left so abruptly. Nor have they ever given more information than was necessary."

"Fate has brought you two together," she eyed them. "Thus, I give you Reyna as a guide. She will teach you everything you need to know. You may go."

The two of them backed out of the room. Derrick turned to Reyna, stunned, only to find her glowering furiously at him.

Chapter 10

"So, what? Did you really think you could just stay here forever? Safe in a little den of peaceful women to cater to you..." Reyna crossed her arms over her chest. Derrick got the distinct impression that if she hadn't, she would have reached out and punched him.

"No! I..." he began.

She threw a hand up in between them, narrowly missing his face, her finger jabbing at his nose. "*You* are a pampered little princeling who knows absolutely *nothing* of the struggles of his subjects. *That's* what fate gives me to work with? How am

I supposed to train *you*, of all people, to survive?"

"I know I..." he tried to say.

"No! You *don't* know. That's the point!" Reyna dropped her hand and her voice, words dripping venom. "*I* would never make the choices you have. The choice you *want* to make, the choice to *hide*, is disgusting. *I* have a backbone. And now, somehow, I have to teach *you* how to grow one!" She threw her hands up in inarticulate frustration.

"I don't know what to say," Derrick said softly. He shifted from foot to uneasy foot, his face shrouded in confusion. He opened his mouth to speak, then snapped it closed. He looked like a fish, freshly pulled from the creek.

Reyna studied his face. It looked so open, so... *vulnerable*. She felt her heart clench. Her cheeks colored with embarrass-ment.

Stop Reyna, you need to think! she chastised herself. What was she going to do now? She gritted her teeth and turned on her heel, stalking towards the trunk of the tree and, more importantly, *away* from him.

"Reyna, wait. Can we talk about this? Reyna!" Derrick pleaded. He started walking, trying to catch up to her. "Please! Let me at least defend myself!"

She whirled around so fast he had to stop or run into her. He overbalanced a little, but managed to stay back. *Can't even keep his feet while walking. Imagine giving him a weapon. He'd run himself through by tripping over the damn thing.*

"*Can* you even defend yourself?" she sneered. The question seemed to catch him by surprise. He gaped at her, struggling to find a response and coming up with nothing.

"That's what I thought." She spun around once more, stalking off in the direction of her treehouse.

"Reyna! Can we at least just talk about this tomorrow, then?"

"No, we can't. I have things to do," she answered, her words clipped. It was a lie, but she didn't care. She needed to get away from him. When he was near, her self-control tried to escape her, like tendrils of smoke billowing through the bars of a cage. He tried once more to follow her, but she flitted down the trunk like a large, furless squirrel.

Her feet hit the ground hard. She squared her shoulders, hands fisted at her sides. No one bothered her as she stalked home, a wild panther on the trail of its prey. Everyone and everything blurred around her.

Instead of her own tree, however, her feet led her to the ground hut where Marlee and Denali were staying. It was past time Reyna had checked on the little girl, and the guilt she felt over waiting so long – over being delayed from doing so by a spoiled, useless man – threw another log on her banking anger.

"Yes? What is it?" a very disheveled Marlee croaked as she answered the door. She had large bruises under her eyes, making it look like she hadn't slept in weeks. Her blonde hair was matted to her forehead and hung loosely at her shoulders. Then her eyes widened in recognition.

"Reyna!" she cried, throwing her arms around her friend in a crushing hug. Her shoulders shook as sudden, deep sobs racked her thin frame.

Reyna's heart broke as she held Marlee. There was nothing she could do to help. Nothing other than hold her and let her know that she wasn't alone. And for Reyna, that just wasn't enough. "She's been asking for you," Marlee managed to say through choking sobs. "She's not awake very much anymore, but when she is, she looks for you." Hearing that made a physical pain punch through Reyna's chest and sharp stabs pricked her eyes until they began to tear up.

Slowly, trying her best not to startle the poor kid, Reyna made her way over to where Denali lay on her cot. She looked so tiny. So helpless. Reyna lowered herself to the floor, leaning over until she could put her head on Denali's shallowly rising chest. Her heart was beating, but it was weak. Reyna drew back, hands clenching into fists in anger.

"R...Reyna?" came the voice, softer than the mewling of a kitten. Reyna sat bolt upright, trying to swipe away the tear that had managed to start a trail down her cheek.

"Hey, Denali."

"Will you...stay? I...miss you." Reyna bit down so hard on

the insides of her cheeks that she tasted the coppery tang of blood. She had to stay strong. She couldn't cry in front of Denali.

"I can't, sweetheart. I have a big job to do for the queen." Denali's eyes closed, and her head lolled back. "But I'll come by and see you whenever I can, ok? I promise!" Reyna watched for another minute or two to see if Denali had heard her, but there were no indications either way. All she could do now was hope the little girl had heard and gotten some measure of comfort out of her words. And pray. Pray to any god or power that was listening, to spare Denali's life.

When Reyna left the hut, Marlee was stretched out on her own cot, twitching fitfully in a light doze. Reyna covered her with the blanket that she'd somehow managed to throw off, then fled.

Ariadne put down her sewing and looked up at Reyna expectantly. "Well? You look ready to either breathe fire or cry enough tears to fill a river. What happened?"

Reyna took a deep breath before launching into the story of everything that had happened in the queen's audience chamber and her visit to the ailing Denali. When Reyna told her mother who Derrick was, Ariadne's eyes grew so wide that they looked in serious danger of popping out.

"And now I'm supposed to teach him all the things that he doesn't know?!? How could I ever teach a spoiled prince how to gut a deer?" Reyna put her head in her hands, voice hitching on tears. "Especially when all I can think about is Denali. She's slipping away, mother. She won't even respond to my voice anymore."

"Denali is her mother's responsibility, though I understand your grief over her plight. As to the boy... he doesn't know how to survive on his own, that's true, but it has nothing to do with being spoiled," Ariandne said, her voice calm. Reyna opened her mouth to argue, but her mother stopped her with a raised hand. "There was a time when *you* didn't know how to gut a deer, either. And it had *nothing* to do with being spoiled, did it?"

"No," she admitted, albeit grudgingly.

"Alright then. Now, where is your charge?"

"My *charge*?" Reyna spat. A warning flickered in Ariadne's eyes, and Reyna bit off the rest of her retort. She gave a nonchalant shrug instead. "I don't know. It's not like I would bring him home with me..." She fought the urge to cross her arms over her chest. Ariadne noticed, chuckling low in her throat.

"What?" Reyna demanded.

"Sweet child, maybe you should go find him. He *is* your responsibility," Ariadne said, biting her lip to stop herself from laughing. Reyna felt her face burning as she turned and marched out of their house, her mother's unuttered laughter still ringing in her ears.

She didn't leave to find him, however. She buried herself in her thoughts, once again, seeking the sanctuary of her work tent. It was the only place where she felt completely at ease. Denali, Derrick, her mother, the Queen... they could all go to blazes, for all she cared. She needed time to herself.

Still, her mind raced. She had no desire to train a coward. But, she had a direct order from the queen.

She paused. Or did she? The nature reading had said so many things... Could this journey actually be used to her advantage?

Her eyes lit up. If Derrick was to take over the throne, then they would have to go to the castle. The castle where King Julius lived...

A fierce grin lit her face. Maybe this wouldn't be such a horrible job after all. Reyna could use Derrick to avenge Anteros.

I'll hide my true purpose until I can finally make my move. By the time anyone knew what was happening, it would all be over, and her revenge would be complete. Tucking that knowledge into her heart, she climbed to her feet and left her tent.

It was fully dark now, and only a handful of houses shown with lantern light. Sighing heavily at the prospect of being laughed at again, she made her way back up her home tree.

A lantern sat on the table, next to a steaming bowl of vegetable soup. Her favorite comfort food... and her mother knew it. An overwhelming feeling of love enveloped her. She went to find her mother, but Ariadne had already gone to bed. Reyna had been lost in her thoughts for longer than she'd intended. Settling down, she ate, blew out the flame in the lantern, and went to bed. That night, she dreamed.

People ran everywhere, trying to hide from a shadow that chased them from above. Flames spewed; lives guttered out. The fire's colors burned so bright. Her people's screams, so loud...

Reyna awoke in a cold sweat. She didn't fall back asleep that night.

When the sun rose the next morning, Reyna sprang out of bed. Whatever that dream had been the night before, it didn't matter in the cold light of day.

She'd come to the conclusion that the only way to carry out their mission was to teach Derrick what he needed to know as quickly as possible. She would teach him courage and convince him to leave with her. Then they could strike out for the palace.

Reyna took off at first light to find Derrick. The earlier they started, the more time they had for lessons. She was going to make sure that they didn't waste any more time.

Reyna's steps held both urgency and purpose. Not many women were out and about, which was normal for this time of day. She walked with purpose to Naida's hut and took a deep breath.

This was it. If she accepted Derrick as her student, then there was no turning back. Fate would embrace her. Gritting her teeth, she knocked sharply, her heart beating rapidly against her ribs.

After a few heartbeats, Reyna raised her hand to knock again. Then she heard movement inside. Taking a step back, she crossed her arms and cocked a hip, fixing a scowl on her face. The door opened slowly, and a tousle-haired Derrick blinked into the light of the morning sun rising behind Reyna's shoulder.

"You're here. I didn't think I'd see you today," he yawned, shading his eyes.

"It's time to start your training," she growled.

Derrick rubbed at his face. "It's a little early, isn't it?"

"The earlier we start, the more work we can get done. Get dressed. I'll wait." She turned her back on him to emphasize her point. When she heard no sounds behind her, she prepared to spin around again, to berate him for wasting daylight. Then she heard a heavy sigh and the squeal of hinges as he closed the door. She grinned. Her first victory over royalty. It wouldn't be her last.

As long as Derrick did what she said, her plan could actually work. Reyna picked at her fingernails as the door opened behind her.

"Well, tell me where to go and what to do," came Derrick's voice from behind her. He sounded sincere enough.

Reyna felt herself starting to warm to the young man. She admired Derrick's ability to put his pride aside and allow her to train him. Most men would have mocked her, but Derrick knew he did not have the skills to do what had to be done.

She glanced over her shoulder at him, and saw both grief and vulnerability in his warm, chocolate eyes. She clenched her jaw tightly, fighting the urge to ask him what was wrong. The man didn't need comfort. He needed toughening up.

"This way," she said, turning towards the edge of the woods and walking. No sound of footfalls followed her.

Irritation reared in her chest like a wild horse. She spun

around; mouth open to chastise him. Instead, a flush crept over her cheeks. He *was* following her. He'd paused only long enough to grab a wooden crutch, which he was now leaning on heavily.

"Thank you for waiting. That was kind of you." He offered her a tentative smile.

Reyna gave Derrick a curt nod, not trusting her voice at the moment. She was furious with herself. She had automatically thought the worst of him. His ignorance, though maddening, came from a good place. It made him unique, like Anteros.

Her heart clenched. She tilted her head in the direction they were to walk, and started again. This time, she deliberately kept her pace slow.

They were crossing the threshold between the clearing and forest when she finally trusted herself to speak. "Why do you even have that thing? You didn't have it when we saw the queen." Though she tried to hide it, a little suspicion crept into her tone.

"The crutch? You're right, I didn't. Before, when I made my escape, I ran through a stable blindly, to get to Apple. I somehow managed to step on a rusted pitchfork or something. Naida told me that it would have killed me if I'd been in the forest alone for much longer." He brightened up, smiling at her. "So, I owe you my life." The look of gratitude in Derrick's eyes forced Reyna to look away in shame.

His foot? She hadn't noticed that injury when she was treating him. Then again, she was more concerned for his vital organs. Another lesson that she's managed to botch at the first opportunity: *Always check the entire body.*

She needed to teach Derrick how to care for and protect himself. Those were the Queen's orders. But Reyna realized that *she* had work to do as well... on herself. It humbled her. Growing up, she'd been the one with all the right answers. She went over her lessons constantly. Now, this pampered princeling not only made her doubt herself, but whether he intended to or not, he rubbed her nose in all the things she'd done wrong.

"That still doesn't explain why you have it now, but not then," she grumbled.

He chuckled bitterly. "I didn't have it because I was stubborn. I thought it was healed enough to get around on my own. I was proven wrong." He sighed. "Going up and down the ladder really took a toll on me. I ripped my stitches out, and barely made it back to Naida before I collapsed from the pain."

"Didn't she tell you to take it easy?" Naida was a *very* talented and gifted healer. She *always* gave express care instructions after an injury.

"She did," he hedged. "But I, perhaps a little pigheadedly, thought she was wrong. I felt so much better, I just went back to doing what I did *before* my injuries." He stumbled, cursing softly under his breath. Reyna had to disguise a snort of laughter as a cough.

He was *somewhat* like her, she could admit that. He didn't like to be told what he could and couldn't do. And it seemed he had a penchant for breaking the rules, and licking his wounds afterwards. Wounds that, ironically enough, came as the consequences of him breaking said rules.

"Did you learn anything?" Reyna asked, unable to hide the amusement in her voice.

Derrick snorted. "If I didn't, I'd be an idiot."

"And, *are* you an idiot?"

"The pain that I went through after she cleaned and sewed it up again..." He winced. "I hope not."

Reyna sucked in her breath in both sympathy and remembrance. All the pain she'd recently experienced, both physical and emotional, flooded back to her. She shook herself, swallowing the lump forming in her throat. Soon, she would be able to move on from grief. Soon, she'd be before the king with a knife at his throat.

"We stop here." Her voice sounded more raw than she'd intended. Judging by the questioning look on Derrick's face, he'd noticed. "Since we have to wait for your foot to heal, *again...*" He flushed with embarrassment. "I think we should start with basic foraging lessons."

He opened his mouth to thank her, but she glowered at him, and he thought better of it. He eased himself down on the ground, and placed his crutch to the side, and waited for her instructions.

Then a loud shriek rent the air, followed by bawdy laughter. Derrick's head snapped up and he grabbed at his crutch, trying to get up as quickly as he could.

"Don't bother getting up," she told him, chuckling. "That is normal around here." He gave her a clueless look, and she bit her cheek to keep herself from laughing harder. "It's just the leshy." Three women ran by, followed by a creature with the upper torso of man and the lower body and legs of a goat. He had horns on his head, and a long, bushy beard that hung to his navel.

"Leshy?" His face turned thoughtful for a moment. She opened her mouth to explain to him what a leshy was, when he grinned. "They like to chase women for fun, right? And they tickle their victims to death." He sobered as those last words left his lips. "Do they ever catch the women?" he asked, apprehension in his voice.

"No. It's just a game for us. They know they will never actually catch us, just as we know they will never actually hurt us."

"No! I will not kiss you, demon!" rang out a mirthful voice, followed by the sad whining of something akin to a dog. Then a woman burst through the underbrush, laughing as she ran. The leshy, giggling like a child, followed in her wake. They watched as the woman stumbled and fell. The leshy stopped, letting her get to her feet and start running again before he gave a hunting cry and sprang forward. The other two women burst out of the bushes to his right and left, making him choose which one to follow. He spun around, looking at all three grinning at him. Faster and faster he spun until he got dizzy and lost his balance on his little goat legs, crashing to the ground. The woman to his right stepped forward and helped him up. He shook his head and steadied himself, then took a few steps. She darted back, and they all ran off again.

While Derrick was distracted by the amusing exploits, Reyna disappeared into the undergrowth. Mushrooms, roots, berries, and a variety of nuts were easily found in the forest, and she would give him a valuable lesson in recognizing what he could eat safely. She'd come unprepared, thinking he was capable of walking on his own. So, she took the hem of her tunic in one hand and held it out in front of her, forming a kind of sling between her hand and her waist.

She got to work. It took her about an hour to gather everything she wanted. When she came back Derrick was sitting where she'd left him, but with his crutch in his hands, ready to swing it at an intruder. She stopped in surprise. He put the crutch down, not meeting her eyes.

"I wasn't sure if it was you coming back, or... something else," he said quietly. The fear in his eyes made him look half his age. She felt like she was seeing him as he must have been as a child.

"I'll always come back." Her cheeks colored and her eyes went wide as she heard the words that had just come from her mouth. *Why* had she said that? It had just slipped out!

But the look on his face tore at her heart. He wanted to believe her, but the underlying pain of betrayal shone through his hopeful gaze. *Had the king really been so cruel to his own son?* Reyna wondered. Had someone said similar words to him before, then betrayed him?

She shook her head to clear it, focusing on the task in front of her. "We're going to get started with how to live off the land. Well, everything that *I* can teach you. There are so many things to cover. Ephiny will doubtless test you on everything you've learned once I've gone through all of your training. So make sure you pay attention!" She barked the last sentence at him, and he jumped.

Good. He needed to pay attention. She sank down beside him, legs crossed, and began laying the forest's treasures in front of him.

"What is all this?" he asked, intrigued.

She gave him an irritated look, and he immediately looked contrite. "These are just some things that you can and can't eat if you're in the woods," she said. "Whenever you run out of food, or want to ration what you have, you can eat and use these for different purposes. Now, this is called a honey fungus."

Apparently, he couldn't resist. "What does it do? And why is it called a honey fungus?"

The glare she shot him was deadly. "If you keep your mouth shut and *try* to exercise some *patience*, you'll find out," she growled. He clamped his lips together and motioned for her to continue.

"Now, if there are no more interruptions..." she asked, her tongue sharp. He shook his head. "This is called a honey fungus." She pointed to a cluster of mushrooms. They seemed to be one solid unit, with flat, round caps spreading out from the center. All the caps had little divots in the middle, as if someone had jabbed their finger into it. The cluster was about the length of her booted foot. "These you can eat. They grow on dead stumps and at the base of willow or beech trees." She waited until he nodded. He shifted, looking as though he desperately wanted to speak. She sighed. "Yes?"

"Do you have to cook them a certain way, or can you eat them raw?"

She was taken aback. He'd actually asked an important question.

"Either is fine," she answered, recovering her composure

quickly before continuing. "This is a cloudberry." She handed it to him. The berries were every shade imaginable between yellow and orange, with strange bumps. They seemed to glow on their bed of stark white flowers. "They have a tart taste to them."

"I've seen those!" he said, and his entire face lit up. "Naida used those in a paste she made to heal my cuts!"

Reyna smiled at him, "Yes, these are great for fighting inflammation in wounds." She had to bite back her laughter at the self-satisfied look on his face. "There is one I don't have called black locust. It grows on a tree that you can't fail to recognize if you see it. It's straight with a very narrow crown, but it's the bark that makes it memorable. The bark is reddish brown, but the grooves in the bark are gray with an orange tinge." He gaped at her, and this time, she *did* laugh. "The leaves are a dark bluish-green on top, with a brighter color underneath. The flowers are white, and hang down in drooping clusters." She sighed, unhappy with her description. "I *wish* I would have found some to show you, but I didn't want to go too far and leave you defenseless."

"Hey!" he said, indignation coloring his voice. "I was doing just fine with my crutch, thank you."

"Yeah, you're a real killer." Rolling her eyes, she fought *hard* to keep the amusement off her face. What was *wrong* with her? Maybe Varia was right. She *was* too soft when it came to men.

"Let's get back to the lesson. The black locust fruit is dark orange-brown with irregular markings on them. They hang from the branches in flat, smooth pods. Sort of like pea pods."

"That tree sounds like it would be beautiful to see," he mused.

"It is. I haven't seen many, but the ones I have…" Reyna trailed off, memories swimming to the forefront of her mind. She shook her head again. *Focus!* "This plant," she pointed at a clump of bright orange flowers, bursting from a bed of perfectly round, flat leaves, "is the nasturtium. The flower has a peppery taste, and it's sometimes used against infection when it's made into a drink. It can also be made into an unguent to clean a wound."

Reyna continued to go through the lesson, showing him every plant, fruit, seed, nut, berry, and mushroom she'd found. "Everything I've shown you so far can be eaten. These are by no means the *only* plants you can eat, but it's what I found."

"They all grow in different types of terrain, don't they?" Again, she was shocked by his astuteness. "I've read a few books about plants when I was home. But none of the stuff you showed me today was in it."

"Yes. Once you're healed I recommend we set out and explore different regions to give you an idea of what to find in different terrains."

Derrick balked. "I'm a wanted man. I can't be caught by my

father's soldiers..."

Reyna's jaw tightened. "Right, of course," she mumbled. She took a deep breath. "Now, *these* ones, make sure you remember *everything* I'm about to say," she said meaningfully. "This is called a Death Cap. If eaten, it can make you vomit and cause intense pain in your abdomen. If you eat half a cap or more, you're dead. They grow in woods made up of trees with broad leaves, like maples." Reyna's fingers accidentally grazed Derrick's knuckles. She cleared her throat, ignoring the sensation. "This is the fly amanita," she said, indicating the last mushroom before quickly moving her hands back into her lap. The fungus had a vibrant red cap, dotted with white spots. The underside was covered in white gills.

"So, what I'm seeing is that anything with white gills under the cap is poisonous."

She gave him a genuine smile. "That won't be true for *all* mushrooms with white gills, but that's a good rule to live by. Good eye on the mushrooms." She set a clump of large leaves with wide, purple flowers in front of him. "This is Wolf's Bane. Ingesting a small amount will cause vomiting and nausea. A *large* amount, however, will slow down your heart until it stops beating completely."

"Just guessing here, but would that be painful?" he asked, grinning at her.

"*Very*," she nodded, smiling back.

While she had been foraging and giving lessons, the sun had climbed directly overhead. She hadn't even noticed. She sprang to her feet.

"What? What is it?" he asked, alarmed.

"It's past the midday meal already! I wasn't keeping track of time at all."

The alarm left his face, and he relaxed again.

"That's nothing to be so worried over," he grinned.

"Is that so?" she asked, her mouth quirking into a half-grin. "I always thought pampered little princes didn't skip meals," she teased.

He rolled his eyes in mock affront. "How *dare* you, peasant? No part of me is little!" He crossed his arms over his chest and stuck his nose in the air.

"*Peasant*? Really, *your highness*, just how many people can vouch for such a remarkable claim?" she asked, raising an eyebrow. After a moment's thought, his arms fell away and his jaw dropped, cheeks flushing. She burst out laughing deep, belly laughs that shook her entire body as she watched him try to recover from his embarrassment. She wiped tears from her eyes and took a deep breath, willing herself to calm down. "What? Women can't make bawdy jokes?"

"No! I mean, yes, but..." He blushed again, searching for the right words. "I'm just going to stop talking before I get myself into any more trouble." She laughed again, then held out a hand to help him up. He eyed it warily. He doubted her? Really? After everything she'd already done for him?

"What? I'm not going to drop you," she said, waving her hand in his face. *What is his problem, anyway? I'm only trying to help.* "I don't trust you, and I don't even like you. But I'm not cruel enough to drop an invalid when I offer to help them up," she said, her anger rising. He hesitated a few more seconds, then grabbed his crutch and took her hand firmly. She hauled him to his feet with little effort, and he looked surprised.

"Is there a problem?" she asked.

"No! I, um, just didn't realize that you could pull me up like that." He realized his mistake when he saw her face cloud over. "I didn't mean—" But Reyna had already turned her back on him and was crashing through the undergrowth, back to Syrinx.

"Maybe I should just leave you out here to wander," she spat over her shoulder.

Contrary to her words, however, she made sure that she was always *just* in view for him to follow.

Reyna felt furious. He was such a typical man! Always thinking that he knew what women could and could not do. Well, she'd show him!

She took a deep breath and unclenched her fists. Alright, she *did* have to admit that she had more strength than most women, even when she was compared to the other Wreya... *No.* That was no excuse. And while she was angry with Derrick, she realized she was more upset with herself.

The next morning, she found Derrick already dressed when he opened the door. *Good.* He had begun taking all of this seriously. As he should... for *his* sake. He stood there, leaning on his crutch, staring.

"Well? Are you going to invite me in?" she asked, a little gruffly. She felt the sting of yesterday's words looking at him, and it stoked the fire of her anger once more.

"Yes! Please, come in!" He shuffled to the side of the door so quickly he almost stumbled. She found a smile tugging at her cheek at his awkwardness, but she pressed her lips together to quell the urge.

"Aren't we, um, working outside?" he asked.

"Obviously not," she answered, pointedly looking around the room. "Today, I'll *try* to teach you how to make some basic medicines. So, *try* to keep up, ok?"

He scowled at her, and she had to bend down abruptly to fetch a mortar and pestle so he wouldn't see her smiling. She did that a lot around him... Damn him for having his cute moments. "We're going to help Naida by replenishing some of her stock of medicines. Don't worry, I won't let you mess anything up," she said matronizingly.

Derrick narrowed his eyebrows. "What makes you think

I'd mess it up? Can't men make medicines?" he asked, his voice cold. "Besides. I've read a few apothecary books here and there."

She turned on him with a predatory smile. "Oh, no, princeling! I would never *dare* tell a man what he can and can't do."

He opened his mouth to snap back at her, then her meaning appeared to dawn on him.

"Reyna, look. I'm sorry for what I said yesterday. It was out of line, and I should never have assumed what you could or couldn't do. Can we start over?" Irritation still coated his tone, but she wasn't sure if it was aimed at her... or himself.

She took a calming breath. She couldn't let him be the bigger person. "Alright. We can start over. But if you make wrong assumptions about the wrong person again it *will* go badly for you."

"I understand," he answered, his tone meek. "So... we're making medicines today?" he prompted.

"Yes. Let me get what we need from the store room." She paused at the door in the back of the hut. Reyna looked back at him pensively. "And get a stool to sit on. Take your weight off that leg."

"That's kind of you, Reyna," he said. He sounded like he meant it.

She shrugged. "You need to be healed enough for weapons

training."

Reyna gathered the ingredients they needed without even having to look at what she was grabbing. She'd helped Naida more times than she could count, and knew every bottle and bowl on every one of her over-cramped, myriad shelves. Returning to the table, she saw that Derrick had pasted a broad smile on his face. She could *also* see that it was fake. It didn't reach his eyes.

"What are we making?" His voice sounded strained.

"This is one for headaches," she told him, laying out the ingredients for it. She named everything in front of him, pointing it out as she went. "I'm going to test you as we go. I'll tell you the steps, and you make the unguent. I've already identified everything for you. Are you ready?"

"I think so," he answered. He seemed nervous: the false smile had fallen pretty quickly, once she had begun listing the herbs.

She nodded. "First, take a pinch of garlic, and put it in the mortar."

His hand found the right bowl, but it hovered over it, hesitating. "How much is a pinch? How do I know if I took too much? Or too little?" More of those important questions. The ones she hadn't thought him capable of asking.

Reyna gentled her tone a little when she answered. "There's no real way of telling, I'm sorry to say. Nadia taught me to just pinch the powder and use whatever doesn't fall off."

"How is that accurate?" he asked with an incredulous look.

Reyna shrugged. "It seems to work for her. Her medicines always do what they should. I don't think that small of a difference is going to matter. Well, I mean, as long as it's not a lethal ingredient." She shrugged again.

His face blanched. "If you're sure..." He took a pinch, letting all the excess flake off his fingers before putting it in the mortar. "Alright. Now what?"

"Two flowers from the feverfew plant." He did as she said. "Add a stalk of helenium, and one red nettle." He followed her instructions, never once needing her to correct him on choosing an ingredient. "Now, fill the mortar the rest of the way with water. Use the pestle and grind it all into a thick paste."

He was so focused on grinding without spilling any water that he didn't notice when Reyna left the table. She started a fire in the fireplace, then grabbed a large fern leaf and a small earthenware pot.

"Is this good?" He gestured to the yellow, runny mess in the mortar. "It doesn't really seem like medicine." His lip curled in disgust. "Are you supposed to *drink* it?"

"No! Of course not," she laughed. "Here." She handed him a cloth. "You have to strain it."

He looked confused. "What's the leaf for?"

"Watch and learn." Smiling, she laid the large leaf on the table. Starting at one end, she began to roll it tightly.

"Shouldn't you roll both sides evenly?" She shot him a withering look, and he put his hands up in surrender. "Sorry! I did it again. Just pretend I never said that."

She went back to the leaf. When one end was rolled tightly, she picked it up, holding the end tightly so it wouldn't unravel, and grabbed the pot, bringing both over to Derrick. He watched as she held the tight end of the leaf over the pot, then she handed it over and stared at him, waiting.

He gave her a blank look. "What do I do?"

"Put the cloth over the mortar, then strain the water into the pot." He took the cloth and carefully laid it over the mouth of the mortar. Slowly, he tipped it upside down over the tunnel the fern leaf formed. The yellow water ran out, filling up the pot. When no more came out, he put the mortar back on the table.

"Now, this is the excess that you don't need." She dumped the liquid into the fire. "Next, scrape what's left into the pot." He did, then she put a thick stopper into the top of the pot.

"We did it?" he asked softly. She nodded. "I...I made medicine? That can *help* someone?" He turned wonder-filled eyes to her. She nodded again.

His eyes glistened with unshed tears. He swiped at them and grinned. "So! What's next?"

With Reyna giving instructions, and Derrick making the medicines, they worked through unguents for fever, breathing problems, and venomous bites. They had just corked the oil for the venom when the door opened and Naida walked in.

"Oh! You're still working? Let me break up your lesson. It's almost midday, and I have some work of my own to do."

She was very politely kicking them out. Well, kicking *Reyna* out: Derrick was living in a part of the hut, and he silently retreated to the room he was staying in.

Naida, already hard at work, had her back turned to Reyna, hands flying between ingredients and a stone bowl. Reyna slunk out, feeling dejected. The child-like joy that had lit up Derrick's face when he'd done something that would help a stranger warmed her heart. Maybe he would grow a little more backbone and confront his fears; if he did, Derrick would make an amazing king.

Too bad there's no unguent for that...

CHAPTER 11

When the knock at the door came the next morning, Derrick was ready. He'd come up with a truce, and he felt excited to present it to Reyna. He knew that he'd said the wrong thing to her plenty of times over the last couple of days, and he'd thought he'd found a way to fix it. Pending her agreement, of course. He flung the door open, a smile on his face.

"The queen demands your presence." Derrick's face fell. It was the woman who'd held a dagger to his throat just a few days back. The woman turned and stalked away, exuding rage from every part of her body. "That *wasn't* a choice. Come. Now."

Derrick didn't move.

"How about we try this again?" He grinned; Reyna was starting to rub off on him. "Hello...my name is Derrick. How have you been since we last saw each other?" He spoke slowly, nodding encouragement. "Your turn." He wanted to be polite and patient, but this woman really rubbed him the wrong way.

"My name is Varia. Now follow me," she ground out between clenched teeth.

He gave her the syrupy-sweet smile his mother had often told him was the most infuriating form of smugness she'd ever seen. Varia looked ready to breathe fire. "There! That wasn't so bad, was it?" he asked, cheerfully pretending not to notice.

She ignored him and began walking again. Derrick saw that her hands had curled into fists at her side. He smiled again, this time to himself. He'd never been one to actually try to upset someone; in Dragonspear, being willfully obstinate got you beaten if you were lucky, and killed if you weren't. And he hadn't forgotten how that blade had felt along the skin of his neck. Putting this woman out a bit seemed a fair recompense for that, at least.

He followed Varia in silence. She led him to the same ladder he'd climbed a few days ago, when he'd gone to petition the queen. *Did she ever leave her treehouse?* he wondered. He hadn't seen her around the village.

As Derrick climbed the ladder, his nerves began roiling in his gut. Had he done something wrong?

Varia led him to the audience chamber. He wondered idly if that was the only room of the treehouse he would ever get to see. She opened the door for him, staring at him coldly as she waited for him to enter. He suddenly wished that maybe he hadn't been so flippant with the woman who now stood between him and freedom.

A blanket of foreboding covered him as he walked through the door. A slight breeze brushed the back of his neck as the door swung shut behind him.

"Derrick! Thank you for finding the time to meet with me. Sit down! Sit down!" The queen indicated a wooden chair that had been drawn up to the opposite side of her desk.

That... was unexpected. "Varia told me you *demanded* to see me," he said slowly, confused.

Ephiny sighed, laying her hand over her eyes. "Varia is a little over-zealous at times. She's a wonderful guard, don't misunderstand me. Sometimes, though, she takes her job and my title a little too seriously." She straightened herself and smiled. "So, let me start with this. *Do* you have time to meet with me? Or would you prefer a later time?"

Derrick considered what the lands of Ulster would be like if *she* were the reigning monarch. *People would not be afraid to approach the palace to petition for an audience, at least...*

He jerked out of his silent reverie when he realized that she was still waiting for an answer. "Um, no." He cleared his throat. "Now is fine. I just... wasn't sure what this meeting was about. I have to admit that I'm a little apprehensive."

Ephiny's eyes widened, then she covered her eyes once more and groaned.

"Varia?" he ventured.

"Varia," she agreed. "I'm so sorry that you were left in the dark. I simply wanted to meet with you so I could give you a lesson in diplomacy. *That's* something that Reyna can't teach you.

"And not just because she isn't a queen," Ephiny hurried to clarify. "She simply doesn't have the patience to work through a problem. Most of the time, she's impulsive and rash."

Derrick grinned. Didn't he know it. He'd cut himself on her sharp tongue more than once...and gotten lost in her dark blue eyes, too. Blue as the darkest depths of the ocean. He felt that he could drown in those eyes, like a sailor pulled under the water by a beautiful mermaid...

"Derrick?" she asked. "Is your mind still with us?"

He blushed, and she favored him with an indulgent smile. "Yes! It is now. Please, forgive me."

"It's alright. Let's begin before duty calls me away." The warmth of her words put him at ease.

"Of course. I appreciate this very much, my queen," he said, using the respectful tone he'd learned at court. "I had no idea that you would honor me by teaching me yourself."

"You don't have to address me like that. Please, just call me Ephiny. I wanted to make sure that you were ready for your duties when you assumed the throne."

"Thank you." He felt lucky the words made it out of his mouth. The idea of taking his father's throne still made his stomach clench, and Reyna's harsh denunciation still rang in his mind. *Could he ever grow a backbone?* Well, if the encounter with Varia taught him anything, it was that maybe, he could...

...or maybe it was a fluke. The idea of facing his father still made him want to run away and never look back.

"Shall we begin?" Ephiny asked.

He nodded, perking up his ears, listening intently.

"The first thing you need to realize about your court is that everyone has their own agenda," she began. "Even the people who you deem trustworthy and close to you. *Especially* the people close to you. Be wary of *everyone*. You can never be too careful."

"*That* is something I wish I'd known all my life," Derrick muttered. Then a realization hit him like a wave of lava crashing against a rocky cliff. "There's so much I don't know!" he burst out. His voice quavered; his cheeks flushed with both anger and embarrassment. His *true* nature, his weak, shallow self, peeking through.

"It's nothing to be ashamed of!" Ephiny cajoled. "As a child growing up, there was no need to teach you the intricacies of court life. And as a second son, you would have been told only those things that were common knowledge already."

Derrick sneered at the memories of his life in the palace. He'd been kept as an ornament, it seemed. Trapped in his own world, like an animal in a cage.

"I was a meaningless decoration," he replied. "The 'spare heir.' The one they could throw away."

"And it was lucky that they did. Otherwise, you wouldn't be here." Her face looked so earnest that he couldn't help but trust her. He let the hint of a smile bloom on his face.

"Now, another important thing to know is that flattery is as good as currency at court," the Queen continued. His eyes widened in realization. He bit his lip, but he had to ask.

"How do you know when they are sincere?"

She smiled gently at him. "Therein lies the problem. You may never know. I will tell you that I am ever only sincere, but whether you choose to believe it remains on you. Take everything with a grain of salt, and try to paint a picture of the person's character from what you know. From there, see if the words line up with what facts you have about them."

For the next hour, Ephiny took him through official protocols and the ins and outs of courtly life. She had just finished going through a list of ranks; making sure to tell him how to address each, and what each rank's responsibility was both to him as their liege and to the people that lived on their lands. She was explaining how each rank should be treated when they came to court when a knock came at the door. Derrick had been so engrossed in her lesson that the sound startled him.

"Come in," Ephiny called wearily. Varia entered, bowed to Ephiny, and presented her with three scrolls.

"Those are the reports you requested, my queen," Varia said. Derrick had a feeling that Ephiny had asked Varia to call her by her name dozens of times, if not more.

"Thank you, Varia." Ephiny waited until Varia had bowed and slipped through the door before she spoke again. "I'm sorry, Derrick. It seems that our time is at an end." She paused. "But before you go, I want to discuss one more thing."

"Of course! Anything you want to tell me, I want to hear. I thank you for every minute that you've spent with me. You've opened my eyes to so many things I never knew."

She gave him a tired smile. "Having this weight of responsibility on your shoulders is not for everyone. Some can carry it, but abuse their powers."

"Like my father." The words slipped out before he could stop them. He put his hand over his mouth, wishing he could take them back.

Ephiny chuckled. "You never have to censor your words here, Derrick. You are free to speak your mind. 'Freedom' is at the core of most of our laws. Freedom of choice, especially. Don't be afraid to interrupt if you need to. Now, let me finish this part quickly.

"There are those who crumble under that weight of responsibility, and those are the ones whose land and people suffer. But there are those who can stand the weight of the crown, and use everything they have to help their people grow and *prosper*. Those rulers are the ones that legends are written about, the ones whose stories are handed down through the generations. You have to choose which one you will be. You will have petitions brought to you... just as you came to me with yours." She smiled at him again, and he returned it. "You have to choose if you will be fair and just, or if you will serve only yourself. That is all. Now, I apologize, but I have work to attend to. If you have questions, I can meet with you again," she offered.

"No, what you've said makes sense. Thank you, again." He rose and went to the door. With his hand on the smooth wood, he turned back; Ephiny was already breaking the wax seal on one of the scrolls with a worried look on her face. He swallowed his questions and silently vowed to be more curious when the two had another meeting.

When, or if.

He made his way to his hut in a thoughtful daze. Ephiny's words churned in his mind. It was easy to say which leader he *wanted* to be. The problem was only whether or not he *could* be that leader...

That night, Derrick fell asleep to imagined scenarios flitting through his mind, practicing his diplomacy.

He sat on his father's throne, looking down at the floor. An older man, maybe twice Derrick's winters, bent down on his knees, trembling in fear. He felt a feral hunger wash through him as he tasted the man's terror.

"Well?" he barked, watching the prisoner flinch.

"We've done it, Your Majesty."

"That seemed to take a little longer than it needed to, didn't it?" Derrick asked. The miserable wretch said nothing, and Derrick felt his lips stretch in a malicious grin. "Not to worry! We will correct any mistakes. And gain back any lost time."

Men – his men – filed into the room, picked up the one on the floor and started dragging him out. The poor fool caught between them started pleading for his life, but Derrick just laughed. A cold, high laugh...

Derrick woke, sweat beading his forehead, breath coming out in ragged gasps. That had been one of the worst dreams he'd had in a long time.

But...was it a dream? It had felt so real. Like he'd been sitting there in the room, watching himself.

He did his best to stay awake for the rest of the night, afraid of what else might worm its way into his mind. *Or out of it.*

But with all of the mental and physical effort he'd expended, he couldn't stay awake very long at all. The rest of his sleep, thankfully, was deep and dreamless.

Derrick opened the door slowly the next morning, wanting to see who had come to call before he actually had to face them.

Reyna stood on the porch, gazing out at the horizon behind her, the sun reflecting off her chestnut hair. He let out a breath he didn't know he'd been holding. When she turned back to the door he saw she once more wore a scowl, and that her arms were crossed obstinately across her chest.

He immediately felt like he'd done something wrong. He opened the door the rest of the way.

"Where were you yesterday?" she snapped, marching into the hut like she owned it.

"I had a lesson with Ephiny." That stopped her in her tracks.

"She already gave you her lesson?" Reyna softened. "She must think very highly of you if she's worked you into her schedule that quickly."

"I'm sorry that I didn't clear it with you first," he tried to joke, bowing to her.

Her cheeks glowed red and she turned away. "You don't have to clear it with me, but it would have been nice if you'd left a message for me. I'd freed up my whole day to teach you, and I had nothing to occupy my time."

"Varia didn't really leave me much time to follow her," Derrick sighed. "But, I'm here now and you're here now. You can teach me whatever you want, now that we're together."

"Yes, I guess we are... together now." She paused, as if she was still trying to process what he'd said. "Well, come on then. Today is going to be an all-day affair. I'm combining two lessons to make up for yesterday."

"Do I need to bring anything?" he asked. Once the words were out of his mouth, he wanted to take them back. What was he going to bring? He had nothing.

"No, I'll take care of it. Come on. I need to make a stop at home. I left everything we needed there in case you weren't home again."

Reyna walked out the door, and unlike Varia, she didn't look back. She simply trusted him to follow her. It meant something to him, that someone trusted him.

"How is your foot?" she asked once he'd caught up to her.

"Better. Naida says it's healed but needs exercise because it's gotten stiff." Derrick stopped for a moment and rotated his ankle around to show her.

"Good. We may have a fair bit of walking to do today, and tomorrow we start your weapons training."

His hands grew sweaty. "Weapons training?" His voice cracked a little as he said it.

"Yes. You'll get two days of that." She stopped and gave him a serious look. "All day on both days."

Derrick swallowed as he noticed how painfully close they were. Then she spun around and clamored up the tree they'd stopped beneath.

When had they arrived under this massive tree? Derrick had been too busy watching Reyna's chestnut curls dancing on the breeze to notice it. What was wrong with him? He shouldn't be noticing things like that about her. She'd made it clear that everything she did for him was against her will, and that she was only doing it for the prophecy.

A clattering sound caught his attention and he looked up. "Do you need help?" he asked.

Reyna climbed down the ladder, laden with so many things that he was worried she would fall off. He reached up as high as he could, trying to take one of the bundles from her, but she slapped his hand away.

"No. Not yet." He couldn't even see what all she had. "I *should* make you carry everything, to build up your strength. But I'm just a *peasant*, so I guess that means it's my job, right?"

She grinned at him as she plunged into the woods next to her tree. She felt lucky that her tree house was on the very outskirts of the clearing. They could reach the forest much quicker from here than it was from his hut.

He felt like he had a bubble of joy growing in his chest. She was teasing him. He beamed foolishly. "That's going to be something that you'll never let me forget, isn't it?"

"Absolutely not, princeling. Now, I know it's going to be hard for you, but there's going to be a point later when I need you to be silent. Think you can handle that?" She winked at him and turned back to her trail.

Once they had reached a thickly wooded area, Reyna put a finger to her lips, then motioned him forward. He crept along as quietly as he could, but to his own ears, he sounded like a dragon crashing around the forest.

Reyna didn't seem to notice. She took the rope she'd brought and made a noose, then looped the entrance in front of an animal's den. Derrick hadn't even noticed it until she'd finished laying the trap.

Reyna fidgeted with the strap of her pack. She looked like she wanted to say something.

"Whatever it is, you can say it," he offered gently.

She looked up at him, the shock plain on her face. "You... are strangely perceptive of the people around you."

He took her hand and lightened his tone. "Reyna... I mean

it. If you ever have something on your mind, you can talk to me. I'm a good listener, and I would never betray your trust."

She gazed at him for a long time, her expression unreadable. Then she shook her head suddenly. "Right. Simple snares are meant to be set up at dens, like this one. Now, this is a twitch-up snare. It takes a little work, but it's very good if you're looking for food in a predator heavy area. It pulls the animal straight up, making it so other animals can't reach it."

"I'm not sure if I'll be able to make the trap myself."

"You'll be fine," she replied – a little brusquely, to his mind. "Now, *you* make the next trap. I'll talk you through it." Reyna stood and motioned for Derrick to follow her off the path.

"Where are we going?" he asked, confused. "Aren't we staying on the trail?"

"I'm going to have to set up a deadfall trap. Let's go." She led him deeper into the forest, stopping only when she noticed some change in the terrain that completely evaded him.

"Go get a heavy object. A big log or rock will do." He stared blankly at her for a few moments. She returned his look with an impatient glare, then shooed him along.

After a few minutes searching, he came back with a large rock. "That's great!" she said. "Put it over here."

He set it down as instructed. "How are we going to use this thing? Are we going to use a tiny catapult or something?"

That sent Reyna into peals of laughter. His cheeks reddened. She'd been so impressed with his questions before this!

When she finally caught her breath, she shook her head and began laying out the specifics for the dead fall. But even after her explanation, Derrick had *zero* confidence that he was going to be able to build the trap. He started by propping the rock on some sticks, as Reyna had told him. He was setting up the last one when he accidentally brushed it, and the rock smashed down on his arm.

He let out a bellow of pain, and Reyna almost fell over as she belted out her laughter. *Why* was he so *incompetent* in front of her? He cursed himself.

"I guess I should have warned you about that," she said as her chuckling subsided. He saw the mischievous grin on her face, and realized she'd "forgotten" on purpose. Well, he'd show *her*. Derrick straightened and tried again.

"Good," she nodded. "Now put this bait under there and let's go." Just then, a terrible scream rent the air. Derrick jumped, his heart racing.

"What was that?" His eyes searched the area around them frantically.

"Relax. It's just a rabbit," Reyna patted him on the shoulder.

When they reached the den, he saw a rabbit dangling in the noose.

"I-I've never seen anything like this," Derrick swallowed.

"That's because *you* don't have to do any dirty work, princeling. We *peasants* are here to do it for you." She gave him a curtsy, and continued. "Alright, next lesson, princeling. Let's teach you how to skin and gut a rabbit."

Derrick blanched. "You-you're not serious. Are you?" He could feel his face turning green as his stomach threatened to reject the morning's breakfast.

"Of course I'm serious," she replied. "It's survival. How would you cook it and eat it if you don't skin it?"

He had no answer for her. Reyna's directness both shocked him and, in a strange way, made him more comfortable with the task before him.

She handed him the dagger and rabbit. "Just do what I tell you, like we did with the medicines." Her face softened, along with her voice. "You'll be just fine."

He looked from the knife to the rabbit, his stomach churning once more. "Alright. I'll do my best."

"You're going to be king. You can't be afraid of a little blood and guts," Reyna said simply.

Derrick paused. He'd never considered that, but she was right. How could he lead his soldiers into battle if he couldn't stomach skinning a rabbit? He gathered up all his courage, nodded, and made the first cut.

When Derrick finished, he held up the carcass. It no longer resembled any rabbit *he'd* ever seen.

Reyna nodded with pride, bringing relief and gratification to his heart. "Perfect. Let's go."

Derrick turned his head towards hers, to ask where they were going. His lips brushed the corner or her mouth. Reyna froze, her dark eyes went wide. She stared at him, lips barely parted.

He *wanted* to apologize. He *wanted* to tell her it was an accident. Instead, he dipped his head forward slowly. He waited for her to either slap him or move away.

Her lips were so soft he felt like he'd touched clouds. His mouth was on hers, and she gasped. Heat flooded him, making his heart race. He wanted to hold her, touch her, grab onto her and never let go. He watched her eyes flutter shut. Her mouth moved to meld with his.

Suddenly, she stiffened and jerked away. He gaped up at her, open mouthed. "Reyna, I—"

She was shaking. With laughter. So hard that she snorted...

Derrick felt like he'd taken a blow to the gut. *A joke?* She thought the kiss was a *joke*? Had she felt nothing? That look in her eyes... It had felt so intimate. His breath hitched, and he choked back the hurt that wanted to rip through his throat.

No. I won't allow her to affect me like this. All this time he'd thought they were becoming friends. That maybe, they'd grow closer on their journey.

He knew now that he was wrong. He couldn't help the feelings that were starting to grow towards her, but it was all...

just a joke.

Angry and embarrassed, Derrick turned and stalked off. He wasn't trying to get to the village; he wasn't trying to get *anywhere,* really. He just knew that he wanted to get away from *her.*

"Derrick! Where are you going? Come back!" He could hear the strain in her voice as she called to him. But no. She didn't need him. She never needed him. He kept walking. "Derrick! Wait! You'll get lost!"

Yeah, probably. At this point, he didn't care. He wanted to go somewhere to hole up and lick his wounds.

"Derrick!" She was right on his heels now.

He swore to himself. *Why* did she have to be so fast? Anger radiated through him as he whirled around to face her.

"What?" he roared. Reyna skidded to a halt. "Something wrong?" he asked, voice hard.

"I'm sorry if I overreacted to your little joke, princeling. It wasn't meant to offend you. I was surprised. That's all."

"Right. Let's go." Derrick replied flatly.

The walk to Reyna's home went by in a blur of sullen silence. To their mutual surprise, Reyna's mother greeted them as they walked through the door.

"Ah, there you are!" She greeted them warmly. "You must be Derrick. I've heard so much about you. My name is Ariadne." He noticed that Reyna had gotten pink in the face when her mother mentioned that she knew about him.

He couldn't help but wonder what she'd said about him. He reached out and shook the proffered hand in front of him, "Yes, I'm Derrick. It's a pleasure to meet you, Lady Ariadne." He pulled the hand he was holding closer, then dropped a kiss on the back of it.

Ariadne giggled like a much younger woman at that. "Let me get out of your way. And *Reyna...*"

"Yes, mother?"

"Do *not* destroy my kitchen."

"Yes, mother," she grumbled. Ariadne gave Derrick another welcoming nod, and left.

"What did she mean by that?" Derrick raised his brow at her. He felt more intrigued now than angry.

Reyna blushed and busied herself with pulling things out of cabinets. "When I was seven, I wanted to bake my own birthday cake. Mother had some kind of a problem with whatever duty she had that day, and she had to stay late. So, I got started by myself."

The corner of Derrick's lip quirked. "Had you cooked before?"

"No..." Reyna chuckled. "Anyway, I went to put my cake over the fire." She paused, closing her eyes for a second. "I didn't know I'd put too much yeast in it and went to play. When mother came home, she let out a scream I'll never forget. I ran in and saw that the yeast had bubbled and risen so much that the pan fell into the flames. The batter charred and burned, but not before it started inching its way across the floor."

Derrick burst out laughing, picturing a seven-year-old Reyna shocked at her mistake. Reyna scowled at him, even as her cheeks turned a brighter shade of red. *Good*. She deserved a little embarrassment, after what she'd put him through that afternoon.

"I'm sorry. It's just such a funny story," he said, though his tone still held mirth. He laid the rabbit on the table and changed the subject. "Do I get to eat what I cook?"

Reyna took a deep breath, and nodded. "Yeah. Why wouldn't you?"

He shrugged. "Would you and your mother eat with me?" It was an olive branch; he hoped she'd take it.

"How about you just cook the food first, and *then* we'll worry about who's around to eat it, alright?" She teased him.

He nodded. *I probably deserved that.* "Fair enough. Ready when you are."

They fell back into their normal flow, Reyna teaching him while the pair endured mutual teasing and comfortable banter. There was something so easy about being in each other's company, especially when they were alone together.

Derrick finished up the last of Reyna's instructions with a

flourish. "Now what?" Derrick slumped into the chair beside her.

"Now, we wait. Occasionally we stir the stew, but otherwise we just... wait. "

They sat in silence for a while. Neither seemed inclined to bring up the events of the day; the wounds were still too raw. Then Derrick had an idea.

"Do you have a library?" She raised an eyebrow at him. "I wanted to see if I could find any more information on the prophecy."

"Most of our knowledge scrolls are in the queen's possession. I could ask if we could borrow them."

"I would appreciate that. I know this is mostly one-sided, with you having to teach me everything, but when it comes to doing research, I'm pretty good at it." He grinned at her, and she gave him a blank look. She turned back to the food, and fell once more into silence.

CHAPTER 12

Against all her better judgment, Reyna had to admit: Derrick impressed her. He'd taken all of her lessons to heart. He had proved to be a good listener, and a quick study. He asked intelligent questions, and never assumed he knew better than she did.

But as much as she tried, she couldn't keep her mind off of the kiss.

She knew it was a joke. It *had* to be. There was no way he cared for her in that way. Besides, she wasn't ready to open her heart again. Granted, she never told Anteros how she had felt.

Not before... it didn't matter anyway. *It's not like Anteros saw me that way either.*

Reyna frowned. She had to stop thinking about it. If she let it, it would take over her mind, rendering her useless for the day ahead.

They only had two days left before Derrick had to pass Ephiny's test. Reyna worried she'd missed something that would help him pass... but she could always explain to Ephiny she'd teach him more on their journey. At least he had the basics to get him by. And she felt confident that Derrick would pass anything that had already been taught to him.

Still, this morning was going to be an interesting one.

Reyna had finally decided to teach Derrick combat. And she had resolved to do something she knew to be controversial among the Wreya: sword fighting.

No doubt the entire village of Syrinx would be watching. Even though it was a private lesson, Reyna had no doubt that plenty of them would hide in the trees around the arena to watch.

Reyna crawled under her bed and pulled out what looked like two flaps of leather, folded over haphazardly. She set the longer piece in her lap and, with trembling hands, peeled back the leather.

It was the sword Anteros had used to teach *her* to fight. Tears pooled in her eyes, but she refused to let them fall. Her fingers brushed the hilt, remembering how he'd shown her where to grip it. She closed her eyes, and in her mind, watched him go through the warm-up routine that happened before every lesson, as he demonstrated some basic thrusts and parries.

She'd thought then that he was one of the warriors that she'd heard stories about as a child. With a sword in his hand, he was a force to be reckoned with. He'd been so powerful, so fluid in his motions. She had aspired to be just like him.

Now, he was gone. Felled by the arrow of a coward! Her eyes snapped open. Heat and anger rushed through her, and her hand wrapped around the hilt of its own accord, gripping hard.

"I *will* avenge you, Anteros. I swear it!" she growled, voice choked with tears. She swallowed them down along with the painful lump in her throat, then wiped her eyes. "And I will never forget you," she whispered.

Rewrapping the sword, she picked up the other blade, cradling them both to her chest, and set off for her destination.

Even though Derrick's hut was across the large clearing that held the bulk of Syrinx, her eyes still felt like burning red embers when she knocked on his door. He greeted her with a smile, and her spirits lifted.

"It's good to see you," he said. She could tell that he meant it. They'd crossed the threshold from strangers to... what? Friendship?

Reyna crossed her arms. Thankfully, she was holding them by the hilts, or she might have cut herself, folding them against her body. "You say that *now*. Wait until you see what I have planned for you."

Derrick's smile slipped a little and he furrowed his brow. "And...what *exactly* are we going to be doing?" he asked.

"You'll see," she teased, giving him a quick grin.

"Oh, no. I don't like that look." He grinned back and shut the door behind him. "Can I carry that?" he asked, pointing to her bundles.

She could feel the sorrow cross her features. Derrick knitted his brow and he pulled back his hand.

"It's alright, I don't have to," he assured her gently.

She nodded. They continued to walk in silence towards the training grounds to work.

She had thought herself ready for this. She wasn't, but the time was fast approaching: she would soon be gifting Anteros'sword to Derrick. To the *prince*. Not only was it a necessity, but she had to *try* to move on from her grief somehow.

This could be a way to honor his memory.

They entered the arena of bare, packed earth. A wooden shed sat at one end, the area full of targets, straw dummies, and training weapons. She ignored it all.

"This is our training arena," she announced. "We leave our worries and troubles outside the ring. You cannot focus if other emotions rule your mind. Always remember that anger clouds the mind more than any other emotion. It will make you rash and impatient. *That* leads to death."

She saw Derrick swallow, hard. She continued. "We have to work on your focus in an environment where you have no distractions. This way you can fall back on the peace you'll feel here automatically when you're faced with *real* enemies." Reyna handed him the top bundle, then sighed heavily and unwrapped her own sword. Timoria gleamed, giving her a glimpse of her own haggard face. She swallowed, hardening her resolve, and wrenched her gaze away from the shining metal to watch Derrick.

He opened the last flap of leather, and his face filled with awe. "This is... wow, 'beautiful' isn't enough to describe it."

Reyna nodded. "Grip the hilt like this," she said, wrapping her fingers around the middle of the hilt. "Don't grip it too hard. You never know how long you have to fight, so if you grip too hard your fingers will go numb. With an improper grip you might even lose your hold completely." She watched as some of the power relaxed out of his grip, and nodded in approval.

"Now, let's practice." She walked towards the center of the ring. Derrick hung back. "What are you waiting for?"

"Shouldn't we be using training swords?"

"You need to practice with the real thing. You don't have

the luxury of years of instruction. Your muscles have to get used to the weight right away." She made it to the middle of the arena, then turned around in a readied stance. Derrick still hadn't moved.

"What now?" she asked, suddenly irritable. "I'd like to start *some time* today, you know."

"But, if we use real swords, won't I hurt you?"

She burst out laughing, so hard that she actually doubled over. When she was able to recover, she took a deep breath.

"There is *nothing* you could do that I can't defend against. Do *you* trust me to control my power enough not to hurt you?"

"You're pretty confident that I couldn't get through your defenses," he said, joining her. He sounded hurt. "What makes you say that?"

"I've had years of training with the apprentice of a blacksmith. He had much more power than you do." Derrick's face went scarlet at that, and she huffed out a sigh. "He spent *hours* every day working the bellows and shaping metal. He had more strength in his arms than almost any other man." Reyna paused, looking down at the sword in Derrick's hands. She choked up, blinked, swallowed the lump in her throat. "That... that was the sword he taught me with. He used it when we trained."

Derrick looked at the blade in his hand once more, awe and

appreciation spreading over his face. "Then I will cherish it all the more," he said. His voice sounded gentle, respectful.

She nodded. Her heart felt full. "Now, the first thing you want to do is create a strong base." She spread her feet about a shoulder's width apart, one foot slightly in front of the other. Derrick mimicked her moves. "If I can push you over, your stance isn't strong enough." She walked over to him, put a hand on his shoulder, and *shoved*. Derrick overbalanced and landed flat on the ground.

"Your feet were too close together. You need to put this one further back." She tapped his leg with her foot and helped him up. He tried again. She pushed once, twice, but he stayed upright this time. He grinned at her.

"Good! Now, sword fighting isn't always *just* about swords and standing strong. It takes a lot of self-discipline and thinking quickly on your feet. You'll have to be able to feint, use other weapons, or resort to hand-to-hand combat when the situation arises." Reyna tried not to notice the intent expression on Derrick's face as he listened. It distracted her from the lesson. *It's so cute and silly at the same time...* "First, let's try a feint. If I come at you with an overhead strike, show me what you would do."

"I would block it?" He thrust his sword up.

"Yes. *That's* how you would block an overhead strike." She raised Timoria high over her head, acting like she was going to perform a very powerful strike. Derrick swung his own sword up in a high parry. Reyna brought her foot up and kicked him in the gut.

"Oof!" he groaned, falling backward and holding his middle. "Why did you do that? I thought you were going to slash down!"

"Exactly. A feint is meant to trick your opponent into reacting in a way that you want them to. If you can set someone up to react the same way over and over again, or if you exaggerate your movements enough that they believe what they see. Then you can catch them by surprise. It *could* be the difference between life and death." She gestured for him to take his stance again.

"This time, parry." She slashed down and he parried, a boyish grin lighting up his face. She repeated the gesture in one flowing motion, the sword circling over her head again from his parry. He went to meet her again, but she stepped to the side, sweeping the blade low and whacking his front leg with the flat of the blade.

"What did you do wrong?"

"Agreed to spar with you?" He smirked, rubbing his injured shin.

Reyna glared at him. "No, that's what you did *right*. I made you think that I was repeating myself. You gave me the same reaction twice, so I was able to surprise you."

"Got it." He nodded, ready to try again.

They sparred back and forth, using only the techniques she'd shown him, both changing up their moves, trying to surprise the other. Derrick proved a quick study, but not even four hours later, he began to show some favoritism to his injured foot.

Reyna easily parried his last swipe and stepped out of reach. "You're done," she said, her tone brooking no argument.

"What? I did what you said!" he spluttered.

"I'm not denying that."

"Then why are we stopping? I'm not even tired!" Derrick burst out.

Reyna was kind enough not to point out that he was soaked in sweat, panting to keep his breath, and both his arms and legs trembled with every move. She pointed at his foot with the tip of her blade.

"You have to rest that for tomorrow."

He opened his mouth to argue, but she held a hand up. He closed it again, scowling at her. "And there is a theoretical part of this lesson, so sit down and listen." She followed her own directions and plopped down to the ground. He came and sat next to her, still looking surly. Reyna held back a grin, "Sword fighting is not just hacking at each other until somebody dies, you know."

"Really?" His voice lost some of its gruffness.

She continued, "There are four main strikes that are usually fatal."

Derrick rested his chin on his hand. "*Usually?*"

"Well, it depends on if they're wearing armor, and how skilled they are. At that point the blow may just wound. The sword will glance off the metal unless..."

"Unless what?" He leaned forward eagerly, their knees almost touching. The heat of his body traveled to her own knee, making it feel hot and tingly. She ignored it as best she could.

"Unless you can hit hard enough to break it."

His face lit up. "Don't get your hopes up!" she added quickly, and his face fell. "Only a very few have been able to do it. And... well, they had much more strength than you do."

He leaned away, his back straightening, his jaw set in sudden determination.

"Guess we'll just see, won't we?" he bit out defiantly.

She smiled, letting him have his moment of assuredness. "Now, each of the four cuts can be done in reverse, too, so you really have *eight* options." He raised an eyebrow at her, but didn't question. "The first is the overhead strike. If you come right down the center of their body, it's guaranteed to be fatal." He winced appreciatively, and she had to bite back a giggle. "Then you have the horizontal strike. It's usually about even with your gut, but still effective at other heights, too. From one side to the other. Third, is the right shoulder to the left hip."

She reached over to him and drew a line across his chest. Her finger felt like she'd held it in a candle's flame as it raked against his tunic.

"Last, you start from the left shoulder and slice down to the right hip," she added, her voice sounding a little husky. Again, she drew the line. Again, neither one breathed until she pulled back.

"And the reverse is true for all of those," he answered, his voice rough as well.

She nodded, at a loss for words, She tried to understand why she had a burning sensation in her fingertip, and what it meant.

She made herself refocus. She didn't have time to feel things. She had a mission. Snapping back into control, she took a deep breath. "Any sort of hand-to-hand combat mixed in with your sword fighting is usually a surprise to an enemy. A lot of men get tunnel vision and can't do two things at once. They only see the sword. Not the fist that knocks them flat." She paused. "They *do*, however, see the sword that stabs into their gut while they lie there." She saw him shudder. That made her apprehensive.

Would he be ready before he met a real enemy? She would keep working with him, of course, but there was no telling when they would meet their first obstacle on the road.

She bit her lip, bringing herself back to the present moment. It didn't matter what she thought. This was her destiny. The only thing she could do was prepare for it as best she could.

"Are you ready?" she asked.

He gulped and gave her a look like his stomach wanted to rebel and void its contents. Immediately.

"Yeah. Let's get started." He settled back into a defensive stance, raising his sword to the ready position.

She couldn't fight back the grin that sprang to her lips. She found that look of intense concentration on his face endearing.

No! She couldn't think like that, they were sparring!

Actually, I shouldn't be thinking about that at all.

Derrick lunged forward, taking advantage of her distracted state and slashing at her ribs. She jumped back, just out of reach, and just in time.

And that's *why we pay attention during sparring sessions!*

"I see you're eager for more bruises," she teased, sidestepping him and coming in for a flurry of blows. He managed to defend himself, though a few of his blocks looked clumsy and uncoordinated. She had to give it to him, though, he was *very* eager to learn everything she had to teach. "Where did *that* come from?"

He smirked. "Was I wrong to attack first?" He swung again, this time an overhead strike that changed mid-swing to a diagonal slash.

Reyna blocked it easily, making his sharp edge slide down

her own. The momentum of his blow shifted, making all of his weight follow the blade down. Derrick overbalanced and landed hard on his knees, using one hand to catch himself. Reyna took a step forward and touched the tip of her weapon to his neck.

"Attacking first can be a good thing, so long as you follow through on your attack and know what you're doing. Sometimes the best defense is to be the aggressor."

He looked up at her with that boyish grin again. Reyna ignored it, though it took more willpower than she would be comfortable admitting. "Alright, let's see what else you can do," she said. "I'm going to slow down my attacks. I want you to focus on your technique. The speed will come later. I want your moves to come naturally before we go full force."

He paled a little at her words, but he pushed himself to his feet and retook his stance. "Alright. I'll give it all I've got!"

The two of them danced around each other in a slow ballet. Reyna corrected him any time he made a mistake, and he made sure to apply her lessons the next time he used the move. He was a *very* quick study. She felt a sting of jealousy that she hadn't picked up the sword this quickly.

Not that she'd ever *say* that.

The two of them pirouetted all around the training arena, slashing and parrying, hacking and ducking. Sweat coated their bodies, and their lungs struggled for air. For once, Reyna's mind didn't wander towards the uncertain future. The physical exercise and the workout brought her relief. More than that, it brought her joy. Even though they moved at half the speed, the effort both of them put forth began to exhaust them.

Reyna refused to be the one to say she was done. Her arms ached, so much so she wondered if she could climb the tree to get to bed that evening. She kept fighting anyway.

Derrick's breathing became erratic, and he gulped for air. Still, he refused to submit, either. For the moment, they were at an impasse.

She felt surprise that he'd lasted *this* long. He was just a prince, a boy who'd never had to lift more than a finger in his entire life. Yet, he had stamina equal to hers. Almost.

"Had enough?" she asked, knocking him down and touching the tip of her blade to his throat... again.

He raised his hands in surrender and she lowered her sword. "Yes," he gasped out. "I know that if *I* don't say it, *you* never will, and we'll be here all night. As it is, we are late into the afternoon, and my stomach is growling like an angry bear." His stomach chose that moment to rumble, as if to make his point.

Reyna laughed. "Alright, let's get something to eat." She turned, heading back to the village.

"I don't have to cook it, do I?" he asked warily.

"You don't want to show off your new culinary skills? I would *love* another demonstration," she laughed again.

It felt *good* to laugh. She hadn't been able to laugh like this in weeks.

Derrick groaned. "I don't know if I have it in me. I can barely lift my arms."

Reyna couldn't lift hers, either, but Derrick didn't need to know that. "Tomorrow is going to be a lot of fun for you, then." She tossed him a wolfish grin.

"I can hardly contain my excitement. You *do* know I need to be alive and breathing for this to work, right?," he muttered, limping as he hurried to catch up to her.

"Oh, yes. Nothing saying you have to be *well*. But no, you don't have to cook." He let out an audible sigh of relief and she chuckled.

"Where are we going? Or, should I stop following you, now?" Derrick asked. They were back in the village center and garnering quite a few stares. Reyna thrust out her chest, lifted her chin. They could stare all they wanted.

"You're coming home with me. I'm sure mother made enough to feed an army." They kept walking. Disgust flickered among the faces that watched them.

"Uh, Reyna? Why are they all staring at me?" Derrick murmured. "They know that I'm here. What's going on?"

"It's not you they're staring at," she answered in the same

tone. "They're staring at me."

"Why?"

Reyna chuckled darkly. "It's because I'm carrying a sword. The Wreya don't use them. We view them as the weapon of choice for a man."

They had almost made it to her tree. She could feel the glares hot on the back of her neck, as if the women thought they could set her ablaze with their stares.

"You don't use swords because they're the weapon of choice for men?" Derrick seemed to be having difficulty processing this. "If you know you will be going up against them, don't you think it would be better to learn how they work?"

She was already crawling up the side of the tree, her sword in its scabbard at her waist. She used the bark, instead of the ladder, as her guide. Derrick glanced at the ladder, then back at her rising form. He made his decision.

Rubbing his hands on his trousers, he took a deep breath and strode to the tree, his face set. Derrick let his fingers roam over the bark until he had a good grip, then he started up.

Reyna, meanwhile, had reached the platform, and was already tapping her foot impatiently. The way they'd all looked at her... She wanted to scream in their faces. They couldn't fight men if they didn't have the same weapons as the men. But saying so would only be a waste of breath. The Wreya stuck to their out-dated traditions. New insights were never greeted with an open mind. They could say what they wanted about her. When the time came, Reyna would be ready.

"There you are! I was wondering—" Ariadne stopped. Her eyes fell to the sheath at Reyna's waist. "Where did you get that?" she asked quietly.

Derrick finally made it to the platform. Reyna hadn't heard him approach through the sound of blood pounding in her ears.

"Anteros made it for me." Reyna raised her chin in defiance.

"You shouldn't have that," Ariadne scolded her. "You know what the Wreya believe. What *we* believe," she corrected herself.

"I do. And I don't care. This sword means everything to me. None of you closed minded women would *ever* understand."

Adriane's eye went wide, looking as if she'd been struck. Reyna's arms flew in the air. *Why stop now? Air it all out.* "And you know what? When we finally *do* go to war with that monstrous tyrant of a king, I'll be ready to cut down every soldier that crosses my path. I am *not* going to stand idly by, and let that vile man take away my freedom!" Her blood thundered in her ears, and every inch of her felt as if a dragon had breathed its flames directly down her throat.

"Come inside." It was an order, and a bucket of cold water on Reyna's outrage. Only her mother knew how to eviscerate her anger, cutting it out like a pestilence. She felt an almost physical shock as the rage dimmed within her, slowly replaced with shame.

Reyna's head drooped as she obeyed. Derrick slunk in after her. "I'm glad that you could join us, Derrick," she said. "I've made too much for us to eat." Derrick forced a smile, and let her usher him in.

Reyna sat at the table, looking thoroughly chastised but nonetheless tearing into the venison steak on her plate. There were also green beans and potatoes, roasted and spiced to perfection.

"Reyna! Where are your manners?" Ariadne hissed.

"What? I'm at the table, ready for dinner. What do you want from me?" Reyna shrugged. Her anger had been tempered, but not extinguished. And she was *hungry*.

"Go and wash up! Put on some clean clothes, too! Dinner guests shouldn't be able to smell you!"

Reyna's face went scarlet. "It's not like he hasn't smelled me all day," she muttered.

"You weren't eating then!"

Reyna rose from the table and disappeared deeper into the treehouse.

When Reyna came back to the table, Derrick smelled of lavender and honey. He wore new clothes ,and looked comfortable and happy. Reyna could only suspect her mother had taken a deeper interest in the boy than she had let on to her daughter. She sat down, catching Derrick's eye. She glanced at him, then lowered her gaze to her food. Her face might have shown him what she was thinking, and he didn't need to know how handsome he looked.

Ariadne chattered on, and both of them answered with noncommittal grunts. When the meal was over, Derrick offered to wash the dishes.

"Do you even know *how*?" Reyna teased.

"What is *wrong* with you, Reyna?" Ariadne cried. "You're talking to a guest! Show some respect." She hissed those last words under her breath.

"I apologize, princeling... for my utterly *despicable* behavior," Reyna simpered, giving Derrick a curtsy before turning and marching away.

"Not to worry, my royal disposition has not been wounded." They shared a smile.

When morning arrived, Reyna didn't want to leave her bed. She'd been plagued more and more lately by a nightmare: a baby dragon sitting in the ruins of its egg shells, crying out in fear and pain.

She snuggled even further into the dark depths of her furs, wishing that yesterday had never happened. *What* had gotten into her? She'd worn Timoria on her hip, out for everyone to see. She groaned. Maybe the anticipation of this journey was beginning to strip her of her Wreyan ideals.

No. That's not true. Her ideals had begun to change the moment she saw one of her loved ones murdered.

Resolve strengthened her muscles, and she crawled out of her bed, readying herself for another day of Derrick's training. It would be his last. *Finally*! She'd waited long enough. Her muscles were sore. She hadn't had a workout this good since Anteros had trained her.

She squeezed her eyes shut to keep a tear from escaping, took a breath, and readied herself to leave. She was halfway to the door when she turned back on an impulse and pulled Timoria out from under it. She belted it on her hip with pride, squared her shoulders and raised her chin defiantly.

She wasn't born a Wreya, but she'd lived as one for all of her sixteen winters. Now she was coming to realize that the way of her people was *not* how the rest of the world worked. She had spent so much time outside Syrinx, she had begun to feel as if she didn't belong here anymore.

Grabbing her bow, she slipped out of her treehouse and made her way to Derrick's hut. Eyes from the few people that were already awake snapped up and glared her way. Reyna rolled her eyes.

As usual, when Reyna arrived Derrick was up and ready for her.

"You're late this morning," he teased.

She gave him a playful scowl. "I thought I'd let you get your beauty sleep."

"Today is our last lesson, right?" Derrick asked. The tone sounded casual, but the look on his face was anything but.

Reyna nodded. "But like I said, all the lessons will continue when we set out. There will be new things I will need to show you that aren't easy to come by here. Additionally, you need to practice your weapons craft...there's a lot more we can work on while we stop for the day and rest."

Derrick shifted and crossed his arms over his chest as Reyna continued, letting a sly smile cross her face. "Ephiny only cares that you know the basics so you don't die when she turns you loose into the hands of fate. Anyway, ready to get started?"

"After you, my lady." She punched him in the arm. "Ow!"

"I am a *far* cry from a lady. Don't forget it."

Derrick rubbed his arm, but he grinned anyway. She rolled her eyes, but she was grinning, too.

Once they reached the training area, Derrick went to his usual spot in the middle and drew his sword. "I've been think-ing about all my mistakes and I think today I have a better chance."

"Not today," she said, shaking her head.

He sheathed it again, looking confused. She went to the training shed and rummaged around.

"What are we doing?" He asked.

"Here," she replied, and thrust a long object at him. Instinct alone made him catch it.

Derrick looked down and saw a quiver in his hand. Reyna pulled out a bow and gave it to him.

"Pull back the string," she stated. He gave her a black stare. "I need to see if it's long enough for your reach," she said patiently.

He stood motionless for a moment more. She growled and put his hand on the carved grip, then extended his right arm straight out to his side.

"Keep that there," she barked. She took his left hand and put it in the middle of the string, curling his fingers around it so the string rested in the first bend of the middle three fingers. "Now, pull that back until your fingers rest in the corner of your mouth. Do *not* let go of the string." He did as he was told. It wasn't long before his arms started shaking.

He couldn't get the string to his mouth; it stopped over his right shoulder. "It doesn't look like it's long enough," he ventured.

She put her head in her hands in defeat. She couldn't bear

to look at him. Derrick's quavering voice found her anyway.

"I can't hold it anymore. Can I let go?"

She nodded, looked up. He brought his hands together slowly, rather than releasing the string.

"Try mine." She held it out to him. He waved her away. "Go on, try it."

"I can't. It's yours."

"I'm not giving it to you to *keep*, you idiot. Just to try the length. Mine has the longest draw length in the village." He opened his mouth to ask why, but she gave him a warning look. He took the proffered bow instead.

He held the bow in his hands, exactly as before. This time, the string went to the corner of his mouth. He beamed at her.

"I thought so," she said. He let the string down and gave it back to her. "We'll just have to take turns. Come on."

He followed on her heels as she strode briskly towards a straw dummy on the other side of the field. She stopped at a short line dug into the dirt and filled with small rocks so rain wouldn't wash the line away. "You stay here," she commanded. He did as he was told.

She walked further forward, stopping in front of the dummy. She pointed to a section of straw that had been dyed brown. "What's this?" she asked.

"The heart?" he guessed.

"Yes and no. Yes, the heart is there, but it's not as large as this circle. This is also where the lungs are located. Once you pierce *any* of this area with an arrow, your target won't get very far before it either bleeds out or its punctured lung bursts." Derrick paled considerably, the image vivid in his mind.

"Now *this* is where a man differs from an animal," she said. She pointed down lower, at the abdomen of the dummy. "In a *man*, hitting this area will also almost always kill. Unless they have a *very* skilled healer or magic available to heal them. On an *animal*, this will puncture the stomach or intestines, leaking the juices into the meat so it sours and you can't eat it." She stared at him until he nodded in understanding. She walked back to where he was standing.

"The line marks ten yards. I want you to stare at the target, at the place that you want to hit. Tilt the bow a little so the arrow doesn't fall out of the little groove here." She showed him a divot above the handle, close to where her hand rested on the bow. "Once you're sure you have what you want to hit in your line of sight, release. Your stance and how you aim your bow will greatly impact your accuracy. I imagine it'll be difficult to do in a real battle, but for training we will focus on proper technique and ways to aim standing versus on one knee. The more you practice, the more you'll know what stance you want to take. It will become second nature." He nodded.

"I'll show you the standing position first, then it's your turn. Feet shoulder width apart." She demonstrated, and he copied. "Always stand sideways when you can to make yourself a smaller target. Focus on what you want to shoot, then bring your hand up to your line of sight. Tilt the bow, then take a deep breath." Reyna breathed in, letting it out slowly. Derrick followed her example once again. "As you finish your exhale, release. This makes for a more accurate shot. Also, if you have to shoot more than once, it will make you more consistent."

Reyna demonstrated, taking in a deep breath. Derrick watched with wide eyes as Reyna's arrow flew towards the target and buried itself a third of the way into the center of the brown circle.

"Amazing!" he breathed.

She ignored the compliment. "Your turn. Take your stance." She watched as he moved his feet into position, but he still squared his body to the target. Reyna gently took his shoulders and pulled them into the correct position. He didn't notice; his eyes were focused on the target.

"Raise the bow to your line of sight." He aimed the bow and arrow. Reyna pushed the top until it correctly lined up to his target. "Don't squeeze the handle or the arrow. It'll mess up your shot." She heard him take a deep breath, let it out. Then he released the arrow.

It wobbled a bit from his shaking hands, but it landed at the very bottom ring of the brown circle.

"I did it!" He jumped in the air, whooping. Reyna laughed.

"Good job! Not bad for a first attempt. Not bad at all."

His whole face lit up with the power of his grin, and she found herself grinning back. "Now, do it another hundred times, and we'll move on." He groaned, and she hid her smile.

Time passed. They tried different positions and techniques. When Reyna deemed Derrick's arms too weak to hold the bow steady anymore, she took it from him and had him retrieve his arrows. He put them all back in the quiver and brought them over to her.

"So, what now?" Derrick asked eagerly.

"Slow down," she teased him.

"You'd better stop abusing me. I may have to impose a royal decree upon you, peasant," he responded with artificial haughtiness.

Reyna rolled her eyes. "Okay, *princeling*." She pulled a set of daggers out of her boots and handed them to him.

"Time to learn about knife fighting," she said. She pulled another set out and turned the daggers over, holding them so the blades turned inward, the flats laid gently along her inner arms. "The pommels of these are heavy and hard. If you don't want to kill an opponent, there are a few places you can hit to incapacitate them for a while." She gestured for him to stand still, arms at his sides.

"No, thank you. I don't want to get beat up again," Derrick said, and put his hands up in surrender.

"I'm not going to hurt you... much," she countered with a mischievous grin. He sighed and did as he had been asked.

Before the final lesson began, Reyna went over the final piece of advice she had for him.

"The last place you want to strike is a blow to the side of the head. Sometimes, it can be enough to make them faint on the spot... or kill them."

"You're not going to demonstrate *that,* are you?" he asked nervously.

She chuckled. "No. Of course not."

"That's a lot of different ways to kill someone," he mused.

Reyna smiled. "Yeah. Ready to practice?"

He nodded. They had just taken up positions across from each other, when Varia strode up to them.

"The queen is ready to administer your test."

"We haven't finished training!" Reyna spluttered.

"Follow me. *Now.*" Her voice offered no debate.

They had no choice but to follow.

CHAPTER 13

Derrick did as he was told and followed Varia. He felt like a little duckling chasing after its mother. Reyna's face fell as he passed her. His gut twisted and his hands slicked with sweat as he thought, *she doesn't think I'm ready. Gods know she's right.*

They came to the queen's treehouse and kept walking. "Wait, where are we going?" he whispered in panic.

"Quiet!" Varia bit back.

Derrick's fear began to rise within him. His knees weakened as Varia led them through an alcove of young trees to the beginning of a well-worn path.

Every so often along the trail, saplings had been bent to make arches. Further down, older trees formed full arches that draped long tendrils of flowers on anyone who passed. Derrick chanced a look back at Reyna, hoping to glean some information from her expression. To his surprise, Reyna stared, wide-eyed, at the scenery around them. Had she not been there before? He hiccoughed, his feet missing a step as he stumbled over some roots. Sweat slicked his palms.

"What did you say?" Varia asked, turning to face him with a raised eyebrow. Her face said he was pond scum stuck to her boot.

"Nothing! I was just... admiring?" Derrick held his breath.

Varia eyed him in disbelief, then twisted around and brought the procession to an end.

Derrick's jaw dropped. They had come to a halt before a sandy arena. It looked much smaller than the one Reyna had been training him in, but still intimidating nonetheless.

"This is the queen's private training ground. To be invited here is the greatest honor," Reyna leaned in and whispered into his ear. Her astounded eyes held frozen to the center of the arena.

Derrick had been so busy looking around, he hadn't seen what her sharp eyes had immediately landed on. Ephiny stood in the arena's midpoint. Next to her sat a table covered with a large fur. Next to *that*... stood Ariadne. She had a grim smile on her face, and an apologetic gaze glued to Reyna. The two seemed to be having a silent conversation, which made the hair on the back of Derrick's neck stand up.

"What's going on?" his voice trembled.

"Welcome, Derrick. This...is your test," Ephiny gestured. "Don't worry about it too much, alright? I just want to make sure that you've been taking Reyna's lessons seriously. This will not impact your travel plans. In fact, you will be leaving here in three days' time."

"This test, however, is still important. It will assure me of your safety once you leave Syrinx. It will also mean you will become the first man to learn our ways, earning the name of Wreya. This is a title that no other has ever claimed, and would mean you would be granted sanctuary among us if the need should ever arise. Do you understand the importance of completing your test to the best of your ability?"

Ephiny sounded vulnerable. Derrick was willing to bet that *some* of the Wreya didn't want him here at all; now or in the future. Such a decree must have caused an uproar among the women behind closed doors.

He couldn't help but let his gaze flick to Varia. She returned his look with a murderous glare. "I understand," he said, returning his full attention to the queen. "I am truly grateful for this opportunity and your gracious hospitality."

"Mother, what are *you* doing here?" Reyna burst out from beside him.

"Reyna, it was a last-minute decision. I couldn't have told you even if I'd wanted to." Reyna's face had betrayal etched in every line. She felt like even her mother was against her.

Her head fell; staring down at her boots. Derrick saw her eyes shimmer in the sunlight, and he knew they were full of tears. The urge to reach out and hold her, comfort her, to never have to see her face like that again, came on so strong he barely held himself in check.

"Isn't it good enough that I vouch for him?" she asked, her voice almost a whisper. "I could recount the lessons I've given him, his progress, his strengths and weaknesses. Wouldn't you want my opinion of his skill? I *am* his teacher after all." Reyna spat the last out suddenly; anger and hurt threading her tone. His heart leapt at the passion in her voice. He bit down on a smile that threatened to show his fondness for her.

"How *dare* you speak to our queen that way!" Varia roared. She advanced on Reyna, hand resting on the hilt of her ever-present dagger.

Reyna's eyes flashed and she gave a feral grin, issuing a challenge without saying a word. Varia mirrored the smile. Derrick's breath caught in his throat. Why didn't Reyna draw her *own* weapons in defense?

Pull out your knife! Defend yourself! What are you waiting for?

"Varia!" Ephiny's voice cut the air like a newly forged sword cut cloth. Varia whirled around, clasping her right fist to her left shoulder, and looking at the ground in deference. "You're dismissed."

Varia's head shot up. Derrick felt surprised that there was no audible crack from the speed of it.

"My queen..." she began.

"Silence! Zoi will take over your duties. Send her here at once. You're officially on a fourteen-day mandatory leave, effective immediately."

Varia gaped at her, shocked. Then she slowly turned towards the village, shoulders slumped, head hanging. Once Varia was out of sight, all attention turned back to Ephiny.

"Derrick, I'm sorry to say that some of the women are apprehensive about you staying with us. Even if it *was* to save your life." He raised an eyebrow, and she gave him a tired sort of half smile. "And no, Varia is not the only one. Should you need to come back here, this test will earn you a right to sanctuary here, even if I am no longer here. There are many jobs among us that we share. Passing this test will prove you can pull your weight among our people."

Derrick felt a palpable relief at these words. The consequences were nothing compared to what his father would have declared. Yet, he wanted to prove his worth to the Wreya; and to himself. "I'm ready, my queen. Allow me to show you, and all the women who don't want me here, that I am willing to do any job, and work hard to find an accommodation in your village."

Ephiny's smile beamed. "Somehow, I knew you would say that. It seems you are finding the courage that's been buried deep within yourself. Let's prove you've truly found it today."

Derrick squared his shoulders and thrust out his chest. Reyna chuckled softly behind him.

"Yeah. Buried inside the heart of a mouse," she muttered.

He shot her a heated glare. She returned it with an innocent bat of her eyes and a shrug of her shoulders.

Still, Derrick felt glad no one else seemed to hear her teasing words; while he hated to admit it to himself, he agreed with her wholeheartedly. His confidence shriveled up inside him, drying out his mouth as it shrank.

"Then let's begin!" Ephiny said, giving no indication she had seen their exchange. She motioned for Derrick to join her at the table. He started forward, and Reyna made to follow him.

"No, Reyna." Ephiny spoke softly, but every single person knew it to be a command.

Reyna stopped dead in her tracks. "I'm not even allowed to watch?" she spluttered.

"You may *watch*. You may *not* aid him in any way. You will stand beside me, and you will say nothing. And Derrick, if you should need an assistant," she continued, turning to look him in the eye, "Ariadne or I would help you."

Derrick couldn't believe it. The queen of the Wreya, offering to be *his* assistant for such a menial task, painted an even grander image of Ephiny in his mind. He couldn't help but compare her to his father, *again*. It seemed that the more time he spent with her, the lower down his father dropped in his eyes.

Not that he was very high to begin with.

"I ask again. Are you ready to begin?" she asked.

He licked his lips nervously, then squared his shoulders and lifted his chin. "Yes. I am ready, Queen Ephiny."

The queen swept her hand over the table's surface. "Step up and choose which of the five tasks you would like to complete first."

In front of him sat a woven basket, covered with a lid that hid its contents; a bottle of some kind of unguent; a living rabbit with a coil of rope; and a small bowl with folded scraps of paper inside it. He had no idea what he would have to do for most of these tasks...but he had a hunch about what he was supposed to do with the rabbit. Derrick took a deep breath then pointed.

"Alright Derrick. I need you to humanely kill this rabbit, skin and gut it, and cut off all usable meat for cooking. Do not waste any part of this gift. We do not want its death to be for naught." She took the knife at her waist and presented it to him, hilt first.

The *queen's* dagger. He took it, starry-eyed and with a hand that trembled only a little, as he tried to fix this moment into his memory. He hoped he could one day be a ruler this kind, this generous…

He stared at the rabbit, then took a deep breath. There were *so* many steps. And he'd only done it once, with Reyna's guidance.

He steeled himself. He could do this. He *would* do this! Today he would either prove Ephiny – or his father – right about him.

He grasped the rabbit, quickly snapping its neck. A clean break, one he thought a teacher would be proud of. Derrick glanced at Reyna; she had turned away, not even watching.

Does she really doubt me that much? A spark of anger surged in his chest, narrowing all of his focus down to a single point. Gritting his teeth, he returned to the task at hand.

He finished with the skin and managed to gut the rabbit without slicing the stomach, letting out an audible sigh of relief. Proud of his job, he looked back to his teacher again. Still, she stood with her back to him.

His frustration grew. Reyna was forbidden from helping him, but still he needed, *wanted*, her support. "Would it kill her to look at me?" Derrick grumbled.

He became so focused on cutting the meat into chunks that he didn't notice when Ariadne slipped an empty bowl over to him. He put the meat in the proffered bowl and stepped back from the table, stretching the muscles that had cramped while he'd been bent over his task.

"I'm finished," Derrick said, wiping his hands on the cloth of his trousers.

"Are you sure? Once you request my judgment there is no more leniency to correct a mistake," Ephiny warned.

Derrick's eyes scanned his work once more. "Yes," he stated, more confidence in his voice than he actually felt. He prayed his efforts were good enough.

Ephiny picked up the skin. "Clean, straight lines." She placed the skin down and inspected the carcass. "Very little waste, good." Finally, she looked over the bowl of meat.

"You've passed your first task. Good job, Derrick. Now, choose what you wish to do next."

"That one," he answered, pointing at the unguent. He had no idea what he was supposed to do with it, but he was determined to prove himself.

"This is an unguent for cleaning out wounds, as well as for pain. You need to identify the herbs that are in it by smell alone. Once you've named them," she pulled a basket out from under the table and dumped its contents, "you will find them and show them to me."

He stared at the jumble of plants and herbs. His face turned pale, and sweat beaded his brow. He had memorized what Reyna had shown him, but all of the herbs on the table were ones he'd never seen before. Derrick closed his eyes.

"Are you ready?"

"No." The word had been crawling up his throat and would not be shoved down.

"Derrick, are you okay?" Reyna asked, whipping around.

Derrick's eyes widened, worried she would be reprimanded. But Ephiny didn't move to stop her.

"Calm down," she said, holding his eyes with her own. "You *know* what you're doing. This entire time, you've just had to trust yourself."

Ephiny held up a hand. Reyna's head fell. "Sorry my queen," she murmured, her voice now contrite. She didn't see the look of gratitude on Derrick's face, but Ephiny did. The queen hid her smile behind the pretense of a yawn.

With renewed confidence, Derrick took the jar and opened it. A bitter, pungent odor assaulted his nose. "I can smell willow bark," he said. He took another whiff, and a sharp stab of wet earth went straight up his nose. "Ginger, I think," he coughed out, trying not to sneeze.

He stuck his nose down into the jar, inhaling so deeply now it stung.

"Rosemary," he declared. He put the jar down and smiled at

Ephiny.

She shook her head and his smile slipped. "I'm afraid you only got *one* of the three," Ephiny said, passing his mentor the jar. "Reyna?"

Reyna brought it up to her nose and closed her eyes in concentration, "White willow bark, Devil's Claw, and..." she inhaled again and took a moment to think, "boswellia."

Ephiny clapped, "You'll have to take a few more lessons if you want to be on the same level as Reyna." She chuckled, then gestured for Reyna to step back.

Derrick approached the table. He didn't have a *clue* what two of those ingredients even *were*. How was he supposed to pick them out from a pile of herbs? He sighed heavily and began to pick them up, one by one, bringing them to his nose and trying to match what was in the unguent.

When he was finally as sure as he was going to be, he pushed his three choices in front of Ephiny. "These," he stated. Ephiny waited. "I'm sure."

She looked down at his choices and was about to speak when someone walked into the arena. She was shorter than Reyna, with white blond hair, and ice blue eyes. Derrick stared at her. There was an aura around her that he couldn't name, but it drew him to her.

"Zoi! How good of you to come. Please, come stand over here until we need you," Ephiny called out.

The woman stood to Ephiny's other side. "Now, Derrick, these *are* the right herbs, but you couldn't identify their names on your own." Ephiny thought for a moment. "You pass... but barely. Another mistake like that and I won't be able to offer you the sanctuary you seek."

Derrick hung his head, embarrassed. He looked at the objects that were left. A flash of movement caught his eye: Reyna, tossing her hair irritably. The gesture made him smile, taking away some of the tension that knotted his shoulders. Reyna was watching him intently. He forced his attention back to the table. After a moment, he lifted the lid of the woven basket.

"Now what do I do?" he asked, looking at an array of mushrooms. There were seven, each one a different kind. His heart sank. His nerves had him drawing a blank. Would this task cost him his safety?

Ephiny's eyes narrowed on him. "Find me the one that is deadly."

Derrick looked hard at each mushroom. Bright colors usually meant deadly as a rule, he remembered. He saw one that was bright blue. His eyes searched its cap and stem for any other clues, and he'd half stretched out his hand towards it, when a memory from his first lesson came back to him. He smiled as he pulled his hand back, and started checking the gills of the mushrooms.

The first rule Reyna had taught him: stay away from anything with *white* gills. His eyes darted around the basket's contents. Only one had white gills: a perfectly normal looking little brown mushroom. He picked it up and put it in Ephiny's outstretched hand with confidence.

"Good. Now, this task," she indicated the bowl with the pieces of paper, "we will save for last. I have a task for you that is not found on this table." It stung a little that she hadn't given him any praise or encouragement. Maybe she had to keep this demeanor in public.

He'd succeeded in the mushroom test, and Ephiny's response had been the same as if he'd correctly predicted the weather of the moment by looking at the sky. It felt...disheartening, to say the least.

"I will need Ariadne's assistance for this," Ephiny continued. Ariadne stepped forward, waiting for her instructions. "I need you to come before Derrick, as if petitioning him. I will then judge him on his moral character." Ephiny's eyes flickered to Zoi and back.

Derrick stood waiting, radiating patience.

Ariadne stepped toward Derrick. "Your highness, I have some cows that I keep in a pasture. My neighbor has a chicken coop. She's demanding compensation for her chicken coop because my cows trampled it. However, my cows only trampled it because her dog got into my pasture and frightened them."

Derrick stood for a moment, thinking. If this had been brought before his father, King Julius would have had the petitioner killed for wasting his time.

But Derrick *wasn't* his father, and refused to think like him. He didn't know the value or extent of the made-up damages, so he couldn't order a specific amount of coin as reparation. He was *pretty* sure that he couldn't ask questions. He continued to mull over the issue. He wanted to do the right thing, but he didn't want to appear weak by asking for help.

Finally, he made up his mind, "You will repair the damage to the chicken coop." He began. Ephiny's smile slipped a little. "*And* your neighbor will repair your fence, because it was her dog who frightened your cows."

"Well done!" Ephiny nodded. Derrick breathed an internal sigh of relief. "You were fair, and made sure that both parties were happy in the end. A compromise is often the best course of action. I award you another passed task."

"Now, for your last test; choose a slip of paper from the bowl. Upon this paper you will find the name of the weapon you shall be wielding in a friendly sparring match with Zoi."

"I will do my best. However, from what I've seen, your warriors are *very* well trained." He grinned softly at Reyna, who had a tiny hint of a smile at the corners of her mouth. Derrick put his hand in the bowl and rummaged around for a moment or two. His fingers closed around one of the slips, and he handed it to Ephiny to read.

"Knives," she read.

"Come," Zoi said, pulling daggers from her boots and leading him away from the table. Ephiny, Ariadne, and Reyna trailed after them. Reyna cleared her throat. When he turned to look at her, she flipped him a dagger.

"I will judge this based on your overall performance, and I will let you know when to stop," Ephiny said. She waited, staring at Derrick. He flushed, not knowing the reason for the pause.

"Your stance," Zoi snapped.

Derrick hurried to correct his mistake. He opened his mouth.

"Begin!"

"Thank—" he tried to say, but Zoi had already lunged.

Derrick *just* managed to jackknife his body back far enough that her swing flew harmlessly past the front of his body. There was apparently no room for pleasantries during sparring. She came at him again, one hand swung in a high arc, aimed for his throat, the other low again, to his gut. He managed to deflect the low blow, and duck the high. Derrick smirked at her surprise and saw the opening she'd given him.

He dove to the ground in front of Zoi, rolling to the side and standing up. Using the pommel of his dagger, he gently dug into her lower back. A killing blow, were he intending to kill.

His eyes flickered to Reyna, and he saw a proud grin on her face. Those few seconds cost him, however. Zoi charged at him again, eyes and blades flashing angrily. He panicked. He narrowly fended off her first attacks, and she *wasn't* holding anything back.

"Zoi! Enough!" Ephiny called.

Derrick silently thanked her for the intervention, because he had no idea how he could survive this otherwise. Just like his training with Reyna, they were using live steel... and neither of them wore armor.

Zoi charged at him again, seeming deaf to Ephiny's shout. He realized suddenly that she might be one of the women in the village that didn't want him here.

He wasn't fast enough to dodge her next slash, and she scored a hit across his left shoulder. The smile she gave him looked almost deranged.

"Varia sends her regards," Zoi deadpanned. A chill ran over Derrick's body as she lunged forward. He swallowed hard, his clumsy stumbles barely keeping him out of reach of her blades. She was too fast. He was about to die. He couldn't escape the onslaught of swings.

Suddenly, he glimpsed a flash of movement, and felt a rough push. He stumbled backwards, falling to his knees as warm liquid steadily dripped down his shoulder.. He closed his eyes, knowing he had seconds left to live. Seconds spent on his knees, like the coward he was. Anger burned through him. He clenched his jaw and wrenched his head up, determined to look his executioner in the eye.

"What?" he gasped.

Zoi was still fighting. With Reyna.

Just like she had stood between him and Varia, she now made herself his shield once more. His chest swelled with a torrent of feelings, but he didn't have the time to sort through them all.

"Varia can go to hell!" Reyna spat, "and so can you! I won't lose another friend. Especially... not... to... one of... my OWN people!"

Zoi remained unfazed, her cool voice cutting through the air. "The rumors are true, then. You lead with your emotions. It will be your ruin, you know."

Derrick's attention was glued to Reyna, watching her in all her vicious fury. When something touched his injured shoulder, he hissed in pain and flinched away.

"Calm down, Derrick. It's just me." Ariadne knelt next to him, pressing something against his cut. It stung like hellfire, and he bit down on a cry. "I'm sorry," she said. "I know it's not pleasant, but it'll stop the bleeding and help you heal faster."

He gave a curt nod and tried to relax, bringing his injured shoulder closer to her, his eyes drawn instinctively back to the deadly dance in front of him. Zoi had a gash across her cheek;

blood wept from it, sheeting down her cheek and dripping to her neck. Reyna had nothing but a wolfish snarl on her face. She jumped high to avoid a slash from her opponent, snapped out her foot, and caught Zoi in the face with a sickening crunch.

"I'm sorry this happened," Ariadne murmured, grabbing Derrick's attention once more. "Ephiny will give you extra protection until you leave. It'll only be for a few days." Derrick nodded and took a deep breath as Ariadne pressed the herbs firmly into his wound.

"Why doesn't Ephiny stop them?" he questioned.

Ariadne looked up at her daughter. "It is our way. There must be a clear victor once a fight has been initiated."

A scream rang out from the two women. Zoi was on her back, Reyna on her chest, legs on either side, pinning her arms to her sides. Derrick saw that the blonde's hands were empty. Reyna had her own daggers crossed over Zoi's throat.

"Enough! There's a clear winner here," Ephiny bellowed. Chests heaving, both combatants looked to their queen. "Let her up, Reyna."

Reyna still had that wild look in her eyes. She didn't move.

"Reyna," Ephiny said softly.

Giving a last warning growl to Zoi, Reyna climbed off of her. Ephiny took the rope from the table in her hands. She helped Zoi to her feet, then tied her arms behind her back.

"You have taken liberties that were not allowed to you. You've gone against my wishes."

Reyna ran over to Derrick and Ariadne. "Thank you, Mother, for helping him," she said. She looked into Derrick's eyes. "I'm sorry, but we have to leave today. I won't stay here and risk you being attacked again."

Ariadne looked to her daughter and nodded, her own eyes suddenly wet and shining. "I understand, my darling girl," she said. "Just know that I will miss you terribly. I'll be right here, waiting for you to come home safely to me again."

Ariadne clasped Reyna's shoulder. "Now, don't linger. There's a sack of coins under my mattress. Take Phanes. Buy your supplies in Cybele. You don't have time to pack." She pulled Reyna in tight. They held onto each other for a few precious moments, then parted with tears running down both faces.

"I love you, mother," Reyna said, her voice hitched.

"And I you, my little Rey of sunshine."

Reyna pulled Derrick to his feet, then strode angrily away. Derrick followed her, a little confused as to what had just happened. "Who's Phanes?" he asked.

"He's one of our horses. She wants us to take him as a pack horse. He'd only slow us down. Your horse..."

"Apple."

"What?" She turned to face him.

"Her name is Apple," Derrick clarified.

She raised an eyebrow at him, then marched away again. "*Apple* is in our pen, along with Andromeda. *My* horse," she added before he could ask.

"We can't leave now. Ephiny hasn't—"

"We're not waiting here for a meaningless title. You'll be dead by the morning. If Zoi has turned on the queen and sided with Varia, then most of the Wreya have made their decision. Their betrayal could mean the end of Ephiny's reign. You are *not* safe here, and neither am I."

Reyna moved fast; they were in front of his hut. "Hurry up and get your things."

He obeyed, taking only the small bag of his belongings and rushing back out to Reyna's side. They continued on to her treehouse, where she climbed up the ladder at lightning speed. She returned a moment later, a money pouch tied to her belt.

"Come on," Reyna gestured.

He followed her to the pen that held the horses. Reyna whistled, and a beautiful chestnut mare cantered over. Reyna quickly saddled and bridled her.

"Here, Apple!" Derrick called as she worked. Apple came running up. She nuzzled him affectionately, letting him know just how much she'd missed him. "I know, girl. I'm sorry."

Reyna flapped her hand impatiently, then swung herself into the saddle. Derrick mounted Apple as well. He saw that

Reyna's bow was loaded in a strange tube that hung from her saddle. He would ask her later about it.

Reyna gently kicked Andromeda and the horse sprang forward. Derrick leaned into Apple's ear and whispered, "Come on, girl! We have to keep up."

Without a backwards glance, Reyna and Andromeda plunged into the forest. Derrick held on for all he was worth, urging Apple to stay right on their tail.

CHAPTER 14

Reyna didn't know how long they'd been riding. The only thing guiding them was her rage-fueled tunnel vision. She could hear Derrick on his mount behind her over the blood pounding in her ears, and that was good enough. Thankfully he held his tongue, leaving her alone to brood and get them as far from her home as possible.

"Reyna! Wait!" Derrick called.

Reyna growled low in her throat. *So much for* that *idea. Apparently the Fates hate me today.* Still, it *did* pull her out of her angry haze, and she hauled on the reins. Andromeda came to a stop, nostrils flaring.

"Thank you!" Derrick gasped.

"What's wrong?" Reyna snapped in reply.

"Apple hasn't been pushed this hard before. She may hurt herself without a rest. She's stubborn, and she'll run herself into the ground, following you. Could we slow our pace just a *little*?"

Reyna's eyes fell on the pretty palomino. Her nostrils blazed, and her sides heaved as she gulped air. Derrick was right. Apple hadn't stopped despite her clear exhaustion, not once had she slowed her pace.

Reyna gave the horse a rare, warm smile. "Yeah. We can do that. On the road, though, we may get into some trouble. She'll need to be fast to get us out of those situations. We'll have to work on building up her endurance."

"Of course. I know *both* of us need to work on that. Don't we, girl?" Derrick reached over and rubbed Apple between her ears. She whickered at him and turned her head to butt him affectionately.

A pang of jealousy pierced Reyna's chest. Andromeda had been given to her as an adult mare; Derrick had had Apple since she'd been a foal. There was a mutual respect between them, a love they shared that was completely different from her own bond with Andromeda.

She clicked her tongue and Andromeda started forward at a

light canter. Apple snorted as she fell in again.

She sucked in a shallow breath when she realized where she was. In another hour the trees would begin to thin at their current pace. Soon they would be out of the forest and within sight of the city.

An unease had settled within Reyna; a fear that one of the Wreya would catch up to them before they made it to Cybele. It hurt. Syrinx had always felt so safe. Now it held a death sentence for both Derrick and Reyna for helping him. The only comfort Reyna clutched onto was that it was still a refuge for her mother.

"There!" Derrick cried.

Reyna's hand flew to her bow, drawing it and an arrow from its sheath in one smooth motion. She twisted in her saddle to see where Derrick was pointing. Following his finger, her eyes scanned the woods while deftly stringing the bow.

"What? I don't see anything!" she growled, furious at herself for not being able to spot whatever Derrick's untrained eyes could see. She squinted, but still saw no danger.

Derrick beamed. "Black locust! Dark blue-green leaves, white flowers, and reddish black bark!"

She looked again and saw that he was right. She chuckled softly. "Do you see the strange colors in the grooves of the bark?" she asked. He nodded, and her prickly demeanor melted away.

"Could I go look at it more closely?" Derrick asked. His childlike tone pulled at her softer side.

She turned Andromeda around, listening closely to the silent forest. No one on the trail; peace surrounded them.

"Knowing my people, they've seen our flight as a victory. We are probably safe now," Reyna relented. "Go ahead. I'm right behind you."

Derrick wheeled Apple towards the tree. Reyna followed at a sedate pace, enjoying the forest now that she wasn't tearing through it. *What if I never see it again*? Reyna closed her eyes and begged the nature spirits around them that this wouldn't be the last time she rode beneath the forest's eaves.

Derrick was out of his saddle, his nose almost touching the tree trunk as he looked deep into one of the grooves. "It's wonderful," he breathed as he pulled away.

"I'm glad you were able to see one for yourself. We should be in town soon," she said.

The color drained from Derrick's face. "So soon?" he asked, his voice soft.

Reyna felt pity for him. He hadn't asked for this journey. Derrick had nothing but the *very* basics she'd taught him and, well, *her*. She would continue to protect him, no matter the cost. But why?

Reyna shook herself, not wanting to analyze their fated connection any longer.

"Yes," she finally replied. "But don't worry, princeling, I'll always be here with you." Derrick swung himself back into his saddle, then guided Apple to follow once more. Reyna kept their pace at a leisurely walk.

The cries of children and the smell of cooking reached them before they ever left the forest. Reyna sat up straight and stern in her saddle, chin tipped at a defiant angle. Derrick did his best to mimic her pose.

Reyna led him through the outskirts of town, heading for The Mangy Wolf. Derrick followed her as she opened the heavy door to the stable. He looked apprehensive, but Reyna didn't have time to ask.

"The soldiers could still be looking for you. It's best you stay here where you won't be seen. I'll buy all the supplies and come back as fast as I can. I'll get Sarah to bring you some food." She turned to go.

Derrick gave her a curt nod. "I'll make sure the horses get rubbed down and fed. I know we'll be leaving again soon, and they'll feel better for the extra care."

Reyna cocked her eyebrow. "You know how to do *menial labor*, princeling?" she teased. It had been a few hours since she'd had the opportunity. It felt good. "I must say, I'm impressed." She winked at him and left.

Reyna rounded the side of the inn, looking around for anyone who might have seen them. Not a soul around; a good sign.

When she opened the door to The Mangy Wolf, memories of Anteros hit her so hard she stumbled. But she recovered herself quickly, and swept the room with a shrewd look. Not a hint of red cloaks anywhere, she was glad to see. Still, a tiny voice in her head told her to stay on her toes.

Sarah stood over by the door to the kitchen. Reyna walked over to her and gestured for her to step to the side, where the two women could talk without being overheard.

"Reyna! It's been too long since I've seen you around here!" she said with a smile that quickly disappeared. "I'm so sorry about Anteros. I know he was a friend of yours."

Tears made Reyna's throat thick, and she fought to get her words out. "Thank you, Sarah. Yes... he was my best friend. I know that sounds strange, coming from a Wreya, but it's true."

Sarah put a sympathetic hand on Reyna's shoulder. Reyna refocused herself. "I, um, have a friend that I'm trying to help. He needs to get as far away from here as possible. He's in the stable right now, with Andromeda and *his* horse. He's going to need dinner brought out to him later."

"Of course! I'll get one of the girls to..."

"No! Please, Sarah. I would prefer it if *you* took it out. I trust you." Reyna took a coin out of her pouch.

Sarah batted Reyna's hand away. "That's too much! You know that, silly girl."

"No," Reyna said again, "it isn't. You've always been kind to me. And Anteros." Her voice cracked. "Thank you. I don't know if I'll ever be able to come back, but I'll always keep the both of you in my thoughts."

Sarah took in Reyna's words. "I'm going to miss you, Reyna," she said, pulling the young woman into a fierce hug. A tear trickled down her cheek, soaking into Reyna's hair. "I'll take it out myself, don't you worry."

"Thanks, Sarah. I know I won't find anyone who cooks as well as you do. I'll miss that every day, I'm sure," Reyna laughed, but there was no mirth in it. Sarah pinched her cheek good-naturedly, and disappeared into the kitchen. Reyna stared after her for a few seconds, then left the tavern.

Reyna's next stop was Morken. He was the only person in Cybele who knew the ins and outs of both tanning and blacksmithing. She frowned, realizing that Ariadne would once again be the one to bring the furs in, now.

Reyna's eyes fell to her boots. If it hadn't been for King

Julius and his soldiers, she wouldn't even *go* on this quest. Screw the Fates, she wouldn't give up her home for anything less.

She felt anger burn away the sadness, and she looked up wanting to glare her fury at one of those cowardly guards. Her eyes darted around, but no matter where she looked, there was a distinct lack of red cloaks. The hair on the back of her neck stood up. Striding along as quickly as she could without actually running, she went to Morken's forge.

"Morken? Are you here?" she called, walking into the smithy.

No clanging of hammer on anvil reached her ears. Her hand went to her waist, hovering just above the pommel of her dagger. The fire still burned, but no work sat cooling by the hearth.

"I'll be there in a minute!" Morken growled angrily from somewhere within.

Reyna let her hand drop away from her weapon. She couldn't help but smile at the older man's gruff nature. She stood back, crossing her arms over her chest.

Morken stormed into the room. "Now, what do you... Reyna!" His whole face brightened, and the gruffness fell away. "It's been a while," he breathed. "I didn't know if I would ever see you again after..." He swallowed hard.

"I know, Morken," Reyna said softly. "Did they... where is

he?" The lump in her throat choked her.

"They took him. I wanted to bury him under the trees just outside of town. I know how much he loved your forest." Anteros had loved the Forest of Gaia. So much so that when they had begun practicing together, Reyna had asked the nature spirits to not only guide him to the clearing, but also that he remember and not need the help from a Wreya to find it again. She felt a sudden sense of déjà vu. She'd also asked the forest to guide *Derrick*; but back to Syrinx rather than a meeting place.

"Morken, I came to get supplies from you. I'm heading out on a long journey, and have to leave in a hurry. I have nothing with me." He raised an eyebrow at her, but didn't say anything. "I'd also need some light armor for me, and a bow and the same armor for... someone about Anteros' size."

"That's easy enough. I still have both of those from Anteros. Would that do?" he asked. She could only nod.

Morken headed into his adjacent house, and Reyna knew he'd left to give her time to cry if she needed to. Gritting her teeth, she looked up instead, willing her tears to stay in her eyes, rather than run down her cheeks. When she thought she had herself under control, she swiped the back of her hand over her eyes.

Grief was a new layer in Reyna's soul. It came and went without mercy.

With uncanny timing, Morken came bustling back; just as

she was finished.

"Thank you, Morken,"she said, proud that her voice betrayed none of the heartbreak she'd been pushing down.

He waved her thanks away, grabbing some canvas sacks before coming over. "Now, I'm guessing that you'll not want to run through the whole village, just to get everything you need."

Reyna smiled. "If there was an easier way to gather everything, I would do it."

"Well, that's what I thought. Here." He handed her one of the bags, and she almost staggered under its weight. "That's food, medicine, bandages, cooking pots, and just about everything along those lines that you might need." She opened her mouth to say something, but he held his hand up, commanding her silence. "Now, this one here,; this has extra clothes, more bandages, furs, and canvas." He gave it to her; this time she was ready for the weight. "Your hands are going to be pretty full. Can I assume you're headed to the stable at the Wolf?" She nodded. "Then I'll have you put this on here." He pulled some light armor out from under his work table.

She gasped. "It's beautiful!" she breathed, setting aside her sacks and taking the intricate half breastplate from him. It had delicate scroll work around the edges, interspersed with leaves and deer etchings every few inches. The edges of the bracers and shoulder plates matched exactly.

"Glad you think so. Anteros spent the better part of a year

making it for you."

Reyna froze. Her chest fluttered as if she were falling. It took all of her strength not to fall over. *No. That couldn't be true...could it?*

"He was saving it for your name day," Morken continued. The tears she'd managed to hold back came streaming down her face. She didn't care who saw.

"I thought... well, I know he would still want you to have it."

Reyna began donning the armor with shaking hands. When she came to the breast plate, her hands shook so badly that she couldn't buckle it on. Without a word, Morken came over and buckled it for her. She nodded her silent thanks.

"And here is Anteros' armor." This time, he gave her a leather backpack. She saw a quiver of arrows and the curve of a bow sticking out of one side. For a moment it felt as if she'd left her body, floating above, staring down at the backpack. Anteros had once worn what was inside; his missing presence within the armor hung heavily in the air. She could still picture him... and the loss was razor sharp.

Reyna collapsed against a workbench. "I don't know how I could ever repay you, Morken," she whispered, reaching numbly for her money pouch.

Morken shook his head and backed away from her. She looked at him, bewildered.

"No. I won't take a single coin from you."

"Come on, Morken. I can't take all of this without paying for it." She dug into the pouch. Her mind felt fuzzy and she felt disconnected from her body. Nothing that was happening felt real.

"Reyna." His tone startled her. Her wide eyes snapped up to his face as she swung back to reality. "I said *no*. Your coin is no good here."

"But! I can't just—"

"*NO!*" he bellowed, making her jump back. He glared at her until she put the coins back.

"I loved that boy. Like my own son. And he..." Reyna had never seen Morken get emotional before. "He loved you, you know..."

Reyna gaped. "A-as a friend. Of course. I was his best..."

"*No,*" his brow furrowed. "He *loved* you." As suddenly as he'd made the announcement he quickly shifted back into his normal gruff self. "Now, is there anything else you need?" he asked.

"I don't think so..." Reyna thought about it, her entire sense of self still reeling. Then it hit her. "Where are the soldiers?"

Morken's brows drew together, and he growled, "They have some *secret* plan for— *something*. Mythos was spouting off at the mouth about how he was going to be the one to *finally* get the Wreya."

Reyna's jaw dropped. She looked like a fish, gasping for

air. "How? No one can find Syrinx. No one knows the way except..." her head shot up. "I'm sorry, Morken. I need to go! Thank you for *everything*!" She started gathering up all the bags he'd given her.

"You're alright, Reyna. Stay safe, girl!" he called after her as she ran out the door.

Reyna ran as fast as the extra weight would let her. She made a bee line for the stables where she'd left Derrick. When she finally burst through the door, he was gone. The horses huffed and whinnied in greeting. She looked around frantically, her vision red.

"*Derrick*," she hissed. Movement caught her eye near the end stall.

Derrick came out of his hiding spot, grinning at her. Reyna glowered at him in return, striding forward. She threw one of the sacks she was carrying at him, then dropped the rest where she stood. He caught it on instinct, stumbling back a step as it knocked the breath out of him.

Before he could straighten, Reyna cocked back her fist and punched him square in the nose. With a pained cry, he dropped the bag and fell over, curling up in a defensive ball. She dropped on top of him, pummeling whatever part of him she could reach.

"*How could you*? I protected you! I saved your miserable, rotten hide! And all this time, you stayed with us so you could sell us out to your father?!?" she screamed.

"Reyna! Stop! Please!" he managed to choke out. But Reyna couldn't stop.

He was going to lead all those soldiers to her home! They would take away everyone and everything she loved. And *he* was the one leading them! Her love for Anteros *had* blinded her, and made her soft on a man. Varia had been right about her all along. Reyna's stomach twisted in self-disgust. Hot tears of betrayal rolled down her reddened cheeks.

"You won't show them the way, you selfish bastard. I'll kill you first!" she shouted. She opened her mouth to spit another expletive when he planted his feet and bucked his hips up hard.

With a surprised cry, she flew over his head. Then he was sitting on her chest, one wrist in each of his hands. He leaned over her so his weight pinned her to the ground.

"How could you do that to me? Everyone I love is there!" She was crying openly now, great sobs wracking her body.

"Reyna! Look at me!" Derrick's voice was firm, yet pleading.

She didn't want to, but defiance made her. One of his eyes was already swollen, mostly shut. His nose was a little crooked at the end; she'd broken it. *Good.* His lip was split, and was bleeding steadily. She felt no remorse at all.

"Reyna! Just stop!" Blood dripped down his chin, and she twisted as far to the side as she could.

"I don't want your *traitor's* blood to touch me!" she

screamed.

"*What* are you *talking* about?" he yelled into her face, so forcefully she froze. She glared daggers up at him. "If you promise not to hit me, I'll let you up. Okay?" he asked, his tone once more modulated. She grunted at him. "I'll take that as a yes."

He let go of one wrist, and she cracked him in the side of the head. He trapped it again, glaring back just as fiercely.

"*What. Are. You. Talking. About*?" he ground out between clenched teeth.

"Like you don't know!" she spat.

"I *DON'T*! So why don't you tell me what I *supposedly* know?" She went limp, but could tell he wouldn't fall for that again.

"I trusted you." Her voice caught in her throat, and the rawness tore at his heart.

She had the same look of betrayal that she'd had on her face when she'd seen Ariadne standing in the arena for his test. The one she'd never wanted to have again...

"Your *father's* army is camped outside the forest, ready to march on Syrinx! The man who *murdered* Anteros is at the head of it!"

"But they won't be able to find it... Right?"

"Unless they know the way. I've asked the spirits that guard our forest to allow you to find your way to our village, in case you ever needed to on your own. Now, I know why you *really* wanted to live with us. You wanted us to drop our guard, to befriend you…" She looked away. "All so you could kill us! You are the only one who could lead them. Who *would* lead them." She reared up and head-butted him in the face. A loud *crunch* rent the air, and his hands flew up to his face as blood gushed from his nose. A choked gurgle escaped his throat.

Her left fist snaked out and cracked him in the temple. His eyes fluttered from the blow. He toppled off of her. "I'll kill you for this!" she roared.

She straddled him, pulling her dagger from its sheath and touching the tip of it to his throat. Derrick's hands slowly came away from his face. Blood poured from a cut over his swollen eye, and a bruise was already darkening under the other. Both lips were now split.

"Any last words, *traitor*?" she hissed.

Derrick looked up at her, his eyes pleading. Reyna refused to let herself be swayed. Though her heart ached, she steeled herself. The rage was now fading into a dull, angry simmer. She had to protect her people. If she killed him here and now, he couldn't lead that army into her home.

"Reyna. Please." His voice trembled. She realized with shock that it wasn't *fear* making his voice quaver… it was tears. "I would *never* betray you, or any of the women in Syrinx. Not even Varia or Zoi. I *hate* my father with every fiber of my being.

I would die before I *ever* led his soldiers to your people."

Gently, and *very* slowly, he pushed the hand that held the dagger to his throat down until it rested over his heart. "I'm asking you to do the same thing you once asked me. You know me. Trust yourself. I know this isn't an unguent to identify, but please... trust in what you know." He put his hands on either side of his head. "If you *truly* think me capable of what you've accused me of, then plunge that dagger in." His voice shook, and a tear mixed in with the blood on his cheek. "I won't stop you," he whispered. "I put my life in your hands."

Reyna felt her bottom lip begin to quiver, and she bit down on it to make it stop. *What am I* doing? Something cracked in her heart when she saw the vulnerability and trust in Derrick's face. Her hands trembled.

A horrible, inhuman scream thundered through the stillness. Reyna jumped, the tip of the dagger sinking into Derrick's chest. He screamed; but true to his word, he didn't fight her or try to move in any way. Horrified, Reyna wrenched it out.

"What was *that*?" she wondered aloud. Derrick didn't move.

Reyna dashed out of the stable, searching for the source of that scream. More people milled through the streets, gossiping and chattering, trying to figure out what had happened, just as she was. No shouts of discovery came, and the minutes dragged on; Reyna's heart was in her throat. She looked around wildly.

The scream came again, eliciting fear in her heart. But it came from... *above* her.

Dreading what she'd see, she dragged her eyes up to the sky, just as a massive shadow slid over the ground. At first, Reyna couldn't understand what she was seeing; her mind simply *refused* to accept it. She blinked hard, and looked again. No, it really *was*... a dragon. And it was headed in the direction of the forest.

CHAPTER 15

Fear froze Reyna's muscles, and for a long moment, all she could do was stare. Its poisonous green scales glittered in the sun. Its massive body swam through the clouds, making a hole big enough to fit the entire Mangy Wolf inside... and then some. A dull patch on the dragon's back caught her attention, and she could *just* make out the tiny figure of a man. He was *riding* the dragon.

The fell beast dipped lower, circling something in the distance. Reyna bolted back into the stable. Derrick still lay in the same place, his eyes closed. She couldn't spare a second to check on him, though she silently thanked him for feeding, watering, rubbing down, and resaddling Andromeda. Reyna swung up into the saddle gracefully and snapped the reins. The horse lunged forward at her command.

Reyna raced through town until she reached the gates. She glanced up at the sky, but the monster was hidden by the walls surrounding Cybele. Reyna gave Andromeda a hard kick, launching them outside the town and in the direction of the forest. Her head whipped around, searching. She couldn't find it. Reyna clucked to Andromeda, speeding her to the forest's edge, pulling on the reins only when they came upon the remnants of a large camp. Her eyes took in everything in disbelief.

Then her heart stopped. Large, dragon-sized tracks started in the middle of the camp, heading straight toward Syrinx. Fear paralyzed her, but somehow, Andromeda understood her need. She burst into motion, following the dragon's path.

The creature's large feet and bulky body had flattened everything in its path. With such a massive wrecking ball the soldiers wouldn't need the nature spirits' permission to find their way through. Syrinx, the last safe place in all of Ulster out of reach of the king, was in deadly danger.

Derrick! How could he? He had given away their secrets, and it was all her fault. Reyna's heart pounded so hard it threatened to break through her chest.

She clung to the reins, urging Andromeda to go even faster. They crashed through the beaten path, leaping over the broken trees and trampled underbrush. The Forest of Gaia wept in pain all around her. Wind howled and pushed against them, forcing the trees to bend in submission under its gale.

A deafening roar ripped through the air. Andromeda reared back, her own cry muted by the horrific barrages. Reyna clasped her ears on instinct, hitting the ground in a painful *crack*!

She lay there, paralyzed, feeling the ground shaking beneath her. Reyna gritted her teeth and clawed into the dirt. With all her strength, she managed to push herself up onto all fours. Andromeda lay just a few inches from her, unable to stand, helpless to fight the power surging around them. It pulsed, knocking them back down each time they tried to get up, to move.

Finally, after what felt like a lifetime had passed, it stopped. Reyna gulped for air, catching the breath that had been brutally knocked out of her again and again. She pulled herself to Andromeda and wrapped her arms around the steed's neck.

"It's okay, girl." she breathed, "it's okay. We... we have to keep going." Andromeda rolled up from the ground with a sharp neigh of defiance.

"Good girl," Reyna said with a grim smile. She swung her bruised body up onto her horse and they tore off towards

Syrinx.

The smell of smoke became stronger the closer they got to the village. Her heart rose to her throat as she screamed at Andromeda to go even faster.

Now the scent of cooking meat filled the air. The rancid stench of burning hair mingled with its cloying sweetness. Andromeda stopped suddenly, right outside the last copse of trees before the village. She dug her hooves in and would go no further.

"Come on, girl. Don't quit on me now," Reyna begged, touching her heels to Andromeda's sides. Finally, Andromeda took a begrudging step. Then another. She moved forward at a walking pace. Reyna's anxiety was building. They broke through the last few trees. Reyna's mouth fell open.

Syrinx stood before her in ruins. The crackling sound of the burning fires across the village was deafening. Frames for weaving were knocked over and broken, some so splintered they were almost unrecognizable. Animal pens had been pulled apart; the creatures once housed there missing. Remnants of blood splatter and broken bone lay in the corral. Fires burned everywhere.

The heat pulsed on Reyna's cheeks. The treehouses had been ransacked; food, medicine, cookware, weapons, clothes, even furniture had been thrown off the platforms with reckless abandon.

One piece especially caught her eye: a beautiful, hand carved crib. Horses and flowers had been painstakingly picked out of the wood with a chisel. Now it lay broken and abandoned, with some of its slats broken out and shattered from its fall to earth.

Something still lay in the broken crib... a doll, perhaps. As they got closer, Reyna gasped, then leaned over Andromeda's side, emptying the contents of her stomach. She lost her balance and slipped off, landing unsteadily beside her horse.

"How could they?" Reyna cried over the motionless babe. A little girl. No more than a winter or two old. Her limbs were splayed at odd angles, and her sightless blue eyes stared up at Reyna accusingly. "I'm so sorry I wasn't here," she whispered.

Reyna's legs could no longer hold her up. She fell to her knees, her face in her hands, and sobbed. It felt like hours, days. She had to pull herself together. She owed the Wreya this much. Once this village bustled with the voices of her people. Today it only held her own sobs and the pop of burning wood.

"I will avenge you, all of you. I cannot give you all the burial you each deserve, but I can honor you," she wept. "This is my punishment. I'm so sorry you all had to pay for my sins." She knew she had to bear witness to their death. It was her fate.

Once the weak feeling in her legs left her, she gained her feet again. She let her gaze roam over the village a second time. This time, she could distinguish some of the bodies. When Reyna realized that some had been burned to ashes, she wanted to retch all over again.

Her mind reeled, envisioning what happened to the Wreya, each thought worse than the next. Some were probably eaten by the dragon – the animals alone may not have been enough to sate its hunger. Others died at the blades of Mythos' men. But... some of the women could have been carried off by the soldiers, who would probably rape them and sell them into slavery. She couldn't bear the thought of it.

She came upon a woman leaning up against the trunk of a tree, head bowed, hands clutching the terrible gash in her stomach. Reyna saw something pink and glistening before she turned away. Another lay face down in a pile of ruined furs, a bloody gash across her back. A gash that could only be made by a sword.

Then she caught sight of sunlight glinting off of something silver, near one of the trees. Reyna started towards it, fury and shame warring within her.

When she reached the glimmer of silver, she saw that it was a chest plate. Gleaming, except for the dark stain of blood near the top. Its owner's throat had been slit.

A fierce pride burst in her heart. Her people would *not* give up their village without a fight! She bent over, looking closely at the sigil that had been pounded into the metal. If she'd had any doubt at all about who these soldiers belonged to, she confirmed it now. A growling dragon's head glared up at her, as if angry at her for disturbing it.

King Julius. King Julius *Dragonspear*. Reyna pulled back her leg and delivered a powerful kick to the breast plate.

Reyna's head snapped up. *Mother!* She'd been too shocked to even *think* about her mother when she'd seen the wreckage, but now she sprinted for her home.

When she got there, she saw that the ladder had been drawn up. Most likely an attempt to keep the soldiers out.

"Mother? Are you up there?" she called, her voice shaky.

No answer. Maybe her mother was hiding, or unconscious.

At once, Reyna began to climb the trunk that she'd climbed hundreds of times before. With every second that passed, her heart beat faster. Beads of sweat popped up on her forehead, but not from the physical exertion it took to make the climb.

Her feet hit the platform that her house was built on, and she stood for a second, trying to steel herself for what she might find on the other side of the closed door.

"Mother?" she asked again, but this time her voice managed only a whisper. Reyna's hand shook as she raised it to the smooth wood of her own front door.

Closing her eyes, Reyna took a deep breath, then burst into her home.

Bowls of nuts and berries had been upended and ground into the floorboards by heavy boots. Reyna's hopes that her mother had escaped death began to evaporate.

No. No, she's going to be here. She has *to be!* Reyna's blood pounded in her ears, drowning out all other sounds. She went into the guest room. Everything had been overturned and thrown around, like a child having a tantrum. Then she moved on to her mother's room.

Horror stabbed into her like a stiletto. There were smears of blood on the floor. On the walls. It wasn't enough to kill anyone, but it *did* confirm a struggle. There was one room left to search...

Reyna's heart skipped a beat, and her knees buckled, spilling her onto the floor. There, on the bed where she had spent her last sixteen years, lay her mother... a spear through her throat. It had been shoved in with such force that it had gone through the wooden lattice work frame that held her mattress, and buried the tip a finger length into the floor.

An agonizingly inhuman scream tore itself from her throat, pouring all the anguish from her soul. She sobbed and screamed until it felt like someone had used a sharp knife to split her open, then scooped out all of her insides with a roughly hewn wooden spoon. Leaving the raw edges gaping.

Syrinx was destroyed. She had no home. Her mother had been murdered, brutally so; she had no family. Anteros had been murdered, and Derrick... Derrick had betrayed her, leading an army into her home to destroy her people; she had no friends. Now, she had nothing to lose. She laughed, and the sound carried a tinge of hysteria.

Reyna struggled to her feet, crossed the room, and tore the spear from Ariadne's throat, throwing it aside. Gently, she closed her mother's glassy eyes, then reached into her coin purse, pulling out one for each. The coins' purpose was twofold. They kept the eyes closed, but it was also to pay the ferryman when her soul went to the underworld. Next, Reyna took Ariadne's cold hands, and crossed them over her chest.

"Mother. I'm sorry. All of this is my fault. If I had it to do over again, I would. I swear I will avenge you. I miss you," she choked out. "You were such a good role model for me. You taught me so many things..." she trailed off, wiping her face on her sleeve. "I'm so sorry, Mother. I love you." Reyna's voice broke as she covered her mother in one of her furs. She would mourn her mother for the rest of her life. And she swore to herself that she would do whatever was necessary to kill King Julius...and the child he had sent like a wolf in sheep's clothing to gain her peoples' trust.

Reyna dropped the ladder through the hole and climbed down. She straightened up with a sudden thought. *Denali!*

She walked through the area with the community huts, eyes wide, ears open. After a few moments, she heard muffled sobs. She ran towards the sound; even if it *wasn't* Denali or her mother, it was someone *alive*.

She came upon a burned-out shell of a hut. When she got close enough to see, she realized that she knew the woman who sat, rocking back and forth, with a bundle in her arms. Tears had cut tracks through the dirt, blood, and smoke that stuck to her face.

"Marlee?" Reyna asked gently. Fear rose in her, but she tamped it down for her friend's sake. The woman moved so slowly, as if fighting an invisible body of water. Marlee looked at Reyna, her gaze empty. "Are you alright?" Reyna asked. "Where's Denali?"

At that, Marlee burst into gut wrenching sobs. Reyna's heart twisted. "Marlee?" She tried again. "Where's Denali?"

Still sobbing, Marlee extended her arms. Reyna's hands trembled as she accepted the bundle, wrapped in a filthy blanket. Twitching fingers pulled aside a flap of material.

Denali's blank eyes stared up at her, a large red gash painted under her chin. Someone had slit her throat. Reyna's mouth fell open as fresh grief assailed her.

"They *lied*!" Marlee spat with sudden venom. She turned feral eyes on Reyna. "*They lied*! They told me that they would give me the medicine she needed if I would lead them through the forest!" She threw herself onto the ground, sobbing and pounding the dirt with her fists, screaming out her heartache and her fury.

"You? It was...you? *You* led the soldiers here?" Reyna's voice rose steadily as the words left her. She laid Denali's lifeless body aside with care and stood up, rage hardening her tone, and her heart. "*You* did this?" Reyna's voice had become a low roar, and she balled her hands into fists. Reyna stepped forward, advancing on the distraught woman.

"Reyna! Don't!" Derrick lunged forward and grabbed her arm.

Reyna didn't even stop to think about how he could have gotten here. She just spun around and punched him in the face for all she was worth.

Derrick screamed louder than Marlee had. *I'm just going to add to his list of injuries,* Reyna thought with a dark grin. Reyna turned back towards Marlee, stalking her with a predatory calm. Derrick sprang after her once more; this time, he wrapped his arms around her just below her elbows, so she couldn't lash out at him.

Trapped, Reyna struggled to free herself. But Derrick held on stubbornly. Finally, Marlee looked up, as if seeing Reyna for the first time. She blanched, fear in her eyes.

"Go!" barked Derrick, "get out of here! I don't know how long I can hold her!" Marlee climbed shakily to her feet, then turned and ran, tripping on some of the wreckage as she went.

"Let me go! I'm going to *kill* her! She murdered my *mother! My people*!" Reyna screamed and screamed until her voice was all but gone.

Eventually, her energy flagged and tears took over. When the fight drained out of her, she collapsed against Derrick's chest. He loosened his hold, and she spun around in his arms, throwing her own arms around his neck. She sobbed into his shoulder as he held her. Her knees gave out, and the unexpected extra weight of her dragged them both down to the ground. How long they sat there, neither of them knew.

Eventually, exhausted and heartsick, Reyna collapsed into a fitful sleep.

Derrick carried her back to the hut he had used while he was staying in the village. He hoped it wasn't completely destroyed.

He was in luck. It was still standing, and the damage looked minimal. He carried Reyna into his room, laid her down on the bed, and tucked the furs all around her. Watching her sleep, and seeing her so vulnerable, made her seem much younger than her sixteen winters. Derrick stretched out on the floor, right next to the bed. Anyone coming into the room would step on him before they could get to her.

CHAPTER 16

"Mother!" she screamed. "Please don't leave me!"

Ariadne looked at her daughter with eyes unfocused, staring through her as if she didn't know her daughter at all. It cut Reyna to the quick, as if someone had shoved a sword through her heart. Ariadne turned away, and never once looked back.

Derrick woke up at the first soft cry, expecting some kind of danger. He sat up quickly, trying to pick out shadows in the dark. Nothing moved except for Reyna, tossing and turning in her sleep. He brought out the lamp, giving them some light.

He set it in the open doorway, casting a soft glow into the bedroom. Derrick watched her, worry creasing his brow.

Reyna couldn't lay still, rolling from one side to the other. She uttered soft mewling sounds; tears streamed down her cheeks as the little sobs escaped. She looked like a lost child.

And she is. The thought caught him off guard. His strong warrior now seemed so vulnerable. It hurt him to see her in this state. Reyna threw out an arm and reached out for a mother who would never come again. Derrick wiped a tear from his own cheek.

When Reyna turned to face the wall, Derrick lay down on the edge of the bed behind her. He took a deep breath and wondered if he was *really* ready to be hit in the face again when she woke up. He turned on his side, slipping an arm around her.

She stiffened, and he thought for sure he'd awoken her. Derrick lifted his head a few tentative inches, just enough to see her face. Reyna's brow furrowed, and her bottom lip trembled. Then she relaxed into a deeper sleep.

He let out the breath he'd been holding. As he lay there, he listened to Reyna's ragged gasps ease into steady breaths. Peace softened her features.

Derrick's eyes began to grow heavy. His head slowly sagged down onto the bed.

Gotta keep watch, he reminded himself firmly. *Can't go to sleep.*

He startled awake a few hours later, when Reyna moved under his arm. She'd slept without moving an inch from where she laid, her restless turning, for now, assuaged.

She rolled towards him. He closed his eyes and resigned himself to fate. She was going to hit him for crawling into bed with her.

When the blow didn't come, he slowly cracked one eye open. She lay there, still asleep. He relaxed, sighing in relief. Reyna rested her arms on top of each other and pillowed her hands beneath her cheek. A moment later she tucked her head right into the hollow of his chest and curled into him. He adjusted his arm to cradle her. He began to doze off again.

"Get off of me!" Reyna screamed.

She woke up disoriented, and unsure of where she was. And she'd woken up pressed against Derrick's chest. At first, she thought she was imagining it. But when she pinched herself as hard as she could, and *still* felt the weight of his arm on her, she knew it was real.

Derrick immediately climbed off the bed, throwing his hands up in surrender. *Here comes that punch.*

Instead, in the morning light, she could see his face. It made her wince. His right eye was swollen shut, and a nasty cut decorated the other. His nose was off center. *You broke his nose, Reyna. And for what? He didn't even do it.*

The blood stain across his heart was so dark. Memory flooded her. The stable. He placed the dagger over his heart. He'd trusted her. The dragon screamed and the point of her dagger pierced his skin...

"I'm sorry!" He looked at her with pleading eyes. "You were crying in your sleep, and reaching out for someone. I thought it would calm you."

"Oh, no. What did I *do* to you?" she moaned as she fell back against the wall.

"It's alright." He actually smiled a little as he said it. "You thought I led the army here. I don't blame you at all. It was the only logical assumption at the time. I would have reacted the same way. Though, I *do* thank you for staying your dagger. Well, *most* of it," he teased.

Horror and shame filled her. She'd almost *killed* him for Marlee's sin. And he had the grace, the kindness of heart, to laugh about it...

"I am so ashamed," she whispered, "and more sorry than I could ever find the words for." Her voice trembled. She'd sworn to him that she would always be there for him and at the first opportunity, she'd broken her promise. *She* was the traitor. Reyna swallowed. "How did you get here in time to stop me from going after Marlee?"

"When I came to, you were gone. So was Andromeda. You were talking about Syrinx, so I figured that's where you were headed. I followed the path made by my father's dragon and got there just in time to hear Marlee scream." He reached a hand behind his head and scratched the back of his neck sheepishly. "I'm, uh, not so good at restraining people, apparently."

"What do you mean?" she asked, raising an eyebrow.

"I grabbed your wrist, trying to hold you back, and you hit me in the face." He blushed, looking everywhere but at her.

"Derrick." Her voice dried up in her throat, and she had to try again. "Derrick..." Her voice came out stronger this time. She turned red, swollen eyes to him. "I know that I can never make it up to you, and I can't put into words how sorry I am. Or how ashamed I feel." Reyna's voice broke. "I betrayed you. In every way." She choked up, and her eyes glassed over again. "I broke my word to you."

Derrick crossed the room and sat back down on the bed. Tears leaked from her eyes as she stared forlornly into her lap.

"Reyna. Look at me." She didn't move. "Reyna." Still nothing. "Please?" She still refused to face him. Her stubbornness overcame even her guilt, apparently.

Hesitating only slightly, he reached out a hand, placing it under her chin. He tilted her face up until she was looking at him. He let go, hoping that she wouldn't look away. "I forgive you. I understand why you did everything you did. I saw what they did... I don't blame you."

Her gaze began to slide away from him. "I would have done the same in your place. Just maybe not as effective as you." She gave him a weak smile. "I can't imagine what you're going through. Let me help. Let me be a friend."

"I don't understand how you can say that. Have you *seen* what I've done to you?" she whispered.

"No, not really. I was just sort of guessing... from the pain," he grinned at her.

"Maybe you should hold your thoughts until after you see, then. Come with me." Her authoritative tone had crept back, and Derrick felt relieved.

He hadn't lied; he really *didn't* hold her actions against her. She'd had no other possible answer for who betrayed the Wreya.

And she hadn't killed him. That meant something.

When he walked into the main room, she was backing out of Naida's workshop. She handed him a mirror. He took it and inhaled a deep breath, trying to prepare himself for the shock. Derrick held it up and stared into the nearly transparent glass.

"Oh, it's not so bad! I think it makes me look more daring and handsome," he said, putting his hands on his hips and throwing his chest out. Out of the corner of his eye, he saw Reyna biting her lip to keep from laughing. "All the ladies will love me now, because I'm so *dashing*!" he cried, strutting around the room like a peacock.

Reyna laughed, unable to hold it back anymore.

He stopped and placed the mirror down carefully. Gently, he asked her, "Is there anything you want to get from your house while we're here?"

"No!" she cried, throwing her hand out to block the door as if he were about to rush out anyway. He hadn't moved, but her reaction told him that something had happened there. Something tragic, if it was enough for her to never go back.

"Ariadne?" he guessed.

For a moment she couldn't speak. "Yes." She barely got the word out. "I think we should just go. The Draco Lingua is waiting for you."

He nodded, forcing himself to remember what they were setting out to do. "I'll just wash up."

"Argh!" She groaned in frustration. "We have to go back to Cybele."

"Why? That town *really* doesn't agree with me."

"I left all the supplies there. In the stable."

"But *I* didn't. Everything is packed up in the saddle bags. Even if they *are* a little over full. I figure it would show you–"

Without warning, she flung her arms around his neck and hugged him.

"Thank you," she breathed. She let go, quickly. "Are we all ready, then?"

"I think so," he said quietly.

She noticed that his hands had balled into fists, to keep them from trembling. "It's alright, Derrick. We'll get through this," she assured him.

"I wish *I* knew how to be so confident," he spat bitterly. "I did what I could to try to help, but it's so hard to change who I was before. I know it doesn't happen overnight, but I'm trying."

"You *are* changing! You're growing! You heard the prophecy. You will find your courage, and *we* will find the Draco Lingua." Reyna walked out into the bright sunshine, and for a moment, looked like a fairy of the air, floating down from the sky to spin gracefully on the breeze, coming to alight on the wretched earth around them. "Come on," she said. Derrick squared his shoulders and marched out after her. She looked around. "Where are the horses?"

"Apple! Come on out, girl," Derrick called. She raised a quizzical eyebrow at him, but he continued. "It's okay!"

"You *do* know that horses can't under..." Reyna stopped midsentence, eyes going wide.

Apple came prancing up to Derrick, tossing her head playfully. "*There* you are,"Derrick grinned. "Did you bring Andromeda with you?" The horse whickered, and he rubbed her velvety nose.

"Andromeda doesn't listen to anyone. And she *certainly* wouldn't follow another..." Reyna ate the words she hadn't had the chance to say. Andromeda came out of the trees, from the same spot Apple had emerged.

"You were saying?" Derrick asked, grinning wider at her bewilderment. "Apple is the smartest animal I know. I don't know how she does it, but she seems to understand everything people say. And she can communicate that back to other horses if need be. I'm thankful to have her."

Reyna came and stood close to Apple. "You can understand me?" she asked, a little skeptically.

The palomino stared at her with those big, liquid, brown eyes.

"If you can, don't bite me, okay?" Reyna stretched her hand out, stopping a foot away from Apple's nose. "If you want me to pet you, come the rest of the way."

Apple hesitated, then took a step forward and nudged Reyna's hand gently.

"See? I told you," Derrick said, crossing his arms over his chest smugly. "And you didn't believe me."

Reyna rolled her eyes. "That doesn't prove anything. Any horse could come forward for attention when a hand is stretched out in front of it."

"Go ahead, then. Tell her to do something else. Be my guest."

"Don't get too cocky, princeling." She turned her attention back to Apple. "Can you walk three circles in a row for me?

Then stop, then walk one more?"

Apple swung her head towards Derrick, as if to ask if Reyna was being serious.

Derrick nodded. "Show her, girl."

Apple walked away a short distance, then deliberately walked three slow circles in a row. She stopped, looking up at Reyna to make sure she was watching, then she walked another slow circle in the opposite direction.

"Satisfied?" Derrick smirked.

Reyna rolled her eyes once more before going back to Andromeda. *That smirk is about to get a smack.* "You're right. She *is* the smartest animal I've ever seen," she said, smiling at the palomino.

Apple tossed her mane.

"And it's a good thing too," Reyna continued "At least I know *one* of you has some sense."

"Hey!" He glared at her through his blackened eyes.

"What?" she asked, all innocence. "Apple? Could you come here please so I can repack all the saddle bags?"

Derrick bristled, his cocky attitude evaporating. Apple walked over to Reyna and stopped so the saddlebags were in front of her. Reyna whistled. "Wow. Smart *and* considerate. You should take notes, princeling."

Derrick's face flamed. "Traitor!" he muttered under his breath.

Apple swished her tail at him.

"Could you please have Andromeda come, too? I'd like to distribute the weight evenly. That way, neither of you is working harder than you have to." Apple snorted a few times in Andromeda's direction, and the chestnut mare came to Reyna, mirroring Apple's position. "That is absolutely *amazing*!" Reyna smiled. "Can I pet you? Just flick your tail twice for yes."

Apple flicked her tail twice.

Reyna patted her beautiful golden flanks, then focused on the saddle bags that Derrick had had to overfill in order to bring everything to Syrinx. "I don't suppose you could tell *Derrick* to come here, huh?" she laughed.

Apple tossed her mane.

"See if I ever bring *you* treats again," Derrick muttered, face surly as he came to stand beside Reyna.

"Let me test your knowledge a little," Reyna eyed him.

"*Another* test? Really?"

"Why do you want to split things of the same nature up between different saddle bags when you have two or more people in your party?"

Derrick gave her a blank stare, then shrugged. "I don't know." He felt stupid, and that the answer would be so obvious when she said it.

Reyna explained, "If we ever get separated, you don't want me to have all the food. And *I* don't want you to have all the medicine."

Derrick sighed. *Yeah. Totally obvious.* "That makes sense," he said aloud. "Can I help you with something?" He gestured to the saddle bags.

"Absolutely! Here, hold this." She started taking some things out and handing them to him; some she put on the ground, instead. "I had planned on doing this right after I bought everything, but... things went a little wrong." She blushed, turning her face from him so he wouldn't see the guilt that still plagued her.

It didn't matter whether she faced him or not; his intuition told him everything he needed to know. "It's really okay, Reyna. I don't know how many times you need to hear it, but I'll keep on telling you until you believe it."

"Just let me get this done so we can leave," she said, and cleared her throat.

Derrick stayed silent, holding whatever she needed and letting her take it out of his arms when she wanted it.

Finally, just a leather backpack remained. A bow and about a dozen arrows stuck out of one side. Reyna picked it up and held it to her chest for a moment. Then she looked up, eyes rimmed with red. She held it out to Derrick. He took it, holding it like he had everything else.

She stared at the pack pointedly. "Open it."

"Oh. Sorry." His cheeks flushed. Derrick untied the leather

thong holding the flap closed and pulled out the bow. It was beautiful, with exquisite detail " Where did you get it?" he asked, eyeing the wolf carvings along the riser and limbs.

"It belonged to my friend. The one whose sword you're carrying."

Derrick's gaze turned somber. His growing affection for Reyna battled with his jealousy and grudging respect for a man he'd never met. Reyna cocked her head at him.

Derrick noticed her curious gaze and explained, "It's beautiful. I would love to carry it. I only worry that seeing me carrying his weapons will bring you grief."

Reyna's heart lurched in her chest. *How can he be so kind, so considerate of my feelings? Look what I did to him,* she thought, wincing at his busted lips and swollen cheeks.

"I don't want to cause you pain," Derrick added, pulling her from her thoughts.

"No." she sighed, "I *want* you to carry them. There is no one more deserving. It would be a shame if they sat on a shelf collecting dust." She looked into the eye that could open the most, pouring her soul into her words. "There is no one more worthy. No one more caring. More loyal. More *just*." Feeling how vulnerable her words sounded, she shifted uncomfortably and gave him a weak grin. "Don't worry, we can work on the courage part later."

Derrick chuckled. "That may take a while." Then, without

warning, he yelped and covered his mouth with his hand.

"Are you alright?" Reyna cried out. She placed a panicked hand on his shoulder, her eyes searching his face for some new injury.

"Yeah." He took his hand away and blood ran down his chin. Reyna gasped. "No, it's okay! My lips just split open again. That's all."

Reyna shook her head. "You have to stop saying it's okay. I can't believe I did this to you."

Derrick shooed her away. "Like I was saying, I was just worried about how it would affect you."

"I don't know how you can care about my feelings after everything. But, I'm grateful, really," Reyna said, her brow set in a deep furrow.

"You'd do the same for me." He started to smile until he felt his lip start to tear a little more.

She didn't answer. She couldn't stop looking him over to assess his injuries.

Derrick's half-formed smile disappeared in the growing silence. "You *would* do the same for *me*, right?"

She laughed. "Of course. I would." Reyna turned and dug around in her saddle bag.

Derrick suddenly remembered that he'd wanted to ask her something, "Reyna?" She turned to him, expectantly. "That tube looking thing on the side of your saddle... for your bow.

What *is* that?"

She looked, "It's called a scabbard. Just like for a sword." She frowned. "I don't have one for yours. Sorry." Her eyes flickered over to her treehouse. "It's not a problem. For now, I can put it with mine."

"What about that whole, 'splitting up what you have bit?'" he teased.

"Oh! So, you *were* listening!" she chuckled. "That's really good to know." He stuck his tongue out at her. "You know, that is *way* more effective now that your face is so beat up." She joked, although the guilt still ate at her.

Derrick gave her his best courtly bow. "Why, thank you, my kind lady! You flatter me."

She giggled, feeling her heart lighten. *What am I* doing? "Alright, that's enough of the theatrics!" she snapped, suddenly serious. Derrick stiffened, giving her his complete attention. "We need to get this finished. We have to get to that talisman so you can take the throne. Now, empty this last bag."

Derrick did as he was told, pulling out pieces of gleaming armor. "Wow! This is really nice!" he said. He looked it over, inch by inch, his eyes wide. Then he screwed up his face.

"What's wrong?" Reyna asked.

"I never thought... that I would *touch* a suit of armor in my lifetime," he said slowly. "Now, I'm going to be wearing one."

"Anteros made it. It was his," she said with a sad smile.

Derrick scratched his head. "Do you really want me to have all of his things? Won't it bother you?"

"No. It won't bother me. Promise. I'm wearing armor that he made, too. Morken said... he'd planned on giving it to me for my name day." Suddenly the reality of the situation hit her. Anteros had loved her and he never got that chance to tell her himself. Reyna clutched her chest, feeling that pain, that loss washing over her.

Derrick wanted to reach out and comfort her. Instead he searched for words to bring that peace. Talking about someone who'd passed was helpful; telling their story could be healing. He decided to compliment the man who clearly had Reyna's heart.

"The detail he added is exquisite. He was a *very* good blacksmith. Not everyone can do that. Did he make the bow, too?" He took the weapon out once more and inspected the etchings. "The details on the wood sort of look like the same craftsmanship as your chest plate."

Reyna's smile didn't meet her eyes. "That was the intention. But no, Anteros didn't make the bow."

"Well, whoever did, made a work of art." Derrick admired the piece.

Reyna let out a low, raw chuckle. "I did it. I made it for him on *his* name day, two years ago."

Derrick's eyes almost popped out of his head.

"*You* made this? It's absolutely breathtaking!"

"Hey, don't sound so shocked, princeling." She swatted at him., "Listen, we don't have time for this. Put on your armor and get that bow put away."

"Of course," Derrick rushed to comply.

He managed to get the bracers on without issue, but the chest and shoulder plates were like a different language to him. After watching him fumble around for a moment, Reyna came over and took the chest plate and looped it around his midsection. She was almost hugging him, trying to make sure no parts ended up twisted or tangled. Reyna was *very* aware of Derrick's head right above hers and the heat of his breath on her hair. It sent a warm shiver down her spine, and she had to remind herself to pay attention to what she was doing. She buckled it on, just as Morken had done for her. Then she attached the shoulder plates with practiced ease.

"Mount up, Derrick. We're out of here." She grinned.

CHAPTER 17

Reyna urged Andromeda into a canter. Derrick rode in her wake. They followed the blackened path left by the dragon and King Julius' soldiers. Reyna's head swung back and forth, taking in the scenery, a frown marring her face. Derrick's eyes followed Reyna's as she took in the sheer destruction of the forest.

"I can't believe they did this," Derrick breathed.

Reyna's deep connection to the Forest of Gaia was starting to sever. The voice which guided her through the trees had weakened, and Reyna could feel the sprites weeping in her chest. Black veins spread out from the char marks on the trees, creeping slowly off the dark path. "What the soldiers have done, both here and at Syrinx, will poison the entire forest. Unless the nature sprites can overcome the damage and repair this, the forest will wither and die."

Derrick gaped at her. He turned his head away, looking at the path they were following. Anger brewed inside him. "I hate him," he growled. "How can he have no regard for the land he supposedly wants to rule? It's like he doesn't think. I mean, what happens to the animals, the nature sprites if they can't repair the forest?"

Reyna just looked at him, waiting for all the pieces to come together. "No...they'll all *die*?" His voice rose. "My father is going to *pay* for this!"

"I'm sure he has a lot more to pay for as well," Reyna said darkly, mulling over the true reason she agreed to this quest. *It would be so easy to tell him... he might even understand.*

"I won't argue with you on that." Derrick's jaw tightened. "So, if we pick up the pace, will we catch up to the army?"

"Oh, no. We're not going after them. We are only using this path for now to get to the edge of the forest. If they don't have a rear scout, then they've definitely set traps ahead, since this is the path of least resistance. No, soon we're getting away from this area and taking a route that no one would think to follow."

Derrick pursed his lips. "Won't it take longer?"

She cocked her head and raised an eyebrow. "Yes...and? This is the safest route. Is your father or the talisman going anywhere that I don't know about?"

"Well, no. But the longer we take, the longer people are being oppressed. I hate knowing they're suffering. That's all."

Reyna's face softened. She looked at him with something close to, but not *quite*, affection. A blush creeped up Derrick's neck and burned his cheeks.

"Yes, I know it's difficult," Reyna said. "But that's a price we'll have to pay in order to achieve what we're setting out to do. *Believe* me, I don't like it either. But in the long run, we're going to make it so this *never* happens again." Reyna's fierce gaze gave Derrick a surge of courage.

That happened a *lot* when he was with her. They shared an understanding smile just before they left the edge of the forest.

Hours passed, with Derrick checking over his shoulder every few minutes, his paranoia getting the better of him.

"Don't be such a worry wart," Reyna chastised him.

"It's hard not to. You haven't seen what my father's men are truly capable of. I've watched as they flayed men alive, and heard the screams from my room as a woman was beheaded in front of her own children." Derrick's face tinged green at the memory.

"I haven't seen what he's capable of?" she whispered, eyes blazing into him.

"That's not..." His voice trailed off. She'd lost everyone she'd ever cared about; in one way or another. Whether they'd been murdered or left behind when they fled. He inhaled a sharp breath. Was he the only one that was left in her world?

"I can't imagine what it was like growing up with him as a father. But I promise, I understand the depths of that man's cruelty and what that has done to the men who follow him," Reyna snarled, a deep scowl set on her face.

Derrick shuttered. "Remind me never to get on your bad side... again."

They chuckled. Reyna shook her head. "The plan, for now, is that we keep heading as far east as possible before we lose light."

"I'm just glad you're leading. I'm terrible with directions if I don't have a map or some sort of guidance," Derrick said, worry coloring his voice.

"I may not have been this way before, but the light guides me. The placement of the sun. And as I said before, we can't take the main roads. We both know your face is plastered at every village along the way." Derrick shuddered again. "Don't worry, eventually, we'll find a village that's off the beaten path. It just might take a few days," she explained.

He felt a pang of dread twist in his stomach. "That's fine. It doesn't matter when we find a village..."

Reyna eyed him, knowing he was putting on a brave face.

"I've got this Derrick. We've got this."

All he could manage was a quick nod in reply.

The sun had dipped down under the horizon and the last few streaks of light were almost gone. Derrick had begun dozing in his saddle while Apple continued to follow behind Andromeda.

"Wake up, princeling." Reyna's voice startled him awake. She coughed to cover her laugh when he had to scramble to grab the saddle horn so he wouldn't fall off.

"What happened?" he asked, feeling his heart beat so hard he was afraid it would break through his ribcage. His eyes darted around from side to side. He squinted into the gloom.

"Nothing happened," she rolled her eyes. "It's time for your first lesson in making camp."

He felt drained. His limbs felt so heavy that he could barely move them. And his mind was clouded to the point where he couldn't think. "I'll do my best. Forgive me if I need another lesson tomorrow night." Derrick had never been in the saddle this long before. His legs screamed, and his nerves were shot from startling at every unknown noise.

"Do we have enough light?" He could *just* see the shape of Reyna on Andromeda against the dark horizon.

"We traveled longer than I usually would. We can just set something simple up so you can rest. I just wanted to put as much distance between here and..." her chest squeezed, "Syrinx."

With a start, Derrick realized he didn't know whether she trusted him. He wasn't sure. He'd noticed her watching him once or twice out of the corner of her eye, and it made him uneasy. He couldn't read her face. It didn't matter that he hadn't actually been the one to betray the Wreya, his family had. He sighed heavily. Would he *ever* shake off the cloak of his father's sins?

Apple stopped, and Derrick could hear sounds ahead. Even though he *knew* it was Reyna dismounting, his hands grew sweaty on the reins, and his breaths came in shallow bursts. He was just about to call out to her when he felt a hand on his leg: it took every ounce of his control to remain calm.

"Here, let me help you," Reyna said softly. "It's dark and I don't want you to step into a hole. Can't have you break your ankle, princeling." Derrick forced himself to relax and to take her hand as he swung his other leg over. "You're okay to jump down."

"How do you know that it's safe? You must see in the dark like a cat," he joked, trying to cover his exhaustion, his fear.

"Yes, actually. Well, maybe not like a cat, but my night vision has always been better than others." His mouth hung open in wonder. A soft chuckle off to his left let him know she saw him, "Come on. I'll help you."

Derrick felt her warm hand grab his. He stiffened, hiding the rush in his stomach at her touch. "You're not going to lead me off the side of a cliff or something, are you?"

She didn't reply, and Derrick's smile slipped as nerves took over. "Reyna? I don't have your eyes. Is something out there?" he said in a whisper.

"There's nothing out here," she snapped.

Derrick flinched. "Why are you mad?"

"I'm not going to lead you off a cliff, okay? If I'd wanted you dead, I would have killed you by now."

"It was just a joke," he frowned.

"Stay here. I'll be right back." Her hand slipped from his.

His hand felt cold and empty. When she'd held it, something had sparked in his chest, like pieces of flint clicking together to start a fire.

Muffled sounds from Reyna opening and closing one of the saddlebags broke the silence in the dark. Something heavy thudded to the ground.

"Ok, I'm back." She took his hand again, leading him forward a few steps. "Sit down."

He did as he was told. When his hand hit the ground, however, something warm and soft met his fingers. "What's this?" He asked, wondering if he was showing his ignorance.

"Sleeping furs," she said, her voice flat.

Apparently he *was* being ignorant. Would he ever stop embarrassing himself in front of her?

He felt her fingers at his throat, and froze. He barely even breathed. Unconsciously, his hand went to the place on his chest where she'd stabbed him. He heard a sharp intake of breath right next to his ear. Her fingers fell away, taking his cloak with them.

She took his hand and put the cloak in it. "Cover up and curl up in this." Gently, she pulled back on his shoulders, helping him to lay down without missing the furs.

Lightning sparked through his shoulders, radiating out from the points where she'd put her hands. He felt more alive and awake than he had all day.

"Thank you, Reyna," he said, his mouth dry. "I think my eyes have adjusted. At least I can make out a little more now." He turned his head and took her hand, giving it a squeeze. "Thank you for all you've done for me. I wouldn't be here now, if it wasn't for you." That spark flickered through each and every one of his fingers, making his palm tingle. "I don't know how I can ever repay you, but I swear to you, I will do my best." With great difficulty, he let go of her hand.

He lay there, listening to her movement. Reyna's pause worried him. Her guilt and self-punishment was painful.

"Go to sleep, Derrick." Her gentle tone sang through the air.

He couldn't help but grin, even if she *could* see in the dark. She'd called him by name! Not *princeling*. He stared up into the inky vastness of the sky as she made her own pile of furs, curling up in her cloak. *We're really doing this. We're going to find the Draco Lingua, together,* he thought, heart racing. As he drifted off to sleep, he marveled at the journey ahead of them.

The next morning, Derrick's mental alarm bells sounded. A feeling of *wrongness* swept over him. He struggled to pull himself from the quagmire of sleep. He needed to warn Reyna.

His eyes flew open suddenly, and he stared at the tip of a sword pointed at his throat. His first instinct was to back away, to try to make a run for it. He let his eyes travel up the blade until he saw the shapely hand, wrapped around the hilt. His heart began to slow its frantic racing.

Reyna stood over him, a predatory grin on her face. "Well good morning! Don't worry, you're safe. Did you get your beauty rest, princeling?"

"Morning." He put two fingers on the flat of the blade, then pushed the tip away from him.

She chuckled as he got to his feet, brushing dirt and grass from his clothes. "Don't worry about making yourself look presentable, princeling. You might as well wait." She grinned at him wickedly. "You'll just have to do it twice."

Derrick was about to ask her what she meant when she tossed the sword in the air, caught it by the blade, and offered him the hilt. Derrick took it, his eyebrows raised. *Oh no. This isn't going to go well for me. This is going to hurt...*

She crouched into a ready stance, Timoria in her hand. Derrick groaned. This would *definitely* not bode well for him.

He mirrored her stance. "I can barely even see," he complained. The sun hadn't even risen yet, and he had no idea how long he'd been sleeping, but it hadn't felt like very long at all.

"Training starts early today, we can't waste daylight. We need the sun for riding."

A sword at my throat first thing in the morning is training? I could have used more sleep.

She grinned at him again. "You didn't think I'd let you go through this quest without making you work, now, did you?" Derrick said nothing. "Come on, we're wasting time." She punctuated her words with a lunge. Derrick barely got his sword up in time.

"Hey! A little warning. It's not like we're using wooden swords here!" A rush of adrenaline hit Derrick, and he suddenly felt much more awake.

"Do you think an enemy will give you a heads up before they attack?"

His cheeks flushed scarlet. She was right. She was *always*

right. It irritated him to no end, but he had to admit that it was the truth. Scowling at her, he lunged himself, taking her back a few steps.

Reyna beamed. "Oh, good! I knew you wouldn't leave me without a dance partner."

"This is *not* what pops into my head when I think about dancing," Derrick bit out, parrying an overhead blow from her.

"Good! You're getting much better at being able to read the next attack."

He grinned at the compliment, then took a whack to the shin with the flat of her blade.

"Focus, princeling!" she snapped, angry that he'd let her get to him. *That was such an easy block! How could he miss that?*

"I'll make you a deal." He slashed at her torso. Her sword swiped through the air in an easy block.

"I'm listening." She spun around, throwing a back slash at him. He managed to dive under the blade.

"If I can disarm you, then you have to dance with me at court... as payback." His eyes blazed, and she laughed at his vehemence.

"I think I'm safe making *that* deal," Reyna rolled her eyes.

He forced his face into an uncaring gaze, hiding the pain of her cool dismissal. He ran at her, slashing out at her shins as she did.

"And you'll have to wear one of those courtly dresses, too." His eyes narrowed. "Are you in? Or are you too afraid?"

She growled at him. His grin slipped when he saw the fury in her icy eyes. He gulped audibly, then did what he could to fend her off her renewed attack.

Back and forth they sparred. Derrick gritted his teeth in determination, holding his own for the first time. He began to smirk with pride.

"What are you smiling at?" Reyna asked, feeling suspicious.

"I'm not doing so bad. I thought you'd have me flat on my back by now." He swung, then ducked and followed up with a parry.

Her eyebrows rose and she barked out a laugh.

"What? What's so funny?"

Rather than answer him, she let him charge her. She swiftly side stepped, throwing a leg in front of his shins and using the pommel of her sword to hit his shoulder. Derrick tripped, tried to correct himself, and landed flat on his back.

"You mean like that?" Reyna asked, a smug look on her face.

The realization hit him. He glared at her. "You're telling me that I wasn't even defending myself properly? You just didn't take me down because... you didn't *want* to?"

"Well... *yeah*. I didn't want to waste time with you having to get up every time I knocked you down." She offered him her hand, but he slapped it away.

Derrick struggled to his feet, breathing heavily. He cleared his throat, trying to hide his exhaustion. Reyna looked composed, even with sweat sticking her dark hair to her forehead.

"We'll spar every morning and every night. I want to make sure that you can take care of yourself," she said. Her voice softened for a moment, towards the end. Derrick couldn't be certain whether she genuinely cared or if it was his imagination running away with him.

He set to rolling up his cloak and sleeping furs, then packed them into his saddle bags. Reyna cocked an eyebrow at him. He ignored her and climbed onto Apple's back. He sat in the saddle, waiting patiently for Reyna to mount up.

She laughed, "My, my, aren't we touchy this morning? I don't suppose you'd want some breakfast before we go?"

"I'm not hungry." No sooner were the words out of his mouth, than his stomach gave a mighty grumble. He pretended he didn't hear it.

He refused to look at her. Out of the corner of his eye, he watched her pack up her own things, then mount up. He fell in behind her, wincing from the pain that flooded his body. He was suddenly *very* glad that she couldn't see him. Less than an hour after they broke camp, his legs chafed where they clung to Apple. Somehow, the horse could tell, and she tried to smooth the ride for him.

"Come on, princeling, you need to keep up," Reyna threw

back over her shoulder.

He waited for her to face forward again, then he stuck his tongue out at her back. He knew he was being childish, but it gave him a small measure of satisfaction to do it anyway.

As they rode, the sun crept across the sky. They were headed directly east. Derrick had no idea where they were. So far, they'd ridden through plains and fields of weeds. He saw no landmarks that he could recognize, even after the hours he'd spent poring over maps in his free time in the palace. Reyna gave him plenty of sidelong looks, waiting for him to say something. He studiously ignored her.

As the sun beamed brightly down on them, Reyna pulled an apple from one of her saddle bags and began eating it slowly. Each crunch came louder and more obnoxious than the last. Derrick refused to turn away from her as she ate. His stomach growled, louder than at camp. Still he would not eat or speak. Whether he was punishing her or just making himself miserable, he wasn't really sure.

They rode in silence until the sun began to sink again. Derrick's body was sore. He wished that they could stop for a day or two, just enough time for some of the pain to go away.

"There's a village up ahead. We can stay there tonight." She turned to face him, but he couldn't give her more than a stoic grimace of pain. "That bad, huh?"

With a tremendous effort, Derrick spoke through clenched

teeth. "I don't know what you're talking about," he said, and forced a shrug of his shoulder. "But staying at a village would be nice. Especially since you said it could be days or even weeks between villages." He kept his face relaxed, trying not to show the relief bubbling up inside him.

When they reached the village, Reyna led Derrick to the door of an inn. She helped him dismount, then walked him inside, taking most of his weight on her own shoulders. Slowly, she brought him over to one of the tables and eased him down on the wooden bench. Derrick bit back a cry.

"I'm going to take care of the horses. I'll be right back." She pulled out a handful of coins from her pouch and gave them to him. "Get yourself something to eat and book us two rooms. Actually, I should be back in enough time to book the room. Just eat."

Reyna's words echoed in his head. She was taking care of everything. And he couldn't help her. His insides wrenched in shame. *How am I supposed to be a king, when I can't even take care of myself... much less a kingdom?* He sighed heavily and put his head on his arms. They hadn't traveled as far into the night as the day before, but Derrick would have happily passed out right there at the table.

"You poor thing. You look exhausted." The breathy voice came from beside him.

Derrick jerked back, sitting tall. A woman stood before him, rouge on her cheeks, kohl rimming her eyes, and berry stain on her lips. Her bosom nearly hung out of her bodice.

She winked at him, "See anything you like?" She laughed as she brought her arms together.

Derrick looked away from her quickly. "Just, um, just dinner, please."

"Just you, sugar?" she asked sweetly.

He shifted uncomfortably, his eyes looking everywhere but her. "N-no. I have a traveling companion."

"So, two, then?" She asked. He nodded at her. The woman placed her hands on her hips. "Is there anything else?"

"T-two rooms, please." She winked at him and nodded her assent.

Derrick blushed, realizing that he'd looked up at her face again. She disappeared. The color had *almost* gone back to normal in his face, when Reyna came back in.

Her eyes immediately found him, and he gave her a genuine, beaming smile. He'd never been so glad to see her. He felt too embarrassed to talk to the bawdy woman himself.

"Everything has been taken care of. As soon as we get rooms, I can have our saddle bags brought up. Have you eaten?" She looked concerned, which made the blood rush in his ears. "Are you alright?"

"Fine. Just a little sore. Nothing a bath and bed can't fix. After dinner, of course. I'm starving!" His hands shook and his stomach twisted.

"Well, you wouldn't be if you'd just swallowed your pride and had breakfast. Or even had eaten something in the saddle like I did," she mused.

"Here you are!" The woman had come back, and Derrick averted his eyes. She set down two plates with sausages, potatoes, and a hunk of fresh bread for each. "And your keys." She placed two iron keys on the table. "The rooms are right next to each other, honey. If you need anything, you just let me know." The woman's eyes raked over Derrick.

Reyna looked from him to the girl and back again. She bristled. Derrick tried to read her expression, but her walls had gone up as if she'd hung a curtain over her face.

"I... um... I'd like a bath after dinner. I-if that could be arranged?" He counted out coins from the handful that Reyna had given him, handed them to the bawdy woman, then pushed the rest across the table to Reyna. She took them without a word, then set to work cleaning her plate.

"Eat. We'll be getting up early," she ordered.

Great. He thought. *What have I done now?*

Reyna ate slowly, almost like it was a chore. He finished *much* faster; he'd been ravenous, after all. Derrick got to his feet, swaying a little. "Do you need help with anything?"

"I'll be alright. Go ahead and enjoy that bath. I'll see you in the morning. Don't stay up *too* late. That woman has her eye on you, you know."

He gave her a quizzical look, then took one of the keys and made his way to the stairs at the back of the open room. Reyna watched him go before letting her eyes roam through the room.

There was a fireplace that took up a third of one wall. There were tables and chairs ringed around it. Some old women sat in rocking chairs, knitting, while children played in the light of the dancing flames. The bar sat along the opposite end of the room, and it was pretty easy to tell the men who wanted to drink from the men who were there looking for...company.

She noticed though, that two of the tables were completely free of the women. It was strange for her to see, being as in Syrinx there had been women everywhere. And as the night grew later, she saw that it stayed that way. Those tables must have been for the decent men, then. She took a moment to beg whatever gods were listening that Derrick would turn into the kind of man that would choose the empty table; every time.

Meanwhile, Derrick made his way upstairs, one slow and painful step at a time. He'd just cleared the landing when he saw a maid bringing buckets of hot water to one of the rooms. When she saw Derrick limping, she dropped her empty bucket and ran over to help him. He swallowed his pride and allowed the woman to fit herself under his arm.

He leaned on her as she helped him to his room. "Thank

you," he groaned.

Derrick saw a tub, full of steaming water. His already weak knees buckled under him. Catching himself on the door, he told himself, "Pull it together, *princeling.*" He cleared his throat. "Thank you for the help. Could you have the saddle bags brought up, please?"

"Of course, sir!" The maid scurried off, and Derrick looked at the rest of the room.

The space was small and had no window. A wash stand stood in one corner, and the bed took up almost half the floor. A small desk sat on the other side of the bed, and the bathtub had been pulled out into the middle of the room. He looked longingly at the hot water. He wished he didn't have to wait for the woman to return with his bags before soaking in the luxurious water.

Derrick began taking off his boots when there was a knock on the door. By the time he reached it, no one was there, but his saddle bag lay on the floor just outside. Derrick dragged it into the room and locked the door behind him. He struggled over to the bed, sitting down and disrobing. He gritted his teeth as he eased down his trousers, his inner thighs bright pink and inflamed. He sighed heavily, worried about the pain the water would cause his raw skin. *Now how to get in the tub without screaming...*

Reyna had really helped a lot when she'd taken his weight,

coming into the tavern. There was *no way* he was going to ask her – or anyone for that matter – to help him get into the bathtub. No, this pain and humiliation were his alone.

Derrick ground his teeth and hobbled to the tub. The hot water felt wonderful on his calf muscles. He let out a sigh of relief. Then, before he lost his nerve, he dropped all the way in, sitting on the bottom of the tub. Derrick had to shove his fist into his mouth to muffle his scream. His thighs felt like they'd been set on fire. Tears leaked from the corners of his eyes. He sat rigid, refusing to move a muscle. With any luck, he could get his body acclimated before he started to wash up.

Derrick forced himself to relax and when he closed his eyes the only thing he could see was the swirling countryside they'd ridden through all day. *I can do this...*he thought tiredly. He began to drift off and the blackness of deep sleep enveloped him.

Chapter 18

Reyna sat in the common room, eating slowly and listening into the various conversations around her. No one seemed to be talking about Syrinx, the soldiers, or even the missing prince. It eased some of the tension in her shoulders, but not all of it. *I need to find out where those bastards are headed,* Reyna growled to herself.

"Anything else for you, sweet?" The overly familiar waitress made a point to place a soft hand on her shoulder after dropping off more food. Maybe it wasn't Derrick she was too friendly with, but simply how this woman was. It still was a bit much for Reyna's liking.

Reyna shifted away from the woman's touch. "Um… actually, a bath for me as well after I'm done eating. Nothing else, though, thank you." She fought against the urge to squirm away and put more distance between the two of them. Instead, she paid for their tab.

Just as she thought the conversation over, the woman spoke again. "Well, if you change your mind, gorgeous, you just let me know." The waitress winked.

As she walked away, Reyna heaved a sigh of relief. "Not likely," she muttered.

Once her food and drink were long gone, and Reyna realized her eavesdropping would provide no more helpful information, she headed up to her room. She pulled out the key and unlocked the door, taking stock. It looked no different than the rooms at The Mangy Wolf, and it brought her a tiny sense of comfort. The bed stood in one corner, carefully made with a well-worn but clean quilt. A basin of water stood on top of an aged and notched wooden pedestal. A small desk with a rickety leg and some paper sat under the one window.

"At least the world isn't completely different than it was back home," Reyna comforted herself.

Reyna started digging through the saddlebags for a change of clothes. Her hand brushed something smooth, and she pulled it out. A glass bottle of unguent. Taking the lid off, she took a deep breath, inhaling the spicy scent of herbs. Reyna smiled. This was the perfect medicine for healing Derrick's legs, at least a little, before they set out again in the morning.

The door burst open. Reyna's hand went immediately to the hilt of her dagger, the bottle transitioned smoothly from one hand to the other.

"Sorry, ma'am. Didn't mean to startle you," the stable hand declared, carrying an empty tub. Reyna sighed with relief as he was followed by three women with buckets full of steaming water, which they dumped into the tub before filing out. The door shut behind them.

Reyna started pacing the small room. Derrick needed this unguent. But he'd just refused her help. He'd be fine though, at the moment he'd simply be bathing... Reyna's cheeks flushed.

"Stop being such a coward, Reyna," she chided herself. "Should I just leave it in front of his door? No, that won't work. He's probably in for the night...." Reyna stared at her fingernails. "I could just knock, and *then* leave it. No, that won't work, either. Someone could walk by and take it." Reyna bit her lip. "Damn it. Why do you even care? Just *give him* the medicine."

Reyna gripped the bottle in her hand and opened the door. Her hand shook as she raised it to knock. "It's fine. It's just Derrick," she breathed. She gave three sharp knocks, then stepped back and waited. The door opened warily, showing a sliver of Derrick's face.

"Reyna." His tone was unreadable, and she swallowed hard, trying to find her voice.

"Um, hi. I wanted to give you this. It should help with your legs." Reyna noticed the water dripping from his hair.

"Thank you," he answered, a softness reaching his dark eyes. "Here I thought you were upset with me again."

"Wait, what?" Reyna crossed her arms over her chest defensively.

Derrick chuckled, "Downstairs. You ordered me to eat as if… I don't know, maybe I made it up."

Reyna blushed, "It wasn't you. Sorry about that."

"It's fine." Derrick continued to hide behind the door. "Anything else?"

"No, that's all." She turned to go.

"Reyna." His voice was soft.

Her heart jumped. "Yes?"

"I need the bottle."

Her face colored, and she dropped her eyes. "Right! Sorry!" She thrust the bottle at him and hurried back to her room.

When morning came, Reyna came down to find Derrick already eating.

She grimaced. "I don't know whether I should be angry at myself for not waking first or impressed that you beat me downstairs."

"Maybe a little bit of both?" he grinned. "Thanks again for the unguent. It helped a lot."

"You're welcome. I'm glad," she said, sitting down. "We're going to have a hard day's riding today. We'll be parallel to the mountains. Those foothills can be treacherous." A serving girl brought her a plate of bacon and eggs. "Besides, we'll need to watch out for giants." She took a bite of toast.

Next to her, Derrick choked, "Giants. Did you just say *giants*?"

Reyna looked at him, meeting his gaze before nodding firmly. "They like to live in the mountains and sometimes come down into the foothills for fresh meat." *How does he not know this? Everybody knows this.*

Derrick took a swig of his water. "Giants aren't real," he said firmly. "All the accounts I've read of them were discredited by any number of my teachers. There was always a rational explanation: a freak thunderstorm, or an earthquake. Stuff like that."

Reyna cocked an eyebrow. "Really? Huh. Well, if we find one, you go right ahead and tell him he's not real. That he's a stormcloud, or something. If he hasn't eaten you already, of course." She turned back to her food, leaving Derrick to stare at her as he tried to process her words.

"They're real," Derrick's voice dropped. "Not some fairy tale?"

Reyna shook her head, continuing to eat. Derrick, meanwhile, had lost his appetite. Suddenly, the doors to the inn burst open.

"Help! Someone please help me!" A disheveled woman ran in, eyes red and flooded with tears. "My boy! He's been taken! Please! Somebody, help me!" She fell to her knees, sobbing.

Before Reyna knew what she was doing, she was on her feet and crossing the room. Derrick stared after her.

"Let me help you up," Reyna said, pulling the woman to her feet. She was like a child herself, letting Reyna lead her. Derrick moved over as Reyna gently pushed on the woman's shoulder, making her sit on the bench. "Okay. Now, tell me what happened."

The woman gulped and took a breath. "My boy, Kai, and I were out gathering some mushrooms in the foothills. He was running around in the tall grass, laughing and singing..." She paused, choking back her tears. "The ground... it shook. I thought it was a rockslide. Then Kai screamed. I ran to where he'd been playing— I was too late. The giant had Kai slung over his shoulder. Kai was still crying and screaming for me." She dissolved into sobs.

Reyna felt her lips curl into a snarl. "I'll get him back," she said. The woman looked up at her, the hope in her eyes tearing at Reyna's heart.

"You said it was in the foothills that this happened?" The

woman nodded, wiping her tears away. "I'm done with break-fast anyway." Reyna stood up, slung her saddlebags over her shoulder, and strode towards the door. She didn't bother looking back, but she knew Derrick was scrambling to follow her lead. He cleared his throat.

"Um, Reyna? Don't you think you're being a little... hasty, here?" His voice sounded concerned, yet argumentative.

"No. That little boy needs help. No one else seems to be willing to go after him." They entered the stables.

Derrick searched for the right words to say. "How do we know the boy's alive?"

Reyna buckled her saddlebags onto Andromeda's back. "How do we know he's not?" she shot back.

"Reyna." Derrick put a tentative hand on her shoulder. She looked at it, then up to the pity on his face. Her eyes narrowed. Undaunted, Derick pressed on, "I know that you couldn't do anything for your people. That doesn't mean you have to go charging into danger at every opportunity... or try to rescue everyone you come across. You can't save them all."

Reyna threw off his hand in disgust, then mounted. "If you'd like to stay here, I won't argue." Clucking to Androm-eda, Reyna rode out of the stable and towards the mountains. When she didn't hear the telltale clopping of hooves behind her, her features hardened.

She *hadn't* lied. If Derrick didn't want to come with her, she wouldn't push him. But, still, she was disappointed.

Reyna found the foothills a few hours later. Small clusters of trees and large boulders dotted the landscape. Reyna's ears were pricked for any signs of danger. She made her way from boulder to boulder, using them for cover in case the giant returned. Reyna scanned the mountain, searching carefully for a cave. Her mother had always said giants preferred to dwell in caves.

Then she found it. If she'd approached at any other angle, the rock crevice would have hidden it from view. She could have searched for *weeks* and never found it. Maybe Fate was helping her after all. Her breath whooshed out of her in awe. The largest cave she'd ever seen loomed in front of her. The whole of Syrinx could have fit inside it. She had a sinking feeling that the boy... Kai... was being kept here.

Reyna made for a small copse of trees to the left of the opening. Before she managed to duck under them, she heard the pitiful wailing of a child. Reyna's heart thumped in her chest. She dismounted Andromeda in the thickest shadows she could find. "Stay quiet," she whispered to the horse.

Crouching, she snuck to the very edge of the copse. Reyna's eyes raked the surrounding area. She saw Kai, and her stomach knotted. He was tied to a metal spike sunken deep into a small boulder.

Reyna's brow furrowed. *They're using him as bait! They*

knew someone would try to rescue him... Reyna's anger and disgust bubbled up inside her. *Screw it. I can still do this.*

Staying low to the ground, she sprinted for Kai, diving behind the boulder and coming up in a roll to land on her feet. Kai stopped screaming and the ground began to shake beneath them.

The giant came to the mouth of the cave. He towered over the landscape. *If I climbed on Derrick's shoulders, I'd still only be half his height!* The pale, yellowish skin looked mottled, as if it had spent years away from any sunlight. Reyna wrinkled her nose at the filthy loincloth that hung from its hips. *Remind me to never get close enough to look under its skirt.* He looked directly at Kai, then scoured the landscape. His eyes rested momentarily on the trees. The giant showed no sign of alarm. His head swiveled back to Kai. Reyna flattened herself against the boulder, holding her breath. After what seemed like hours, the giant strolled back into the cave.

"Kai, I need you to be careful. We don't want them to get suspicious again, okay?" Reyna whispered.

"Are you going to take me to my mama?" he asked, his voice wobbly.

Reyna nodded. "Now start screaming again so they don't come back."

Kai threw back his head and screamed again.

"Good. Keep going." Pulling the dagger from her belt, she

started sawing at the rope that bound him. When she finally cut through, she scooped Kai into her arms. Though he was small, he had some weight to him. "Quiet now!" she hissed.

Taking a deep breath, she ran hard for the trees. The giants would come either way, and she didn't want them to be sure which way they'd headed.

A mighty roar shook the tree tops and vibrated in her chest. She fought to keep her balance as the impact of his feet hitting the ground made her *own* running treacherous. One thunderous step threw her to her knees, sending Kai tumbling out of her arms. She knew by the terror on his face that the giant was right behind her.

Unbidden, Derrick's words came back to her: *you can't save them all*. Now, she wouldn't be able to save even *herself*, much less Kai. They were going to die.

Thwip! The familiar sound shot through the air. A bellow of triumph came from behind her, as thundering footsteps came to a halt. Reyna looked up at the giant as he clasped his eye, crying out in pain. He took a few unsteady steps, and the earth thundered as the giant collapsed to the ground.

She squinted toward the fell beast, and a beaming grin split her face. The giant was trying to get something out of his eye... something that looked suspiciously like one of Reyna's arrows. Kai stood by, eyes wide with fear, mouth gaping open in a silent scream. In the far off distance, a chorus of roars echoed from the depths of the cave.

"Reyna! Over here!" Derrick. He'd come for her.

Fresh adrenaline coursed through her body. She shot to her feet and scooped up Kai in one smooth motion. With unnatural speed, Reyna crashed through the tree line to find Derrick already on Apple's back.

She handed Kai up to him, then slapped Apple's hindquarters. "We've woken the rest. Go! And don't look back! I'll be right behind you!"

Derrick didn't need to be told twice. He held one arm around Kai as Apple plunged forward, racing for all she was worth. Reyna swung herself up into the saddle. Another bellow came from behind her. Hurriedly, she kicked Andromeda's sides, spurring her to action.

The small figure of Derrick on Apple drew further and further away. She was thankful that he'd listened to her. Reyna, on the other hand, looked back every so often to ensure the other giants weren't following them. When the village came into view on the horizon, Reyna relaxed.

"There she is!" came a booming voice as she entered the village.

Reyna's eyes darted all around, searching for danger. No one charged her. No one drew a weapon. She took a second look around. The people were... *applauding* her? The distraught mother rushed forward with Kai clutched in her arms.

"Thank you! Thank you so much! You've saved my son!" the woman cried.

Reyna dismounted, making her way over to where Derrick stood silently, holding Apple's reins. "It wasn't all me," she told the woman. "I had help." Reyna put a hand on Derrick's shoulder. His face flushed.

"What are your names?" asked a man in the crowd.

"My name is Reyna." She looked at Derrick, who stared stubbornly at his toes. She had to make a decision. In her gut, she knew these people had been won over. Biting her lip, she turned to Derrick. *This is for the best.* "And this is Prince Derrick Dragonspear."

Dead silence met her revelation, and Derrick gave her a furious glare. Without saying a word, he swung himself gracefully into the saddle, and Apple cantered off heading back out of the town. Reyna stared after him.

"Sorry everyone, don't mind him. He doesn't... like being the center of attention." She shifted uncomfortably.

A young man took Reyna's hand. "How can we thank you?"

"No one can know which direction Derrick and I are headed. I would consider it a boon if you would keep this a secret. That's all the thanks we need," Reyna said, wondering if maybe she'd made the wrong choice as Derrick disappeared from view.

"We have no love for the king here!" a young man exclaimed. Defiance colored his hazel eyes, and it made her heart soar.

She grinned. "Neither do we. But I can promise you, as sure as I'm standing before you now, that we will do everything in our power to change the law of this land."

"Bless you!" the mother called out, kissing the top of Kai's head.

The young man looked at Reyna with something akin to awe. "If ever you need safe passage through these lands again, you can count on us."

"Thank you." Warmth spread through her. It wasn't just the fact that a *man* had offered her aid, but that *anyone* had. Tears welled in her eyes. *Maybe I don't have to do this all alone.*

"Typhon speaks on behalf of us all m'lady," an elderly man grumbled, patting his thick belly.

Reyna felt the clock ticking as Derrick presumably got farther and farther away from her. A mix of worry and anxiety filled her. "I'm so thankful to you all. I will pass the message along. But, I'm so sorry. I must be going. We have a long ride ahead and I'm afraid my partner will beat me there," she said, forcing a chuckle.

Reyna remounted and set after Derrick. She heard several "goodbyes" and "safe travels" called out behind her. The sun was now at its highest point. She began to see Derrick's figure ahead in the distance.

"Hey! Get back here!" She urged Andromeda on. In a few minutes, they drew level with Derrick. "Let me explain!"

"Why did you tell them who I was? You know the danger this poses. Now the soldiers will be after us any minute!" His eyes burned.

Well, *two* could play *that* game. She matched him, glare for glare. "Did you see any soldiers in that village?" Reyna turned towards the left, forcing Derrick to follow her.

"Well... no," he answered.

"Did you pay *any* attention to the looks on their faces?" she snapped. He was quiet for a moment then shook his head. "They were *thankful*! I made the decision because you need the people behind you. They need to know you're nothing like *him*. If they love you, they will rise up and form an army once you have the Draco Lingua. Or did you think your father would just hand over his crown?"

"I didn't think about anything beyond getting the artifact," he admitted, now feeling a bit sheepish. The bubble of anger he'd been holding onto deflated.

"Any good deed you can put your name to, will spread. If

we're *lucky*, it'll spread far and wide. You *need* that support." Reyna slowed Andromeda, and Apple followed suit. The horses were grateful for a break after their mad dash from the giant, and subsequent hard ride out of the village.

"I, um, managed a few of those before I reached the forest," he mumbled.

"That's great! Did you give your name?" He shook his head, and Reyna cursed under her breath.

"I didn't need to!" he defended himself. "I couldn't help everyone, so I managed to help one person per town. I was on the run. Wanted posters of my face were on every village news board. I was terrified every single time. And every single time, their eyes would go wide, and their mouths would fall open. They recognized me. Of *that*, I have no doubt. Still, my name floating out there will give my father and his men an idea of where we're headed. Did you take the time to think of *that*?"

"I did. I spoke to the villagers. They will not say a word. They have no love for your father. If the soldiers come sniffing, I'm sure they will send them looking in the wrong direction." It was a good thought...a hopeful thought. Reyna stiffened. What if she was wrong?

Derrick shook his head. "I guess we'll see. What's done is done."

They fell silent for a while. They continued to travel back towards the mountains. The town became a small light in the distance.

"Maybe we should avoid the foothills... give ourselves a little space," Reyna finally said.

Derrick nodded. "How far will we go before we stop for the night? We didn't set out as early as we wanted to."

Reyna winced. That was his polite way of telling her that she'd been reckless when she'd made that promise and gone after Kai. "It doesn't matter how far we get. We can stop right before sundown." More silence followed. "Thank you, by the way." Her voice was soft. He had to lean in closer to hear her.

"I'm sorry, I didn't quite catch that."

"Thank you," she said, speaking up.

"For what?" Derrick's brow furrowed.

"For coming after me." She sighed, refusing to meet his gaze. "If you hadn't... I wouldn't be here. Neither would Kai. That took real *courage*, Derrick. Even if you don't think so. I owe you my life." Her cheeks colored, but it wasn't dark enough yet to hide her embarrassment. "I'll think things through next time before I go running in."

Derrick laughed, but offered no explanation as to why. She glared at him, fairly sure that he was poking fun at her. *How like a man.* With a sniff, she faced forward again, and urged her horse on, making conversation impossible unless they called out to each other. After what had happened with the giant, they'd come to the unspoken agreement *not* to draw any more attention to themselves; unfriendly or otherwise.

Time went by, filled with more silence. Reyna squinted at the skyline, judging roughly how much light they had left before dark. She pulled up on the reins, hopping lightly off Andromeda's back. "Let's make camp."

She pulled out her sleeping furs and cloak, made up her bed, and plopped down on it, pulling a strip of dried beef from her saddlebag. Taking a swig from her water skin, she sat, staring, and chewed slowly while Derrick did the same.

As soon as he'd swallowed his last bite, Reyna clamored to her feet, drew her sword, and walked to an open area, settling into her sparring stance.

Derrick looked up at the sky and groaned. "Do we *have* to spar tonight? I'm exhausted."

"We spar *every* night. That's how this works. Or did you forget that we have a job to do? It's even better when you're exhausted. It'll help you keep your focus in a real fight." She paused, letting him ready himself. "And the shot you made today? It was excellent. I'm glad you paid attention during our lesson." Derrick grinned with pride and Reyna lunged.

CHAPTER 19

The days began to fall into a pattern, each morning and each evening the same. The day started with a sword fight and ended with a knife fight. It wore Derrick out more than he would like to admit, and he was grateful that they spent most of the day in the saddle, or else he'd collapse from weariness. He chuckled to himself bitterly. *Don't let Reyna catch onto that thought she'll have you sparring twice as hard. At least her unguent has healed and strengthened the skin on my legs.*

Another change he'd noticed: their sparring was honing

Reyna's muscles even more; the physical activity melting what little softness she had. She wasn't the only one, however. Derrick found his body changing right alongside hers. He'd developed muscle in his arms and legs, and the soft belly he'd acquired from all the rich palace foods had melted away. Even his cheeks now had a sharper angle to them.

"I think I see a village!" Reyna's face brightened as she pointed excitedly, breaking Derrick from his reverie. Derrick followed her finger. It *did* seem to be a small town. Derrick smiled. It had been three weeks since the giant adventure, and likewise since they'd seen people.

The sun was beginning to set, and he knew what was coming. They hobbled their horses and gave them their evening feed. but he didn't bother with food or furs. He drew his sword as silently as he could, and charged at Reyna. She laughed, easily sidestepping him and drawing her sword in one smooth motion.

"Eager for another beating tonight, aren't we?" She gave him that cocky grin he loved so much. "Well, I'm only *too* happy to help, princeling. After all, that's what us *peasants* do, right?"

"One of these days, I will beat you, wench." He'd taken to calling her that in the same teasing manner that she called him "princeling".

Reyna grinned and something shifted behind her eyes that he couldn't read. "Only if I'm old and gray, and you somehow keep your youth, princeling." She smirked, giving no hint at all of the attack that followed. *CLANK!* He barely managed to bring his sword up in time.

Reyna finally called a halt to their training as the sky became cast in the reds and purples of sunset. Derrick was sore, sweaty, and covered in bruises. To his surprise, Reyna seemed to be sweating and panting, too. Derrick puffed his chest, pleased with himself. She pushed sweaty curls off her forehead, then slid Timoria back in its sheath.

"Have I managed to land *any* hits on you, yet?" he panted with a wry grin. He slid his own sword home, knowing the answer.

"Of course not, princeling." She narrowed her eyes playfully and his heart skipped a beat.

"Someday I'll wipe that smirk off your face." She batted her eyelashes at him innocently. Derrick looked away as his stomach tightened, and took a swig of water to mask the movement.

"You have such wonderful fantasies, princeling. You should become a bard." Derrick chuckled as she continued, suddenly looking serious "Have you named your sword yet?" Her midnight blue eyes sparkled in the gloom.

"I have."

She stared at him expectantly. "*Well*? Are you going to tell me?"

"Nope. One of these days, when we have another long

stretch of open land, we'll play a game I used to play in the palace. Maybe then you'll guess it." Derrick shrugged. He grabbed his pack and started settling his bed into place.

"I'm not going to stop just to play a game," she snapped. He grinned that infuriating grin of his, and watched as her eyes flashed like lightning in a storm. She tossed one end of her furs away from her, spreading them out.

Reyna stuck her nose in the air and turned her back to him. Then she crawled into her own furs. Derrick softened as he gazed at her.

Shaking himself, he added, "Don't worry, it's a game that can be played on horseback." No answer. Derrick put his hands behind his head and stared up at the stars, "Goodnight, Reyna." He received a muffled grunt in reply. He chuckled low and deep in his chest, and fell asleep with a smile on his face.

"Derrick..." a whisper. He stirred, but didn't wake. "Oh, Derrick..." A feather light touch on his cheek made his eyes snap open. Reyna was sitting on him, face inches from his own. His heart raced. Was this a dream? It had to be. Reyna giggled. She leaned forward and pressed her lips to his. They were cool, not at all like he'd imagined. His eyes widened, then closed as the kiss swept him away.

She wriggled against him. He let out a gasp. She grinned at him knowingly, then jumped away, beckoning to him. He scrambled to his feet, staring at her, dumbstuck. Reyna picked up a lantern and disappeared into the fog.

Fog? When had the fog rolled in? The thought was dim, and easily pushed to the back of his mind at the sight of Reyna's playful gesture to follow.

"Where are you going?" he asked, hurrying to keep up with her. "Reyna!" He couldn't see her anymore, and the light from the lantern was muted but visible in the fog. Derrick ran after her, doing his best not to fall behind.

Reyna's giggling echoed in the air just ahead of him. "Wait! Where are we going?" he asked again. Suddenly, the sound of hoofbeats reached him. Faint at first, but drawing nearer. Derrick's heart jumped. Was it his father's soldiers? Had they finally caught up with them? He couldn't focus on them right now, though. Reyna turned back and blew him a kiss. Grinning like a fool, he picked up the pace.

Where is *she? I can't see through this fog!* He searched the murk intently, trying to make out the shape of her body, when a blinding flash of light engulfed him. Derrick cried out and fell to his knees, eyes shut tightly, hands fisted at his sides.

"Derrick!" Reyna's furious voice cut through the sudden silence.

A sudden force cracked across his head, and he saw stars. He fell over from the blow, his eyes still shut, now leaking pained tears. Hands wrapped around the cloth of his tunic and yanked him, none too gently, to his feet. "If you don't open your eyes, so help me!" Reyna's voice, again; again it was angry, not seductive. Derrick's eyes snapped open, only for him to flinch away. Reyna's face was mere inches from his, and her hand was cocked back, ready to crack him again.

"R-Reyna?" Wetness seeped into the legs of his trousers, and he looked down. Brackish, foul-smelling water came up to his knees. His eyes darted around. The smells of rot and decay filled his senses. Shimmering gasses floated over small paths of dry land that led through the water. "Where... where are we?"

"Oh, you don't know?" she asked, her voice cold and mocking. He shook his head, cringing away from her. "We're in a bog, Prince *Idiot*!" she screamed, pulling him from the water and onto dry land, "You were *stupid* enough to follow a will o' the wisp!" He gave her a blank stare. Reyna closed her eyes and took a deep breath. When she opened them again, her voice sounded gentler. "A will o' the wisp is a fairy who disguises itself and carries a lantern to lure unwary people into bogs. Sometimes over cliffs. So, be glad it wasn't *that*. Come on," she sighed, taking his hand and tugging him behind her towards

Apple. "Here. Get up." She put his hands on Apple's saddle, then turned to mount Andromeda. "What was it they used to lure you, anyway?" She stared at him, frowning.

Derrick stumbled over some quick lies as his cheeks heated. "My... my mother." He swallowed. "How did you know to follow me?" he asked, trying to change the subject.

"You were rolling around in your furs. It woke me up. I saw you stand up, so I called out to you, but you didn't answer. You had a stupid grin on your face, walking like you were drunk. I gathered everything up and by the time I was chasing after you the fog had rolled in. I was afraid I was going to lose you. Lucky for you, I didn't."

"So... it was you I heard," he mused.

"What are you talking about? If you'd heard me you would have stopped," she griped.

"No, I mean, the hoofbeats. I thought it was my father's soldiers, hunting us down."

"No, just me." She laughed darkly at the comparison. "Come on, we need to get going." She led Andromeda along one of the thin land bridges. They lapsed into silence. Derrick could feel the anger still radiating from her, so he hung his head and kept quiet. He took Apple's reins in a loose hand, and followed.

Hours passed, and the light in the bog never changed. It sent a chill down his spine. What manner of cursed magic was this?

He understood now why Reyna was so furious with him.

Every now and then, he thought he saw a flash of movement in the brackish water, or a pair of eyes watching him from the shadows of a submerged tree root. Giving in to fear, he closed his eyes and wrapped the reins tighter around his fist.

"Falling asleep on me, now?" she asked, sounding irritated. Derrick's head jerked up and he looked at her, twisted in her saddle, narrowed eyes fixed on his face.

"No! I, um, I kept seeing things in the water," he admitted, feeling sheepish. Her eyes widened, and a little fear crept into her voice when she spoke.

"Pull your tunic over your nose! Now!" He jumped at the urgency in her voice, and his fingers fumbled in his rush to comply. "Do *not* take it off your face until I tell you to. Derrick, I need you to listen to me on this." He nodded to show he understood. Some of the tension left her shoulders, and her gaze fell to Apple. "Can you keep up with me, girl? I need to get us out of here, fast." Apple gave her a determined whinny

"Yah!" She flicked the reins on Andromeda's back, and the horse bolted. Derrick felt suddenly *very* thankful that he'd wrapped the reins around his hand several times. Apple's powerful muscles bunched beneath him, and he barely had time to grab the pommel before she exploded with power, surging after them. Derrick closed his eyes again, hunching down low over Apple's neck.

The pair made it out of the bog with no further incident, thanks to Reyna's quick thinking and quicker horse. "There's a river not too far from here, so that's where we're headed," she said. "We may stop there for a day or two so we can regroup. I have no idea where we are now." She didn't look at him, but he felt the accusation in her tone. *Great. This is* my *fault. We probably went* miles *in the wrong direction now because of me...*

"There! I can see it!" Derrick squinted his eyes, but even then, he could *barely* make out the dark winding ribbon in the distance. Relief swept through him. "Reyna...I'm sorry. I didn't know. I could have gotten you killed." His voice broke, his mind conjuring up an image of her face pale as death, sightless eyes staring up at nothing.

"It's alright." Her voice was flat, but her eyes looked glassy. "*I'm* not the one who needs to finish this quest. *You* are." I'll do whatever it takes to get you there. I'll do everything I can...for as long as I can." Her voice had a bitter undertone to it, and he wondered if she knew something he didn't...

They reached the bank of the river unmolested, and Reyna heaved a sigh of relief as she dismounted. Derrick's feet were dead beneath him by the time he hit the ground. Even so, he drew his blade, dropping into a defensive crouch. Reyna turned at the sound of steel scraping on leather. Her eyes softened as she looked at him, at how his sword shook in his hands.

"Not tonight, princeling. I'm just not up for it." She started her evening ritual of laying out her furs. Derrick missed his scabbard twice before he managed to sheath his sword. He made it to Apple, then had to grab her saddle to stay upright when his knees buckled. Relief flooded him, and he was more grateful than he would care to admit that she was changing their usual schedule. He rested his head on the soft leather, closing his eyes. He felt arms wrap around him, and he stiffened, afraid it was another will o' the wisp.

"It's alright. It's just me." He relaxed into her, and let her bear him down to the ground. When she let go, he found himself reaching out to her, wanting to wrap himself up in her warmth.

She dug through his things, then set about making his bed for him. He watched her out of eyes narrowed down to the thinnest of slits, fighting sleep with as much vigor as he'd planned to spar only minutes ago. She helped him crawl into the furs, then covered him up.

"I...don't want...can't sleep..." he mumbled.

"It's alright," she said softly. "You didn't sleep much last night, and rode another day besides."

His eyes were closed now, but he wouldn't stop fighting the darkness that wanted to pull him down. He heard rustling; the thump of furs close to him, and he flinched away from the sound.

"Shh...it's me." Something warm wrapped around his hand, pulling it out from under his furs. It took his muddled mind longer than it should have to figure out that she had taken his hand in hers, anchoring him to her. Keeping him safe. He stopped fighting, letting himself slide down the slope into the inky blackness.

"Love...you..."he mumbled. Her fingers tightened around his for a moment, then relaxed again.

When morning came, Derrick felt much better. He woke up slowly, like he was emerging from the bottom of a deep pool. The first thing he noticed was that something was touching him. Something warm. He looked down at his hand, and saw that Reyna still held his.

His heart swelled. He could only remember bits and pieces of the night before, but what he *could* remember was so clear, it seemed wreathed in brilliant light. She'd claimed *she* was the one who couldn't spar. Her warm arms around him, helping him down into a bed that *she'd* made up for him. Holding his hand all night long...to comfort him.

She looked so peaceful now, as she slept. Like an angel. Somehow, she looked much younger than her sixteen years. She'd done so much for him... he couldn't rub in her face that she'd outslept him today. He used the time to watch her, this... amazing woman. She used sharp words and a cold demeanor as a defense mechanism to cover the sweet, loving person she hid beneath. The one he saw, every now and then, peeking out.

She shifted, and he snapped his eyes shut in haste. If she could do little things to let him save his pride, then he could return the favor. She remained silent, but he could feel her eyes on him. Was she watching him the way he'd watched her? Could it possibly mean she felt something, too? He *knew* she was awake; and yet, she didn't pull her hand away. He tucked his chin down into the furs, so she wouldn't see the start of a smile. Derrick felt something soft on his cheek, and it took everything he had, not to twitch. She ran her fingers down the side of his face, then pulled away.

She gently disentangled her hand and got to her feet, taking great pains to be as quiet as she could. He planned to lay there for a minute or two longer, then pretend to wake up. He heard some different sounds, and focused hard, trying to figure out exactly what she was doing. The hiss of flames was followed quickly by the smell of food cooking. On the open plains, they hadn't cooked anything, because the land was so flat, the fire could be seen from miles away. The warmth of the furs, and the hypnotic sound of the flames, soon had him lulling back in a half doze.

"Hey. Time to get up." Reyna shook his shoulder until he opened his eyes. He'd fallen asleep again. Yawning, he managed to drag himself up into a sitting position. She brought him a plate with two strips of bacon and a fried potato on it. "I've been trying to figure out where we are since I woke up, but I have no clues to go by."

"I'm so sorry. It's my fault." He felt miserable and was about to tell her so, when she laughed wryly, shaking her head.

"Were you stupid? Yes." He bristled. She didn't need to say it like *that*. "But you didn't know. I can't expect you to understand what's going on, or how to protect yourself, if you don't even know what you're protecting yourself *from*." She tilted her head back and looked at the fluffy clouds floating above.

"Can you teach me how to survive the things I don't understand So I can be ready if we encounter them?" he asked, biting into the bacon.

"If I did that, we'd be here for weeks. There are so many creatures that we *might* encounter." She sighed and shook her head. "No; unfortunately, I think the best way to deal with anything new is a case by case basis. I promise to be more patient if...*when* something happens. Just try to remember something useful from all those books you read, please?" He opened his mouth to give an indignant retort, but saw that she wore a good natured grin. He smiled back, picking up the potato and taking a bite.

"So, what's the plan for today?" He could see that she hadn't touched her food, and his eyebrows furrowed with worry. She looked down at her plate, then passed it to him. "Not hungry?"

"No. I'm just...well, don't worry about it. As for today's plans...what would you like to do?" She spread her arms wide to encompass the squat trees and bushes surrounding their campsite. "I'm afraid you won't have *too* many options, though."

Derrick looked around, his gaze falling to rest on the river. He grinned as a conversation from one of their lessons came back to him. *Those lessons seem like ages ago...* He finished both plates of food quickly, then took the plates to the water's edge to wash.

"So, you *do* remember how to wash dishes," she laughed. "I'm *very* impressed." He stuck his tongue out at her as he packed away the plates, walked over to her, and gave her one of his best courtly bows before extending a hand out. "Are you taking me to the ball? I'm afraid I'm a bit under dressed," she laughed again. She held out her hand anyway, and he pulled her to her feet.

"If memory serves...you promised to teach me how to swim." She stared at him for a second, then realization dawned.

"Yes. I suppose I *did* promise that, didn't I? Well, there's no better place than this river. The current looks to be gentle, so it shouldn't be *too* difficult for even a know nothing princeling to learn." She gave him that playful grin that melted him inside. "Don't go in past your waist until I say you can."

"Yes, mother," he grumbled, earning him a glare. Derrick

took off his boots and tunic, then ran towards the water's edge. He'd already promised her that he wouldn't go in past his waist; and he'd keep his promise. For now. He couldn't help but feel elated. She was going to teach him to swim! He splashed in and turned around.

Reyna had taken off her armor and weapons, laying them in a neat pile that she could get to quickly if a situation arose where she needed to. She stood her boots next to them, and she walked towards him. He caught himself staring at her.

Suddenly, Derrick felt something grab his ankle. It wasn't smooth and slimy, so he had a pretty good idea that it *wasn't* seaweed. It felt like a hand.

There had been no one else in the water when he'd gone crashing in. Reyna's words flashed through his mind: *There are so many things we might run into.* He barely had the time to hope that this wasn't one of them before he felt a hard tug, and he sank a few inches into the water.

Heart hammering in his chest, he pulled himself towards the shore, struggling to walk back. Reyna had made it in ankle deep by now, being careful to watch where she was stepping. *I have to get back to her.*

"Uh, Reyna?" he said, still struggling to gain the shallow end. "There's something in the water here!" Whatever it was, didn't let go.

"Yes, princeling. There are many things: fish, rocks, seaweed…" She started ticking them off on her fingers. He started shaking his head.

"You don't understand, something has my—" Whatever it was gave a powerful wrench, and he felt his feet pulled out from under him. He tried to cry out before his head went under, but ended up with a mouthful of the murky river water instead.

He squirmed and kicked trying to get away from the iron grip that encircled his ankle like a manacle. His efforts earned him a foot on the bed of the river, and whatever held him loosened its grip at his sudden burst of motion. His head broke the surface of the water, and he sucked in a lungful of air. He saw Reyna's eyes lock onto his. He reached out to her for help, and the last thing he saw were those beautiful, midnight blue eyes go wide with fear and understanding as he was yanked down again. He barely managed to draw a breath in time.

Reyna dove in, swimming towards him with fast, powerful strokes. She only paused long enough to scoop up a large, sharp rock. Using her free hand, she grabbed his wrist and heaved on it, throwing all her weight behind it and kicking hard.

It was enough to halt his backwards momentum. But only for a few seconds. He drew his finger across his throat, eyes panicked, pointing to himself. It was the only way he could think to let her know that he was almost out of air. She still had his wrist, and she pulled him close, her body sliding through the water as she drew nearer. Reyna put her hand on the back of his head and pressed her lips to his. He was so startled his lips parted of their own accord. Reyna seemed to be waiting for exactly that, because she blew a blast of warm air into his mouth.

She drew back, kicking hard to get to his ankle as she pulled herself down his body. With a start, Derrick realized that she'd just given him her air. Guilt crashed through him like a tidal wave.

Derrick felt a second hand on his leg. She'd anchored herself to him, but thankfully, it wasn't the hand with the rock in it this time. Her legs were right in front of his chest, and he wrapped his arms around them tightly, doing the only thing he could to help anchor her to his body. He felt strange currents around his foot, but when he looked, he couldn't see anything through the brown murk.

Then a dark cloud passed in front of his face, and the taste of iron passed his lips. He shuddered. The hand that had trapped him gave way, and he felt Reyna's legs kick frantically. He let go immediately, trying to shield his face from the possible impact. While his hands were still in front of him, she grabbed his wrist and swam upwards with fierce and desperate strength.

Reyna turned to look back at him, and Derrick almost let out the last remnants of his precious stolen air. Reyna's eyes were...*glowing*! They were bright blue, like her eyes had been hit by bolts of lightning then held the live bolt within her irises.

The pair surfaced and he sucked in great gulps of air. His heart still hammered in his chest.

"Come on. You need to get out of the water." Her voice sounded breathy, and when he stole a look at her, he saw that her chest was heaving, too. The realization that she'd almost run out of air *completely* made his jaw drop.

She pushed him ahead of her, shoving him roughly in the middle of his back. He turned back, looking at her eyes. They were once again their deep, midnight blue. Had he been wrong? Had it been a trick of the water, or his brain, starving for air?

He stumbled, and she jerked him to his feet, none too gently. She wouldn't let up, making sure to keep him moving forward.

"What *was* that?" he asked, once his feet were back on dry ground.

"*That*, was a rusalka." For all of her forceful pushing, her tone was conversational. He relaxed a little.

"A, uh...a water fairy?" He coughed, and a tiny rivulet of moisture dripped down his chin. He wiped it away quickly, embarrassed.

"Exactly," she told him, then hesitated. He waited, giving her time to find the right words. "They're born from women who were murdered near water. It's why they try to kill people. It's mostly men they're after," she said apologetically.

She looked him over, head to toe. He thought he caught a flicker of heat in her eyes. Then again, he'd thought her eyes had shone like a bolt of lightning, too. "If you want to put on some dry clothes, there are a few bushes over there that you can change behind." She pointed over her shoulder.

He followed her finger. Yes; there were *indeed* bushes that would cover him completely, but they were pretty far away from their camp, in his opinion.

"I, um, I don't think we should separate right now," he said shakily. She chuckled, and he knew she had probably guessed he was afraid of being alone.

"You'll be fine. They can't come on land. If *you're* not going to change, then *I* am. I don't want the blood of that overgrown *sea slug* on me any longer than it needs to be." Reyna grabbed a change of clothes and headed towards the bushes.

CHAPTER 20

Reyna was relieved she had a reason to duck behind the bushes. Honestly, the whole rusalka attack had shaken her.

It wasn't so much that she didn't *want* to save Derrick from harm; she was afraid that the more she had to, the higher the chance that she would *fail* to save him. No one was *that* good, and she was strong enough to admit that.

Her hands shook as she worked on opening the ties on her tunic. Derrick's bravery in the face of the giant had been tremendous, but his lack of experience placed a target on his back. Yes, she wanted to murder King Julius more than anything. He needed to pay for all the evil he'd sown, and all the pain reaped from it. Lately, though, she'd begun to realize that killing him wasn't the *sole* reason for her to be on this quest.

Oh, she would most *certainly* strike the moment the opportunity arose. But putting Derrick on the throne was becoming more and more important to her.

Throughout the time that she'd known him, she'd learned little things about him, in starts and bursts. As she strung them all together, she learned to appreciate who he was at the very core of his heart. She'd found herself liking him more and more.

She blushed as she pulled a new tunic over her head. She found he was taking up more and more of her thoughts the more time she spent with him. Her heart thudded in her chest when he looked at her with that softness in his eyes, and when he said her name in that gentle way of his, it undid her. She'd had to hide under her cloak of anger and sarcasm, unwilling, unable to let herself feel this way about a man. But she'd also allowed her caring, kind self to show more and more.

Reyna swore under her breath. She couldn't let herself be soft; being soft meant being weak, and she couldn't be weak. Derrick needed her strong, and protective, and, if need be, hard as stone.

She looked down at herself in satisfaction. Fresh clothes always made her feel better. She really wanted to wash the soiled ones, but she'd be damned if she washed them in *that* river.

"Alright. Your turn, princeling." Derrick was still staring out at the river when she returned to their camp.

"I, um, I think I'm ok." His voice still had a nervous edge to it, and she couldn't even imagine what was going through his mind.

"No, you are most certainly *not* ok," she warned. "I'm not travelling with you looking like *that*." She gestured at his clothes. "Besides, how would it look to the people you meet? You're a prince. You should present yourself as one."

Derrick saw her point. He hung his head like a scolded child and grabbed a change of clothes from Apple before tracing her path into the bushes.

Reyna smiled as he disappeared into the greenery. When he was nervous, his eyes widened a little, and she felt as if she could look through them down into his soul. She set about packing up their camp. They didn't have much, and it only took her a few minutes.

The sound of bubbling water made her whip around. Derrick wasn't back yet... She drew her bow from her sheath, nocked an arrow, then trained it on the swell of bubbles on the water's surface. Her breathing came in shallow gasps, and her heart raced. Her body, however, gave off a sense of calm, cool menace.

The bubbles started to spread out with the ripples, and something worked its way to the surface. A head crowned the water; long, green hair flowing from it.

The rusalka. Even though the creature had been scaly with shark's teeth and bulbous eyes when Reyna had fought it underwater, she knew it for what it was. Now, it had taken the small form of a child, rising from the water. Her long hair fell in a wet mass over her shoulders, and her simple dress appeared to be sewn from leaves. She was beautiful... except for the huge gash that took up most of her right cheek.

Reyna gave her a cold smile, acknowledging her handiwork. When the little girl's form had completely emerged from the water, she raised her flashing eyes to Reyna, causing her to suck in a breath. The rusalka's eyes flashed a bright, poisonous green.

"Please forgive me for my intrusion," she said, her voice soft and lilting. "I would not dare to steal from you. Please, allow this lowly rusalka to apologize. I would never knowingly take your prey."

"What's that supposed to mean?"

Reyna jumped at the sound of Derrick's voice. She'd been so focused on the creature in front of her that she hadn't heard him approach. Her face flushed in anger at herself for letting her guard down.

"How *dare* a lowly mortal speak to me?" the rusalka hissed, turning a furious glare his way. He flinched. That didn't make sense. Reyna was mortal, too. So, why was this creature talking to *her*? And...why was it *apologizing*?

The rusalka turned back to Reyna, eyes downcast in deference. "I offer you a gift. Please, take it and accept my apologies." Before Reyna could speak, the fairy sank back below the surface of the water. She began turning to Derrick, wanting to ask him about this strange occurance, when the bubbles started again.

She froze. Something else was coming up. Something *big*.

Both of them stared in wonder as a raft popped to the surface, water running down the sides. It was woven from purple reeds; a kind of seaweed even Reyna had never seen before.

"Wow." Derrick stared in awe. Reyna felt it as well, if she was being honest with herself. "I don't understand. Why did she treat you differently?" Derrick asked.

Reyna shrugged. She had no answer for that. "Maybe because I bested her? I really don't know." She heard a whicker, coming from in *front* of her. She knew Andromeda and Apple both stood *behind* her. Worry flickered across her face as she turned forward, yet again.

Her mouth dropped open. Two gray horses stood in front of the raft, half submerged.

"They're beautiful," Derrick breathed. Reyna grabbed his arm before he could take a step.

"Stop! Those are kelpies! Don't go near them. They aren't safe." The kelpies stood in the water, pawing impatiently. They lashed their seaweed manes and tails, which looked stringy, almost like watercress, and dark blue.

"What do they want?" Derrick no longer looked awestruck, so Reyna released him. The raft grew to the size of a small house. It bumped gently against the shore.

"It seems that we are being given a method to travel up the river," Reyna said, astonished. "I had planned to follow the river until we found a town, anyway. That way we could get our bearings again." She paused. "I've never heard of a rusalka *helping* someone before. I don't know if it's safe," she admitted, biting her lip.

"Well, look at it this way," Derrick said. He looked thoughtful. "She could have left us alone once we were out of the water and looked for prey elsewhere. Instead, she came to the surface and spoke to you. From her attitude, I don't think she does that very often. Then she *apologized*. And gave you a gift. I've never read about anything like that, and it seems like an awful lot of work, just for one meal. I think it's safe."

Reyna thought through his logic. Everything he said made sense...

"Alright. But if we die, I'll kill you."

"You have my permission," he said, laughing.

"I will find a way. *Trust* me." He nodded, but the smile never left his face.

"Alright," she sighed. "Let's do this." Reyna called out to Andromeda, who came forward with hesitant steps. She whinnied nervously, eyes bulging, and refused to get within twenty feet of the raft.

Sighing heavily, Reyna turned to Apple. "A little help here?"

Apple tossed her mane, then pranced forward. She nudged Andromeda's flank, then nipped it, before walking onto the raft by herself. Andromeda hesitated once more, but finally followed suit.

"That was the hard part. Let's go," she said, gesturing for Derrick to go first. She made one last sweep of their campsite, making sure they'd left nothing behind, before stepping into the boat herself.

"So. Where are you taking us, exactly?" Derrick asked. The kelpies ignored him, and neither one of them moved. "Excuse me, I'm talking to you!" They remained motionless. "Do these things not listen to mortals, either?" he grumbled. "Maybe *you* should talk to them," he said, throwing up his hands and sitting down grumpily.

She tried to fight her laugh, but lost. "I can do my best, but I guess we'll see." She cleared her throat, and spoke with as much authority as she could muster. "If you can understand me, look at me." Derrick looked up at her, at the command in her voice. He stared at her, fear on his face. The look cut her deeply. She'd *never* wanted him to look at her that way.

She doesn't know, Derrick realized. Once more, her eyes blazed a white hot blue.

Having nowhere else to look, her eyes landed on the kelpies. They both stared at her. She cleared her throat, willing her voice to come out strong and unaffected. "Take us to the next village," she said.

The kelpies faced forward again, and their manes grew long, the seaweed braiding itself into ropes that snaked down to the raft. They threaded their way into the mess of woven plants that made up the raft itself. It jerked as it started forward, and Reyna wobbled a little. She sank down, sitting by *choice* before she was thrown off her feet. Her leg scraped a thorn, and she swore. Reyna turned her leg so she could see it better. A small drop of blood beaded up on her skin before she wiped it away.

CHAPTER 21

Derrick knew his fear shown on his face, because hers collapsed into hurt and betrayal.

But her eyes! And there was no excuse this time. No brackish water between them, no lungs screaming for a breath of air to distort his senses. Her eyes had shown with crackling blue energy.

She sat silently, watching the kelpies tread the water, and very pointedly *not* looking at him. Derrick cursed himself. That look, the breach of trust it signified...he had never wanted to see that look on her face again. He'd seen it the first time when her mother had been brought to his trial without her knowledge. Now, *he'd* been the one to put it there.

He rested his head on his arms, where they crossed over his drawn up knees. Her *eyes*. They'd changed again. Why? And more importantly...*how*?

The raft lurched forward, and Derrick heard her swear under her breath. He looked up and saw that she was examining her leg. She mirrored his position without looking at him, and he saw that her shoulders shook. She was crying.

Anger and shame filled him, but he didn't know what to say. So, like a coward, he said nothing, and let the silence stand between them.

Derrick didn't know how long it stretched, but the sun had passed the halfway point of the day before Reyna picked her head up. She still sat hunched over, but she swiped at her eyes and watched the riverbank. Feeling like he had to do *something*, he cleared his throat. She stiffened at the sound.

"Do you remember that game I told you about? When you wanted to know what name I'd picked for the sword?" She remained silent. "I said that it could be played on horseback?" he prompted. Silence. "It could be played here, too." She didn't respond. He hung his own head and sighed.

"What kind of game?" she asked stiffly, though she still refused to face him. Derrick beamed anyway, thankful that she'd answered.

"Well, it's sort of a game to get to know someone," he explained. "You ask a question. It can be anything at all. The person you're asking *has* to tell the truth." She said nothing. "Do you want to play? It would pass some of the rest of the day."

Too late, he realized his mistake. By asking her to play, he'd unwittingly opened the door for her to ask what had made him look at her like that. He winced.

"Alright." She still kept her eyes trained on the shore; it was like he didn't really exist.

"Do you want to start?" he offered, resigned to his fate. She shrugged.

"What did you name your sword?" He chuckled wryly. He should have known that she wouldn't let that go.

"Tharros." It meant 'courage'. Her shoulders went rigid. "I know you didn't ask me why, but I'd like to tell you, anyway." He took a deep breath and spoke quickly, before he lost his nerve. "I wanted to stay true to Anteros. From the little you've told me about him, he had plenty of courage. I can only hope that I can use it to make him proud."

He heard a soft sniffle from her. "The second reason...is because of you." She turned to face him now, midnight blue eyes swimming with tears. "You taught me what *real* courage was. You face every danger you meet head on. You march in and stand up for those who can't stand up for themselves. You're fierce and gentle, hard and soft. You know how to be everything to everyone. You know what they need, somehow. And you work to make sure they get it. No matter what it costs you." She looked down, but he saw a solitary tear fall to the seaweed of the raft.

"My turn," he said gently. "Will you tell me why your mother travelled to Syrinx?" She was quiet so long that he didn't think she would answer. Then:

"She was a slave. Sold by a man who'd kidnapped her from her family. Her owner beat her within an inch of her life, raped her, then threw her out, leaving her for dead." Reyna's hands balled into fists. Her voice came out rough and angry. "My father found her. He nursed her back to health. They fell in love." She smiled sadly, picking at a stray frond of seaweed. "She said that she'd never felt more loved in her entire life. He'd find joy and wonder in even the simplest of things. He had to leave, though, before he ever knew she was with child. She made it to Syrinx, almost at death's door again, and heavily pregnant." Her eyes flicked to his. "Kind of how you were." She looked away again. "The Wreya found her and brought her into their society. Taught her their ways, their customs. *Our* customs." She took a breath. "I was born a short time after. She named me after the people who saved her."

They continued back and forth for almost an hour, talking

about their pasts, learning about each other, understanding each other a little better. He told her about the time he'd tried to step in and save that girl from Stravos, and how his father had made him watch after he had failed. How he'd blamed Derrick for all the horrible torture and perversions that had been done to her, before she'd been brutally murdered. How he no longer stood up to anyone for fear of what consequences his actions might reap on the innocent. Reyna cried for him.

"Your father is a coward. A sick bastard who can only be happy when he's hurting others! One day, I'm going to shove my blade so far up his ass that I'm going to split him open. Then I can look to see if there's actually a heart in there after all." Derrick knew she wasn't the only one to think that way. "And your brother?" She gave an involuntary shudder. "*That* monster is going to get what he deserves, too. Mark my words. If it's the last thing I do, I'll see to it that he pays for his cruelty!" Derrick had to put a hand over his mouth to keep from chuckling at the heat of her vitriol.

Time passed, and orange light streaked the sky as the sun set. "I suppose I don't have to tell you that there won't be any sparring tonight," she said around a wide yawn. "I think I'm just going to go to sleep. I'm exhausted." Derrick looked at her in the gloom. Her face was a little haggard, and she looked weary. She grabbed her furs and spread them out. It hurt that she put them on the other side of the raft from him.

"Yeah. I might as well, too," he said, trying to keep the connection from the boat going. "You never know when you'll be safe enough to sleep deeply." She grunted an answer. Sighing, he followed her lead. He was sorely tempted to move his furs closer to her, but he gritted his teeth and fought the urge. She'd never asked about his frightened expression, and he'd been too timid to ask about her eyes. Derrick kicked himself mentally for being such a fool.

When Derrick awoke the next morning, he didn't know where he was. He'd been in a strange place...whether it was a dream or some in between world, he didn't know. Things hadn't made sense, but the more he tried to remember exactly *why*, the faster it all slipped away. He looked around, saw the kelpies and the raft beneath him, and everything came back to him. *Everything*.

He looked across the raft to her pile of furs. She was still in them. That was two days in a row that she'd outslept him! He allowed himself a moment of congratulations before sobering. He wanted to do something for her to make up for what he'd done.

Since they were on a raft, he couldn't make a fire and cook for her. Maybe he could do her daily maintenance on her weapons? He couldn't think of anything at the moment, but as soon as something popped up where he could do something nice for her, he would jump at the opportunity.

She moaned. Was she having a nightmare? Carefully, he crossed the raft, not wanting to startle her or the kelpies.

"Reyna? Are you ok?" She was buried so deeply in her furs that he couldn't even see her face. Another moan. *That* one sounded like she was in pain. "Reyna? Hey! Are you ok?" he tried again. He was digging through the pile of furs, trying to uncover her. When he managed to unearth her, he gasped.

Reyna's face was ashen. Dark bruises stood out under her eyes. Sweat made her forehead slick, and her lustrous, chestnut curls hung limply from her head, some plastered to her face. Her face scrunched up in pain, and she moaned again. He shook her gently. Her eyes fluttered open. They looked dull and glassy.

"Derrick? What... is it? Is something wrong?"

"Do you feel alright?" he asked hesitantly.

"I'm a little... sore all over, and my leg really itches." She pulled her leg out from under the furs. Then it was *her* turn to gasp. "My leg!" He shifted so he could see better.

Black lines ran under her skin, radiating out from a little hole in her leg. The skin around it was deathly pale and shrivelled, like a waterlogged corpse long forgotten in a mire.

"It's poison," Reyna said clinically, as though the wound were on someone else's leg. Derrick jumped to his feet, running to the horses, digging through the saddlebags.

She gave a hollow laugh. "Don't, Derrick. I have nothing for poison with me." She looked up at him. "I didn't think this would be the way I would go." She chuckled darkly. "Killed by seaweed."

"Stop!" Derrick tried to tamp down the hysteria rising in his voice. "Don't talk like that! You're going to be ok. I'll make sure of it," he vowed.

"Listen to me, princeling. I don't know how long I have. No matter what happens to me, *you're* the one that needs to keep going. Raise an army. I'm sure there are plenty of down-trodden people who would flock to your cause. Find them. Remember who you are. Remember that you are doing this to protect them." Her voice hitched. "Remember that courage you've found, and let it burn through you." She sat up, and Derrick put an arm around her when she wobbled. She smiled her thanks. "When I die—"

"You're *not* going to—"

"Okay, *if* I die," she cut him off forcefully, "I want you to put me in the sea. Something about the water has always been soothing to me. It's healed the hurts in my soul more than a few times." He kept his mouth shut, even though he wanted to tell her there was no need to make these plans. "Please..." her voice broke. "Please, don't put me in the ground. It's so claus-trophobic. And..." She looked up at him, sunken eyes begging. "Will you sing to me? When Denali was sick, no one could get her to stop crying. I don't understand why though. All I did was sing to her and she calmed right down. Sometimes, when I sing, it makes people happy." She paused. "So, would you sing to me?"

His lip quivered when he answered, and he wasn't proud of it. "Of course, Reyna. Whatever you want. Let me get you something to eat, first." She shook her head. "Please," he begged. "You've got to keep your strength up."

"No," she answered weakly. "I'm not hungry. You go. Get something in your belly." She lowered herself back down. Her eyes closed again. Derrick grabbed a bag of food, set it down next to her in case she changed her mind, then sat down gingerly next to her furs. He looked at the kelpies, plodding along. He got on his knees. They may not care, but he had to try.

"Please! I know you can hear and understand me! I know that I'm beneath you." His voice cracked from pain and fear. "*Please*! Can you go faster? Can you take her somewhere that can help her? She's dying..."

One of the kelpies turned its head and stared at him with one baleful eye. It watched him for a moment, seeing the tears streaming down his face. It turned back around.

Nothing happened. Heartbroken, Derrick crawled back to Reyna and lifted her into his arms as gently as he could. He opened his mouth to sing. He went through every song he'd ever learned, until his voice was hoarse and his throat was raw. Derrick didn't move the rest of the day. He didn't eat or drink.

He did nothing but hold her.

The bump of the raft hitting the shore woke him from the fitful sleep he'd sunk into. He sat up, looking around. They were next to a dock. He whipped his head around. A village loomed behind him in the early evening. The kelpie looked at him expectantly.

"Thank you! Thank you for bringing us here. I'm not going to let her die!" He packed her furs up, then had the horses follow him as he picked Reyna up in his arms and stepped onto the shore. When he looked back, the raft and kelpies were gone.

He had to find a place where he could take care of her. An inn. There would be one near the middle of town. Grateful that he'd developed some extra muscles, he hoisted her against his chest, cradling her like a child, and marched forward.

"Is she dead?" Derrick's head whipped around, looking for the speaker, but he saw no one. "I'm over here." A boy crawled out from between some broken crates. His face was dirty, and his clothes were torn. Just one more innocent who was suffering under his father's rule.

"No. She's not dead. But she's very sick. I need to find a place to keep her, and someone who can help her. I don't know how long she has."

"What's her name? She's pretty."

Derrick smiled weakly. "Yes, she *is* pretty. Her name is Reyna." The boy froze, looking from Reyna's face to Derrick's.

"Then... *you're* Prince Derrick, aren't you?" His eyes were wide. Derrick took a chance and nodded. Just like Reyna had done after saving the boy from the giant.

"Come with me! I don't live far!" The street urchin darted down a side alley that Derrick hadn't even noticed. He did his best to follow, trusting Apple to get both of the horses where they needed to go.

"How do you know who we are?" Derrick panted. "Who *I* am?" He almost ran right into the little boy as he whipped around, a fierce expression on his face.

"Shh!" he hissed, finger to his lips. "It's not safe to talk here!" Feeling embarrassed and chastised, Derrick clamped his mouth shut, following at the boy's heels. Derrick felt glad that he had a guide, of sorts, for where he was going, because he would have been lost in the twists and turns they ducked through.

By the time the boy finally came to a halt in front of what looked like a run down boarding house, Derrick's muscles burned with exhaustion, and Reyna shook in his arms. The boy opened a side door and ushered him in, staying back to look up and down the streets, making sure no one was watching them.

Derrick's eyes had to adjust to the gloom. Only one taper was lit, and its quality was poor. It hardly gave off either heat or light. Derrick's heart squeezed painfully in his chest. Then fire coursed through his veins, and hatred for his father had him seeing red. This was *all* going to change! The courtiers and nobles be *hanged*. They would *all* be cutting down the majority of their luxury and riches for as long as it took for his people to get on their feet. Then maybe some luxuries could be returned to them. No, not everyone would be able to live like kings, but they would at least be able to feed, clothe, and shelter their families. His soldiers would *help* the people and keep the peace. *Not* abuse them for their own sport. If he found out any *one* of them was being cruel, then he would be relieved of his duty, and given a punishment that suited the crime.

After a few heartbeats, a thin, ragged woman entered the kitchen. She stared at him with wide eyes, her hands trembling and worrying at a dirty, frayed handkerchief. Derrick started.

"Hello, ma'am. I'm so sorry to come barging in on you." He wanted to say more, but the little boy came barreling into the room, grinning from ear to ear. He threw his arms around the woman, and she immediately picked him up, snuggling him to her chest.

"Mama! You'll never believe who she is!" he was so excited, he could barely get the words out between fits of giggles. When his mother didn't answer right away, he kept talking. "That's *Reyna*!" he breathed in a hushed tone, full of reverence.

His words seemed to wake his mother from her trance. She gasped, and moved to make tea. He followed behind her like a little shadow, doing his best to help her as she went.

Mother? Derrick had thought the woman a crone. *Another victim of my father's cruelty.* "I'm sorry," Derrick interrupted. "How do you know about us? I mean, I assume you've seen a poster or two of me, but how do you know about her?" *And why aren't you turning us in for the bounty?*

"Oh! I'm sorry. I was just so excited! I'm Bray, and this is my mama, Caela." He turned to beam at Caela, and Derrick saw the love they shared reflected in their eyes. It cut him deep, and made him miss his mother. "We know about you because news of you two is *everywhere*!" Bray whispered, conspiratorially. "A lot of people talk about how Reyna went to save that boy from the giant! And how you went to help! And then, stories have been passed around that you fled to the Forest of Gaia, but that you helped someone in every single town that you passed through. And there were projects you did to help all of us, and the king wanted to murder you for it." Derrick's mouth fell open. How had so much information gotten around so quickly? Moreover, so much *accurate* information?

"I need to put her down," Derrick grunted. Reyna wasn't exactly heavy, but he'd been carrying her for a while. Shame crested over him like a wave. He hadn't asked for a healer right away. He hadn't asked for medicine. He hadn't even asked for a soft place to lay her. "Please. Tell me where I can find a healer. I'm afraid she'll die if she doesn't get help." Derrick's voice broke. If she died, it would be all his fault for standing there gossiping like an old woman when he should have been taking care of her.

"Please! Follow me!" Caela finally came to life. She turned quickly and led the way out of the kitchen. Derrick hugged Reyna closer to his chest, and set off after her. Caela came to a halt at the back door of the common room. This probably led to their *own* living quarters. She opened the door and let Derrick precede her into the room. "Please, use my room." Derrick lay her down as gingerly as he could, but still a soft mewl of pain escaped from her.

"I need to find a healer right away. One that deals in a lot of poisons." Caela thought for a minute, then called Bray into the room.

"Mama? What is it?" One quick look at Derrick's face, and the boy grabbed his hand, pulling Derrick along. "Come on." Derrick didn't even have time to nod in agreement as he was pulled out of the room. He fought to catch his balance. "You have to be quick, ok? And keep your hood up. There are still soldiers swarming the town." Derrick marveled that so much anger and bitterness was compressed into this little boy's body.

"Where are we going?" Derrick asked, eyes darting everywhere. There were *indeed* a lot of soldiers. It felt strange to see so many of them after not seeing any for so long. Bray must have deemed him worthy of finding his own way, because he released Derrick's hand.

"Madame Oonagh is the best healer in town. The problem is, her shop is right in the middle of the town square. That's where all the soldiers like to be." Bray grimaced, and it made Derrick wonder if he'd seen something in the town square that he'd rather forget. Something told him that a good part of his kingdom was in the same situation. His eyes darkened at the thought and his lip curled into a snarl of its own accord.

"We'll be able to get there, though, right?"

"Yeah. I'll make sure no one stops you from going in!" Bray's face grew fierce, and it was all Derrick could do to stop himself from smiling. The two of them did their best to meander their way into the square without drawing any attention to themselves.

Derrick didn't need to ask which shop belonged to Madam Oonagh. Dried herbs and small bones decorated the lintels of the door, and when he stepped inside, the sharp smell of myriad spices burned in his nose. More animal bones, herbs, and even crystals littered the shelves. Racks of potion bottles and unguents were crammed in the empty spaces so thickly that he had to move very slowly in order not to knock into anything. There was a counter at the far end, and a door leading to a room behind it. There was movement and soft noises coming from that room, and his heart started to race. He sprinted towards the wooden counter, doing his best to dodge around all the barrels of slimy things and potion ingredients. By the time he reached it, his eyes had grown wild with fear and desperation.

"Please! You have to help me!" he cried, voice trembling. He was hoping that someone was back there. He didn't want to think about *what* could have made those sounds and noises if they weren't human.

"Who are you and what do you want?" came a wizened old woman's voice. *This must be Madame Oonagh.* And from the sounds of it, he didn't think she was very friendly.

"Please! My companion...has been poisoned by some sort of seaweed. And... is dying." His voice broke, and he raised his head to find a woman standing in the doorway, watching him with beady little eyes that seemed to be judging him. He flinched back. He hadn't heard her approach.

"What are her symptoms?" she asked, voice calm and measured. Derrick described Reyna's ailments as best he could, his voice riddled with emotion.

"How did you know it was a woman? Whatever, never mind. She's feverish, and sweating a lot. She's in so much pain..." he trailed off, voice hitching. "There are black lines running under her skin from the wound; and she's so weak that she can barely move." The healer nodded, her eyes narrowing as she listened.

"Just a hunch. It sounds like she'd been poisoned by a particularly potent strain of Soul Reaper seaweed," Madame Oonagh said. "But there *may* still be something I can do. There's an herb that can counteract the poison, but it's rare and can only be found in one place." Derrick's heart leapt into his throat with hope. She didn't say anything else, and the silence stretched uncomfortably between them. Derrick almost couldn't hear over the pounding of his heart, echoing in his ears.

"Well? Do you have it?" he asked, voice trembling with anticipation. Madame Oonagh shook her head, and her expression became grave.

"No. And I need to warn you, it's not an easy cure. Not to find the ingredients for, not to make, and not to endure. Things *will* get worse for her before they get better. *If* everything is done correctly." Derrick frowned.

"If?"

"The herb is called Fadegrass, and it's known for its ability to counter most poisons. But if it's not prepared properly...it can be dangerous. Even deadly. What are you willing to give for her life?"

"Anything. Everything. I don't care. I'll do whatever it takes to help her." Derrick paused. Something just came back to him. "You said you had a hunch. What gave you the hunch that it was a woman?"

She smiled at him knowingly, and it dropped years from her face. Standing before him now was a beautiful young woman with silver blond hair and startling violet eyes. His mouth fell open. Before his eyes, she changed back into the old crone once more. He knew he was being rude by staring, but he couldn't help it.

"Love will make you pledge your very soul... then come to collect it in ways you never imagined." Derrick had to force himself to rip his gaze away. "You won't just find this herb growing in the ground. It can only be given by passing a test. You must be willing to give everything..." she trailed off, and Derrick saw that her eyes were far away. He wanted her to tell him what he needed to do, but he didn't want to rush her. "The only place to find Fadegrass is in the garden of a troll." She paused once more, letting her words sink in. "You won't be able to just fight the troll and push your way into the garden, mind you. There is a test you must pass. And all magic comes with a price."

"What test? What do I need to do?"

She shook her head sadly. "I can't tell you that. It's different for the ones that have gone. There are only a few that have ever made it back with the herb to tell the tale. And of those, only one or two are still alive. The others went mad until they were locked away, or killed themselves to escape the memories."

Derrick swallowed hard. It didn't matter. If he didn't go, Reyna was dead. If he *did* go, and he died along the way or the troll killed him, Reyna was dead. But what if he went, survived, and brought back the Fadegrass? Reyna might still die, but it would be because the cure wasn't prepared properly...and she might *not* die at all.

"Where do I go?" The woman smiled at him.

"Follow the river north for a day. Then you'll see the caves." She fell silent, and Derrick waited, growing more and more impatient. He wanted to be off.

"How will I know when I found the right place?"

"You'll know," she said cryptically, then disappeared into the room behind her. Derrick could only assume that it was a work room. He smiled bitterly as memories of his time in a work room learning from Reyna came to the forefront of his mind. Then he swallowed hard and steeled himself. He would do this! She'd saved his life more than twice over, and by his reckoning, he only had one rescue under his belt. The giant was all he had on his tally. He had to even the score.

Granted, even if there was no tally, I'd save her just because of how I feel about her.

A tear beaded in the corner of his eye. It wasn't just that he had debts to pay. He needed her. Not just for this quest, but in his life. She was the best friend he'd ever had, and all he'd ever done was put her in danger.

Or hurt her. He thought back to the look of absolute pain on her face when she'd seen his reaction to her eyes changing. No. There were many reasons that he had to do this. And he refused to let himself fail. He would save her. He had to...

When Derrick left Madam Oonagh's, he found Bray waiting for him. Apple stood beside the boy, letting him scratch her ears. The little boy beamed up at him.

"Did she tell you if she could help her?" Bray asked. Derrick nodded. Bray looked behind Derrick, as if he expected someone to be following. "Well? Where is she?"

"She's not coming." Bray looked confused, then opened his mouth to say something. Derrick held his hand up to stay the boy's questions, then launched into the story of what Madam Oonagh had said, and what Derrick was setting off to do. "Thank you for bringing Apple. You must have known I'd need her."

"I didn't bring her. I was just standing here, waiting for you, and she came ambling up. So, we waited together. She's not just a pretty pony, she's really smart, too." Apple whickered at him in thanks, then turned sideways so Derrick could mount up.

"Please..." The words stuck in his throat. "Please watch over her. If I don't make it back, and the worst happens...put her in the sea. Don't bury her. She doesn't want that." The tear that had tried to get out earlier, now ran down his cheek, and it wasn't alone. "I've got to go. But, please...put her in the sea." Bray only nodded.

Derrick gave him three coins. Bray was speechless. Apple had everything in her saddlebags that he would need. He had no idea how all of that had come together, and he really didn't care. He was just thankful that it had happened. Madame Oonagh had said a day's journey...

"Be careful and come back alive. I don't want her to die," Bray said, his voice wobbly.

"Me either, Bray. Me either." Derrick clucked to Apple and she sprang forward, heading towards the river...*again*. It was that damned river that had done this to begin with. The rusalka that lived in it. The seaweed that had come from it. And now, it was leading him to his death. Possibly...probably.

"Let's go, girl. If we go fast, we might be able to cut some time off." Apple snorted, then opened into the fastest gallop she'd ever run in. Derrick tried to tell himself that the tears now streaming from his eyes came from the wind that tore at them; but he couldn't lie to himself...

CHAPTER 22

The sun had just begun to sink as Derrick reached the caves. Madame Oonagh had been right: he knew immediately which one he needed to go to. Bright colors lit the cave's walls,, and soft music came from the entrance, floating out into the night. It soothed him, and he felt a strange pull toward the cave. Apple whickered loudly in his ear, nudging him to get his attention.

"I guess I needed that. Thanks, girl." Derrick snapped out of his reverie and patted her velvety nose. "It looks like that's the one we need to go to." His voice wavered, and he took a breath, strengthening his resolve. *For Reyna.*

He made certain to loosen Tharros in its sheath. His palms were sweaty, and he hastily wiped them on his trousers. He gripped the pommel of his sword and marched resolutely towards the cave. The music wrapped around him like a lover's embrace. He closed his eyes and leaned into it, but kept his hand on the pommel nonetheless.

"Who disturbs my cave?" a sweet, sugary voice called out to him. It surprised him. Madam Oonagh had said a troll lived here. From what he knew about them, they were ugly and misshapen, their voices gravelly and low. Whatever was in there, was definitely *not* a troll. At least, not one that he had read about. He wasn't sure if he should answer the question or not.

For Reyna. He took a chance.

"My name is Derrick. I've come here to find some Fadegrass." He swallowed hard. "Are you alright? I was told a terrible troll lived here. One who devoured wanderers." As he spoke, he edged his way closer to the mouth of the cave. "Go, Apple," he murmured to his oldest friend. "If I don't come out within a day, go back to Reyna, ok?" She whinnied and tossed her head sadly. He patted her for what might be the last time, kissed her nose, and gently pushed her away before he entered the cave. He froze.

In the cave was an oasis like he'd never seen before. A massive pond spanned the ground, dotted with little islands. It looked like each one had some kind of different, strange plant or flower growing on it that he'd never seen. On one were white flowers, shaped like stars, that had a tinkling string of musical notes floating out of them, lulling him into a sense of peace. One had what looked like a blackberry bush, except it was covered in flat, dark red pods. As he watched, the pods filled out, looking like overfilled pea pods, before going flat and empty again, like they were breathing. His eyes rounded and his jaw dropped in amazement.

"See something you like?" a voice asked, lilting.

"I, uh, have never seen plants like this before. Are all of them magical?" A shimmer of blue white light sparkled in the air next to him, and he flinched away from it, hand almost creeping to his pommel again. "Who are you? We need to leave. There's a troll that lives here, and he might kill us. Do you know which one is the Fadegrass?" he spoke with all the urgency his fear for Reyna mustered.

"I am Moonflower, and this is my garden. Of course, I could tell you which one the Fadegrass is. I *did* plant it," the voice gave a silvery laugh, and Derrick's attention swiveled to *her*, rather than the plants. She wasn't human, that much he knew. Long, silvery hair flowed over her body like a waterfall, and her eyes sparkled violet as they met his. She was tall and slender, with a glass-like fragility. "The troll won't come. Not yet. Will you walk with me?"

Swallowing hard, Derrick nodded, letting his arms hang nervelessly down at his sides. But even just taking a step forward seemed difficult. He felt like he was paralyzed.

"Are you afraid of the troll? Does it hurt you?" he asked gently, wondering if maybe he should take her back with him. It would be cruel to leave her as a prisoner in the troll's cave.

"Afraid? No, of course not," she laughed, as if Derrick had been a child and asked an impossible question.

"And you won't get hurt for helping me?" he asked.

"Why would I help you?" she asked. There was no bitterness in her voice, no anger; just curiosity.

Derrick felt his shoulders slump in defeat. He *really* should have known better. No nonhuman creature had done anything helpful for him since he'd discovered how different they were from all the accounts he'd read. Except the rusalka. And really, she didn't count.

Anger filled him as he thought back to her idea of help. Reyna lay dying now, because of the poison from the reeds the rusalka had used to make the raft. His hands clenched into fists at his sides.

"You're right. You have no reason to," he said. Then he thought back to everything that Madame Oonagh had said about the herb. But Madame Oonagh hadn't described the plant to him! Could he take a tiny bit of every plant in here? That would guarantee he had the right one.

"If you want to leave here and be free, I will escort you somewhere safe," he told the woman, before slipping into the pond. The water stopped just below the junction of his legs, making him slosh about with every step.

"I thank you for your kind offer," the woman called out from the shore. He gave her a curt nod, then turned towards the first little floating island. He reached for it, intending to snap off one of the smaller stems.

"Stop!" The woman's voice had hardened, and sudden dread slithered down his spine. He pulled his hands back obediently. "What is it you want from this cave?" she asked, her voice now rough and throaty.

He turned to look at her. "I'm searching for Fadegrass. My friend has been badly poisoned, and I need to save them." She stared at him, as though she was looking down into his very soul.

"Your friend is that important to you?" she asked softly.

"Yes! More important to me than anything else in the world," Derrick said, keeping his voice firm.

"Then I will make you a deal. I will give you questions to answer. If you tell me the truth, I will give you the Fadegrass. Lie to me, however, and I leave you for the troll to find. Do we have an accord?"

Derrick didn't even have to think twice.

"Agreed." She waved him over to stand with her. He sloshed up, pulling himself to the shore, and tried not to think about how he was now going to be answering questions in wet breeches.

There was a strange contraption next to her that resembled a kind of scale; it was golden and covered in delicate tendrils of gold filigree. A golden feather floated over it, circled in a blinding white light. Derrick gaped, entranced at the sheer *beauty* of it.

"Drop your weapons." It wasn't a request. Derrick did as he was told. "You've told me why you've come," the strange woman said. "Your friend is in grave danger?" Derrick nodded. "And you would do anything to save her, wouldn't you?" Derrick nodded again.

"How did you know she was a woman?" What *was* it about him that gave everyone the impression that he was trying to save a woman? Was he *that* transparent?

"I don't have to answer your questions, mortal man. Are you ready to answer mine?" Derrick nodded, swallowing hard.

"Are you here *only* for the Fadegrass?"

"Yes." She gave him a hard look, and from somewhere deep inside him, words started to spill out. "I'm here to save her. I know you're the troll. If I can leave here without having to fight you, then I will consider myself lucky. I don't want to kill you. And if you kill me…" he trailed off and his voice grew gravelly. "Then she dies."

"What responsibility do you fear the most?"

"I…I fear the throne. I love the people; and I want them to be happy. Not suppressed by my father or brother," Derrick said. "I want to take care of the people. *My* people. They've been through so much…" he trailed off. She waited. "I don't think I'm going to do well enough to help and protect them. I think someone else might be better suited for the job. Someone who has been taught the way of politics their whole life, but with the love of and for the people that I have." Tears stood in his eyes as he looked away in shame at his admission.

"Last question. If you had to choose between your friend and your people…which would you sacrifice?" The question caught him by surprise.

"I would give my life for either of them. To choose between them…" Derrick closed his eyes, and the tears fell. "I would choose my people. It would kill me inside. Break my heart and tear at my soul. But I would have to choose the greater good over my own happiness." His voice was broken now, and his hands shook.

"Look at me, mortal." Derrick slowly dragged his gaze up to meet hers. As he watched, her form grew until she stood taller than he was. The pale, smooth skin changed into something rough and mottled, green and black and covered in boils.

Before Derrick could even move, the troll's scaly, clawed hand shot out, lightning quick, and punched through his chest. Her claws wrapped around his heart, and with a tremendous pull, the troll's clawed fingers ripped out of Derrick's chest...holding his still-beating heart in her clutches. Derrick screamed and sank to his knees, his chest in agony.

The troll strolled over to the gold scales and dropped Derrick's heart on one side. The feather sprang to life and started fluttering, until it flew to the other side and settled down. Ethereal music began to play, soothing him even as his chest throbbed and burned around the gaping hole.

"This is the Feather of Truth," the troll said, and even its voice had changed to something akin to rumbling thunder. "Your heart will be weighed and judged. If your answers are deemed to be truthful, I will get you the herb you seek. If you are deemed to be untruthful, I will crush your heart and you will die where you kneel." Derrick nodded, sweat dripping from his forehead. He couldn't move. The pain was still debilitating, even over the balm from the melody surrounding him.

Both of them waited as the two sides of the scale swung and bounced... until, finally, they leveled out. The troll shook, her body collapsing into itself as it transformed back into the beautiful fae woman from before. She reached up and took

Derrick's heart from the scale, stepped in front of him, and plunged it back into his chest.

Derrick screamed once more, and collapsed where he'd been kneeling. His breath keened in short gasps. The troll stepped into the pond and headed towards one of the little islands, far from where Derrick had intended to start. She returned with an herb that looked like nothing Derrick had ever seen before. The petals were completely clear and looked like they were made of glass. The very center of the flower pulsed blood red.

"Is this it?" Derrick asked, voice feeble. Pain still crashed through him in waves. The troll nodded and pulled him to his feet. Then she handed him the Fadegrass, handling it with great care.

Derrick took his weapons back, and held on to the flower as gently as he could. He shuffled his way over to the entrance, whistling for Apple. She came at once, and he managed to crawl up into the saddle before the pain overtook him and he passed out.

CHAPTER 23

Derrick woke up hours later, still groggy, but feeling like the pain had lessened – in fact, it was almost to the level of discomfort he was used to after a typical long stretch riding. Apple spun her neck back and nuzzled him, jerking him wide awake.

Apple had gotten them back to the village. He'd spent the whole ride unconscious.

Panic swept through him and he immediately groped his tunic for the herb. He breathed a sigh of relief when he felt the petals. It wasn't damaged. He felt energized, his head and limbs tingling with excitement. Everything was going to be ok. *Reyna's going to be fine.*

Apple whickered and jumped behind a small building. Derrick startled, and he overbalanced, having to save himself by jumping off her back before he fell off. He caught himself on the wall, and Apple moved closer to him, blocking him from view.

"What's wrong, girl?" he whispered. He peeked over her back and sucked in a sharp breath. Soldiers patrolled through the streets. More than what he'd seen the day before. Had something happened? Had they found Reyna?

"Go on. Find your way back to Reyna. Take care of her until I get there." He patted Apple's flank and urged her on.

Derrick took a deep breath, and headed towards the town square. It was only three blocks away. He could make it. He *had* to.

He hunched his shoulders down and kept his face averted. Taking another nervous breath, he steadied himself, slowing himself down to an amble, doing his best not to look conspic-uous. He was halfway there, and some of the weight lifted off of his shoulders.

"You there! Stop!" The harsh voice felt like someone had taken a chunk of ice and shoved it down the back of his shirt. He said nothing, just kept on walking. "I said *stop*!" Derrick glanced over his shoulder. A soldier headed towards him, and his heart beat faster.

Derrick bolted. He didn't know where he was going, but he needed to get away from here. He heard the soldier behind him calling for backup.

Derrick's heart pounded in his chest as he darted through the winding alleys of the village, his eyes constantly scanning the surroundings for any sign of the soldiers hot on his trail. Reyna's life hung in the balance, and he knew that he had to get to the healer with the herb as soon as possible. He took a sharp turn down an alleyway, almost colliding with a merchant carrying a crate of goods.

"Watch where you're going, boy!" the merchant shouted, but Derrick barely heard him over the sound of his own ragged breathing.

The soldiers were getting closer, their footsteps pounding on the cobblestones as they closed in. Derrick's mind raced as he searched for a way out.

Suddenly, he spotted a pile of hay in the corner of a nearby stable, just inside the open door. He dove into the pile, covering himself as best he could.

The soldiers thundered past the stable, their boots clattering on the stones. Derrick held his breath, praying that they wouldn't think to look in the hay, to stab it with swords to flush him out. But one of the soldiers slowed down, peering into the stable as if he sensed something was amiss.

Derrick's heart leapt into his throat as the soldier approached. But he forced himself to remain still, praying that the hay would conceal him. The soldier walked past, seemingly oblivious to his presence, and Derrick breathed a slow, silent sigh of relief.

As soon as the coast was clear, he scrambled out of the pile of hay and resumed his frantic run through the village. He knew that he couldn't keep running forever; sooner or later, the soldiers would catch up with him.

As he dashed madly down the alley, he spotted a tattered cloak lying on the ground, abandoned by a beggar who had probably fled the village in fear of the soldiers. Inspired, he snatched it up and wrapped it around his shoulders. He pulled the hood over his head, obscuring his features, and slowed down to walk as casually as possible through the streets. It was a risky move, but he had to try *something*.

To his relief, the disguise seemed to work. The soldiers were still searching for a young man with short, dark hair, and they didn't pay any attention to the beggar in the tattered cloak.

Derrick made his way to the healer's shop, his heart beating a rapid tattoo against his ribs. He burst through the door, panting and sweating, and handed Madame Oonagh the herb. She led him to the back room, where she began to prepare the Fadegrass immediately.

She ground the leaves into a fine powder, and mixed it with a rare oil from a distant land he'd never heard of. As she worked, she went over the herb's qualities again.

"Fadegrass is a rare and powerful plant," she told him. "It's known for its ability to counteract poisons of all kinds. Unfortunately, that's the only thing that *is* known about it. How and why it does what it does, or *what* makes it so potent against poisons, no one knows. It's known for its unpredictability. If it's not prepared correctly, it can have horrible side effects. But if we do it right, it should save your friend's life." Derrick ground his teeth. He'd heard all of this before. Couldn't she just do whatever she needed to do to make the elixir and be done with it? Every second he stayed here, was another second the soldiers might find him.

Together, he and the healer worked tirelessly to prepare the Fadegrass for what seemed like hours.

"It's a good thing that I paid attention when she taught me herb lore," he joked, trying to calm his own nerves.

"Check in here!" A voice rang out from outside the shop. Derrick froze. The soldiers had found him.

He dropped to the ground and tried to creep out of the work room without being seen. The front door burst open, and Derrick froze again. He hid himself behind the far end of the main counter now, trying to stay out of sight. "Hello!" the nasally voice called. "Come out here! I hear you back there!"

Madame Oonagh poked her head out, looking at the soldiers with the most terrifying scowl on her face Derrick had ever seen in his life.

"What can I do for you, gentlemen?" she asked fiercely.

"We're looking for a young man who could be hiding in your shop." He motioned some of the soldiers forward to start searching.

"While you search, then, I have to go back to work on a commission," Madame Oonagh growled as she returned to the room. The soldiers set to work. "I won't be finished with this for another half an hour," she said to the empty air. The soldier raised an eyebrow at her, but she ignored him.

Half an hour. Could he stay hidden for that long? Maybe. But not in this shop. How would he get out and find a better place to hide? The soldiers were getting closer to him. He had to make a break for it.

He waited for an opening, took a deep breath, and *ran*.

Seconds of silence went by, then an uproar from the men in the shop as they clattered after him. He ran off in a random direction, jumping wagons, ducking past livestock, doing whatever he could to stay ahead of them all.

What was he going to do? There wasn't really anywhere nearby that he could hide for long. Tears of frustration welled in his eyes as he realized that the only thing he could do was to head back to Reyna. He'd have to come back and get the medicine later...somehow. He didn't want to waste any more time. He didn't know how much longer she had. He slowly worked his way back, trying to take a circuitous route. He stuck to the alleys, eyes and ears honed to any potential threat or observation. When he finally arrived at Reyna's safehouse, he slipped in quietly through the back door.

Twenty minutes later, Derrick was being let into Caela's bedroom. Reyna looked like a corpse. Her skin looked dry and mottled gray, and her chest didn't seem to be rising or falling. Derrick's heart stopped. The world grew silent as he crept forward, slowly lowering himself down onto the bed. He reached timidly across the bed and took one of her hands in his. He could feel the barest flicker of a pulse in her wrist. Alive. But only just.

"Just hold on, Reyna. It's going to be alright," he said, his voice thick, and he squeezed her hand gently. "Madame Oonagh is making the potion right now. Just hang on a little longer. Please."

He didn't really know how long he sat there, holding her hand and murmuring reassurances. Eventually, there was a knock on the door, and Bray stole into the room.

"I made sure to sponge her off every hour," Bray said reverently, nodding towards a bucket of water and cloth that sat at the foot of the bed. "I got the water fresh two hours ago." Bray looked like he wanted to come sit as well, but he stayed where he was.

"Come here, buddy. You don't have to stay over there. I won't bite." Bray rolled his eyes at Derrick, then came and sat next to him.

"I wish I could help her, too," Bray muttered, looking down at his little hands as if they were useless. Derrick grinned.

"You can! How about you go and get the medicine from Madame Oonagh for me?" The little boy looked up at him with wide eyes. "I know it would be much more dangerous for me to go. That way, you're helping her *and* me. What do you say?" Bray just grinned.

"Madame Oonagh has plenty of us kids in her employ to keep things discreet."

"Well, that's interesting," Derrick smiled weakly. "But I bet Madame Oonagh's shop has men watching it, and they'd follow you or anyone else that goes in there for the next few days. We've got to be careful." No sooner were the words out of his mouth, then Caela came running through the door. She had something small in her hands.

"One of the little girls just dropped this off," she said, chest heaving with the effort of talking after her run. Bray jumped to his feet in an instant, grabbing the bottle from his mother and rushing it to Derrick. "Here. Give her a mouthful, then rub some into the wound."

"Is this the medicine?" Derrick asked eagerly, yanking the stopper from the flask and almost dropping it in his haste.

"Yes. I'm going to saddle up your horses and pack you whatever food we can spare. You need to get out of here, Your Highness. Soldiers are going door to door, asking everyone if they've seen anything unusual or anyone matching your description." She left in a twirl of her ragged skirts, Bray bounding along behind her.

"Alright, Reyna, we're out of time," he muttered, pouring some of the potion onto her wound and rubbing it into her skin. "Our safe haven isn't safe anymore." Gently, he slid an arm under her shoulders, then carefully lifted her up into a sitting position. It wasn't easy, trying to get the potion into her mouth, but Derrick managed it... even if it *did* take him some long minutes to do. He'd just put the stopper back in the potion bottle when Bray burst into the room. Derrick flinched, startled, then he saw the child's eyes wide with fear, and that he was panting. "They're here?"

"Yes! Come with me. Now! Mother's trying to hold them off."

Derrick exploded into action. He packed up their few possessions in the room and handed them to Bray. Then he slid both arms under Reyna and picked her up, cradling her to his chest again. She whimpered and shook at the sudden movement, and though it stabbed him deeply, he couldn't stop. Or even slow down.

Bray raced out of the room, Derrick on his heels. He'd had

to push Reyna's face up against his chest, muffling her little whimpers and cries of pain. Every single one cut him to the quick. He wished he could spare her.

Bray came to a sudden halt, then doubled back the way they'd come, frantically motioning for Derrick to follow him. Derrick clenched his teeth to stifle the groan of frustration that wanted to claw out of his throat, but stayed on Bray's heels. The little boy led them back into the bedroom, and to the closet that stood in the back corner. Derrick's heart sank. They were finished. They were going to hide in a closet...

King Julius' soldiers were known for being cruel and stupid, but he was pretty certain that even *they* knew to look in the closet while on a manhunt. He'd even go so far as to say they'd probably look under the bed, too.

"Quick! In here!" Derrick opened his mouth to argue, but Bray shifted aside the back of the closet. He now stood in front of the opening to a tunnel.

"Come *on*!" Bray hissed.

He moved, barely ducking past Bray before the boy pulled the doors shut and set up the false back again. "This tunnel leads out to the stables."

"So, this isn't the *first* time that you've smuggled someone out of the boarding house, is it?" Derrick asked, adjusting Reyna in his arms as he crept along the tunnel. Bray just grinned at him. The two did their best to muffle their footsteps as they walked along; thankfully, Reyna remained silent. Derrick's heart pounded, and he told himself over and over that she was only sleeping, or passed out from the pain. She wasn't dead. She couldn't be. His world would stop. His heart would break.

They came out of the wall inside the farthest stall in the stable. Bray went first, making sure the coast was clear. Then he ushered Derrick out. Apple and Andromeda were both saddled, heavily laden with supplies. They looked tense.

"I'll get some rope," Bray offered.

"Rope? What would I need rope for?" Derrick asked. Bray looked at him like he had grown a second head. Derrick flushed.

"You'll need to lash her to the horse," Bray answered simply. Derrick pursed his lips and tried not to kick himself. If even this *child* had more common sense than he did, then how could he expect anyone to follow him? To fight for him?

The fears he'd admitted to in the troll's cave settled once more in his heart. He had no idea what he was doing. He needed Reyna for that.

Bray came back with a coil of rope. He held it out to Derrick, whose face fell. Derrick had no idea how to tie the knots. Bray picked up on his unease, and walked him through the simplest knots. He quietly sat Reyna on Apple's back, legs hanging down as if she were riding, and tied her on as gently as he dared and as safely as he could.

"Thank you, Bray." The boy nodded, then gestured for Derrick to mount up, while he headed to the front of the stables. "Alright, girl,' he said quietly. "Take good care of her for me. She needs you to be the guide." Apple whickered her understanding.

Derrick opened the stall door and let her out. Then he led Andromeda out of hers, and climbed onto her back. He needed to think clearly about what they had to do next, so he couldn't worry about Reyna every second. With Apple, though, he knew Reyna was in good hands...well, hooves.

"Go! Hurry! The soldiers just moved past the side of the building!" Bray whispered harshly.

Taking a deep breath, Derrick turned Andromeda towards the doors. They had just rounded the building when he spotted movement from the corner of his eye. A group of soldiers rounded the boarding house, and Derrick's heart leapt into his throat.

"There! I see him!" Derrick swore and turned Andromeda towards the river. The only way he knew of to get out of town was the path he'd taken on his way to retrieve the Fadegrass, so he directed the horses that way once more.

"Come on, Apple! Let's go!" Apple charged after him, Reyna bouncing haphazardly on her back. He looked back over his shoulder, but the soldiers were on foot. They'd need to find their own horses, then try to pick up his trail. He thought his head start *might* just be enough.

But...a head start was all it would be. He had no idea where he was going, or even what to do next. Reyna had always been the brains on their quest. He looked over at her, and his eyes welled. As soon as he could find a safe place to stop, he'd be able to check on her.

Apple pulled up alongside him, and he gave the rope that secured Reyna a quick visual sweep. Everything still looked in order. He breathed a heavy sigh of relief, and turned his attention to the road ahead.

CHAPTER 24

Reyna awoke to pain. Every inch of her felt as if she were being jabbed by hot pokers. She gritted her teeth, making sure no sound escaped. She hadn't dared to open her eyes yet, because she didn't know her situation. She realized she could hear the steady pounding of hooves.

Had the soldiers gotten to them after all? Where was Derrick? Was he alright? Her heart raced at the thought that anything might have happened to him.

But that was a worry for later. She still didn't know where she was, or why she was there.

Slowly cracking one eye open, she saw the coils of rope that encircled her waist. So, they *had* been captured. And the horse under her wasn't Andromeda. She was riding Apple. Had the soldiers just confused the horses? Or did they just not care if she was on her own horse? Probably the latter.

Letting her gaze roam a little, she saw that she was lashed into her saddle pretty thoroughly. She managed to turn her head, just the tiniest bit. Derrick's worried face filled her vision, and her heart soared. He was still with her. The last thing she could remember, he was singing to her on the raft...

"D-Derrick?" she stuttered, her voice hoarse and raw. When had she last had a drink of water? She sucked in a breath to try again, louder.

"Reyna!" Derrick immediately pulled Andromeda up short and vaulted off her back as Apple came to a gradual stop, circling over to stand in front of him. In her haste to look for him, she hadn't even noticed if there were soldiers around. Now she saw that there were not. She sent a silent prayer of thanks to the universe that her fears had been wrong.

"How are you feeling? Is anything wrong?" Derrick asked. He approached her nervously, hands shaking.

"Why, princeling; I didn't know you were such a mother hen," she croaked. He relaxed, shoulders slumping, a bright and teary smile stretching his face. He busied himself with the rope lashing her to Apple.

"How did you manage to do all this?" she asked, indicating her hempen prison. "*I* didn't teach it to you." She tried to laugh, raising an eyebrow at him. He blushed, turning away from her.

"No! No, you didn't teach me; but I *did* have help. A little boy named Bray." Reyna cocked an eyebrow. "Don't worry, I'll fill you in on everything you've missed."

That wiped the smile off Reyna's face. *Missed? What have I missed?* And exactly how much time had she lost?

She opened her mouth to start asking questions, but Derrick raised a hand. "We can talk about it in a little while. First, I want to get you down and make sure you're still in one piece." She didn't necessarily agree with this plan, but she let it go.

Gently, Derrick's hands fluttered over her, pulling the heavy rope away. Anywhere his fingers brushed her felt like tiny wildfires had started along her skin, burning down into her very soul. She breathed shallowly, trying to hold herself as still as possible.

When the ropes fell away, his arms snaked up around her waist, and he pulled her over the side of the horse, cradling her to his chest. She hid her smile, and heat pooled low in her core. Blushing, she turned her face even more into his chest. He set her on the ground, feather light.

"I need to see to the horses," he murmured apologetically. She waved him away. He hesitated, then busied himself with the animals. She watched him carefully, a teacher ready to discipline a poor or indolent student. But he did nothing wrong; left no steps out. Reyna smiled warmly at him.

The boy he'd been when she'd first dragged him, barely alive, back to Syrinx... had been replaced with this young man. A man who admitted when he was wrong, and deferred to wisdom and experience he lacked, no matter *where* it came from. A man whose courage had grown and bloomed like a wild rose, beautiful and dangerous. He'd developed muscles during their time together, too; he hadn't batted an eye at her weight as he'd picked her up. No; Derrick was not the same soft little prince that he'd been when she'd met him. Now, before her stood a *king*.

Her heart stirred within her chest. This was a king she could happily follow.

"All finished?" she asked as he came over and sat down next to her.

"Yeah. With *them*, anyway," he chuckled. "Now, it's your turn." She stared at him. *What is* that *supposed to mean?*

"Reyna. You've been in a coma for three days. I can't let you do anything yourself right now. You're too..." he faltered under her icy stare. "Your *body* is too weak to do things on its own right now," he amended quickly. The glare didn't leave her face, but her shoulders slumped in defeat. He was right.

"It might be a day or two before all of your strength returns.

Until it does, your body is using all of it to fight the poison." He looked away. "At least that's what Madame Oonagh told me. Now, do you want to eat first? Clean up? I'm at your command, my lady," he said, with no trace of humor or teasing sarcasm.

"I don't... uh, I mean, I *can't*... get to the river on my own to wash up," she admitted. She watched his face flush scarlet, and she felt her own cheeks mirror his. Apparently, he hadn't really thought of what "cleaning her up" entailed. They looked away from each other at the same time.

"I can help you," he told her, voice low and husky. She dared to meet his gaze, and the look of heat and desire in it made her belly flutter. They held that gaze in silence, until he pulled her tunic and trousers off with delicate fingers. Her underthings, though, he didn't touch.

She sat there, knees pulled up to her chest, as he went over to Andromeda's saddlebags and retrieved some clean clothes for her. He piled them on top of the sleeping furs he'd already spread out for her. He took a bar of soap and a washcloth from his own bags, then held them out to her.

"Are you ready?" he asked.

She looked from the soap, to his face, and back again. "I understand you're uncomfortable," he whispered, his voice sliding over her skin like a caress. "I give you my word, Reyna. I will be nothing less than honorable." She knew he was telling the truth.

Finally, she nodded. He lifted her up to his chest again, making sure that his arms were firmly under her knees and across her shoulders. His hands were balled into tight fists, and he kept his gaze straight ahead as he walked slowly into the river, fully clothed. When she started to float, she tapped his shoulder and he stopped.

"I think this is far enough." He gently let her legs go, and she clung to him as they sank down, down, until her feet touched the riverbed. Derrick held his arm out like a support beam, staring resolutely up at the sky.

"I'm right here if you need me." Then he closed his eyes and stood perfectly still. Tears pricked her own eyes as she watched him, and the tiny chip in the walls around her heart grew bigger. She started washing up.

Of course, once he's on the throne, my task is done. He would be taken care of; pampered, even. He would have beautiful princesses paraded before him like they were courses of a meal. He would wed; not for love, but for allies, whomever he chose. And there would no longer be any room for her in his life.

Where would she go? What would she do? Reyna hadn't the slightest idea. Even now, though, she pushed those thoughts out of her head and focused on the here and now.

"Ok. I've gotten everything I can," she mumbled. "I have to take my things off." Slowly, so she wouldn't overbalance and fall, Reyna took off her underclothes.

"If you, um, need help just, uh, tell me. Okay?" his voice sounded a little strangled. Reyna nodded, then remembered that he couldn't see her.

"I will. I'll be alright, though," she told him. She managed to undress and wash up within ten minutes, and she was pretty proud of herself. Still, her legs shook; even with the water's help taking away some of her weight, she felt exhausted. "I, um, I'm finished. How do you want to do this?" she asked nervously.

"Um, do you still have clothes on?"

"No. They're in my hand. I'm clean, so I don't want to put these on again until I can wash them. I just don't have the energy to do that right now." Derrick nodded, brow furrowed while he thought.

"Put your arms around my neck," he told her. Reyna wanted to argue on principle, but she didn't have the energy. She did as he said.

Once her arms were around his neck, he raised one hand up to the top of her head. She held her breath as his hand slid down the back of her hair and stopped at her shoulders. His hand shuffled across to her far shoulder, and curled around it, hugging her to him. "I'm going to put my arm out. Just drape your legs over, ok?"

"Um, yeah. Alright." Reyna gritted her teeth and waited.

Derrick put his arm out, about waist high, and froze. Taking a steadying breath, she pulled first one leg, then the other, over his arm and sighed heavily.

"Are you ready?" he asked gently.

"I-I think so." He turned himself towards the shore, and started to walk slowly. He still had his eyes closed, and his head turned up.

"You'll have to let me know where to go. You'll need to be my eyes."

She had no difficulty getting Derrick where he needed to go. No, the difficult part was making sure she paid attention to directing him, and not thinking about how much she loved the warm feeling of being safe. It was new to her

"You can put me down," she told Derrick. He did, eyes still firmly shut. Reyna crawled under her furs, new clothes in hand, and made sure she was covered entirely before telling Derrick he could open his eyes. Even with her reassurance, he cracked one eye open, then the other once he knew it was safe. He gave her a curt nod, and turned away from her. He still seemed nervous.

"Is everything ok?" she asked, confused.

"Yeah! Of course!" He stopped, then ran over to Apple and dug around in one of the saddlebags. He came back with a hunk of cheese and some dried meat, then took his waterskin from his waist and gave everything to her. "Here. You need to get your strength back."

"Thank you," she answered, taking the offerings. "But I need to know what's happened since I..." she trailed off, embarrassed. She didn't want to accept that she'd been in a coma.

"Let me get cleaned up, ok? Then we can talk about everything that's happened." Reyna nodded. He stared at her and she bristled.

"What?" It came out sharper than she'd intended, but he didn't flinch back from her.

"You're not going to look, are you?" The color drained from her face, and her mouth fell open.

"Are you serious?" she choked out. He shrugged, then started removing his tunic and trousers. Reyna's neck actually cracked from the speed with which she turned her head away from him. She swore under her breath, took the food, then burrowed into the depths of her sleeping furs to get dressed.

"Warn a girl, would you?" she muttered.

When she had everything settled, she stuck her head out again, chancing a quick peek at the river. Derrick stood waist deep in the water, washing up. Cheeks burning, she turned back to her own area of camp and broke off some cheese. She ate like a ravenous wolf. *Or a woman who apparently hasn't had solid food in three days.*

Then she felt the weight of utter exhaustion press down upon her. Reyna's eyelids grew heavy, and her head drooped until she fell the short distance to the ground, curling up in her furs.

CHAPTER 25

Morning light stabbed mercilessly through her eyelids, and she turned away, groaning. Slowly, she raised one eyelid, trying to let her eyes adjust to the bright morning light. When she was awake enough to make sense of the world around her, she looked around, searching for Derrick. Every detail of how he'd helped her at the river came flooding back into her mind, and she bit her lip. Derrick was checking the buckles on the horses' saddles. Reyna got to her feet.

"Stop!" Derrick's cry startled her and she froze, wondering if he saw some danger she'd missed. He was at her side in a heartbeat, wrapping his arms around her. "Why didn't you tell me you wanted to get up?" he asked.

"I'm sorry. I didn't know I needed your *permission*," she snapped.

"You couldn't even *walk* yesterday! What if you'd fallen?" he asked, voice rising in volume.

"Then I would have fallen! And you could have laughed!" she retorted. She took a breath. *It's not his fault I'm embarrassed. Stop taking it out on him.*

"I'm fine," she ground out, teeth clenched. "Go. Saddle up. We need to get moving." Either the authority in her voice or simple self-preservation was enough to get him to listen, thankfully. The longer they stood there, the more her body reminded her that she was *not* at her best.

She reached down to gather her furs, but Derrick ripped them out of reach before her fingers touched them.

"Hey! What are you doing?" she demanded. Derrick raised an eyebrow at her, then deliberately turned his back and finished packing up the last of their campsite. Derrick mounted Apple, then stared down at her mutely. Growling low in her throat, she marched over to Andromeda and managed to climb up into the saddle on her own. She held her head up proudly.

"Do you want to go over the last few days?" Derrick asked, once they'd already been on the road for two utterly silent hours.

"Yeah. I suppose that would help us in the long run," she replied. He started with when she'd gone to sleep on the raft; how bad off she'd been that next morning.

"Don't try to spare me, now," she sighed. "It's all happened already. You might as well tell me all the details."

He paused for a moment, then told her about all the conversations that she couldn't remember. Reyna turned her face away, unable to control the shock that crept across it.

She'd asked him to put her body in the sea! That was something she'd never told anyone before. Not even her mother. And she'd wanted him to sing to her...which he had.

Derrick told her about the town where he'd met Bray. He told her about Madame Oonagh, the Fadegrass, and how he was supposed to get it.

She held her breath, captivated by his story of his time with the troll. When he told her how his heart had been ripped from his chest to be weighed, her eyes dropped to his chest involuntarily.

He chuckled bitterly, then pulled down the collar of his tunic. There, over his heart, was a jagged circle of a scar. She gasped.

"It's alright," he told her stoically. "It got me the Fadegrass." He continued on, taking her with him through the run in with the soldiers.

"King Julius is on our tail, then," Reyna growled. *Why hadn't he mentioned this part first?!?*

"Maybe," Derrick nodded. "But they don't have much to go on. They know where I've been recently, but they don't know for sure if you're with me. And they don't know where we're going."

"Still," Reyna said. "We've been so careful, and now there's a likely garrison just a few days behind us." *Because of me. Because I got sick, and because he had to help me.*

Reyna felt that this was the price she had to pay for being curled up against him for so long. She'd had a little time with him in their own little pocket of time and space, away from the rest of the world. Now, though, they would have to race to that point in time she'd been dreading.

It wasn't that she feared destiny, or even that she wanted to back out of the quest. But reaching their goal meant that she and Derrick would reach their end as well.

"Your father knows you're still alive. We don't know how long it will take to get the talisman, but every second that it takes us is another second that Julius has to rally support amongst his own followers."

Neither one said what they were both thinking. What if they *didn't* show up with the talisman? Because they couldn't? Because they'd failed?

"We've got to get it together, princeling," Reyna said. Derrick nodded, his face ashen.

'We'll need to push the horses more. The cave we're looking for is in the next mountain range. Maybe another three days' ride."

"Let's make it two. Lead the way." She gave him a sort of half bow from her saddle.

Derrick looked at her for a long few seconds, then touched his heels to Apple's sides. Apple leapt into the air, already galloping before her hooves came back to earth. Reyna felt a battle cry creep its way up her throat, and though she clenched her jaw, she couldn't keep it in. It tore out of her, flung to the four winds. Derrick flinched when he heard it, looking at her with an unreadable expression, but she didn't care.

"Go!" she roared. He snapped himself around, then hunched down low over Apple's neck. The race for the kingdom had begun.

CHAPTER 26

It took two days of hard riding, little sleep, and less food, but they did indeed make it in two days rather than three. The pair now stood at the foot of the mountain range that ringed the lava fields surrounding the capitol.

Reyna had mixed feelings, being a day's ride from their final goal. On the one hand, she was so *very* close to carrying out her plan of revenge. For Anteros. For her mother. For *all* the Wreya, and for *everyone* that King Julius had ever hurt. On the other hand, Derrick was the heir to the kingdom, and the king the people wanted and deserved. She *had* to make sure he got the throne. He was the king they needed to heal the very heart of this land. The king the people loved. Reyna shook her head.

The dragons lived in these mountains, and many a wanderer had lost his life looking for them. Derrick had told her that his father had sent multiple units of his soldiers up into the caves, trying to steal a dragon egg for Stravos to raise. With a dragon, no one would dare oppose him. She didn't want to even *think* about how many men had lost their lives, getting that egg.

And they must have gotten one; a dragon had burned Syrinx to the ground, and it had to have done so under some kind of command. The attack was too clean, too targeted to be anything else.

She didn't want to think about *that* dragon. Not when she had no idea how many she'd have to deal with *here*. She wasn't ready for this...

"Alright. It looks like the best way to get up this mountain is going to be from the south side. It's less steep, so we should be able to find some hand and foot holds. It's going to be a long, hard way up, princeling. Think you can manage it?" she smirked. *If he's half as exhausted as I am, he's going to need all the motivation he can get.*

"Well, if a *wench* can do it, then so can I." She scowled at him, and he laughed. "You've got this. *We've* got this."

"Are you ready?" she asked. He nodded. "Take off your sword. You'll want to strap it flat to your back, otherwise it might get stuck on a rock or in a crevice and you'll fall to your death. I've worked too hard to get you here. Don't ruin it for me now, princeling."

"Well! I'm sorry that I've been such an *awful* burden to you," Derrick simpered with another knowing smile. He adjusted the strap holding his sword flat against his back, his movements stiff and deliberate. Reyna caught the tension in his jaw, and the flicker of hesitation in his eyes as he glanced at the sheer rock face towering above them.

She smirked again, unwilling to let him see that her stomach was doing somersaults at the thought of the climb. "Not having second thoughts, are you, princeling?" she teased, cocking an eyebrow at him.

"Second thoughts? Never," he straightened, rolling his shoulders as if shrugging off the weight of her jab. "I'm just wondering how long I'll have to wait for you at the top."

She snorted, her hand already reaching for the first jagged handhold. "You might want to keep dreaming. That's the only place you'll ever be faster than me."

Derrick grinned, but the expression didn't quite reach his eyes. Reyna pretended not to notice.

The rough texture of the stone bit into her palms, but she welcomed the sting. It was a grounding, sharp reminder to focus. Derrick followed close behind, his boots scraping against the rock as he found his footing.

"This isn't so bad," he called up, his voice carrying a hint of forced cheer.

"Don't get cocky," Reyna shot back, glancing down just long enough to catch his smirk. "We've barely even started."

The cliff face quickly proved her right. The wind picked up as they ascended, tugging at her hair and threatening to unbalance her. Sweat slicked her palms despite the cool air, and her muscles burned with the effort of hauling herself higher. She gritted her teeth, determined not to let Derrick see her struggle. A loose rock shifted under her boot, and her heart lurched as she slipped. Her fingers scrambled for purchase, nails scraping against stone.

"Reyna!" Derrick's voice cracked with alarm.

"I'm fine!" she barked, finding her footing again. Glancing down, she met his wide-eyed gaze. "Keep climbing, princeling."

"Could have fooled me," she heard him mutter. But the worry in his tone had faded, replaced by the usual playful edge. "Try not to fall. It'd be a shame to do all this work just to lose you now."

She rolled her eyes and continued upwards, the banter a welcome distraction from the ache in her limbs and the sharp drop below. As they climbed, the rock face grew steeper, forcing them to pause more frequently to catch their breath. Reyna pushed through the fatigue in her muscles and mind both, determined to reach the top.

Derrick's voice broke through the quiet. "You're slower than I thought, Wreya. Should I come back down and carry you the rest of the way?" Somehow, his longer limbs had managed to get him ahead of her in the climb.

"If you've got enough energy to boast, princeling, you're not climbing hard enough," she shot back, grinning despite herself. She reached for the next handhold, pulling herself up with a grunt of effort.

He chuckled, the sound light and almost carefree. "I'll have you know, I'm making this look easy."

"Good for you. Too bad there's no one here to witness it."

They continued trading jabs as they climbed, the easy rhythm of their banter helping to dull the edge of fear that threatened to creep in, and the exhaustion that hid behind it. But the higher they climbed, the harder it became to ignore the pounding of her heart and the strain in her limbs.

When Derrick finally reached the top, Reyna let herself believe that the worst was over. Then she heard his sharp intake of breath.

"Reyna!" His voice was tight, urgent, and it sent a jolt of adrenaline racing through her. She didn't stop to think, just hauled herself upwards with a strength she hadn't known she still possessed, her body moving on pure instinct.

"Derrick, what is it?" she demanded as she swung a leg over

the edge, her breath coming in ragged gasps. But the look on his face froze the words in her throat. Heart pounding erratically, Reyna vaulted over the top of the cliff, her muscles screaming in protest. Her boots hit solid ground and her hand shot over her shoulder, gripping Timoria's hilt. She pulled the blade free in a smooth arc, the whisper of steel cutting through the tense mountain air.

Her breath hitched as she froze, caught in the shadow of the massive creature before her. Derrick stood, just a few paces away, his body stiff as if carved from stone. And a dragon loomed in front of him...

It was enormous, and terrifying. The scales shone with the reflected light of jewels, as if each scale had crushed diamonds embedded in it. Its claws were sharper than Reyna's daggers, and its teeth were serrated and blinding white. It had a deadly beauty, like the powerful crush of the most beautiful waterfall. Its wings were spread wide, casting jagged shadows against the cliff face, its barbed tail lashed and slashed behind it. Smoke curled from its flared nostrils, its deep, rumbling breaths vibrating through the ground beneath Reyna's feet.

Its golden eyes were locked onto Derrick, glinting with something that might have been hatred. The dragon's jaws opened, revealing rows of razor sharp teeth, and Reyna swore she could feel the heat rolling off its scaled body.

Derrick wasn't moving. He wasn't even reaching for his

sword. His mouth hung open, eyes wide with a mixture of awe and fear.

Reyna's own paralysis snapped. With a snarl, she dropped into a fighting stance, Timoria held at the ready. The dragon shifted, its head swiveling towards her, the weight of its gaze a physical thing pressing down on her chest. Her knees nearly buckled, but she held her ground, gripping her sword tighter.

"Derrick!" she barked, her voice cracking like a whip. "Run to the cave!"

Out of the corner of her eye, she'd spotted a narrow opening in the rocky cliffside, just behind the dragon. The dragon's size meant it wouldn't be able to follow them inside. The plan formed instantly in her mind, and she gritted her teeth, praying Derrick would snap out of his stupor.

"Go! Behind the dragon, on your left! Go already!" she shouted, lunging forward with her blade raised. "Damn it, Derrick, move!"

The dragon's head whipped back to Derrick, its maw opening wide. Smoke billowed out, the heat so intense that Reyna flinched on instinct, sweat already beading her brow. Derrick finally moved, drawing his sword with a shaky hand, a far cry from the confident stance he usually took in a fight.

The dragon lunged, its massive body surging forward. Derrick rolled to the side just in time, narrowly avoiding the beast's snapping jaws. The ground trembled beneath its bulk, and

Derrick stumbled closer to the edge of the cliff.

"Derrick!" Reyna's heart stopped as she watched him teeter.

The dragon turned, its focus briefly shifting back to Reyna. She forced herself to meet its glowing gaze, her body taut with tension. There was something in its eyes...something calculating. It wasn't wild fury; or even mindless rage. Could it be hesitation?

"Reyna, don't...!" Derrick's voice was a desperate cry, but she didn't hear the rest. She swept forward, placing herself between him and the dragon. Her blade slashed through the air and the dragon reared back, wings flaring.

It could have struck her. Its claws were outstretched, its teeth inches from her. And in her haste to draw its attention from Derrick, she had left herself wide open.

But it didn't. It leapt into the air, wings beating hard enough to send gusts of wind whipping down upon her. Reyna stumbled but kept her feet planted, her blade trembling in her grip.

"Move!" she shouted at Derrick, sprinting towards him. She grabbed him around the waist and hurled him towards the cave. He stumbled, but she didn't let up, practically throwing him to the safety of the tunnel.

The dragon landed in front of her with a thunderous crash, the force rattling her teeth. Its claws raked into the earth. Its head dipped low, jaws parting as it let out a guttural, bone shaking roar that echoed across the cliffside.

Reyna swung Timoria in a wide arc, but the beast recoiled at the last second, its baleful eyes tracking the movement of her blade. It wasn't trying to kill her, though it could have. Instead, it lingered, as if waiting for something.

Reyna didn't question the reprieve. She turned and bolted, her boots skidding against the uneven ground as she raced for the smaller tunnel. She didn't stop until she reached the entrance, stumbling into its narrow confines. She whirled around to see the dragon watching her. It stood at the cliff's edge, wings tucked in tight, its glowing eyes unreadable. Then, with a powerful leap, it was gone, disappearing over the edge of the mountain into the open sky.

"Go! Get further into the cave," she ordered, shoving Derrick forward. She followed close behind, her senses on high alert for any signs of pursuit. They continued, the way twisting and turning before them, until she grabbed Derrick's arm, signalling a stop.

"We should be safe here. Far enough in to avoid any fire blasts. Besides, we need to talk."

"Talk? About what?"

"I get it. That was more terrifying than anything we've yet faced, and larger than anything you've seen in the pages of a book. But you have to be ready. I can't have you freezing up on me again, Derrick." His lips pressed together into a thin line, guilt flickering across his features.

"You have the courage to face a dragon. You just have to remind yourself that you do," she continued gently, her own words surprising her. It wasn't often that she allowed herself to be so vulnerable, but she needed him to believe it.

"I'll try to remember that," he said, voice barely above a whisper. He swallowed hard, looking away. "I'm sorry. I'll do better."

"I didn't mean it like that," she said, putting a hand on his shoulder. "I'm sorry, Derrick. I just...I'm not good at this. At saying the right things. I don't want this to come between us. I don't want to drive a wedge."

He looked back at her, and the tension in his face softened. "You didn't drive a wedge between us, Reyna. You saved me...again." He offered her a small, earnest smile. "Thank you, Reyna. For everything."

"I don't think we need to keep count of who saved who, and when. We'd be here all day. Now let's see if we can sneak in and out of here without getting caught. I'd be happy to never see another dragon again."

Derrick chuckled faintly. "A sentiment we can agree on. Shall we?" He gave her an exaggerated bow, earning himself an eye roll as they ventured deeper down the tunnel.

The air grew cooler as the tunnel twisted and widened. Faint glimmers of light reflected off the walls, teasing them with the promise of what lay ahead. When the passage finally opened into a cavern, Reyna froze.

The room was colossal; its vaulted ceiling lost in the shadows high above. Piles of treasure stretched out in all directions, glittering under the pale, ethereal glow of gemstones embedded in the walls. Gold coins spilled like rivers across the stone floor, cascading into pools of precious jewels, silver chalices, and ornate weapons. The air shimmered with latent magic, making every breath feel heavier.

"By the gods," Derrick murmured, his voice filled with awe. His wide eyes darted across the room, taking in the unimaginable wealth.

Reyna swallowed hard, forcing herself to focus. The room's splendor was a distraction, and one misstep here could be fatal. "We've got to find the needle in the haystack. Do you remember what it looks like?"

"A golden dragon's skull on a chain." She grinned. "But...you know...*smaller*." He mimed something little with his hands.

"Good. Bravo, princeling. Let's split up and search. Stay alert."

Derrick nodded, his awe replaced with determination. He moved towards a pile of glittering treasure to the left. Reyna took the other side, her steps cautious as she scanned the endless mounds of gold. The silence in the cavern was deafening, broken only by the faint crunch of coins shifting underfoot.

Reyna sifted through piles of gold and trinkets for what felt like hours. Her arms and back ached; from the climb, from facing the towering dragon, from the relentless ride to the mountains. She wanted sleep, and a meal that hadn't been bolted down over the coals of a bare fire.

She caught a flicker of movement from the corner of her eye. Her breath hitched. That *wasn't* Derrick. Her reflection wavered in the polished surface of a golden shield, but just behind it, another figure moved. She spun around, her instincts screaming danger.

The figure darted towards her, sword flashing, and she narrowly dodged the strike. The blade sliced through the air where her neck had been a moment before, the sheer force sending a spray of coins clattering to the ground. She stumbled back, her own blade raised, and her heart stopped as the attacker stepped into the reflected light.

Mythos! The man who had murdered Anteros. His black eyes burned with cold disdain, his lips curling into a familiar sneer. The memory struck her like a physical blow: Anteros, falling from Orestes, the arrow buried in his back. Rage roared to life inside her, obliterating every other thought.

"*You*!" she snarled, her voice trembling with fury. "You killed him."

Mythos tilted his head, his expression feigning confusion. "You'll have to be more specific."

"Anteros!" she spat, her grip tightening on Timoria. "The man you murdered in cold blood. Do you even remember him? Or do you forget the faces of those you murder?"

His smirk deepened. "Ah, yes. The fool who dared to defy the king's soldiers. He made quite the impression, I'll admit. Few have the courage, or the *stupidity*, to stand against me."

Her vision blurred with tears of rage. "You'll *pay* for what you did!"

"Justice, is it?" Mythos stepped closer, his blade gleaming. "You're welcome to try, *Wreya*. But I wouldn't get your hopes up."

With a feral cry, Reyna lunged. Their swords clashed, the sharp ring echoing through the cavern. Coins and jewels scattered as they moved, their strikes fast and brutal. Mythos deflected her attacks with ease, his smirk never fading, while Reyna's raw fury fueled her relentless assault.

The battle raged on, their movements sending treasure flying in all directions. A silver goblet clattered to the ground, a cascade of coins spilling like water as Reyna ducked under a sweeping strike. She pivoted, her blade arcing towards Mythos' chest, but he sidestepped, his laughter grating in her ears.

"I came to this dragon's nest looking for eggs. But all I found in this nest is a rat," he taunted.

"Shut up!" she snarled, slashing at him with renewed anger. Her strikes grew wild, her focus clouded by weariness and her desperation to see him bleed.

But Mythos was fast, his movements precise. He dodged and parried, his expression one of cruel amusement. "Anteros fought harder than this," he jeered. "Perhaps I overestimated you."

Reyna's grip tightened until her knuckles turned white. "*You* don't get to speak his name," she growled.

Their blades locked, and for a moment, they were face to face, the raw hatred in Reyna's eyes meeting Mythos' cold disdain. Reyna's blade clanged against Mythos' with a jarring force that rattled her arms to the elbows. His smirk never faltered, his movements fluid and maddeningly precise as he twisted out of reach and countered with a strike aimed for her side. She blocked it, but the effort was taking its toll. Every muscle in her body burned, and her breaths came in ragged gasps.

"You'll tire yourself out before you could ever even *scratch* me," Mythos sneered, stepping back to avoid a low sweep of her sword.

His words sent a fresh surge of anger coursing through her veins. She lunged again, her blows becoming more haphazard, more desperate. But Mythos sidestepped her with an infuriating grace, laughing as he did.

Behind her, a voice cut through the clash of steel. "Reyna!"

Derrick. She risked a glance over her shoulder and saw him rushing into the fray, his sword drawn.

"Derrick! Stay back!" she shouted, panic lacing her voice. But Derrick didn't stop. He closed the distance with surprising speed, his blade arcing towards Mythos. The smirk on Mythos' face finally disappeared as he deflected the strike, his expression twisting into something darker. Derrick pressed forwards, his movements clumsy but determined.

"Brave," Mythos drawled, his tone dripping with disdain. "But foolish."

Before Reyna could react, Mythos twisted and struck out with the hilt of his sword, catching Derrick in the side. Derrick staggered, but he didn't fall. He gritted his teeth and swung again, narrowly missing Mythos' arm. Reyna joined in, hoping to capitalize on his distraction, but he anticipated the move. He whirled on her, their blades colliding with a sharp clang that reverberated through the cavern. She barely had time to react before he spun back to Derrick, driving his knee into Derrick's stomach and sending him to the ground.

"Derrick!" Reyna screamed, her heart twisting at the sight of him crumpling to the floor, his sword clattering from his grip.

Mythos raised his blade, poised to finish Derrick, but Reyna barreled into him with all her strength. They tumbled to the ground, a spray of coins and jewels scattering around them. She rolled to her feet first, her sword raised, but Mythos was faster than she'd anticipated. He surged up, his blade flashing towards her. She blocked the strike, but her gaze flicked to Derrick, who was clutching his side, blood seeping from between his fingers. Her resolve wavered, and Mythos saw it.

"You should tend to your prince," he mocked, stepping back. "I'll leave you to your tragic little love story."

A golden bow with a matching quiver of arrows lay next to her in a pile of treasure. With a furious cry, she grabbed it, nocked an arrow, and fired in one fluid motion.

The arrow struck its mark, sinking into Mythos' shoulder as he fled into the shadows. His scream of pain echoed through the cavern, a sharp, satisfying sound that eased her rage, if only a little. But there was no time to celebrate. She dropped the bow and ran to Derrick's side, her heart pounding with fear.

"Derrick?" she whispered, kneeling beside him. "Let me see."

"It's not...fatal," he managed, though his face was pale and pinched with pain. Blood seeped through the tear in his tunic, staining the fabric dark red. "You should go after him. Finish him... for what he did to Anteros. I'll...be okay."

But Reyna's hands were already moving, tearing strips from her own tunic to use as makeshift bandages. "Stay still," she ordered, her voice firm but gentle.

She reached into her pouch, pulling out a small bundle of herbs. Crushing them between her fingers, she spread the paste over his wound, her movements deft and sure.

"Reyna…"

"Don't talk," she said, not meeting his eyes. "Save your strength."

He caught her wrist, his grip surprisingly steady. "Thank you," he said, his voice soft. "For saving me. Again."

Her heart twisted at the vulnerability in his gaze. She leaned closer, her hands trembling as they rested against his chest. "Don't make a habit of needing saving," she whispered, her lips curving into a faint smile.

Derrick chuckled weakly. "I'll try, but I make no promises."

Their eyes locked, the tension between them crackling like the air before a storm. Before she could think better of it, she leaned in, her lips brushing against his in a tentative kiss. Derrick responded immediately, his hand sliding to the back of her neck as he deepened the kiss. For a moment, the world around them faded, leaving only the two of them and the unspoken connection they'd been dancing around for so long.

Then Derrick winced, a sharp cry escaping him. "Ow!"

Reyna pulled back, alarm flashing in her eyes. "What's wrong?"

"Something's biting into my back," he gritted out, shifting uncomfortably.

"Hold still," she said, helping him sit up enough to check behind his back.

As she moved his tunic aside, her breath caught. There, tangled in a fold of the fabric, was a golden chain attached to a pendant shaped like a dragon's skull. It was no larger than her palm, but it shimmered with an otherworldly light that seemed to pulse with its own heartbeat.

The *Draco Lingua*. A surge of energy crackled through the air, making the hair on Reyna's arms stand on end. She reached out hesitantly, her fingers brushing the cool surface of the talisman.

"It's incredible," she murmured, awe filling her voice.

Derrick's gaze flicked to the talisman, his expression caught between wonder and trepidation. "What happens now?" he asked quietly.

Reyna met his gaze, the weight of the talisman heavy in her hands. "Now? We finish this. Come on, princeling, let's get you that throne." Reyna stood up, and offered him a hand to help him do the same. Together, the two of them began to make their way out of the dragon's lair.

Acknowledgments

I'd like to say thank you to everyone who has helped me bring Reyna to life. First to Adrianne for pushing me and lighting a fire under my ass to finish the story. Second, to Chris for having to put up with me through all the craziness that writing added to our lives. Because, let's face it. I was already crazy to begin with. To Jessica who showed me that Reyna was a story that others want to read. To Derek for being the editor who put in sooo many hours of work and combing through everything again after I made changes. To Derrick for my amazing map. And to John Gwynne, the author who inspired me to start Reyna's story to begin with.

About the Author

Sabrina Roznowski is a proud military mom who traded her combat boots for author's slippers when crafting enchanting worlds of YA fantasy and romantasy. When she's not busy juggling the chaos of family life, you can find her knee-deep in craft supplies, concocting magical stories that blend heart, humor, and just the right amount of adventure. Sabrina believes every great tale deserves a twist, whether it's an unexpected plot twist or an accidental glitter explosion.

Join her on this whimsical journey where romance meets battle strategy—because who says you can't have a little magic with your motherly multitasking?

Follow Sabrina on Facebook